Everything I Need

THE EVERYTHING series

A.K. EVANS

Copyright 2017 by A.K. Evans
All rights reserved.

ISBN: 978-1-7328858-3-7

No part of this book may be reproduced, distributer, or transmitted in any form or by any means including photocopying, recording, or other electronic or mechanical methods, without the prior written permission of the author except in the case of brief quotations in a book review.

This is a work of fiction. Names, characters, places, and incidents are the product of the author's imagination or are used fictitiously. Any resemblance to actual events, locales, or persons, living or dead, is coincidental.

Cover Artist
cover artwork © Sarah Hansen, Okay Creations
www.okaycreations.com

Formatting
Stacey Blake at Champagne Book Design
www.champagnebookdesign.com

Editing & Proofreading
Ellie McLove, My Brother's Editor
www.grayinkonline.com

Everything I Need

AK Evans

Dedication

To the loves of my life: Jeff, Jaden, & Jensen

Prologue

THE GAS PUMP CLICKED OFF, INDICATING THE TANK WAS FULL. After returning the pump to its cradle, I replaced my gas cap and got back in my car. I fired up the engine and pulled away from the station I'd been filling my car up at since I was old enough to drive.

It would be my last time.

Because today I was leaving it behind.

I was leaving all of it behind.

The pain.

The agony.

The memories.

My home.

Because there are moments in life that change us forever. The entire course of my future was altered in just one single instant.

Sometimes, these moments have beautiful endings. Those are the ones I used to live for. But I don't ask, wish, or hope for those beautiful endings anymore. Now, I just know that I never want to have a life-changing experience ever again because the reality is that the ending isn't always happy. Everything I thought I knew came crashing down around me. Suddenly, nothing made sense and I was left to try and figure out how to go on.

I tried. I tried so hard not to leave. But it had been too difficult. I thought it would help if I just avoided going out, but I was only kidding myself. Even my apartment became too painful a place to be. Every single room had memories that brought me to tears daily over the last three months.

Glancing up in the rearview mirror, I saw my best friend following close behind me. Because she, too, had to find a way to get past the pain.

We needed to start fresh. We needed to be able to make it through a single day without breaking down into tears. And the longer we stayed in Ventura, California, the harder that was becoming.

So, we packed our bags and hit the road.

One thousand thirty-two miles.

That was all that separated us from daily suffering and a new beginning. Or so we hoped.

We were moving to Rising Sun, Wyoming. Neither of us knew anything about the town we were moving to. We picked it because the name sounded promising. It was our hope that living in a place that was synonymous with the one thing that indicated the dawn of a new day would lead to a new beginning for us as well.

Me and my best friend. Charley Meadows and Emme James. Southern California, beach-going girls, were about to become Northwestern Wyoming, Rocky Mountain snow bunnies.

As Emme and I merged onto the Interstate, a fifteen-hour road trip ahead of us, I could only hope we were making the right decision.

One

Charley
Six Months Later

"Morning, Charley."

I had just walked into the kitchen and was greeted by Emme. She was already sitting at the island with her coffee and her breakfast, a bowl of fruit.

The two of us had officially started over. Rising Sun was the best decision we could have made. Neither of us is completely healed; I'm not sure that'll ever happen. But it has gotten marginally better.

While I still struggle to get through the days without wanting to break down or having a moment of weakness, I'm no longer crying every day. I have found that the busier I am, the less time I have to sit and think. So, I've thrown myself into two jobs since arriving.

Currently, I am working as a waitress at First Tracks Diner. I've managed to snag the early morning shifts, which means there's very little downtime and lots of tips. First Tracks is a great, family-owned establishment. My bosses, a husband and wife team, and co-workers all make the diner an enjoyable place to work.

Following my shifts at First Tracks, I work at Brew Stirs,

the coffee stand in the lodge at the Parks Ridge Ski Resort. I haven't worked at Brew Stirs for as long as I've been at the diner; I only started at the coffee stand this season. Initially, I thought that working at the coffee shop would have been laid back. I was sorely mistaken. It is borderline overwhelming.

We are still at the beginning of the season right now since it is only late November, but nevertheless, there is always a line and I rarely get a reprieve throughout my entire shift. I love it, though, because it keeps my mind occupied and the time passes quickly.

Before I know it, my days are over. When I get home, I am typically so exhausted that I hop in the shower and quickly grab some food before I call it a night.

I get a few hours of sleep before I'm back at it the next day. My weekends, when I don't pick up an extra shift at First Tracks, consist of me doing the necessary evils of grocery shopping, laundry, and house cleaning. I'll forgo some of these tasks if I get sidetracked by my art, though. I always try to make time on Saturdays and Sundays for that.

It always used to be my dream to become a graphic designer. And while I had a few paid gigs back in California, I have not even considered that here in Wyoming. It is now only a hobby that I keep to myself to keep me connected to a part of my previous life, a part I can't let go of.

So far, my new hometown is working out well. My jobs are great, nobody in town looks at me with sad eyes and, greatest of all, I have my best friend, Emme, here with me.

Emme, just like me, needed to get out of California after everything that we had been through. Lucky for her, she is an incredible photographer and was able to make the move without the worry of what to do for income. She is incredibly talented, and I am so proud of her for already making a name for herself in a new town.

Both Emme and I are still holding out hope that we will

eventually convince the other half of our foursome to join us. Nikki and Monroe, our closest friends from Ventura, had greater ties to their families and jobs, so picking up to move just over one thousand miles away is not as easy for them as it had been for Emme and me. It certainly was not easy to leave Nikki and Monroe, but neither Emme nor I regret the decision to come here. It has been a refreshing, much-needed start for the both of us.

We really lucked out when we had searched for places to live in Rising Sun. We found an incredible two-bedroom condo that had a clean, modern feel to it. The kitchen was part of the open-concept floor plan of the condo and shared space with the dining area and living room. I found that the kitchen was one of my favorite spots in the house, second only to our bedrooms. Both of our bedrooms were spacious enough to fit king-size beds without making the room seem small. Emme and I were torn between our love for the huge closet each bedroom boasted and the most beautiful views from our bedroom balconies. The bedrooms both had separate, full bathrooms and we also had a half bath in the hallway off the main living space.

Our kitchen was gorgeous with all new stainless appliances, a massive center island, and chic slate gray tile floors. The cabinets were bright white, and our countertops were gray, matching the floors. The style of the kitchen and the entire condo, for that matter, was contemporary.

I sat myself down at one of the island bar stools while I put some granola into a bowl of yogurt.

"Morning, Em. You're up early. I'm guessing you've got a shoot this morning?" I replied.

"Yep. This morning I've got that newborn and family portrait session I was telling you about last week, and then I'm heading off to a lunch meeting with some clients. A newly engaged couple."

I smiled at her. "That's awesome, honey. I think you have been busier here than you ever were back home."

Nodding, she confirmed, "You're right. I have been busier...and I think it's been really good for me. My mind stays occupied when I'm at those meetings or out on a shoot. It's the editing that is toughest since I'm alone with my thoughts then." She paused for a moment, looking away. A couple seconds later, with a shake of her head, she continued, "But enough about my stuff, I'm glad I caught you before you left for work. I wanted to ask and make sure you're still up for dinner and drinks to celebrate your birthday next Saturday night?"

"Yes," I immediately replied. "We have been out twice since we moved here. I think we need this, even though we're keeping it low key."

She looked at me and smiled. Her eyes were a bit sad, but she quickly brushed it off. I'd grown used to that over the last nine months. I'm sure the same was true for her when she looked at me. I couldn't say it was easy, though. Seeing your best friend in a constant state of sadness was heartbreaking.

Sadly, neither of us had the answers for how to make it any better. We'd fallen into our routines since arriving in Wyoming and we'd managed to make some progress, even if it was small.

Standing there, I took in my beautiful friend. She was my opposite, physically speaking. She had almond-shaped green eyes, flawless olive-colored skin, and thick, long brown hair that ended more than halfway down her back. I had round, blue eyes, fair skin, and short blonde hair that sat just at my shoulders. She was just an inch shorter than me at five feet five inches tall, but where I had an athletic build, she had a more petite frame with curves in all the right places.

I returned Emme's smile, knowing mine was just as sad as hers, before focusing on my breakfast. The two of us ate in comfortable silence before I took to getting my stuff together so I could make it to work on time.

It was Thursday, and I was looking forward to having the next two days go by quickly since I had the entire weekend off. It wasn't very often that I didn't pick up an extra shift or two on a Saturday, so I planned to take full advantage of that time off.

"I've got to get out of here and get to work," I started as I walked out of the kitchen and toward the front door. "Have a great day. See you tonight, Em."

"You too, Charley. Later," she called back as she took off in the opposite direction down the hall toward her bedroom.

Several hours later, I had finished up a grueling shift at the diner and was heading out to my orange Jeep Rubicon so I could make my way over to the resort for my shift at the coffee shop. It had been a long week and, after the shift I just had, I was more than ready for this day to be over. I hadn't even turned on the Jeep when my cell beeped with a text. I looked at the screen and saw a message from Emme.

I need wine tonight!

I quickly tapped out a reply.

Sounds like your day is going just as great as mine.

Emme: My newborn shoot went well. It was the engaged couple that did me in!

Me: I'm already wiped from First Tracks. So busy today. Just now headed over to Parks Ridge. I'll be up for a drink when I get back.

Emme: I'll pick up the wine!

Me: Great. Later! xoxo

I put my phone away and started up the Jeep. It was only a ten-minute drive to the resort and I usually had about an hour and a half between finishing my shift at the diner and the start of my shift at Brew Stirs Coffee. Typically, I would use that time to grab a bite to eat, catch up on a good book, or sometimes if I was really exhausted, I would take a quick nap in the car. Unfortunately, I stayed a little later today at the diner to help with the rush and only had twenty minutes before I needed to be at the coffee shop.

I got to work with five minutes to spare and saw there was already a massive line at the counter.

"Hey, Hannah. Has it been like this all day?" I asked.

"All day, girl. And I was late getting in this morning, so Mark was alone during the rush. I felt horrible, so I told him to head out a little early. He just left about thirty minutes ago when there was a minor lull," Hannah answered, bringing me up to speed.

Even though there was usually little downtime at the coffee stand, I'd relished in the fact that I had some kick-ass co-workers. Hannah was Filipino, about five foot four, dark brown hair that fell right to the base of her shoulder blades, and beautiful, big, brown eyes. Her eyes and her radiant personality more than made up for her tiny size. Hannah was, without a doubt, a spitfire. Her personality was something that I quickly realized, after my first three shifts, was crucial to surviving the long, busy shifts at the coffee stand.

"Well, I'm sure he was grateful for your generosity."

"Are you kidding? If he could have shot daggers out of his eyes when I arrived, he would have."

I laughed. I could just imagine the look on Mark's face at having to face the morning crowds alone. That many people needing coffee first thing in the morning and one person working at the stand was a recipe for disaster.

I jumped right into the mix and started taking orders. Before long, the line had died down and I was thankful for the break considering the overwhelming morning I had at the diner.

"I'm going to take my break now, Charley," Hannah stated as she took off her apron.

"No problem. I think I've got it under control for now."

I looked out at the skiers and snowboarders huddled up at the tables inside the lodge. Some had stopped in just to grab some food and refuel before they put in another couple hours out on the mountain. Others had been sitting there for the better part of the day reading a book by one of the fires or watching friends and family members who were skiing or riding their boards. With the brief respite in customers, I decided to make myself a cup of coffee to help me get through the remainder of my shift. Only an hour and a half more until I was finished and could head home to enjoy that bottle of wine with Emme. After that, I just needed to get through one more day of work for the week.

I brought the coffee cup up to my lips, glanced up, got distracted by what I saw, and then burned my mouth.

"Ow."

I dropped the cup down on the counter.

"Are you okay?"

I didn't answer. I couldn't. Not only was my mouth still feeling the effects of the scalding-hot liquid, but I was also staring at the most beautiful man I had ever seen. He had thick, black hair that had a slight wave to it, emerald-colored eyes, and a chiseled jawline. He had a day's worth of scruff on his face, which I found incredibly sexy. I couldn't see his lower half as it was hidden by the counter that separated us, but I could tell by his upper body that he was in good shape. No, not good shape—he was in phenomenal shape. His long-sleeved gray thermal was pulled taut across his arms and chest and I could see the outlines of his muscular body through the thermal. My heart felt like it was beating out of my chest. I was focused on his fantastic arms when I noticed movement. He had tilted his head and drawn his eyebrows together. That brought me out of my stupor.

"Oh, yes. I'm fine. Great. Thanks," I answered. "Can I get you something? Coffee, espresso, hot chocolate? We have muffins, too. Actually, we have a bunch of baked goods."

I was rambling.

I knew it and I couldn't stop it.

That is, until he smiled.

I gasped. His smile was blindingly white and, though I'm not sure how it was possible, his level of hotness skyrocketed.

He pointed to a table off to his right and explained, "I've been sitting over there for the last hour with my buddy and I haven't been able to take my eyes off you. You've had a line for so long I didn't think I was going to get the opportunity to come over and talk to you."

I was back to silent. Yep. He shut me up quick and then he continued talking.

"Are you sure your mouth is okay? That looked painful."

I nodded. I still could not believe this man was talking to me.

He grinned. That was when I knew I was in trouble. That grin made him mouth-watering.

What the hell was going on with me?

I needed to get myself together.

"I'm sorry. Did you want to order something?" I asked, still dumbfounded.

He grinned again. "Two Americanos, gorgeous."

Gorgeous?

My belly squeezed at the endearment, and I tried to quickly shake off my surprise. I got to work on his order.

I finished his drinks and brought them over to the counter. He was still smiling, and I tried to remain unaffected by his beautiful face. As I was ringing him up, he decided to talk again.

"So, Charlotte, how long have you worked here?"

"How do you know my name?" I wondered, caught off guard.

He laughed. "Your name tag sort of gives you away."

Crap.

I was an idiot.

And where was the line that I usually had?

Why now, when I had Mr. Muscles in front of me, was there not a single other customer wanting to get a cup of coffee? And where was Hannah? Surely it had been well over twenty minutes at this point, hadn't it?

"Oh, right. I just started working here this season. And it's Charley."

"What?"

"Charley. Charlotte is my name, but I go by Charley."

"Oh. Okay then, Charley. It's nice to meet you. I'm Wes... and that's short for Westley."

"Hi, Wes."

"I guess I'll see you around, gorgeous."

He picked up the cups and winked before turning and walking back to his table. I watched him walk the entire way back. I was not too proud to admit that the man is a serious piece of eye candy. And now that I could see the lower half of his body, I confirmed what I already knew. The rest of him was just as delectable.

Hannah came back from her break five minutes later and I spent the rest of my shift trying not to think about Wes or glance over in his direction.

Two

Wes

DREAM BIG.
Build a career.
Fall in love.
Enjoy life.

I grew up believing this was how it all worked because my parents drilled this into my head. James and Linda Blackman were the epitome of positivity. They worked hard, made a decent living, and showed so much love to each other and their two children, my sister and me, that it was hard not to believe in the fairy tale.

My dad made a living as a pharmacist and, up until the time he and my mom had their first child, that child being me, my mom spent her days as a nurse. Once I was born, she poured every ounce of energy and love into raising me and caring for our family. Three years later, my baby sister, Elizabeth, was born. Our family of four was the picture-perfect image of happiness.

I had been repeating my family's mantra to myself over the last year. I had dreamt big, no doubt about that. I built a career. That took slightly longer than I would have liked, but I pushed hard and made it happen. I'd been working on pursuing this dream for as long as I could remember. Falling in love and enjoying life...I have exactly accomplished those just yet.

Snowboarding is my life. I grew up riding every single weekend during the winter season with my best friends, Zane, Stone, and Luke. The four of us worked on our craft relentlessly and it wasn't long before our group was approached by several big names in the industry looking to sponsor each of us as one of their riders. We all started as amateurs riding in contests and, eventually, all of us became rep riders. Becoming rep riders for the companies was a huge deal at our young ages, and we were beyond thrilled to be doing what we loved, having others recognize our talents. Even though we weren't at the professional level, we could not complain; we had plenty to be thankful for.

During this time when my buddies and I were up and coming in the snowboarding scene, I managed to meet a girl named Dana. I thought that everything was finally coming together. I had the dream, I was honing my craft and learning the business that I would eventually turn into my lifelong career, and I had met someone with whom I thought I would be able to fall in love and create a life.

As the years passed, I knew I did not want to be riding and promoting someone else's brand. I wanted to do this for myself. Once I finished school, I went to work on building my business. My friends knew what my dream was and they supported me all the way. None of them had the same desire to build the business I wanted—they simply wanted to ride—but they helped me in the beginning when I started making my own boards by hand. As I continued making boards, the guys would test them and give me feedback on which designs and materials worked the best and held up through their riding sessions.

With all of my focus on building a business, there wasn't

exactly a ton of disposable income. I was not making much money during this time to begin with. I knew I needed a bit of an income for the basics and to keep pursuing my ultimate dream, so I entered a few contests and did well enough with prize money to make ends meet. After the basics were covered, any leftover funds went straight into making my dream come true. I knew the greater fortune was just ahead and would come in time. I just kept pushing and working to make it happen.

My days were spent working and carving out bits of time to spend with Dana. We had been together for nearly four years when I proposed to her. I was not able to get her the diamond ring that I truly wanted her to have, but I knew that once I got to where I planned to be, there wasn't anything I wouldn't be able to give her.

Over the next six months, I worked day and night to pursue my dream. My relationship with Dana became strained. She was never into snowboarding and mostly tolerated it, but she argued with me several times that I needed to get serious about pursuing a real career. She felt I was putting too much time into something that was going to go nowhere. Despite numerous arguments, I kept pushing to make it happen. One night, I came home to my apartment after a long day building and testing boards to find all of Dana's things were gone. I walked into the bedroom and found that she had left the engagement ring and a note on the bed. She said she could not marry someone who chose fun and games over a serious career.

I haven't heard from her ever since.

That was almost two years ago.

Now, I had finally made it. I kept up my pursuit and it had paid off. I am not only the owner of Blackman Boards, but I have also built a company that now rivals some of the top in this industry. Blackman Boards is a relatively new player in the extreme sports business, but with a big dream and a lot of perseverance, the company has catapulted to the top of the pack.

Blackman Boards has picked up such momentum in the last eight months that I have finally been able to officially sign all three of my best friends as professional riders and I have just recently acquired a new thirty-thousand-square-foot facility to house the operation.

I was sitting in my new office going over the plans for some of the construction I had planned for the warehouse renovation. The office renovations were just recently completed about two weeks ago and I was satisfied with the results. The warehouse was roughly eighteen-thousand-square-feet of space that would house the entire production process for the boards and accessories. The upstairs and downstairs offices made up the remaining twelve-thousand-square feet of space. My office was probably larger than was needed at nearly a thousand square feet and could easily fit two additional employees, but I had worked hard for this place and wanted to reap some of that reward.

Zane walked in.

"Hey," Zane offered his version of good morning.

"What's up, Zane?"

"Not much. Got in an early workout today and figured I'd stop in before heading out to ride."

"Did you get a chance to try out the new lineup for the Fire series?"

"I was planning on it today. Part of the reason I stopped in was to see if you cared to help me test them out."

I stayed silent and stared.

"Come on, Wes. It's been too long since you've ridden with any of us. Things are going well with the company. Don't you think it's time to get back on the board, even if it's just to spend the day out of the office for once?"

He had a point.

"You know what? You're right. Let me make a call to the foreman on the warehouse project and I'll go. I could ride some pipe today."

"It's about damn time," Zane stated with a smile on his face.

At that, I called my foreman, went over a few details, and grabbed my gear.

Zane and I made our way to the Parks Ridge Ski Resort to test out a stack of the prototype boards from our new Fire model line. The Elements Series would consist of four different models—Fire, Air, Water, and Earth. Each model would be designed specifically for a particular type of snowboarding. The Fire model snowboard was slated to be a board designed specifically for pipe riding.

Over the last six months or so, I had been putting so much of my time and energy into the rapidly-growing business I hadn't been able to spend much time on a board. We made it to the resort that morning and spent several hours testing out the boards. We got through most of them within a few hours and finally decided to head into the lodge for a quick bite to eat.

We went in, grabbed some food, and found a place to sit. I knew Zane was going to take the opportunity to get on my case about not having ridden in so long.

"Feeling good, Wes?"

"I'll admit it, man. It has definitely been way too long. I do not regret taking the time to focus on the company, but I can honestly say it really felt great to get back out there."

"Happy to hear it. Do you think we'll catch you out here more now?" he asked.

"I'm not sure. If I do make it out here, it probably won't be very often. I need to make sure things are going smoothly at the new space," I answered.

I knew it wasn't what he wanted to hear, but he accepted

it. He knew this was my dream.

We finished eating and went over all our thoughts on the boards. It was during our review that I had noticed the line for the coffee stand was long. I glanced behind the counter and saw two women working there; one shorter who was of Asian ethnicity and certainly cute, and another who was slightly taller and an absolute knock out. Zane noticed me looking.

"See something you like?" he asked with a smirk on his face.

"I was just thinking after all this riding I am going to need a bit of caffeine to get through the rest of this day."

Zane looked over behind the counter and laughed. "I'm sure it's the caffeine you need."

"That girl is gorgeous," I announced, not taking my eyes off her. "When that line goes down, I'm getting some coffee."

He shook his head at me with a smirk on his face and we got back to our review of the boards. Afterward, he took off to the bathroom while I looked back to the coffee stand. There were only two more customers in line. When Zane returned a few minutes later, I got up. On my walk over, I noticed the shorter girl with dark hair was no longer there, and it was going to be just me and the knockout. She didn't notice me approaching. As I stopped in front of the counter, she was bringing a coffee cup up to her pretty lips. It was then she saw me and burned her mouth. If it wouldn't have made me look like a complete creep, I'd have jumped over the counter and kissed that mouth better.

"Are you okay?" I asked, feeling genuinely concerned for her.

She didn't answer. She stood there staring at me and was quiet for so long I began to wonder if she even heard my question. I tilted my head and then she finally looked back up at my face and started talking a hundred miles a minute. I found myself oddly amused by her. She ultimately asked what she could get for me.

"That looked painful. You sure your mouth is okay?" I asked, realizing once again that I really wanted to make sure she was alright.

She answered me by way of a nod and I realized she was a bit flustered. I smirked and decided to hand over the ropes to her.

I used the silence as a time to take her in. She was beautiful with shiny blonde hair, big blue eyes, a trim body, and those plump, pink lips.

I ended up giving her my order, learned from her name tag that her name was Charlotte, but that she went by Charley, that she had just started working there this season, and introduced myself to her. With that, I took my order and went back to the table Zane was sitting at and spoke.

"You know," I started. "On second thought, I think I might need to come here more regularly. It was refreshing to be back on the board and it's only going to help on the design of the other models in the lineup if I am out here testing some of them."

Laughing at me, Zane replied, "I do not, for one second, doubt your commitment to the business; however, I'm more inclined to believe your change of mind has less to do with riding the boards and more to do with a different kind of ride from Blondie over there."

I just looked at him and back to her. He was right; there was no use denying it.

"Alright, man, I'm heading out. You want to ride tomorrow?" Zane asked.

"I think I might just do that."

Zane shook his head and laughed. "Good ride today. See you later."

"You too. Catch you tomorrow."

I knew the resort was closing soon, so I decided to wait it

out and make sure Charley got to her car safely. In the meantime, I reviewed our notes on the board and wrote down some more ideas for the other three models in the series.

When closing time neared, I went out, put all my gear and paperwork in my truck, and I walked back to the lodge. I timed it perfectly because as I approached the lodge, she was walking out with her co-worker.

"Hi, Charley."

She stopped and looked at me. Then she turned to her friend and introduced us.

"Hannah, this is Wes. Wes, Hannah."

I nodded to her. "Nice to meet you."

Her eyes got big and she looked to Charley. Then she smiled big. "You too."

After a beat of silence, Hannah not so discreetly and rather loudly declared, "Well, I'm beat. I have to get out of here." She hugged Charley and whispered something to her before she informed her, "I'm off tomorrow, but I'll see you Monday."

Hannah was gone before Charley could say anything.

"I was hoping I could walk you to your car," I told her, honestly.

She hesitated, stayed silent while staring at me, and then started walking toward the parking lot. I took that as a sign that she was okay with me seeing her to her car. I glanced to where Hannah had walked and found that she'd made it to her car.

Charley surprised me when she finally spoke.

"Do you come here often?"

"I've been coming here my whole life. It's the best place to ride. Do you snowboard?"

For a moment I thought I noticed her step falter, but decided to ignore it.

"No. I've never done it. Though, ever since I've moved

here I've secretly wanted to learn," she responded.

"Seriously? If you want to learn, I'd be happy to show you how to snowboard."

"Thanks for the offer, but I don't have a lot of free time."

Suddenly, she stopped, and I realized we were standing next to a bright orange Jeep Rubicon.

"This is yours?" I asked.

She looked away and nodded. When she faced me again, I could see a sadness in her eyes. The last thing I wanted was to make her upset so I decided not to push it. I was taken aback at how much seeing that look on her face affected me.

She seemed to quickly swallow whatever it was and smiled. The smile didn't reach her eyes, though.

"Well, thanks for walking me to my car, Wes. I guess I'll see you around," she said.

I opened the door for her while she climbed in.

"You absolutely will."

Three

Charley

Wes closed my door and waited while I started the Jeep and drove off.

As I drove home, I began to replay everything that had happened from the moment Wes walked up to my stand until I got in my car. I didn't know what I was doing. This was the first time in nearly a year that I even noticed an attractive guy.

Who was I kidding? Wes was not attractive. He was devastatingly beautiful. I had no idea what was going on with me and, quite frankly, it scared me a little.

I had a feeling that Wes planned to make good on his parting words that I'd see him around. I knew this was a bad idea. I could not come to terms with how I felt just being near him, though. My mind was telling me that being around him was going to lead to heartbreak, one way or another, while my heart and body were simultaneously telling me that this guy was a good guy who would be worth it.

I made it home and walked in to find Emme had made good on her promise to pick up wine. She had several bottles set out on the island. I walked down the hall toward her bedroom and stopped in front of her door.

"Hey Em, I'm home," I called as I knocked on her door.

"Hi sweets, I just got out of the shower," she returned. "I'll be out in a few."

"Okay. I'm going to hop in the shower quickly, and then I'll meet you on the couch."

"I'll get the wine poured. Do you have a preference?"

"Sweet red."

"Got it."

I walked to my bedroom, got undressed, and turned the shower on to hot. When the bathroom had sufficiently steamed up, I got in and did my thing. I tried not to let my mind wander, but every time I closed my eyes under the spray of the water all I could see were those emerald eyes and that wicked grin. I finished up in the shower and put on my favorite sweatpants and sleep shirt. Tonight was all about comfort.

I padded down the hall and back into the living room where Emme was parked on the couch with a glass of wine in one hand and the remote in her other hand. There was a filled wine glass for me on the coffee table. She had the television on, but I suspected she wasn't really paying attention to it.

She looked over to me.

"How was the rest of your day?" she asked.

"Interesting, to say the least," I told her. "I got to Brew Stirs and it was busy as usual. Hannah and I were swamped for several hours until it slowed down about an hour and a half before we closed. Then, I burned my mouth on a cup of coffee when I saw the world's hottest guy standing at the counter."

Emme didn't say anything, but I could see her mind working.

"Emme. I couldn't speak. I don't know what happened to me, but it was like I lost control over all of my bodily functions as soon as I saw him. And then, he called me gorgeous. Twice!"

She was smiling. "That's because you are gorgeous,

sweets. So, what happened next?"

"He ended up waiting around until I finished my shift, and when Hannah and I walked out of the lodge, he asked to walk me to my car."

"What?" she practically shrieked.

"Yes. And again, I could not speak so I just started walking and he fell into step beside me."

I then went on to tell her about our conversation and how I nearly tripped when he told me how Parks Ridge was 'the best place to ride' and then almost broke down into tears when he asked about my Jeep. Of course, I told her how he said that I'd definitely be seeing him around. She listened to me and then smiled at me, her eyes tearing up.

"It makes no sense to me, but despite my inability to speak around him, I feel comfortable. He has this way about him that just makes you feel...I don't know, warm. Safe. I know maybe four things about him, but I already feel that way being near him. How is it possible?"

I knew, of all people, she didn't have an answer to that. She would likely never be able to give me that answer, but I asked anyway.

We spent the rest of the night polishing off the bottle of wine. I listened while she told me about her day and the engaged couple who made her head spin. They sounded like the world's most perfect couple. They were so in love and Emme told me she could feel it was a true, genuine love. She just barely made it through the meeting.

We sat in silence for a few minutes and she stared off toward the window when she asked, "Is it ever going to get easier, Charley?"

I took a deep breath and answered honestly when I sighed, "I don't know, Em."

We said nothing after that.

We didn't need to.

Occasionally, Emme and I did that. We simply sat in silence after catching up with each other, somehow finding comfort in the quiet presence of one another. She would refill my wine glass or vice versa. We'd polish off a bottle sometimes and, without many other words, head off to bed. That's precisely what happened that night.

The next morning, I woke before my alarm went off.

I hadn't slept well.

I never did when Emme and I had days that made us remember the past. I knew I needed to get some time in with my art. That always helped when I felt overwhelmed with thoughts about everything we'd been through.

Thankfully, I had a shorter shift scheduled today at the diner and did not have to be in until ten o'clock. This would give me enough time to put a solid hour or two in on my artwork. I rolled out of bed, pulled out my art supplies, and had at it.

I set my alarm for an hour and a half later so that I would have enough time to get ready and still be at work on time. I needed to set the alarm or I could very easily get lost in what I was working on and forget about any actual responsibilities I had.

Before I knew it, the alarm went off, but I was feeling much better. My artwork had a way of refocusing and calming me. I put my supplies away and got ready for work.

I told Emme I was leaving and made my way to First Tracks. I was happy to see that it was busy when I got there.

"Hey, Charley. How's it going?" Greg greeted me.

Greg was one of my co-workers at the diner. He, along with a few others that worked there, was one of the few friends I had made here in Wyoming apart from Hannah and Mark. I loved working with them all but never had an opportunity to enjoy them outside of work, despite numerous invitations from all of them. This was, of course, except for the plans I had finally settled on with Emme and Hannah for a night out this weekend.

Greg made work fun. He was always in great spirits and made the place more enjoyable for not only the staff but for the patrons as well. I'm certain he was one of the main reasons the diner had so many regulars. I blamed his consistently carefree mood on his relationship. He had been dating Tony for just over a year and they were blissfully happy.

"I'm good, Greg. How are you?"

"Tony and I are planning to road trip out to Utah next Friday for a long weekend. I don't work again until the following Tuesday morning, so we'll head back early Monday morning. That said, I'm doing absolutely fine, girl."

"That sounds awesome," I began before it suddenly hit me. "Wait. Isn't Tony originally from Utah?"

"Yep," he beamed at me. His face had lit up.

It was then I realized what this meant.

"Oh, Greg. You're meeting the parents, aren't you?" I asked, the giddiness flowing from me.

He shook his head excitedly and I smiled.

I was happy he had Tony because from what I learned over the last six months here, Greg hadn't received the best reception from his parents when told them he was gay. I really hoped the weekend went well for him.

"That's fantastic news. Congratulations!"

After my chat with Greg I got right to work and, as was typically the case, the day passed by quickly. My shift was over before I knew it. Before I left, I ordered myself a chicken wrap and then walked up to Greg, gave him a hug, and wished him luck.

"I can't wait to hear all about your trip when you get back. See you on Tuesday, Gregory."

I made my way out to my Jeep and drove to my second job. I had just over an hour to spare before my shift started and since I hadn't slept well last night, I figured I'd take a quick nap. I set my alarm on my phone so that I would have enough time to wake up, get my bearings, and eat my food before I started work. With that, I dropped the back of my seat down and fell asleep.

It felt like I had just closed my eyes when I heard a tapping sound. It startled me because I hadn't changed the ringtone on my alarm. I heard it again. I opened my eyes and nearly jumped out of my seat.

Wes was looking in my passenger's side window at me. He had a look of concern on his face. I looked at my phone; it had only been thirty minutes. I looked back to Wes and put the window down about halfway. I didn't know what he was doing there, and he disturbed me, so I figured he could talk first. I stayed silent and stared at him.

"I am pretty certain I walked you to your car yesterday and watched you drive away," he stated.

Okay, that was an odd conversation opener. "You did. So…" I replied, trailing off waiting for further explanation.

"So? So, I pulled into the lot a few minutes ago and saw your Jeep in the exact same spot it was in yesterday all the way here at the back of the lot. Thinking I'd like to make it easier for when I walk you to your car tonight, I decided to park next to you. When I got out of my car and saw you asleep in yours, I was not sure if what I witnessed yesterday actually happened. You didn't just drive away and then come back and park here after I left, right? Please tell me that as kick-ass as this Jeep is that you don't live in it."

When he walked me to my car tonight?

"It's cold out there and all of the heat is going out the window."

"You could put the window up."

So I did.

And then he grinned at me. Damn it. This guy was too

good-looking, and I had a feeling he knew it, too.

I unlocked the door.

He got in the car. I just looked at him.

"You still didn't answer my questions."

"No. I did not leave and come back after you left and I do not live in my kick-ass Jeep," I assured him. Then, I'm not sure why, but I continued talking. "I just got here about thirty minutes ago. I left my first job and had enough time before my shift at Brew Stirs starts that I decided to get a quick nap in before eating and heading in to work."

"Where else do you work?"

"First Tracks. I'm a waitress at the diner."

"Why are you working two jobs?"

"What is this? Twenty questions? I'm not sure I should be answering all of this for someone I just met and know almost nothing about," I informed him.

Then again, I did open my door and allow him to sit in my car, I thought.

Wes smiled. "What do you want to know, gorgeous?"

He seriously needed to stop calling me that.

"Okay. Well, how about you tell me why you are here for the second day in a row and not working even one job?"

"There are two answers to that question. First, I'm here for the second day in a row because yesterday was the first time I'd been here in months and much to my surprise I realized I was missing out on things. I do not want to miss out on those things anymore. Second, I do work. I worked yesterday, and I was up early this morning to work. I've already put in a solid eight and a half hours today."

I looked to the clock on my dash. "It's only two thirty in the afternoon."

He had a full-blown smile on his face at this point. "Like I said, I realized yesterday there were things here I did not want to miss out on."

I stared at him for a beat and decided it was best not to respond. Instead, I reached into the back seat and grabbed the bag with my food. I wasn't really feeling hungry anymore, but I needed a distraction. I took out half of the wrap and started eating. Wes sat there silently and watched me for a few minutes. I was surprised at how comfortable it felt. I had just met this guy, and he was now sitting in my Jeep watching me eat.

I had just taken a huge bite of my wrap when I looked up at Wes and saw him shaking his head, trying not to laugh.

"What is so funny?" I asked, my mouth full of food.

"You're adorable."

I finished chewing and swallowed. "Excuse me?"

"You're adorable."

I harrumphed.

"So, what time do you have to be to work, Charley?"

"In about twenty minutes."

"Do you do this every day? And do you usually have this much time between the job at the diner and the coffee stand?"

"That's my gig Monday through Friday. And most days I do have this much time in between. I occasionally stay a little later at the diner if they are really busy."

I looked at him and it seemed he was thinking. I left him to it. He was easy on the eyes, so I just stared at him. He eventually broke the silence.

"What do you do for fun on the weekends?" he asked.

"Sometimes I pick up an extra shift or two at the diner on Saturdays. Other than that, I do the normal stuff like grocery shopping, laundry, and house cleaning."

He went silent again and had that same look of concern on his face.

I finished half of my wrap, started gathering my things and asked, "And you? Is walking girls to their cars after they have had a full day of work your idea of fun?"

He chuckled. "Well, you'd be the first I've done that with,

so I'll have to get back to you on that. So far, it's been okay, but I'm hopeful that the real fun is coming soon."

Then he winked at me.

Damn.

I glared at him. He laughed.

We got out of the Jeep and I found myself surprised that I wanted to wait for him while he grabbed his snowboarding gear out of his truck, a Chevy Tahoe. Wes walked me to the lodge, confirmed that I was there until closing, and said he'd be back to walk with me after work. I thanked him and told him to have a good time.

"Hi, Mark," I greeted as I walked up to the coffee stand.

Mark was a great guy. He was friendly, caring, and offered a lot in the way of emotional support. He'd not done this for me as I kept things mostly private, but Hannah had told me about how he helped her out of a sticky situation once when an ex of hers showed up at the lodge one day. Hannah's ex would not accept the fact that things were over between them, so when he showed up at the lodge not long after their break up, Mark easily stepped in and played the role of Hannah's new love interest. Hannah's ex never showed his face after that. Mark stood at an even six feet tall with brown hair and brown eyes. He was handsome in that boy-next-door way and he had the personality to match.

"Yo, Charley," he returned.

"Have you recovered from yesterday morning's madness?" I asked.

He scowled at me. "It was miserable here. Thankfully, today has been just steady. I'm off for the night now. I'm working a double tomorrow."

"Okay. Have a good night, Mark. See you next week," I replied.

"You too."

"Thanks."

My night passed quickly as it was relatively steady throughout the evening. I had a few moments to myself and, during those times, I'd find myself looking at the door to the lodge where I knew Wes would walk in at some point, looking to the table where Wes had been seated yesterday, or simply thinking about his handsome face. I still could not quite understand why I was so distracted by this man.

Since Emme and I arrived in Wyoming, I had been approached by guys, but I'd never given any of them a second look. In fact, when I took a minute to really think about it, I realized that I had not been on a date in more than a year. Things had changed so drastically in my life nine months ago that I didn't have the interest in going out to pursue a relationship. In fact, the thought of a relationship that could ultimately end in heartbreak or tragedy terrified me. It puzzled me as to why I so quickly felt comfortable with Wes. During the downtime that I did have, I realized I kept looking to the clock to see what time it was. I couldn't wait until I was finished and he could walk me to my car.

The next thing I knew, Wes walked in and I had just finished cleaning up everything for the night. I had made two cups of hot chocolate with whipped cream on top for the both of us. I figured after spending a couple hours on the mountain he could use something to help him warm up.

"Ready?" he asked.

"Yes. Hot chocolate? I just made it so it's still pretty hot. I kept the lid off so it'll cool a little quicker."

He smiled and took the cup from me. We started walking toward the door.

"How was it?" I asked.

"Good. It feels great to be riding again after so much time off."

"Why did you stop?"

"I've been busy with work. I forgot that I needed to make

time for the things that make me happy," he began. "Don't get me wrong. I love what I do and I don't regret the time I put in, but I'm happy my buddy talked me into coming riding yesterday. It was definitely worth it…in more ways than one."

We made our way outside and approached our cars. Wes put his gear in the back of his truck and his hot chocolate in the front driver's side cup holder while I turned on my Jeep to warm it up. He walked back over to where I was standing.

"Thanks again, Wes—for both the company and for walking me to my car."

"And thanks for the hot chocolate. I've got to admit, though, I'm a bit bummed."

I turned and had my back up against the driver's side door of my car. I looked up at him and asked, "Why?"

"You aren't working again until Monday and I'd really like to see you again before that. Are you free this weekend?"

Damn, I really wanted to see him again.

"I actually have plans with my best friend, who is also my roommate, tomorrow along with Hannah. Maybe another time?"

Another time? Did I just say that?

I bit my lip. This guy had seriously thrown me off kilter.

He curled his hand into a fist and placed it under my chin while he swiped his thumb along my bottom lip pulling it free from my teeth.

"Another time then," he accepted, gently.

I took a sip of my hot chocolate and quickly licked my lips to make sure I didn't have any whipped cream on them.

He looked from my eyes back to my lips. "Damn, Charley."

"What's wrong?"

He leaned closer to me. "I'd really like to kiss you."

My heart started pounding, and I decided to give in to what I was feeling. "I think I'd really like for you to kiss me."

I barely got the last word out before Wes had one hand behind my head while the other rested at my hip and his lips came crashing down on mine. It was firm but slow. I kissed him back, one hand resting on his arm the other still holding my cup of hot cocoa. He teased my lips with his tongue, and I opened my mouth to let him in. Wes shifted my body closer to his, tilted his head, and deepened the kiss. It was delicious.

It was at this moment I was hating that it was so cold out. I seriously wanted to feel more of Wes' body, but we both had too many layers on. He continued to kiss me, our tongues dancing until Wes broke the kiss and rested his forehead against mine while his hand squeezed the back of my neck.

"Wow," I whispered.

"These lips," he murmured before he pressed another soft kiss to my lips. "Gorgeous, Charley."

I felt my face flush and my belly squeeze at his words. I looked back up into his eyes and he needed no further invitation. He kissed me again. It was slightly more frenzied this time; yet, it was still so very yummy. After several minutes of kissing like high school teenagers in a parking lot, Wes pulled away again.

"As much as I want to drag you into my truck and take you back to my place I'm going to wait. You need to get in your car now, though and get warm," he instructed.

After I got in the Jeep, he closed the door and I put my window down.

"Where is your phone?" he asked.

I took my phone out of my purse and held it up to him. He seized it from my hand and tapped on the screen. I heard another phone start to ring and he handed my phone back to me. "Now you have my number and I have yours."

I smiled at him. "Thanks again, Wes."

"No need to thank me, gorgeous. Though, I won't say no if you want to show your appreciation with another kiss."

I pressed my lips together and acted as though I was thinking about it before I reached my hand out to him. He leaned in so I could give him one last kiss.

Gosh, he was such a great kisser.

I could kiss him all night and not tire of it.

This time I broke the kiss. "I should really get going. Good night, Wes."

"Good night, Charley."

I drove home and thought about Wes' kisses the whole way there. As soon as I got home, I hopped in the shower, did my business, threw on some clothes, grabbed a bottle of water from the fridge, and climbed into bed.

Despite the lack of sleep last night, the long day I'd had, and the nap that I did not get to finish I was still so restless. I hadn't felt this way in so many months, mostly because I worked myself to utter exhaustion. But Wes had gotten me all worked up. I rolled over toward my nightstand and opened the top drawer. I pulled out my vibrator and with one hand controlling the vibrator and the other at my breast I thought about Wes' arms around me, his body pressed to mine, his lips kissing me, and I came. Minutes later, though much later than my usual bedtime, I was asleep.

Four

Charley

I HAD A REALLY BUSY WEEKEND.

I woke Saturday morning and spent the better part of the morning doing laundry and cleaning. I went grocery shopping that afternoon and then made some calls to Nikki and Monroe to catch up with them. They were doing well, but both were bummed that my birthday was the following weekend and we wouldn't be spending it together. I tried not to get too upset and knew that, despite my sadness over not seeing them, I was in the right place for me at the moment.

On Saturday evening, I went out with Emme and Hannah. In fact, it was pretty much the first time that the two of us had gone out with anyone else since we moved to Wyoming. We went for dinner and drinks and had a great time. This was mostly because it was a mellow evening out. Nothing too crazy and certainly not more than either of us was prepared to handle at the time.

On Sunday, I slept in. It was glorious. I hadn't realized just how exhausted my body had been. I had received a text from Wes late Sunday morning, which is what woke me.

Thinking of you.

It was such a simple text, but it made me smile. It felt

good. At the same time, it completely freaked me out. Still, not one to be rude, I decided to respond.

☺ I was sleeping.

Wes: Didn't mean to wake you. Though, considering it's nearly 11am, it sounds like it's been a good weekend so far.

Me: I actually wasn't out that late. I think I'm just overworked and exhausted. ☹

Wes: Well that doesn't make me feel any better.

Me: Ok, then. How about—if I hadn't been sleeping when you texted I'm pretty certain I would have replied with, "Same here."?

Wes: Now I feel better.

Me: So, what's the rest of your weekend looking like?

Wes: Getting a workout in and then going to my parents' house later this afternoon. Today is their monthly family Sunday dinner. You?

Me: Nothing too crazy. Catching up on sleep, getting some things done around the house, and helping my roommate on a project she's working on.

Wes: Ok. I'll let you get to it. See you soon.

Me: Later, Wes. ☺

I then got to it.

I spent the rest of my Sunday doing just what I'd told Wes. I finished tidying up around the house, spent some time with my designs, and then helped Emme with a wedding album she'd just finished up for some clients. She was an incredible photographer, but she always asked my opinion on albums she put together before she presented them to her clients. I think she thought with my graphic design passion I would have some incredible insight to changing the albums. She always did such an amazing job, though, that it was rare that I made any crazy suggestions.

After I helped her, I made good on my word and caught

up on my sleep by heading to bed rather early.

Before I knew it, Monday morning had arrived and I was getting ready for another week of work. On the bright side, this week gave me a little something to look forward to as Saturday was my birthday and Emme and I had planned to go out to dinner.

I had an early morning shift at First Tracks so I was out of the house before Emme was awake. The early morning shifts on a Monday were always busy. I thoroughly enjoyed the people I worked with as well as the patrons, but I hated doing this job day in and day out. It was exhausting and, more than anything, I realized I was not feeling personally fulfilled working there. Then again, when I took the time to think about things in my life in general, I was not expecting happiness anymore. I really needed to learn to accept that I'd be doing what I needed to do to survive and happiness or fulfillment was not likely going to be part of the equation anymore. The occasional night out with Emme, Hannah, Greg, or all three of them might be the extent of happiness I'd see in my life.

My shift had ended and I made my way out to the Jeep. The one thing I realized I missed at work today was Greg. I knew he was on his way back from Utah and that got me excited about coming in to work tomorrow. I could not wait to hear all about his trip and the meeting with Tony's parents.

I tapped out a quick text to him.

Hi Gregory. Just making sure you are coming back to WY?

He responded immediately.

Tony and I are on our way now.

Me: Hope all went well for you this weekend.

Greg: It was AMAZING. Tony's parents are freaking awesome, Charley. They are so supportive and invited us both back out for Christmas with Tony's entire family.

Me: That's awesome, Greg. I can't wait to hear all

about it tomorrow. Safe travels!

Greg: Thanks, girl. See you tomorrow!

I tossed my phone into my purse, fired up the Jeep, and made my way over to Parks Ridge. I pulled into the lot and made my way over to my usual parking spot. I noticed Wes' Tahoe was already parked in the spot next to where I typically parked. I felt the butterflies fluttering in my belly. As I pulled into my spot, I realized Wes was in his truck. Once he saw me pull in, he climbed out. I found it odd that he didn't hop in on the passenger's side. Instead, he walked around to my side of the Jeep and opened my door.

"Did you eat, gorgeous?"

I pulled my eyebrows together at his question and answered, "Yes."

"Great. Get out," he demanded and then walked away.

"Excuse me?" I asked, shocked at him giving me orders.

"Today is day one," he replied loudly, now standing at the back of his Tahoe.

I hopped out of the Jeep and walked around to where he was standing. "I'm sorry, I'm confused. Day one of what?" I wondered.

He was rummaging through the back of his vehicle and pulled out his snowboarding gear. He pulled out his boards, turned to me, and declared, "Your snowboarding lessons start today."

I stared at him, my eyes huge. "What?"

"You said you wanted to learn how to ride. I'm going to teach you how to ride."

No, no, no.

I was going to lose it.

I could feel it coming.

I could not do this. I needed an excuse…fast.

"Um, I…I can't do this today," I started, stammering as I tried to come up with a legitimate excuse. "I haven't ever done it before, but I'm pretty certain that my current attire is not appropriate for learning to snowboard."

He laughed and shook his head. Then, he reached back into his truck and pulled out a bag. He held it out to me and urged, "Open it."

I opened it.

Inside, there were all the trimmings for a proper snowboarding outfit, including thermals, pants, jacket, gloves, goggles, and helmet. My jaw dropped and I looked back at Wes, who was still smiling.

"I...You...I can't."

"Yes, you can. You sat here last week and not only did you tell me that you wanted to learn how to snowboard, but also that you basically do nothing to let loose and have a good time. You can't just work your life away and miss out on all the fun. You are going to have a good time today. And you're going to do it with me."

My eyes started to feel wet. "Wes."

"No arguments, Charley. We have a lot of time left before you start work, and we can get a lot accomplished in the time we have. Let's go."

I stood there, staring at him. He continued to grab the rest of the gear and boards out of his truck before he closed the rear door.

"Ready?" he asked.

"I guess I'm learning how to snowboard today," I mumbled.

After he grinned a huge grin and winked at me, Wes walked toward me and gave me a kiss on the cheek.

We made our way into the lodge so I could change into appropriate boarding attire.

Just over an hour later there was absolutely no doubt in my mind that ice packs and Ibuprofen were in my near future. I had been up on the mountain, on the beginner's slope, with

Wes, and I'd fallen more times than I cared to admit. There wasn't a single part of my body that did not ache.

On the bright side, I realized that had it been smooth sailing I would have likely been riding down a trail thinking too much and had a breakdown. I was willing to have a bruised ass if it meant not having to think about things that would have really sent me into a tailspin.

After I changed out of the snowboarding gear and back into my clothes for work, Wes and I walked back out to the parking lot with the bags and boards.

"I appreciate your offer to teach me, Wes. This must have been absolutely brutal for you."

"It wasn't that bad," he replied. "It is expected that you'll fall when you first learn. I sure did. In fact, I can remember trying to teach myself how to do it and I failed miserably. It wasn't until I received actual instruction that I really picked it up. To be honest, I'm really surprised at how well you did."

"What?"

"I'm not kidding, Charley. For your first time on a board, you did fantastic."

I had a feeling he was just being nice because I didn't really think I did all that well. Rolling my eyes, I scoffed, "Tell that to my ass!"

"I'd be happy to," he teased, grinning at me.

I looked at him and rolled my eyes again. "I'm serious. I don't know what hurts worse, my ass or my legs."

"It'll get easier, I promise. Based on what I saw today I am willing to bet you'll be able to ride down a blue trail before the end of the week. Sure, you fell a lot in the beginning, but toward the end of our session you were able to get from the top to the bottom of the hill three separate times without falling."

We approached the cars and I walked to the back of Wes' truck. "Thanks for letting me borrow the board and all this gear," I said. I didn't want to think too much about why he had all of this women's stuff.

"That's yours."

"I'm sorry. What?" I asked, my body freezing on the spot.

"That stuff is all for you, Charley."

"I can't accept this. Are you kidding me?"

I hadn't been snowboarding before, but I was not an idiot. I knew this all must have cost a pretty penny.

"Why not? We're going to ride again tomorrow. In fact, we're going to have lessons every day for the rest of the week."

My body shuddered at the promise of seeing him every day for the next week. I had money that I had no intentions of touching, but with the extra shifts I had picked up at the diner I could afford to buy the stuff he brought. "Okay, but then you have to let me pay you for all of this. How much do I owe you?"

"You aren't paying me for anything."

"But Wes…"

"Charley, listen. Do you remember last week you were asking me if I worked?"

"Yes."

"My name is Wes Blackman. I own Blackman Boards. Everything here is from my company and I don't want your money. I just want to spend time with you and teach you how to ride. Besides, the way I see it, a gorgeous girl like you riding powder with my stuff outfitting you is free advertising for my company."

I stood there staring at him. "You own Blackman Boards?"

"Yes."

"And you want to teach me how to ride?"

He laughed. "That's what I said."

I didn't know what he found so amusing. He was who he was and I was just me.

"Why?" I asked.

"Because I'm intrigued by you. You said you wanted to

learn how to ride and I know how to do that. The fact that you are a great kisser is just icing on the cake."

I didn't know what else to say, so I smiled at him and said the only thing I could. "I don't know what to say, Wes. Thank you."

"You're welcome, gorgeous."

We put my stuff in my Jeep and he put his stuff in his truck. I watched him put his things away and I was, undeniably, a bit bummed. I was hoping he'd be walking me to my car after work tonight.

As if he could see my thoughts swirling in my head he spoke, "I have to go get some things done at my new warehouse for the company. I'll be back later tonight to walk you to your car. You work until close?"

I tried to hide my smile, but it was no use. "Yes, but you don't have to do that, Wes."

"Is someone else going to be here with you?"

"I think Hannah is on until close with me tonight."

"Then I'm coming back to walk you to your car. You are a beautiful woman, Charley. Walking to your car in a mostly empty parking lot in the dark is not an option. Hannah isn't going to be able to protect you and, quite frankly, she shouldn't be walking alone either."

"I can't ask you to do that."

"You didn't. Now, do you want to spend the last three minutes you have left before you have to walk in there arguing about something that isn't going to change, or do you want to spend that time letting me taste those lips again?"

How could I say no? I mean, he refused to let me pay for the snowboarding gear, and I assumed I'd get the same response on asking to pay for lessons. He also insisted on coming back to walk me to my car. Kissing him was certainly no hardship for me.

I took two steps toward Wes and immediately felt his

hands at my hips. I tilted my head back to look up at him while he lowered his mouth to mine. We spent the next three minutes kissing.

Then, Wes walked me back to the lodge and kissed me quickly on the lips before he went back to work.

"So, when were you going to tell me that you were dating Wes Blackman?" Hannah asked as I walked up to the stand. She had a line in front of her, but that didn't seem to bother her as she continued, "I mean, I didn't want to bring it up this weekend because I was hoping you would, but I can't stand it anymore. I want details."

"I'm not dating Wes Blackman," I insisted. "And how do you know him anyway?"

"I grew up here. Wes grew up here. He's a local celebrity. How would I not know who he is?"

I'd been living here for six months and it just became clear to me that I was not getting out enough. If Wes was considered a local celebrity and I hadn't even heard of him, it was safe to assume that I'd kept myself isolated since moving here.

"So?" Hannah pressed.

"What? I'm not dating him. I just met him," I answered.

"And yet he walked you to your car last Thursday. Hmmm," she said sarcastically as she tapped her fingers across her lips.

"And Friday," I corrected. Then, I added, "And he's coming back here tonight too."

"I'm sorry. Did you say coming back?"

"He was kind of already here when I arrived following my shift at First Tracks. He brought a bunch of snowboarding gear and he gave me lessons. He just went back to work, but said he'd be back tonight to walk me to my car again."

Hannah stood there staring at me. Her eyes were nearly popping out of her head and her jaw had dropped. "He totally wants in your pants."

Now, it was my turn to stare at her.

The customer in front of her cleared his throat, which thankfully got her back to work and no longer focusing on my situation with Wes. I jumped in and took the next customer in line so that I, too, didn't have to focus on my situation with Wes.

I was thankful for the distraction of a busy night as it meant I would not have to discuss this whole Wes thing with Hannah. Unfortunately, not having much time to discuss the situation didn't mean that it wasn't consuming my thoughts. Despite my best efforts to not focus on all things Wes, all I could do was think of him and the possibility that he totally wanted in my pants. Somehow, I was certain that was worse.

It was about a half hour before closing time when things started to slow down. Hannah and I took the break in stride and started working on some of our clean-up duties.

"Hey, I wanted to ask you if you'd mind picking up my day shift next Tuesday?" she asked. "I am willing to switch with you and can take your shift this Thursday night if you can do that for me."

"Sure. I just need to see if I can get someone to cover me at the diner. Nearly everyone there owes me a few shifts for covering a Saturday morning shift for them so I'm sure I can make it happen. Consider it done," I answered.

"Thanks, Charley."

"No problem, Hannah."

Five minutes before closing I saw the front doors to the lodge open and in walked Wes. He locked eyes with me and a sexy grin spread across his face. I felt the butterflies in my tummy and felt a smile tug at my lips.

"Yep. Totally wants in your pants, girl," Hannah joked,

snapping me out of my lust-filled fog.

I turned to her with my eyes wide. "Hannah!!"

"What? If Wes Blackman was looking at me like that and wanted in my pants, I'd totally let him."

"You're certifiable," I told her.

"Charley, I'm not the crazy one," she insisted. "Look at him—it'd be crazy for you to let a body like that go to waste."

It was then I realized that I was seeing Wes for the first time in regular clothing and not snow pants. He had on a pair of olive green cargo pants and a black slim fitting pullover hoodie. He looked delectable. I licked my lips and heard giggling. I looked to my left and saw Hannah laughing at me.

"He wants in your pants, girl, no doubt about it. But from what I can see, you definitely want him to get what he wants."

I glared at her.

"Hey, gorgeous," Wes called as he walked up to the coffee stand.

Great. Now Hannah had more ammunition for her whole Wes-getting-in-my-pants idea.

"Hi, Wes. We're just about finished. I just need to close up the register."

"Take your time," he said.

I quickly finished up and Hannah and I grabbed our things.

"Ready," I announced.

We all walked to the front doors and out into the parking lot. Wes turned to Hannah and asked, "Where are you parked?"

Hannah pointed to her car which was closer to the lodge and on the way to where Wes and I were both parked. Wes nodded and we all walked together silently. I took the time to think about the fact that Wes seemed to be a true gentleman. He didn't have to ask Hannah where she was parked, but I believed he was truly concerned and had she been parked elsewhere he would have made sure that she made it to her car safely.

As we approached Hannah's car, she spoke. "Thanks again for covering me next Tuesday, Charley. Enjoy having Thursday off."

"It's no problem at all," I assured her. "I'll see you tomorrow."

Hannah got in her car while Wes and I continued walking to our cars. "You have the day off Thursday?"

"Well I'm still working at the diner Thursday morning, but Hannah needed me to cover her day shift next Tuesday so she's going to swap and take my shift here Thursday evening."

"Got any plans for Thursday evening yet?"

"No. I mean, she just asked me..." I trailed off. We had made it to the cars, and when I looked up at him, he was staring at me with a smirk on his face. "What?"

"Meet me here at the usual time Thursday. I'll give you your lessons and then I'm having dinner with you," he declared.

I stared back. This was not going to be good. I couldn't do this. I could not open myself up to this. "Wes, I'm flattered, but—" I couldn't finish because he cut me off.

"Gorgeous. I've been waiting for the right time to ask you to have dinner with me. I figured I'd wait and give you lessons for at least a week before taking the next step. The way I see it, your girl asking you to switch shifts with her is an opportunity that we should not let pass since it does not seem like you have off very often."

I stared at him a beat. This was going to be trouble. I knew it. Against my better judgment, I accepted his invitation anyway. "Okay. I'll meet you here on Thursday for lessons," I conceded.

"And dinner afterward," he added, taking a step closer to me.

"And dinner afterward," I repeated.

"Do you eat steak?" he asked, his lips coming closer to mine with one hand behind my head and the other splayed on my hip.

"I eat steak," I answered.

Wes gently brushed his lips against mine. He playfully teased my lips with his tongue. I opened my mouth and allowed his tongue to slip inside and stroke against mine. The kiss started off sweet and gentle and quickly grew wet and hot. When Wes kissed me last week, it was the first time I'd kissed a guy in nearly a year. I hadn't had sex in nearly two years. Standing there with his lips on mine and his tongue in my mouth I was once again feeling things I hadn't felt in a very long time. I let out a moan and that made him grip my hip harder and pull me closer to him. Wes groaned and pulled his mouth away from mine.

"If we don't stop now, I'm putting you in my truck and taking you back to my place," he claimed.

"We should probably stop now then."

"Get in your Jeep, Charley," he ordered through gritted teeth.

"Okay."

I did what he asked, mostly because I felt bad. I knew that I couldn't take that next step with him and I had felt the evidence of what our little make-out session had done to him. I put my window down and looked to him. "Thank you for coming back to see me safely to my car."

"Good night."

"Night."

I smiled at him, put my window up, and drove away. When I got home, I took a shower and got in bed. My cell phone chimed indicating I had received a text. It was from Wes.

I'm thinking I made a mistake. I should have put you in my truck.

Me: If it makes you feel any better, I'll admit that it wasn't easy to get in my Jeep. With a little bit of work, I may have been easily swayed to go with you.

Wes: Fuck.

Me: Haha. I'm sorry. I had fun, though. And I haven't had that in a very long time. Thank you for the snowboarding lessons, the gear, and the kisses.

Wes: You want me to come pick you up now?

Me: I'm already showered and warm in my bed. I'm NOT going back out in the cold!

Wes: Fuck!

Me: Good night, Wes. xx

Wes: Sleep, gorgeous.

I put my phone back on my nightstand and tried to get to sleep. I soon realized Wes wasn't the only one who'd gotten worked up and had no release. I slipped one of my hands into my panties and imagined it was Wes' hand touching me. Within minutes, I came and fell asleep, warm in my bed.

Five

Charley

IT FELT LIKE ONLY HOURS HAD PASSED WHEN I WAS WALKING BACK into the diner. Luckily, I had a later start this morning, and I was feeling much better after having some time this morning to draw. I walked to the room off the back of the kitchen and saw Greg.

"You're back, Gregory," I stated the obvious.

"In the flesh, girl."

"Spill," I ordered. "And don't leave out a single detail."

"It was fabulous. Tony's parents are so amazing and so supportive. The whole ride there I was freaking out and Tony kept telling me to relax. He said his parents were awesome and they'd love me. Of course, having a negative reaction from my parents when I came out to them made me even more nervous. Tony's parents already knew he was gay and have accepted him from day one, but it didn't change the fact that my nerves were shot dreading the possibility that they might not like me."

"You poor thing. So, what happened when you got there?"

"Tony's mom came running out to the car with open arms. Literally. She hugged him and then walked right up to me and hugged me. She told me that she'd heard a lot about me from Tony and that it was so great to finally meet me. I had no idea he'd told her so much about me. It was shocking, but it felt so good to know that he'd shared our relationship with them and that they wanted to meet me."

"That's such awesome news, Greg. I'm so happy for you."

"Thanks. I'm on cloud nine right now, girl. Today is gonna be a great day...I can feel it."

I smiled at him and thought how every day he was at work was a great day. He brought such joy to the place as is that Greg in a mood such as he was now would only mean a fantastic time for not only the patrons but the rest of the staff as well.

A couple hours later, I realized Greg was right. The day had been great. The diner had a steady flow of customers and with Greg on cloud nine, he was a blast to be around.

"Not hanging around past your shift today?" Greg asked.

"Can't. I've got plans before my shift starts at the resort," I answered.

"Plans? What plans?"

"I'm sort of learning how to snowboard."

"Are you holding out on me, girl? You've been working here for how long now? Never, in all that time, have you had plans other than the one weekend I'm not here to join in. Now you're telling me you have plans that involve you sort of learning how to snowboard," he stated disbelievingly.

"I'm not holding out on you, Greg. I've always wanted to learn how to ride and Wes has offered to teach me."

"Wes?"

"Blackman. Wes Blackman."

"Are you kidding me? Wes Blackman is giving you snowboarding lessons?"

"Yes. Why? Do you know him, too?"

"Charley. Girl, Wes Blackman is a legend in the snowboarding world. You don't live in Wyoming, especially Rising

Sun, and not know who Wes Blackman is. I didn't know he was offering lessons. That man is one fine piece of eye candy. I might have to sign up for lessons just to spend some time looking at him. Do you think he'll catch me if I fall?"

I giggled.

"There are two problems with that, Greg. First, he's not offering lessons. At least, not that I'm aware of. He kind of just offered them to me. He brought me a bunch of gear, wouldn't let me pay for it, and then gave me my first lesson yesterday. The second problem is…you have a boyfriend. And may I remind you that you just got back from meeting his parents?"

"It doesn't count if the guy I'm getting lessons from is straight," he reasoned. "Besides, Tony is well aware of how I feel about him." He paused to smile. "So, you're getting private lessons, huh? I go away for one weekend and I miss the first piece of action you get since I've met you."

I shook my head and laughed. "You're crazy. I have to go."

"I'll let you go for now, but this conversation is not over."

"See you later, Greg."

"Bye, Charley," he replied.

As I turned to walk away, I heard him mumble, "Unbelievable. Private lessons with Wes fucking Blackman."

I walked out of the diner and to my Jeep with a smile on my face. I still had the smile on my face when I made it to Parks Ridge and pulled into my space next to where Wes was already parked.

He got out, rounded my Jeep, and opened my door for me to step out.

"Hi, Charley," Wes greeted me as he leaned down and kissed me quickly on the lips.

"Hi, Wes," I replied.

"Ready for day two?"

"My body aches in places I didn't know existed," I shared. "So, while I might be mentally ready for day two, I'm going to need you to take it easy on me physically."

Wes' eyes lit up and then he winked at me. "I think I can manage that."

We made our way out to the mountain and I immediately strapped my left foot in. I knew to keep the right foot out of the bindings on the board until I was up at the top of the hill.

Yesterday, when we first started our lesson Wes had come up behind me, caught me off guard, and pushed me. He literally pushed me. It wasn't hard enough that he hurt me or made me fall, but it caused me to take a step forward. I had turned around and asked him why he pushed me and he said I 'wasn't goofy.' I stared at him puzzled and then he went on to explain that he pushed me to see what foot I'd try to catch myself with. That was usually the best way to find out what someone's stance on a board should be. There were two options, regular and goofy. If your left foot leads, it's regular. If the right foot leads, it's goofy. I was, apparently, a regular rider.

Wes and I went over to the magic carpet, another thing I learned about yesterday. For the beginner hill that Wes was using to teach me the basics, a standard lift was not used. There was what was called a magic carpet. It was basically a conveyor belt that ran up the side of the hill to take you to the top. Of course, I thought I was going to easily be able to handle this; however, when I got to the top and had to get off, I literally fell over my foot that was attached to the board. Lovely.

As part of my lesson the day before, Wes had explained what the toe and heel edges of the board were and how I could use either to slow down or even stop myself completely. Yesterday, I spent a good portion of the lesson learning the terms, turning the board sideways so that the tip of the board was pointed forward and then I'd come immediately back to my heel edge. I did this once down the mountain and then went back up and did the same thing, but the second time I would descend a little and only use my toe edge to stop.

We rode the magic carpet to the top of the hill and I got off without incident, thankfully. The rest of my lesson was spent learning how to link from my heel edge to my toe edge. I started at the top on my heel edge looking down the hill. I'd get myself going, turn and stop on my toe edge, start going again, turn, and stop on my heel. I fell a couple times, but not nearly as many as yesterday. I found I enjoyed going to my toe edge to stop much better because not only did I learn that I stopped better and fell less when I did this, but also that I ended up coming face to face with Wes, who was always right behind me. It felt good knowing he was right at my back following me down.

Overall, I had to admit that I had improved, but I was certainly not a professional by any means. Additionally, I was not ready for riding down a trail. Following my lesson, Wes walked with me back to my Jeep so that I could put all my gear away before heading in to work.

"So, I'll be here today riding the pipe while you're working," he informed me as we walked to the car.

"Oh man. I am really wishing I didn't have to work now. I would love to see you do that," I replied.

"I'll show you another day."

"Really? Do you promise?"

He chuckled. "Yes, Charley. I promise I'll ride for you another day."

"How about Friday?"

"Okay. Friday."

"Yay!!"

He smiled at me. We made it to my car and unloaded my gear. I closed the car, locked it, and turned to walk back to the lodge. Wes was standing right in front of me, smiling wickedly.

"What?" I asked.

"So adorable," he started. "You're the only woman I know that gets that excited over watching someone else do something they love."

I sucked in a breath and quickly tried to hide my reaction to his words by turning to walk toward the lodge. We walked back in silence and then he told me he'd be back when I was finished with work.

I walked up and saw both Hannah and Mark at the coffee stand.

"Wes Blackman? Seriously, Charley?" Mark asked in disbelief.

I looked to Hannah and glared.

She giggled.

"He's giving me snowboarding lessons, Mark," I replied.

"Right," he remarked, but it was clear he didn't believe me. "First, he's Wes Blackman. He doesn't need to give anybody lessons. Second, he's not just giving you lessons, Charley. He makes sure you get to your car every night."

"He is being a good citizen and looking out for women who walk in parking lots at night."

"Except that you're the only woman he's doing that for," Hannah put in, grinning at me.

"No. He made sure you got to your car last night, too."

"Charley, he didn't wait around to walk me to my car. He waited for you. I happened to be here with you when we closed. My car was on the way to yours."

I sighed. "Oh, whatever."

I got to work and didn't push the conversation any further. Hannah was there for about an hour after I arrived and then she left. Mark left another two hours after that. I was the only one closing tonight. It was steady, so the hours ticked by quickly. Before I knew it, the crowds had thinned significantly, and Wes was walking back in. I finished up my nightly duties and shut everything down.

"How'd it go?" I asked as we walked out of the lodge.

"It was good. Worked on some new tricks. How was

work?" Wes answered and then asked.

"You're like a legend around here," I told him.

"What?"

"Hannah told Mark about you giving me lessons and walking me to my car at night. Apparently, everyone in this town knows who you are."

"Yeah, I guess so. This town lives for winter sports."

We made it to the cars and I immediately went to turn on the Jeep to warm it up. Wes turned on his truck and then came back around to my door.

"Day three tomorrow," I announced. "I think my legs are not going to be happy."

Wes said nothing. He took that moment to pull me close to him, bend his head to kiss my lips, and then wrap his arms around my bottom. He lifted me up, mouth still attached to mine, and wrapped my legs around his waist. With his left hand under my bottom supporting my weight, he used his right hand to squeeze the muscles on my right thigh. I groaned in his mouth. He did this for quite some time before switching hands and working the left leg. It felt so good. My legs were feeling really sore and his hands were so strong. In the middle of the left leg rubdown, I pulled my mouth from his and rested my forehead against his.

"It's pretty freaking cold out right now. Actually, it's freezing out here, but if you keep that up, I think I could stay out here all night," I offered with my eyes closed and my forehead resting on his.

When I opened my eyes and looked at him, I saw his green eyes were intense. Wes moved both hands to my bottom and squeezed.

"Gorgeous, we don't have to stand in a parking lot to do this. I would be more than happy to take you to my place, let you soak in the bathtub, and then give you a proper rubdown."

"It would be wrong to tease a girl like that."

"I'm definitely not joking," he maintained, his voice low and filled with promise.

I stayed silent.

With my legs still wrapped around his waist, I squeezed my thighs tighter. It was Wes' turn to groan. I leaned forward and kissed him again, knowing that I was torturing myself because I wouldn't very well see the finale out here in a parking lot. I knew the same would be the case for Wes because as I unhooked my legs and stood, he was still holding me close to him and I could feel his hard length pressing into me.

I pulled my mouth from his again and put my hands against his chest. "I'm sorry, Wes. I should really get home."

He smiled at me before he spoke. "Okay, Charley. Drive safe."

"See you tomorrow."

"Looking forward to it."

Wednesday passed in a flash.

Both First Tracks and Brew Stirs were extremely busy, so my shifts were over quickly. Wes and I had our third day of lessons and he walked me to my car that night after I finished work. Of course, as per usual, there was a bit of kissing and moaning before we parted ways for the evening.

It was now Thursday morning and I had time before heading into the diner since I wasn't working the early morning shift. Between working both jobs and getting the snowboarding lessons from Wes, I had been feeling exhausted. It was nice to have a little time to sleep in. Plus, I hadn't seen Emme all week, so I was happy that I'd have some time to catch up with her. I got out of bed and made my way to the kitchen to make some coffee and eat breakfast. I saw Emme sitting on the couch with her laptop.

"Hey, honey. What are you up to?" I asked her.

"I've had so many shoots this week, so I'm going through all of the shots from one of my engagement sessions and getting some editing done. I've got a long day today with a couple of Christmas shoots. One is a family holiday session this afternoon and the other is a corporate Christmas party this evening; so, I'll actually be home late. On the bright side, after tonight I don't have any more shoots until next week. What's going on with you?"

"I have a date tonight," I blurted, biting my lip.

Emme looked up at me, closed her laptop, and walked to the kitchen. "I'm sorry. I think I was sitting too far away in there and couldn't hear you. It sounded like you said you had a date tonight."

"You heard correctly," I told her.

"Is it with that Wes guy from last week?" she asked.

"Yep."

Her brows pulled together. "What have I missed?"

I lifted my shoulders and smiled at her. Then, I launched into it and told her everything that had been happening between Wes and me. I told her about him walking me to my car every night, the snowboarding lessons he'd started giving me earlier in the week, and finally, all of the kisses we'd shared. I ended by explaining how Hannah had asked me to cover a shift for her, leaving my schedule open for this evening.

I wasn't sure what I expected from Emme when I finished telling her, but it certainly wasn't what she gave me.

She stared at me a beat processing everything before she asked, "Is he a good kisser?"

I let out a sigh. "That was not the reaction I was expecting to get out of you. Nikki? Yes. You? No. You and Monroe are my voices of reason. You are supposed to tell me that this is a bad idea. I'm standing on the edge of a cliff and, as my best friend, it is your job to talk me back from the ledge."

Emme smiled at me but stayed silent.

I sighed again. "He's an amazingly talented kisser," I gave in, pausing for a brief moment. "Now, do your job and talk sense into me. Help me out of this mess. You and I both know this is a bad idea and it won't end well. Wes seems like a genuinely great guy and I am worried more that I'm going to hurt him. I can't get close."

"Sweets, I can't do that," she replied.

When I didn't reply, Emme took a deep breath and reasoned, "You need this. You haven't smiled, like really, truly smiled, in almost a year. Sure, you can fake it at work and hide how you really feel, but I know you and from what you told me last week and what you just told me now, I can see how badly you need this. Your face lights up every time you talk about him. You even said he makes you feel safe. I know you need that again. Of all the people you could ask, you should know I am going to be the last one to stand in the way of any potential for you to feel happy again. Especially since I was the reason..." She trailed off, tears filling her eyes.

"Stop, Emme. Don't even say it," I warned her.

She looked at me a moment, sadness in her eyes. "Charley, whatever you decide about Wes is going to be your decision. I'll support you no matter what decision you make, but don't ask me to be the one to stop you from doing something that could bring happiness into your life. I won't take that away from you again."

"Emme, honey..." I stopped, not knowing what to say and not needing to because Emme knew how I felt.

We sat in silence for a few minutes. This always happened.

Here we were again; we had opened up old wounds and would now end it by sitting silently with each other. I needed my art again. Since I had the time before work started, I got up. "Want some tea?" I asked Emme.

"No, thanks. I'm good. I'm going to shower and get ready.

I need to leave shortly anyway. Enjoy your night tonight. I will be home all day tomorrow and I've got nothing planned for the evening except a bottle of wine with my best friend. I want to hear all about your date."

"Ok. Wine and details tomorrow then. Love you, Em."

"Love you, too, Charley," she replied as she walked down the hall toward her bedroom.

I made my coffee, toasted a whole grain bagel, slathered it with some cream cheese, and made my way back to my bedroom. I set my alarm, pulled out my art supplies, and lost myself in it while eating my breakfast.

The alarm sounded all too quickly, and I had to stop. I put away my supplies, got ready, and went to work.

My shift at the diner was over before I even had the chance to check the time. I made my way out to my Jeep and realized how odd it was that I was making the drive to Parks Ridge, even though I wouldn't be working.

I was going to get snowboarding lessons and I was going to have a good time. It felt a bit surreal and I realized I could take the moment to panic or just go with it. I thought about Emme's words this morning and decided to just go with it.

I pulled into the lot and looked to our spots.

Our spots.

I was surprised at how good that felt.

Wes was just parking as I pulled up. I parked next to him, looked over, and smiled. He winked and returned a smile. I felt my belly warm before I stepped out of the car. I walked around to the back of the Jeep so I could grab the gear out of the back, but Wes was already there. He pulled me close to him, bent his head, and gave me a quick kiss on the lips.

"Hello, gorgeous. How was work?"

"It was a good morning. A friend of mine who works at the diner with me is on cloud nine, so everybody else reaped the benefits of his great mood. How has your day been?"

"Work is busy. I managed to get a bunch of work done early this morning before I had to run an errand this afternoon. Now I'm here, and I'm thinking my day just got better."

I grinned at him.

"Ready?" he asked.

I nodded.

We walked toward the lodge, got our gear on, and made our way out onto the mountain.

"I think I'd like to try one of the trails today," I divulged, surprising both myself and Wes.

He looked at me, smiled, and agreed, "I think that's a great idea."

Wes may have thought I was smart, but minutes later, I realized I was an idiot.

What was I thinking?

Moments after my declaration of bravery, Wes had me parked in a lift and we were making our way to the top of one of the peaks. I felt myself getting nervous the higher the lift climbed and, by the time we got to the top and I strapped my second foot to the board, I realized how stupid I was. I looked down from the top and felt my panic rising. I wasn't sure what made me think I could do this.

"I think I was too ambitious. We're really high up and that's a long way down," I admitted to Wes, who was standing beside me at the top.

"You can do this. Trust me. I've seen how much you've improved over the last couple of days. You are ready, Charley. We'll take our time and if you need to stop, just say the word. I've got all the time in the world, so you go when you're ready and I'll be behind you the entire way."

I nodded as I stared straight ahead.

After taking a few deep breaths, I went. I spent the first little bit riding my heel edge trying not to panic. I couldn't see him, but I could feel Wes behind me. I knew he was there and with me as I made my descent. Eventually, I decided I was ready, and I got off my edge and turned the board, the tail pointed toward the top of the mountain. I was riding down the trail, picking up speed, and tried to tame my excitement. The last thing I wanted to do was ruin this glorious moment. I would occasionally slow myself down using my edges as Wes had taught me and then got right back to gliding almost effortlessly down the mountain.

The next thing I knew, I had reached the bottom. I turned on my toe edge and stopped myself completely. As I did, I saw that Wes was right behind me the entire time, just as he said he would be. He slowed and stopped on his heel so he was facing me. A bright smile spread across his face and made my knees weak.

"Gorgeous, that was awesome. I told you that you could do it. I'm so proud of you," he praised me.

My eyes filled with tears as I reached out to Wes. I put my arms around him and hugged him. I held him so tight trying to tell him everything I couldn't say with words. We stood like that for quite some time. When I managed to pull away and look up at Wes, I found his eyes were warm and he had a smile on his face. I think he understood what I needed him to understand. Certainly not everything, but enough that I didn't need to offer any explanations.

"Thank you, Wes."

"My pleasure, Charley," he returned, gently.

After our moment, it took me a second, but I realized how much I enjoyed riding the trail.

"Can we do it again?"

"I'll do that as many times as you want because anything that moves you to the point you smile and hold on to me like you just did is worth doing again."

I grinned at him before I bent down and freed one of my feet so we could make our way to the lift.

Over the course of the next two hours, we rode a few different trails. I did wipe out once, but Wes was right there to help me up onto my feet and at my back again as soon as I took off. Other than when I was already scheduled to be off, I hadn't voluntarily taken a day off from work in all the months I'd been here in Wyoming. Having this opportunity for even a half day of enjoyment felt unbelievably good.

When we decided to call it quits on the riding for the day, Wes and I walked back through the lodge and out to our cars.

"So, I'll need your address," he stated.

"For what?" I asked.

"Please tell me you didn't forget about dinner with me tonight," he pleaded.

I shook my head. "No, but I thought I'd meet you wherever we are going."

Wes gave me a look of disbelief before he explained, "Charley, that's not a date. At least, not in my book. I'm picking you up."

I knew I'd lose this battle; so, I gave in and gave him my address. He lowered his mouth to mine, kissed me quickly on the lips, and stated, "I'll pick you up at seven, gorgeous."

"Okay, Wes."

I hopped in the Jeep, noted it was already five and realized I needed to get home quickly to get ready. After driving slightly faster than was legal to make it home, I parked the Jeep and dashed through the lot. I barreled through the door and ran to my bedroom. Immediately, I went into my closet to inventory my wardrobe. After I had mentally taken everything in, I made my way to the shower and considered my options for an outfit for my first real date with Wes. I finished up in the shower and went back into the closet. I selected my favorite pair of dark wash skinny jeans, a crisp, white short-sleeve top with a scoop neckline that showed the barest hint of the top swells of my C-cup breasts, my black faux-leather motorcycle jacket, and my just-above-the-ankle black booties.

I set everything out on my bed, put on a nightshirt, and went back into the bathroom to fix my hair and makeup. I dried my hair and then used the curling iron to put some loose waves in it. I had a smoky eye, pink cheeks, and a matte pink lip. I had just finished getting dressed and was zipping up my second boot when I heard a knock. I took one last glance at myself in my full-length mirror, decided I looked okay and went to the front door.

I looked out the peephole and saw Wes, so I unlocked the door and let him in.

"You look beautiful," he said immediately after I opened the door and he scanned me from head to toe and back up again.

I shot him a look of contentment. "Thank you." I took a moment to look at him and noted he was wearing a pair of dark wash jeans that fit extraordinarily well, black boots, and a long-sleeved, light grey Henley under his black leather jacket. I licked my lips. "You don't look so bad yourself," I shared.

"Lick those lips again, and we aren't going to be eating dinner any time soon."

Oops.

"Sorry," I lamented, biting my lip.

He just shook his head and tried to suppress a laugh. "Are you ready to go?"

"Yes, let me just grab my purse and keys."

I grabbed my things, locked the door, and walked with Wes to his truck. He held my hand the whole way there.

Six

Charley

WES OPENED THE PASSENGER'S SIDE DOOR FOR ME, CLOSED IT when I got in and made his way around to the driver's side. As he drove, we sat in comfortable silence. Since I hadn't really taken in the views after moving to Wyoming, I enjoyed the scenery. The ride was about fifteen minutes before he pulled into a private driveway. I looked at him and asked, "Is there a restaurant here? I thought we were going out to dinner."

"We are having dinner, but I never said we were doing it at a restaurant," he answered glancing over at me. He then continued, "We are going to my place. I'm cooking dinner for you."

He could cook? Seriously?

I was beginning to wonder if there was anything he couldn't do.

We drove further down the driveway when finally, a massive and absolutely breathtaking home came into view.

"Wow," I murmured quietly.

I'd never seen anything that said mountain home more than Wes' home. The exterior was finished in what I believed was timber from the main floor and up while stone covered the base of the home. There were plenty of large windows, an enormous deck, and many more stone accents around the exterior.

Wes parked in the garage, hopped out, and came over to open my door. As we walked inside I realized that just like the mountain exterior the home boasted, the interior could be described as rustic mountain. While the layout of the home was beautiful, other than this basic furniture, there were no other pieces of decor or personal touches to make it feel like a home.

I found this odd.

"You have a beautiful home," I marveled.

"Thanks. I'll show you the rest later. Right now, I am going to feed you," he responded.

And he did.

Wes poured me a glass of red wine and grabbed himself a lager. He then cooked and plated a piece of filet mignon, a baked potato, and some asparagus for each of us.

"This tastes excellent, Wes. Where did you learn to cook?" I asked.

He smiled and answered, "I'm not a master chef or anything. And I haven't had any formal training. I can do the basics and cook a really good steak. My mom always cooked meals for us growing up, so sometimes, she forced us into the kitchen with her."

"Us?"

"I have one sister. Her name is Elizabeth."

My heart clenched. I wanted to know more but wasn't going to open myself up to that line of questioning. I nodded and quickly changed subjects.

"So, Wes, am I your first success story or do you teach all the ladies how to snowboard?"

"Not only are you my first success story; you're my only story. I've only ever ridden with my buddies. Prior to starting my company, my friends and I rode for fun and then got noticed by other companies. We became rep riders for those companies and competed in contests. When I decided to put all my focus into building my own company, I needed to take the time off to focus on just that. It's been a lot of work, but I'm happy with where Blackman Boards is right now and where it's headed."

"That's incredible. Why didn't you just stick to snowboarding?" I asked, putting a forkful of potato in my mouth.

Wes took a bite of steak, chewed, swallowed, and answered, "I love riding, but I've always had a dream of owning my own company. When I was out riding with the boys and we did so well that other brands were noticing us, I realized that if I was going to be out there promoting a brand, it should be my own. I decided it was what I wanted to do, so I put everything I had into it and never looked back. My parents have always been big supporters of my sister and me pursuing our dreams, so that helps, too."

I nodded and smiled, not saying anything. We continued eating and Wes told me all about his company and his early days of snowboarding.

Wes then turned the conversation to me. "What I want to know is, how is it that you live here in the mountains and have wanted to snowboard, but have never done it before?"

"I actually only just moved here about six months ago from southern California, Ventura to be exact. I've been working a lot so I haven't really had much time for learning to ride," I answered.

Wes' eyebrows drew together, and he had a puzzled look on his face.

"I guess that explains it. You arrived and the season was over."

"Yep," I replied, looking toward the great room and out the floor to ceiling windows there. It was dark out, but

I wanted to change the topic again, so I said, "You've got an amazing view here."

Wes stood, gathered the plates, and took them to the sink. While he did this, I walked to the great room and stood in front of the fireplace looking out the windows into the dark night.

Moments later, Wes came up behind me, put his arms around me, and rested his chin on the top of my head.

"I have always wanted this," he shared, and I grew tense. He must have felt it because he continued speaking, "This home on this land with an amazing view. It's just another reason I've put so much time into my business. I knew I'd be able to have this if I worked hard enough."

"You're rare," I stated.

"Come again?"

"You. You're rare," I repeated. "You followed your dream. In the end, you got what you wanted. That doesn't always happen. In fact, more often than not it doesn't happen."

He turned me around so I was facing him and, with a sexy grin on his face, he pointed out, "I haven't gotten everything I've wanted yet."

The butterflies were fluttering madly in my belly. Wes smelled so good and I could feel the warmth emanating off his large, lean, body. He pressed his knuckles on my cheek and slid the back of his hand down the side of my face. His thumb swiped across my bottom lip after which I moistened it with my tongue. Wes' hand continued to travel downward, along the side of my neck while my hands gripped his shirt at his waist. His fingertips lightly traced along the scoop neckline of my shirt across the swells of my breasts. He then brought his hands up to frame my face and brought his lips down to mine. The kiss was slow and sensual. I needed to feel Wes' skin with my hands so I loosened my grip on his shirt and placed my hands at the hem of it, where I began lifting. He broke the kiss and helped to pull the shirt over his head. I drank in the sight of him. He was beautiful. I bit my lip and put my hands on his chest. Taking a cue from his earlier movements, I lightly ran my fingertips down his chest and across his abs. When I looked back up into his eyes, I saw his emerald-green eyes were smoldering. He lifted my shirt at the hem and pulled it over my head before moving to my jeans. After unbuttoning and unzipping them, Wes slowly pulled them down my legs. He bent down and unzipped my boots and after I stepped out of each one, he slid my jeans off my legs. Wes stood up, took a step back, and stared at me. I stood there in my matching pale-pink panties and lace trim bra.

"So gorgeous," he whispered.

"Wes," I called quietly as I extended my hand to him.

I grabbed him at the waist of his jeans and pulled myself to him. Wes wrapped his arms around me and I relished the feel of his solid body next to my soft skin. It felt so good, and I felt safe and protected in his arms. He unhooked my bra, put his hands to the straps at my shoulders and carefully slid them down my arms. With my bra on the floor, Wes' hands came up my sides and his thumbs rubbed back and forth across my nipples. I moaned as I felt the wetness pool between my legs.

He kissed me again, then picked me up with one hand under my knees and the other at my back. He continued to kiss me as he walked. I didn't pay attention to where he was walking; I was too preoccupied with kissing him, so I just kept my arms wrapped around his neck. He stopped walking soon enough and gently placed me down on a bed, where he settled his large body over mine and carefully adjusted his weight in his arms. Wes didn't stop kissing me, but moved from my mouth down my throat until he'd reached my breasts. He sucked one nipple into his mouth. He licked and teased, paying special attention to one side before moving to the other.

He began moving farther down my body, kissing as he went along. When he finally reached the top of my panties, he gripped each side at my hips and slowly slid them down my legs. He sat back, his ass resting on the heels of his feet while he looked down at me lying in his bed. One of his hands trailed lightly and excruciatingly slowly from my knee up my thigh. Finally, his fingertips were at the sensitive spot between my legs, where they gently slid through my wetness.

"Christ. You're soaked."

Wes slowly slid one finger inside me and then slid it out at just the same pace. It felt remarkable. He continued his assault on my sensitive body, gliding his finger in and out of me while staring at my naked form.

"Wes, please," I breathed. I knew I sounded needy, but it had been nearly two years since I had had sex. I was desperate to feel something. Anything.

"What do you want, Charley?" he questioned me as he looked in my eyes.

"You."

While Wes got up from the bed and removed the rest of his clothes, my eyes took in his entire body. I finally had all the proof of what I knew was hiding under his clothing. This man had an impressive body. It was all lean, hard muscle and absolutely mouth-watering. He opened the drawer to the nightstand and pulled out a condom. I watched as he tore open the foil packet and sheathed himself. When I dropped my eyes to his manhood, I licked my lips.

Wes came back to the bed and positioned himself between my legs. His lips brushed right up next to mine. "This mouth," he growled. "So pretty." He kissed me wet and deep.

With the tip of him positioned at my entrance, Wes slowly slid about halfway inside me and didn't move.

"Fuck. You're so tight."

"Please, Wes. Please move."

"I don't want to hurt you."

"You won't. Please, I need you."

Apparently, that was all Wes needed to hear because he immediately pushed himself the rest of the way in and filled me. Everything Wes did up to this point had been slow and controlled. Once he pushed himself completely inside me, he lost that control. His hips thrust rapidly back and forth. With all of the touching and teasing that led to this point, I was already on the brink of an orgasm. Wes kept pounding into me and I could feel myself getting close.

"Let go," Wes encouraged me as he continued to power himself into my body.

I let go.

It was magnificent.

Wes drew out my pleasure as he slowed his thrusts. When I came down from my orgasm, his pace picked up again, and Wes reached his climax as he groaned and called out, "So gorgeous. Fuck, Charley."

After he came down from his orgasm, Wes moved to the bathroom to dispose of the condom. He made his way back into the bedroom and climbed into the bed next to me.

"Are you okay?" he asked.

"Yes," I replied, curling my body into his.

He moved his hand down my body and cupped me between the legs. "I mean here. Did I hurt you?"

My belly fluttered at his concern for me. "No, Wes, you didn't hurt me."

I stared at him for some time, feeling sleepy. Wes was so close to me, I felt so warm, and I'd just had sex for the first time in two years after spending several hours snowboarding earlier that day. I was wiped out and sleep overtook me.

My eyes shot open.

It was dark, and I was not in my bed.

Suddenly, it all came rushing back.

I had dinner with Wes and then he gave me the most intense orgasm of my life. Now, I was awake, his front to my back, and he was lightly tracing his fingers over the skin at my hip. It felt so good.

I gave my eyes a moment to adjust to the darkness before I turned so I was lying on my back. This meant Wes' hand was now sitting very low on my abdomen. When I looked at him he was up on one elbow, his head resting in his hand, and he was looking down at me, smiling.

"I was just lying here thinking that we ate dinner, but we didn't have dessert."

Okay. I hadn't expected that as his first response but went with it anyway. "You made dessert?"

He shook his head. "No, I bought dessert earlier today. But, now that I'm here I think I need a different kind of dessert," he clarified. After a moment, his hand drifted lower. At the same time, he bent his head so his lips were close to mine. He whispered, "I want to taste you, gorgeous."

I swallowed.

Wes kissed my lips.

Then, he slid down my body and took each of my nipples into his mouth and sucked. After giving them plenty of attention, he worked his way farther down my body and tasted me.

I moaned.

Wes swept his tongue straight through my center before pushing it inside me. After his tongue pushed in and out of me for several beats, he moved his mouth to my clit and slid his finger inside me.

It was glorious.

My hands fisted the sheets and I ground myself into his face and finger. He kept at me, and it wasn't long before I felt the orgasm building deep in my belly. Wes slid his finger out and replaced it with his tongue again. He wrapped both of his arms under my thighs and splayed his hands across my abdomen. It was too intense, and I couldn't pull away with the hold he had on me.

Wes continued his barrage of pleasure while I writhed, my breathing becoming quick and shallow. This only encouraged Wes and his hands moved from my abdomen to my hips, where he gripped me tight and restricted my movement. I reached down, put my hands on the back of his head, and pulled his face farther into me. This made him groan and work his tongue even faster in and out of my body. Seconds later, I was over the edge.

"Oh, Wes," I moaned as I came.

Wes slowed the strokes of his tongue until I came down from my orgasm and before I had any time to think he slammed his cock inside of me.

"Charley," he growled.

Wes pounded into me, stroke after delicious stroke, and I angled my hips to meet his with every thrust. He was relentless and the next thing I knew another orgasm was building. Wes kept thrusting, one hand now supporting his weight on the bed beside my head, the other with a firm hold on my breast. I could tell he was getting close as the noise he was making from the back of his throat got louder. He swiped his thumb across my nipple, then gently pinched the pink bud between his thumb and finger. My body exploded at the same time Wes groaned loudly through his pleasure. His body collapsed on top of mine before he quickly rolled to the side, taking me with him.

We stayed like that for a few minutes, catching our breath before Wes got up to deal with the condom. He came back to the bed, and I could just barely see the grin on his face.

"Best dessert I've ever had," he shared, draping his arm

over my hip around my back and pulling me toward him.

I smiled as I rolled to my side, curling my body tight to his.

After a few minutes of comfortable silence, I spoke.

"I need to find my clothes."

"I think you look just fine without them, gorgeous. Just close your eyes and sleep."

I rolled my eyes and got up to search for my panties. "Wes, I need to get dressed and go home."

"Stay," he urged, now pressed up on his elbow, watching me put my undergarments back on.

"I can't stay. I need to get home; I have work tomorrow. And Emme will worry."

"Emme?"

"Best friend and roommate. She'll panic if I'm not home."

"So, call her and tell her you won't be home tonight so she doesn't worry."

"It's not that. I need to go home, or she'll be alone. I can't leave her alone."

"Why not?"

Now I was beginning to panic. "Wes, please. I have to go. I'll call a cab to get me so you don't have to go back out tonight." I walked toward the door of his bedroom so I could find my way back to the clothes he removed out in the great room. I turned to look back at him. "Thank you for dinner… and dessert. I had a great time tonight."

With that, I walked out of the room to find my clothes. I found my bra and jeans and pulled them on. I located my top, and as I bent over to pick it up, I heard Wes come into the room. I turned around to face him and saw that he had his jeans back on and was walking toward the coffee table where his shirt had landed earlier.

He tugged it on.

"What are you doing?" I asked, putting my booties back

on my feet.

"I'm taking you home."

"Wes, really, it's no problem for me to call a cab."

"It's a problem for me if you call a cab. I'll take you home. I picked you up in my truck, brought you here for dinner, took you once, watched you sleep, ate you once, and then had you a second time. I'm not sending you home in a cab. No man who's a real man does something like that unless he really is a dick and doesn't give a shit. And Charley? I'm not a dick."

Okay, so that was good to hear.

"Thank you," I whispered.

"You don't have to thank me, gorgeous. I would rather have you here with me tonight, but seeing how you insist you've got to get home to your girl, I'm going to make sure that you get there safely."

My belly fluttered again at his words, and I realized I was in big trouble. I didn't respond and decided to finish getting dressed by grabbing my jacket off the chair at the kitchen island. Wes put his boots on and walked toward the door leading out to the garage. He opened the door and allowed me to walk ahead of him. Then, he drove me home and walked me to my door. Once we were there, he kissed me, told me he'd see me tomorrow for my lesson, and waited until I locked my door before he walked away.

I had to admit I loved that he cared about my safety, all the while hating what it made me feel.

Seven

Wes

I FELT LIKE A ZOMBIE.

I'd barely gotten any sleep. After taking Charley home last night, I drove back home thinking about my night with her.

It had been brutal being around her all week giving her lessons and then kissing her every night after I walked her to her car. I could kiss her mouth for hours and never tire of it. The problem was that that was all that was happening and I was having to take care of business with my hand every night.

I was over that.

When I heard her co-worker tell her to enjoy her night off on Thursday, I had to jump at the chance to be her plans for that night.

I picked her up that night and it was the first time I'd seen her not in either casual work clothes of jeans and a t-shirt or snowboarding gear. Though, if I'm being honest, seeing her for the first time decked out in Blackman gear was hot. But standing in front of her all dolled up was something else. She was a knockout, with her form-fitting jeans, sexy-as-hell boots, and just-low-enough shirt. Charley sized me up and licked her lips.

That mouth.

I had to get her out of there and into my truck if we were going to eat dinner.

The dinner conversation was nice; though, I noticed her need to quickly change the topic on a few occasions. I did not want to ruin the evening with her, so I decided not to press for more information in those instances. Clearly, she was not ready to talk, but it bugged me that she didn't talk about family or friends other than to tell me about Emme. I also learned that she'd just moved here from California and, not that I was complaining, but I wanted to know why she moved here.

After dinner and a bit of fun in my bed, she dozed off. I let her sleep for a bit while I sat there thinking about this girl who, until I started giving her snowboarding lessons this week, only ever seemed to work herself to exhaustion. Nobody understood better than me a person's need to pour themselves into their work, especially after a bad breakup. I realized that maybe that's what happened, but I was at least working to build a business. She was waiting tables and serving coffee. This was not to take anything away from what she chose to do, but I couldn't for the life of me figure out why that was all she seemed to have going on, and again, I was surprised to see how much it bothered me.

She woke not more than thirty minutes later, and I knew I had to have her again, but only after I had my mouth on her. The way she came alive for me while I brought her to climax with my mouth and then with my cock was awesome. It was like she was trying to give me everything she could, and I was more than willing to take what she had to offer. The problem, again, was I wanted more.

I had hoped to have her stay and spend the night with me; unfortunately, she all but demanded that she get home because Emme couldn't be left alone. I asked what she meant by that and I could see the panic take over her features. As much as I wanted to know what would distress her so much, I did not want to be the one to cause any more stress for her, so I let it go.

And then, even though I've not let her walk to her car alone after work one day since meeting her, she thinks I'm going to let her get in a cab at that hour? What. The. Fuck. It's like the girl has no care for her own personal safety.

When I got back home after dropping her off, I couldn't stop thinking about her.

Everything about her.

Everything from why she moved here from California to why she seemed guarded so often. My thoughts then drifted to the fact that she rocked my world by actually showing interest in snowboarding and then rocked my world again when I realized she was really good at it. And of course, I couldn't help but think about how great it was to finally sink myself deep inside her and hear her call my name from that mouth. That mouth was so goddamn beautiful.

I finally fell asleep last night, but the alarm went off not even four hours later. I could have easily gone back to bed, but then I'd have to give up something, either time at work, which I really couldn't have happen with the new warehouse, or snowboarding lessons with Charley, which really wasn't happening. So, I got out of bed, showered, grabbed breakfast, and made my way to work.

I walked into the new warehouse that morning and confirmed that everything was still going as it should for the construction and that it was all still on schedule for completion within the next two weeks. It would be finished just before Christmas. After checking on the construction status, I made my way to my office. It was so early that I was the only one there. I found that I enjoyed having that time alone to work without interruptions, and it was when I was most productive.

Being that it was not only the holiday season but also the

beginning of the ski season, Blackman Boards was extraordinarily busy. Boards, boots, bindings, and apparel were being cranked out rapid fire to keep up with the demands.

I had already gotten a solid two hours of work in before the first employees had begun to file in. An hour later, Stone and Luke had both made their way into the offices. As they passed my office, I called out to get their attention. They both stopped and walked in.

"Hey man. How's it going?" Luke asked.

"Good. Construction is coming along nicely, and everything seems to be on track with completion right before Christmas."

"Sweet. It's going to be nice to have everything under one roof again. At least now you'll have the space."

"Agreed," I said.

"So, we're still riding today, right?" Stone began. "I know you and Zane took the Fire boards out and did some testing.

"Yeah. I'm definitely riding today. We got through the entire Fire line up, but I need your input on them. The line is meant for pipe riding, which is why Zane's input along with yours is critical," I answered, looking to Stone.

I turned my gaze to Luke. "I know the pipe isn't your typical gig, but I want you testing them, too. Zane and Stone can give me the usage data I need, but if someone is going to break them, it'll be you."

"I'll do my best. Hopefully you won't have to have a major redesign," Luke answered. "Any idea on the progress of the Air line up?" he asked.

The Air snowboard model would be the second in the Elements Series to be released. The boards in this line would be geared toward the big air and big mountain riding. Luke could ride pipe with the best of us, but big air was his thing.

"We're getting close to completion on the first round. I'm expecting sometime late January on those."

"I'm ready when they are ready."

I nodded to him.

Stone confirmed, "We're meeting four o'clock at the resort, right?"

"Yeah. I'll be there already so just meet me at the pipe."

"Why are you going early?"

"I'm giving riding lessons to someone," I answered, a smile tugging at my lips just thinking of Charley.

"Does this have anything to do with Blondie that Zane told us about?" Luke asked.

"Zane's got a big mouth apparently," I replied, shaking my head. "Her name is Charley. And yes, I'm giving her lessons."

They both grinned at me.

"We were curious why you had so much interest in riding again. He figured she had something to do with it."

I didn't answer.

"Alright, man. Good luck with your lessons. Catch you at four o'clock."

I lifted my chin as they both walked out. Once they left, I got back to work for a few hours before I left for lunch and made my way to Parks Ridge. When I got there, Charley was just pulling in to her spot. I drove up and pulled in next to her. I looked over at her and she smiled.

I almost couldn't handle how beautiful she was.

I got out of the truck, walked around the back of hers, and met her at her door. I opened her door and she hopped out.

"Hi, gorgeous," I greeted her before kissing her on the forehead.

"Hi, Wes," she replied as the most beautiful smile I've ever seen spread across her face.

"What's got you in such a happy mood?"

"I get to see you ride pipe today! I can't wait," she responded.

That felt good.

Really good.

There was a time when I hoped to find someone who would tolerate the hours that I'd put into my work and understand that I might occasionally want to get out and ride, but Charley was not only interested in learning to ride, she was also excited to see me do what I loved.

I smiled at her and we walked to the back of the cars to get our gear. After we made our way into the lodge and up to the mountain, we got on the lift. We decided to do a bit of trail riding so that Charley could ride before she watched me. We went down a couple of trails and I was so impressed at how much she had improved since the first lesson. She really didn't need much instruction throughout the entire time we rode.

With a little time left before her shift started, we walked over to the pipe. After I showed her to the best place to watch from, I made my way to the top of the pipe.

I finished my run and went straight to Charley.

"Holy crap!! That was the most amazing thing I've ever seen. You are so good!" she exclaimed.

I couldn't help but smile at her. She was so excited, and I hadn't even done anything too crazy since I hadn't really trained in quite some time and only recently started riding again. Of course, it was a bit like riding a bike, but I didn't want to risk it and try to be a hero. Clearly, Charley thought what I did was more than impressive. And again, it felt so good that she was so fired up by it.

"Thanks, baby," I said softly as I leaned down to give her a quick kiss on the lips. "Ready to head into work?"

"No! I really want to see you do that again. Promise me you'll do it for me another day?" she begged.

"Charley, I've told you before that anything that makes you smile like that is worth doing again."

She beamed a bright, beautiful smile up at me.

Yep, there was no question about it. I was going to do that again for her.

We walked back toward the lodge so Charley could get to work. Since she only had a few minutes left before her shift started, I told her I'd take the gear, put it in my truck for the time being, and give it to her tonight when I walked her to her Jeep. I let her know I'd be on the mountain testing out some boards tonight and that I'd see her when her shift was over. We kissed, she got to work, and I went out to the pipe to meet the guys.

A couple hours later, Stone, Luke, and I had finished testing the boards. As I had expected he would, Luke managed to break one. Thankfully, it was only one board and I had a feeling that if one would fail, that would be the one. We knew what the issue was so it was a simple enough change that needed to be made. Otherwise, it went well, and we had a blast. I knew, after riding for the first time in months with Zane about a week ago, that I missed riding. After going out with Stone and Luke tonight and having spent so much time with Charley teaching her how to ride, I also knew that I needed to continue to make riding a priority.

The guys left, and I made my way into the lodge right as Charley had finished up. When she got to work, Hannah was there, but Charley closed alone tonight.

"Hot chocolate with whipped cream?" she asked as she held out a cup.

I smiled at her and took the cup. "Thanks. You ready?"

"Yep."

We walked out to the parking lot.

"What are you up to tonight?" I asked.

"Quiet night at home with Emme. Girl time."

Damn. "Okay, then. Tomorrow night?"

She bit her lip. Fuck.

"I'm sorry. Emme and I have had plans for a couple weeks now for tomorrow night," she said and then continued, "But I might be able to forego laundry on Sunday…"

"Sunday morning. Breakfast. I'll be at your place at nine. Does that work?"

"That works, Wes."

We made it to the cars. I put my hot chocolate in the truck and I pulled Charley's gear out of the back. I put it in the back of her Jeep while she leaned in over the driver's seat, stuck the key in the ignition, and turned it on. She turned around as I walked up to her door.

I put my hands to either side of her face and leaned in to kiss her gorgeous, plump lips. She tasted like hot cocoa. I worked my tongue into her mouth and she sucked on it. As I groaned, she moaned. I stepped toward her and pressed her up against the Jeep. Despite all the layers of clothing I knew she could feel my arousal pressing into her belly. I wanted her to know just how hard she made me.

She broke the kiss and whispered out of breath, "Wes."

I looked down at her while she looked up at me with her big, blue eyes. I really wanted to just pick her up and take her home with me. "Sunday is a long fucking time away."

She bit her lip again. "I'm sorry."

"This mouth, gorgeous. The next time I have you in my bed I want this pretty mouth wrapped around my cock."

Her eyes grew wide and she licked her lips.

I kissed her again, picked her up, and put her in her Jeep. "Sunday morning. Goodnight, Charley."

"Goodnight, Wes."

I watched her drive away. Then, I hopped in my truck and drove home. When I arrived, I got in the shower, wrapped my hand around myself, and stroked while I imagined Charley's mouth wrapped around me.

Eight

Charley

"Well? How was it?" Emme asked.

I was sitting at the end of the couch in the living room while Emme sat at the opposite end. I had just gotten back from work, showered, and was now consuming a glass of wine along with my dinner. Emme was an excellent cook and had made chicken fried rice.

"Wes didn't take me out for dinner last night," I told her.

Her eyebrows drew together, and she wondered, "What? What happened? You weren't home when I got back last night, so I assumed you were still out with Wes. I heard you come in not long after I had gotten home. I was already wiped out otherwise I would have tried to get the details as soon as you walked in."

"I was with Wes, but he didn't take me out. He took me to his house."

Emme's eyebrows went from scrunched together to raised. "Oh my."

"Yep. He cooked. And for the record, he's good at that. We had a nice conversation. I had moments where I would change topics because I knew the conversation would go somewhere I didn't want it to go. Then, after dinner we had sex. And for the record, he's really good at that. I dozed off for a bit, woke up to him wanting to eat dessert in the form of me. And for the record, he's really, really good at that. Then, we had sex again."

Emme sat there staring at me with her mouth open. I continued talking.

"I haven't had sex in nearly two years and then in one night in a matter of a couple hours, I have three orgasms. How is that even possible?"

"Maybe because he's apparently really good at giving them?" she suggested. "Wow, Charley. How are you feeling about all this?"

"Honestly, I'm freaked. For more than a year before everything happened, I hadn't really been in any sort of relationship, serious or otherwise. It wasn't for lack of trying. I just wasn't meeting anyone worthwhile. Nine months ago, life changed, and I had no desire to form any relationships. We came here to have a fresh start, and I had absolutely no intentions of getting close with anyone. But then I meet Wes. I can't explain it, Em. It just feels right with him. Comfortable. Most of all, he encourages me. And that? That's what makes me so scared."

"What do you mean?" she asked.

"Well, for example, I told him I had wanted to learn how to snowboard and he goes and decides to give me lessons. I have had an awesome time learning over the last week and then yesterday I rode down my first real trail without falling. Had he not encouraged me and pushed me to do this, I honestly never would have done it."

"He's helping you live life again, sweets," she began. "Let him. Enjoy it and try not to think too much about it."

"That's the problem. I really like him, Emme. I've only known him a week and I already realize how much it would hurt if he wasn't around. The butterflies I feel in my belly every time I know I'm going to see him are crazy. And when I'm with him, I mostly forget about all my reasons that would stop me from pursuing this. It's when I'm not with him or when he says something that makes me think of those reasons that I realize how bad it will be if I get in deep and this ends."

A look of remorse washed over her face. "Charley, you can't do this to yourself. He's making you happy right now. You're going to be twenty-five tomorrow. You have your entire life ahead of you and you can't spend the rest of it not living because you are thinking about the possibility of something bad happening," Emme stressed.

I sat there, sipped some of my wine, and thought about it. Then, I realized I wished I could tell her to take her own advice. Unfortunately, I knew it wouldn't be nearly as easy for her. I just hoped that one day she'd get her piece of happiness.

Emme snapped me out of my thoughts. "So, three orgasms in one night, huh?"

"Emme, I'm telling you—he's really good at everything I've seen him do. But orgasms, he's *so* good at giving those. And tonight, when he walked me to my car after work, he told me what would happen the next time he had me in his bed. Ugh…I'm in so much trouble."

She giggled and then topped off our wine glasses.

"So, when are you seeing him again?" she asked.

"I told him that you and I already had plans tomorrow so he said he'd be here Sunday morning for breakfast at nine o'clock. I think I want you to meet him, Em."

"Whatever you need, sweets. It's your birthday weekend!"

Emme and I spent the rest of the night chatting, watching a movie, and drinking wine. Afterward, we went to bed, and I fell asleep with a smile on my face thinking that I liked the idea of enjoying my happiness while I had it.

I just hoped that it wouldn't be ripped away.

The doorbell rang.

I reached over to my phone on the nightstand and looked at the time. It was six thirty in the morning. On a Saturday. When I hadn't scheduled myself to work. What. The. Fuck.

Then I heard Emme scream and I bolted up out of bed and ran down the hall. When I reached the front door I, too, screamed.

Standing in front of us were Nikki and Monroe.

"What are you two doing here?" I squealed, hugging them as they stepped inside the condo.

"From the time we were in elementary school we have celebrated every single birthday together. Just because you and Emme moved a thousand miles away doesn't mean that changes," Monroe explained.

My eyes filled with tears and I did not even try to stop them from falling. These three women were my life.

"I can't believe you girls came all the way out here," I exclaimed.

"Well you ladies better believe it because here we are," Nikki announced.

Emme and I laughed and closed the door behind them.

We caught up over eggs, avocado toast, fruit, and mimosas. Nikki and Monroe filled us in on all the latest news and happenings in Ventura while Emme and I brought them up to speed on our lives in Rising Sun. I left out Wes. I was not ready for that conversation with them. Emme knew, and I already had too many conflicting thoughts about it. I needed to see where it was headed before I told Nikki and Monroe.

"So, what are the big birthday plans for this evening?" Nikki asked.

"Charley and I thought we'd keep it low key. We were going to go out for dinner and drinks before heading back here for a quiet night with some movies or something," Emme answered.

Nikki and Monroe looked at each other, then to Emme and me.

"No way. It's your twenty-fifth birthday, Charley. You need to get out and do something fun. Other than last weekend when you went out for dinner and drinks, when was the last time since you've moved out here that you two had any real fun?" This came from Monroe, and I knew where this conversation was headed. It did not matter what I said; they weren't going to let me off the hook.

Taking our silence as an answer, Nikki pointed out, "Exactly. You have not done anything to let loose in the last six months. Not even once. You are both going out tonight and we aren't taking no for an answer."

I broke my silence. "I don't know. I just don't think I'm ready for that yet."

Nobody said anything for a beat and then Monroe came over, sat next to me, and hugged me. She pulled away, cupped her hands on either side of my face and reassured me, "Babe, nobody understands more than Nikki and me what you and Em are going through. We get it. Trust us. But you two are our best friends and you've moved away from everything you know and are keeping yourselves secluded. You both just spent the last hour telling us about your lives here. They pretty much consist of working constantly. We realize you are trying to occupy your minds, but you need to have a little bit of fun. We are going out tonight. If it becomes too much, you say the word and we're out of there."

That's when Nikki chimed in and shocked me. "Besides, if Monroe and I are going to move away from the sunshine and sandy beaches of southern California to the snow-covered and cold mountains of northwestern Wyoming you are going to have to do something to convince us that it's worth it. We love you both, but it's fucking cold here!"

I jerked my head out of Monroe's hands and looked to

Nikki then to Emme. Emme was smiling so big. It was the first time in a very long time that I had seen her truly, genuinely happy.

I would do anything to see that look back on her face all the time.

Shit.

"Okay, we'll go out tonight."

Nikki and Monroe looked at each other, smiles on their faces, and high-fived.

Upon inspection of my closet following breakfast, Nikki decided I did not have anything worthy of a twenty-fifth birthday celebration. At that discovery, she insisted we were heading out for the day. The rest of the morning and afternoon were spent shopping, having lunch, and being pampered. We managed to find a dress for me that they all approved of and insisted upon regardless of the reservations I had about it. Emme also found a dress that looked killer on her so she splurged as well. I guess the two of us silently decided that if we were going to do this, we might as well do it right. Food was an absolute necessity, so we grabbed a light lunch at a local burger joint. And as a birthday present to me, the girls treated me to a manicure, pedicure, and a facial. Of course, they joined in on that action and treated themselves as well.

After being pampered, we made our way back to the condo. On the drive back, I called Hannah. Without ever having really experienced the nightlife here in Wyoming, I was not sure where to go for a night out. Hannah grew up here so she knew all the best places.

"You want to go to Lou's," she stated.

"Lou's?"

"Yep. It's technically called Big Lou's Restaurant and Saloon. As the name states, it's a restaurant and saloon in one. They make the best food and offer live music, occasional karaoke, and a great time. The place is always packed, but you are guaranteed to not be disappointed."

"Sounds great. Thanks, Hannah!"

"No problem. Have a great time and enjoy your birthday."

"I will. See you Monday."

I disconnected the call as we pulled in and parked at the condo. We all went in and started getting ready.

Nikki works as a hairstylist and makeup artist back in Ventura, so she took charge of everyone's hair and makeup. Monroe, owner of a dance studio, insists that any night-out preparations should have great music playing in the background so our bodies are primed for a night of dancing. Emme, as always, insists on capturing our memories, so she breaks out her phone and snaps candid shots the entire time.

Once we were finally ready, I had to admit we looked damn fabulous. I was all dolled up in a sleeveless black mini dress. It was banded at the hem and fit snug around mid-thigh, but the bodice was loose with a scoop neckline. I added a pair of four-inch black patent leather stilettos and the combination made my legs look long and lean. Nikki had kept my hair straight and sleek and given me mostly natural makeup with a smoky eye and pink tinted gloss on my lips.

Emme wore a green body-con dress also with a scoop neckline that showed off just enough of her ample cleavage. She had a tiny waist and a generous booty so the form-fitting dress worked with her curves. She finished the look with a pair of black booties. Nikki put loose curls in Emme's long hair and a little bit of shimmer on her face with some gold tones.

Monroe opted for a champagne colored sequin mini skirt with a cream-colored spaghetti strapped plunging v-neckline top that just covered her midriff. She wore that with a pair of pale pink sandals that had one band across the toes and one band around her ankle and a three-inch heel. Monroe had great legs from all the years of dance and her outfit showed off her muscular calves and thighs. Her legs were tied with her plump, pouty lips as her best physical features. Her chestnut colored hair came to mid-back and had natural loose waves in it with hazel eyes that were accented by her subtle makeup. There was only a bit of shimmer to compliment her skirt.

And finally, Nikki. The girl screamed exotic beauty. She had mounds of jet black hair that was super thick and had tons of volume. She put some waves in her hair and kept it big. Her piercing blue eyes against her porcelain skin was striking. She wore a multicolor blue floral and black and white patterned mini dress with a V-neckline and long sleeves and paired it with knee-high black stiletto boots. Nikki looked absolutely stunning.

"Alright, ladies, group picture," Emme announced once we had all finished getting ready.

She got her tripod out and we all huddled together. Emme set the timer on the camera and we posed for a group shot. Once the camera had snapped a shot, we put on jackets and made our way to Lou's.

Nine

Charley

We arrived at Big Lou's and instantly realized Hannah wasn't kidding when she said that there'd be a crowd. It was a large, two-story building that housed Big Lou's, but the outside had that old western feel to it. There were wooden steps that led up to the covered porch, which wrapped around three sides of the main level of the building. There was another set of stairs that led up to the second-floor outdoor balcony. The restaurant was on the main level and we were fortunate enough to not have to wait too long for a table.

As we walked in, I took in the beauty of the place. There were natural wood barn floors with booths that had wooden tables lining the outer walls. Two more rows of them were situated on each side of the restaurant. In between each of the rows were free-standing wooden tables and chairs. All along the entire back wall was a massive bar that had to have at least fifty stools lined up around it. Despite all of the dark wood, most of the restaurant was well lit with modern lighting fixtures.

We followed the hostess to our booth and were seated. Our waitress came over and took our drink orders. Monroe, who may have an occasional glass of wine but mostly preferred not to drink, was our designated driver. By the time our waitress returned with our drink order the four of us had only gotten about halfway through the menu. It would seem that Lou's didn't do anything small. We asked for a few minutes to make our dinner selections and then continued to peruse the massive menu. Once we made decisions on dinner and gave our order to the waitress, we moved into conversation. It was light-hearted and fun, mostly the four of us reminiscing past birthday celebrations. Or, that was the case until Emme changed the topic.

"So, Charley met a guy," she announced.

"And why are we just now hearing about this?" Monroe asked.

"Details, now," Nikki demanded. Nikki was a no-nonsense girl and got straight to the point.

I glared at Emme.

"I was working at the coffee shop last Thursday and he approached me. He ordered some espresso and introduced himself. His name is Wes."

"And she got tongue-tied around him, he called her gorgeous, waited for her to finish her shift, and walked her to her car," Emme elaborated.

"Is he hot?"

I sighed. "He's the most beautiful man I've ever laid my eyes on." I paused and took in all their smiles. "He has these amazing green eyes, dark hair, a wicked grin, and muscles. Lots of muscles."

"See? Now this is the stuff that a girl can leave warm, sandy beaches for," Nikki reasoned.

We all laughed just as our waitress returned with our dinners. As she was putting our food down on the table, she spoke.

"Did I hear y'all say something about the beach?"

"Yes. We just moved here from Southern California a few months ago," I explained while gesturing my hand between Emme and myself. "We're trying to convince our best friends here to leave the beach weather behind and come hang with us in the mountains."

"I'm originally from Texas," she began. "I moved here five years ago and have not regretted it once. I think it's the cold weather and having a hot guy to cuddle up with that helps."

Monroe spoke up. "It's our friend's birthday today, so we're here celebrating with her tonight. Nikki and I are leaving to go back to California tomorrow afternoon, but I wouldn't mind having a dance or two with a hot guy. Any idea where we can make that happen?"

Our waitress smiled. "Upstairs, darlin', she said with a wink. "Enjoy your meals, ladies." With that, she was off.

"And that, my friends, is southern hospitality at its finest," Nikki exclaimed.

We all laughed again and got to eating. The food was incredible, but food was no longer the priority. Nikki and Monroe were determined to have some fun.

Shortly after we were all thoroughly stuffed, a man approached our table. He was the epitome of cowboy. He was tall and wore jeans, a flannel shirt that covered his larger belly, cowboy boots, and a Stetson. He was older, had a round face, and a white mustache.

"Hey girls. Brookie tells me there's a birthday celebration here."

We stared at him, puzzled.

He continued, "I'm Lou. Brooke's one of my waitresses."

"Lou?" I repeated. "As in Big Lou's Restaurant and Saloon?"

"And here I thought my belly gave me away," he murmured. "You've got that right, darling. So, who's the birthday girl?"

Emme, Nikki, and Monroe pointed at me and said, "Charley."

"Guilty," I admitted with a wave of my hand.

"Well, here at Big Lou's we always make sure a pretty girl has a great birthday. After you finish your dinner, I'm sending you upstairs. We've got Elle performing tonight. She's a local, but she's the best. No cover charge for you and your girls tonight and the meals and all your drinks are on the house."

I sat there dumbfounded.

Nikki spoke up. "And Big Lou would be reason number two I can leave sandy beaches behind!"

"That's very kind of you, but I can't let you do that," I interjected.

"Darlin', it's not up for debate. I own the place and you don't want to upset Big Lou. I'll make sure the guys upstairs know the deal. Stay as long as you like and enjoy yourselves. Happy Birthday, Charley."

I was blown away by this man's kindness, "Thanks, Lou."

I looked back to the girls and saw the excitement rolling off them in waves.

We left a huge tip for Brooke, made our way out of the restaurant, and up the wooden steps to the outdoor balcony that would lead into the saloon.

We walked up to the entrance and met who I could only assume was one of the bouncers. He surmised, "You must be Charley." I'm not sure how he knew, but I wasn't going to question it.

I simply nodded.

He moved out of the doorway and waved his hand out for us to pass through. "Name's Cliff. You need anything, you ask any one of the bartenders or bouncers. Happy Birthday, girl."

"Thank you for the hospitality, Cliff," I expressed and then pointed to each of my girls. "These are my friends, Monroe, Emme, and Nikki."

"Hey Cliff," they all said in unison.

"Ladies," he replied as they followed behind me.

As we entered, I had to admit I was taken aback by the size of the place. The upstairs housed several bars along the walls, a dance floor, tons of seating that included free-standing tables throughout as well as booths that lined the walls, and stages for what I assumed was either the live music performances or the occasional karaoke that Hannah had mentioned. It was much darker than the restaurant below but still lit well enough that you could see across the room.

Monroe and I made our way to the bar to get drinks while Emme and Nikki went to find a table.

"You must be Charley," the bartender said as we walked up.

How did these people all just know that I was Charley?

"Yes, that's me," I confirmed. "And this is my friend, Monroe."

"Nice to meet you. What'll it be tonight, ladies?"

"Three vodka cranberries and a bottled water," Monroe ordered.

"You've got it."

As we waited for our drinks, we checked out the scene. Monroe was looking for a dance partner and I was scanning the room looking to see where Nikki and Emme ended up. As I turned my head toward the direction of the stage, I sucked in my breath and felt my body tense.

Monroe felt it. "What's happening, Charley?"

"That's him."

I pointed toward the area by the stage where I saw Wes standing. Sadly, he was not alone. There was a woman with him. She looked about my age with long, wavy blonde hair that sat at her waist. From the distance, I couldn't make out her eye color, but she had stunning cheekbones and a beautiful smile. She had her hand resting on his arm and she was looking at him listening intently while he spoke to her. Then she laughed; and somehow, she looked even more beautiful than she did before. When I looked back to him, he was looking down at her and it was clear he had very strong feelings for this girl.

My belly twisted.

"Who?" Monroe asked, concerned.

"Wes. The guy I was telling you about at dinner. Monroe, I didn't just see him last Thursday. He came to the lodge again Friday. He sat with me in my car before I started my shift and then walked me to my car afterward. Before I left, he kissed me. Three times. And he's a really great kisser, Monroe. Then, all this week he met me at the lodge immediately following my shift at First Tracks and started teaching me how to snowboard. There was also a lot more kissing. I had off this past Thursday and he took me to his place and made me dinner. Afterward, he gave me three orgasms." I paused a moment trying to swallow the tears that were threatening to fall. "How could I have been so stupid? I knew better than to pursue anything."

I looked back to him and he was now hugging the girl. I sat and stared knowing what it felt like to have his arms wrapped around me.

"Oh, Charley. I'm sorry, babe. Do you want to get out of here?"

I stayed silent a beat thinking, then took a deep breath and answered, "No. It's fine. I am not going to let it ruin my chance to convince my best girls to move here," I resolved, forcing a smile.

I looked away and saw that our drinks were ready so we each grabbed two, dropped a tip on the bar, and headed toward the table where Nikki and Emme were seated. We sat, and they immediately knew something was up.

"Talk," Nikki demanded, looking at me.

"It's nothing," I mumbled.

"It's not nothing. I can tell something happened."

"Wes is here. With someone. With a beautiful someone," I explained, discreetly pointing over to where he was standing, still with the pretty blonde holding his arm.

Nikki and Emme looked to where I had pointed and Nikki, as her eyes completely bugged out, questioned, "That's Mr. Muscles?"

I nodded. I then proceeded to fill Nikki in on last Friday's make-out session, the snowboarding lessons for the past week, and Thursday night's sex-filled escapades.

Thankfully, at that moment Big Lou had just stepped up to the microphone on stage. At least I wouldn't have to worry about Nikki causing a scene and coming to my rescue by saying something to Wes. That's just who she was. Fiercely loyal, without shame.

"Ladies and gentlemen, it gives me great pleasure tonight to present to you our very own hometown sensation and one of my favorite pretty girls, Elle!!"

The crowd cheered and that's when I noticed the beautiful blonde that was with Wes was making her way to the stage. This was just wonderful. Not only was she gorgeous and there with him, but she could sing, too.

Maybe I wouldn't be able to stay here the rest of the night.

I turned back toward my friends who were all staring at me with worried looks, except Nikki—she looked like she wanted to rip someone's head off.

"We sit through as many songs as are needed so I can finish this drink and have two more. Then, we are out of here," I told them. Then I murmured, "I must be a fucking masochist."

They nodded and didn't question me.

Two songs and three drinks later, I painstakingly had to admit, only to myself, that Elle was good. As she belted out two originals, I realized she had a beautiful voice and, under any other circumstance, I might have become a fan. I glanced once or twice—okay, maybe more like ten times—over to where Wes was now sitting throughout this. The smile, coupled with a look of pure pride, never left his face as he watched her sing.

Why did the first guy I felt any sort of connection to have to be a jerk? A hot jerk, but a jerk nonetheless. I could feel my eyes begin to sting and knew I had to leave.

"Ladies, it's time to go," I announced as I looked to my friends.

They weren't paying attention to me and that's when I saw Emme's eyes get big and Monroe lick her lips. Nikki declared with a massive smile on her face, "I think reasons three, four, and five for moving to the mountains just walked in."

I looked behind me to see what had them so distracted and realized that Wes may have been the most beautiful man I had ever seen, but these three guys were all easily tied for second place. They were making their way toward the front of the room and stopped at Wes' table to sit with him.

"Damn," Nikki sighed. "Why'd they have to go to his table?"

"Are you ready, Charley?" Monroe asked looking to me.

I nodded, willing the tears not to fall. How could I have been so stupid to think something good was happening in my life? I should have known better.

The girls and I all got up, but since Elle was in the middle of a song and she was a favorite in town nobody else was standing to leave. I glanced one last time over where Wes and his buddies were sitting and saw that he had turned to see the commotion. Despite our best efforts to sneak out of there without him seeing, that clearly wasn't going to happen. He saw me and, at first, he looked surprised. But then he looked worried.

I bet you're worried, buddy, I thought.

My friends and I started walking away, and Wes realized I was not coming over to him. He shot up out of his seat and started striding toward me.

"Charley. I didn't think I'd see you until tomorrow morning."

"I'll bet you didn't," Nikki shot back.

He looked at her and then back to me and his face was puzzled.

"Are you a fan of Elle's? I wish I had known you were coming here."

I stared at him, completely dumbfounded by his ignorance. My liquid courage had kicked in. "As you already know, I've only lived here for about six months, so this is the first I've ever heard her sing. She's good. And she's beautiful." *Just like you.* I paused to swallow the lump forming in my throat. "I didn't know I was coming here. I woke up this morning to find that my other two best friends had come all the way out here from my hometown in California to surprise me and celebrate my birthday with me today."

"Today's your birthday?"

I couldn't help it. My eyes welled up with tears. Thankfully, Emme saw this, stepped forward and grabbed my hand. I tore my eyes away from Wes and looked to her. "Charley, sweets, let's go."

I nodded to her and turned to walk away.

"Wait, Charley. Stay. I'd love to introduce you to my friends and Elle."

I turned back to face him. "Sorry, Wes. I have no interest in playing this game and meeting your very talented girlfriend. Quite honestly, I don't understand why you would even waste your time on someone like me when you have someone like her already."

Wes stepped back, looked confused, and then started laughing.

What the hell was his deal? What did he think was so funny?

Nikki stepped forward at this moment, pointed her finger at him, and scolded him. "You, my friend, are grade A asshole. How dare you? My Charley girl here is gold. Fucking. Gold. And she deserves the fucking world, especially after everything she's been through. I don't care how big your muscles are or how hot your friends are, I could totally kick your ass right now."

Yep, that's Nikki. What did I say? Fiercely loyal, no shame.
God, I loved her.

Right now, I also hated her. She said all that and, now coupled with how I was already feeling, I knew there was no controlling the tears that were about to spill over my cheeks.

"Charley, look at me," Wes ordered, his tone lethal and no longer a trace of humor anywhere in his voice.

I looked to him and a single tear fell from my eye.

"Gorgeous," he paused. "Elle is my baby sister."

"What?" I whispered, another tear falling. Then I realized he told me about his sister Elizabeth. Elle must have been her nickname.

"Christ, Charley. You're killing me here. Baby, don't leave." His voice was strained on those last words. He held his hand out to me and I had no control over myself. My body propelled forward, and I slammed into his chest. He wrapped his arms tightly around me and I just stood there for a moment, feeling.

He bent down and got close to my ear and shared, "I want nothing more than to take you out of here right now, but I can't leave in the middle of Elle's set. Come watch with me?"

I took a moment to get it together and pulled my head back from his chest. I looked toward my girls and noted their worried faces before I directed my gaze back to Wes and nodded. When I glanced over at my friends again, I assured them with a small smile and nod that I was okay.

"Wes, these are my friends—Emme, Monroe, and Nikki."

He nodded to them.

Nikki stepped in front of Wes. "I'm sorry for jumping the gun there. That said, I'll still totally kick your ass if you hurt her."

"Don't sweat it," Wes insisted. "It's nice to know Charley's got good people looking out for her."

That put a smile on Nikki's face. I looked to Monroe and Emme and could see they both shared the same sentiment.

"You coming?" he asked.

"I'm not leaving my friends," I answered.

He smiled. "I didn't expect you to. I've got my three best friends at the table with me, and I'm pretty certain that with friends that look like yours they'll be more than fine with your girls joining us."

I looked back to my friends and saw Nikki and Monroe were smiling big and nodding furiously. Emme just laughed at their reactions. Given her laugh, I assumed she was okay with it, too. Wes turned while holding my hand to lead us all back to the table, where his friends were sitting.

"Charley, these are my buddies—Stone, Luke, and Zane. Guys, this is Charley and her friends, Nikki, Emme, and Monroe."

I did a quick inventory of Wes' friends. They were all huge. We'd seen them when they walked in so I knew they were all tall, each of them easily at least six feet tall. They all also had incredible bodies that were very much in shape proven by the presence of their lean muscles.

Is this how they made them out here in Wyoming?

Stone had blonde hair that he wore in a bit of a spiky mess. He had puppy dog baby blues and a great set of juicy lips. His face was clean shaven, and he had a strong jawline.

Luke had the most rugged look. He had short, light brown hair, brown eyes, and a neatly-trimmed beard. His long-sleeved cream-colored Henley had the sleeves pulled back on his forearms and I saw the man was serious about his tattoos. Both arms were completely inked.

Zane reminded me a lot of Nikki in that his look was raw, exotic, beauty. He had clean cut, black hair that was a bit longer on top with ice blue eyes and the most exquisite bone structure I'd ever seen on a guy. He had a few days' worth of scruff on his face.

Wes' friends all nodded at me and then quickly turned their attention to my friends. Stone had his eyes on Monroe, mostly focused on her legs while Luke grinned at Nikki.

And then there was Zane.

His eyes were boring holes into Emme who, when I had glanced over to her, looked like she had had the wind knocked out of her.

Ten

Charley

It turns out Wes was right. His friends did not mind my friends joining the table. The guys got up and gave their seats to the girls before they pulled a couple of extra chairs up and we all sat down. Everyone turned their attention back to Elle, and while I tried to pay attention to her, I was focused more on what had just happened.

I was mortified by it.

I now knew that Elle was Wes' sister, but when I thought it was a lover he was with, my stomach sank. I jumped to conclusions about what I saw and assumed Wes was playing games. Of course, we hadn't made anything official between us, nor did we discuss exactly what was happening between us, but it simply never crossed my mind that he might have a different idea about all of this. I knew that if I didn't address it, I'd be setting myself up for disaster. But I had no intentions of talking to him about it, especially not tonight. Tonight, I was going to try to enjoy the rest of my birthday.

A little while after my friends and I sat down with Wes and the guys, Elle had finished her set. She walked off the stage and came up to our table. Wes stood and pulled me up with him.

"Great job tonight, Elle," Wes said, kissing her on her cheek.

"Thanks, Wes," she replied.

Her attention was then directed to the words of praise and hugs she got from Zane, Stone, and Luke.

After that, she looked beyond Wes to me, a questioning look in her eyes.

Putting one of his hands to her back and holding the other out to me, he introduced us. "Elle, this is my friend, Charley Meadows. Charley, this is my sister, Elle."

My friend.

Well, there you go. I was his friend.

"It's nice to meet you," I started, holding out my hand to her. "You're really great. You have a beautiful voice."

"Thank you. It's nice to meet you as well."

Then, pointing to my girls at the table, I introduced her to them. They all smiled and waved.

"Are you hanging out for a while?" Wes asked looking at his sister.

"I wish I could. I'm exhausted from my gig last night and then traveling today so I could get back here for tonight's show. I need sleep. I'm going to quickly find Lou, say my goodbyes, and head out."

"Okay. Do that and come back to get me. I'll walk you out."

"I'll be fine, Wes," she assured him.

"It's not up for debate, Elle. Find me after you see Lou," he demanded, giving her a look that indicated he was serious.

Elle nodded and took off.

My heart squeezed at this. I mean, he walked me to my car every night I worked, but he also insisted on doing it for his sister tonight. I was beginning to realize just how good of a guy Wes really was.

Yep, I was definitely in trouble.

"Time to dance, birthday girl," Monroe announced.

After Elle had finished her set, music boomed out from the speakers and people were up dancing and having a good time. At Monroe's declaration, Nikki bolted up out of her seat while I looked to Emme for help. She was getting up out of her seat. I guess she wouldn't be helping me out of this.

Emme looked to me and shrugged. "It's your special day. I'm making an exception for you."

I looked back to Wes, "I guess I'm dancing."

"Have at it, gorgeous. I'll be here until I have to walk Elle out, then I'll be back."

"Okay."

I followed Monroe, Nikki, and Emme out to the dance floor. I couldn't remember the last time I had danced and, doing it now, I remembered just how much I missed it. We had easily been out there for at least three or four songs when I felt a hard body behind my back and hands at my hips. I knew immediately it was Wes. He wasn't dancing, but he was standing there with me while I danced. I turned around and put my arms around his neck. He bent down so his cheek was pressed to mine, his mouth at my ear.

"You aren't moving," I informed him as though it was news to him.

"I don't dance, Charley," he shared.

"So why are you out here on the dance floor?" I wondered, continuing to move while he stood there.

"You are out here wearing this dress, showing off these fantastic fucking legs, dancing with your girls, and the four of you have the attention of every guy in here. I'm just here to make sure they know that you're mine."

I tensed and stopped moving.

"What?" I whispered.

Wes pulled my body closer to his. "Do you feel that?" he asked.

I did.

I could feel his erection pressed into my body. I nodded and bit my lip.

"That's from watching you dance, Charley. Two days ago, I was inside you. Twice. All these guys here are looking at you dance, thinking they'd like to be right where I was. Unfortunately for them, I don't share. The day my mouth tasted the sweetness between your legs, gorgeous, was the day you became mine."

I think I came on the spot. "Wes?" I squeaked.

"Yeah?"

"My friends are here until tomorrow early morning visiting me from California. They came just over a thousand miles to spend my birthday with me."

"I know," he replied, seemingly confused as to why I was telling him this.

I pressed my body into his, whispered in his ear, "I would like to be back in your bed right now so I could wrap my mouth around you. I can't leave my girls tonight, though."

He groaned.

"Enjoy your friends tonight, Charley, because I've changed my mind. Tomorrow, instead of breakfast I'm coming to pick you up after your friends leave and I'm going to make sure you and I celebrate your birthday properly."

At that, Wes stayed close by while I turned back to my friends. When I did, I noticed that Zane, Stone, and Luke were all standing around them. None of the guys were dancing, but my girls did not mind. Nikki was close to Luke and thoroughly enjoying herself. She was not too far from Emme while Monroe danced for Stone. She was literally dancing for him and he seemed to be enjoying the show. Emme, though, was a different story. She was still dancing trying to enjoy herself, but I could tell she was not comfortable. Zane was still caught up in watching her and she knew it. Unfortunately, I knew at that moment I needed to help her out.

"Emme, I need to run to the ladies' room. Come with?" I asked, grabbing her hand.

She nodded, and I could see the relief in her eyes.

I turned back to Wes, told him we were running to the restroom, and we took off. Nikki and Monroe continued dancing and waved as we walked off.

Once inside the bathroom I turned to Emme and could see how worked up she was. It broke my heart.

"Emme, honey," I comforted her as I put my arms around her and squeezed.

She hugged back but didn't say anything. I stood there for a moment while she settled.

Eventually, she pulled her face back, dropped her arms, and spoke, "I'm sorry, Charley. It's your birthday and I'm totally ruining it."

"Stop, Em. It's fine. My birthday would be ruined if I knew that you were doing something that truly made you uncomfortable."

"When, Charley? When will I be able to have a normal night out with friends and not feel this way? Did you see Zane? My goodness, he's beautiful. I see the look in his eye and I know he's attracted to me. As much as I want to dance and just have a good time, I can't do it," she cried, tears pooling in her eyes.

"You'll get there. I promise."

Emme stood there staring back at me, defeat in her eyes. She blinked back her tears and took a deep breath.

"Why don't we go out, get Nikki and Monroe, and head home?" I suggested.

"No, Charley. It's your day. I'll be fine. And I don't want to ruin their only night here. I will just sit at the table, grab a drink, and watch them have a good time. Really—I'll be alright."

"I'm giving them two more songs and then we're heading out. I don't want to hear anything from you. You said it yourself—it's my birthday, so I get to say what we do."

She tilted her head, her eyes warmed, and she murmured, "Thank you."

I winked at her and took her hand as we walked back out.

Emme and I approached the table we had all been sitting at earlier to find Wes and Zane sitting in the middle of a conversation. I glanced to the dance floor and saw Nikki and Monroe both still dancing. Neither Luke nor Stone had left their spots. Nikki was a bit more hands-on; Monroe was just a great performer. I smiled at them, held up my hand with two fingers showing, and they nodded at me. They knew what that meant. We had reached the table, where Wes and Zane came out of their conversation and directed their attention to us. I sat down next to Wes but had Emme right next to me.

"All good?" Wes asked.

"Yep," I answered.

I glanced over at Zane and found him looking at Emme again. Her eyes were focused on the dance floor. Zane's gaze was pensive as he studied her.

I turned my attention back to Wes and informed him that we would be leaving shortly. Disappointment flickered in his eyes. Seeing that made my belly warm and the butterflies started fluttering. I decided to play a little with him.

I leaned into him and whispered in his ear. "I'm very much looking forward to a private birthday celebration with you tomorrow, though."

Pulling back from his ear, I looked at his face and saw his eyes were starting to smolder. Yep. That worked.

I turned my gaze to Emme and saw that she was not only looking at Zane but also that she had a pained expression on her face.

"So Zane," I called out, directing his attention to me.

"Wes tells me you snowboard?"

"Wes speaks the truth," Zane answered.

"Nice. Are you as good as he is?"

Zane glanced to Wes and grinned before he hit me with a full-blown smile. Gosh, he was good-looking already and that bright white smile just took it up a notch.

"Wes spends more time working on the business than he does riding, darlin'. I'm training every day, so it's safe to assume that I'm as good as he is," he replied.

"It's true, Charley," Wes chimed in. "Zane's one of the best pipe riders in the country, and definitely in the top ten in the world."

My eyes nearly popped out of my head. "Wow. That's awesome."

I heard Emme giggling. When I turned toward her, I found that she was still looking out at the dance floor. Nikki and Monroe were trying, with not much luck, to get Stone and Luke to dance with them. The guys were standing there watching my friends but refusing to join in on the fun.

"You've got to get out your phone and snap a few shots," I said to Emme. "At least we could have had pictures of this and used them to help convince those two to move out here with us." I looked back at Wes and shared, "Emme is a photographer and your friends are very good-looking. I think, with a little bit of effort, they could persuade my girls to move out here."

He smiled at me then turned to Emme, "You're a professional photographer or it's something you do for fun?"

"That's my full-time gig; though, I do it because I love it."

"And she's freaking amazing at it. Emme James Photography, best in the business," I added.

At that moment, Nikki and Monroe came up to the table with Stone and Luke following right behind them.

"Is it time to go already?" Monroe asked as she walked up.

"I was just getting started."

We laughed. Monroe could dance all day, every day.

Nikki chimed in, "Seriously! I'm thinking we need to at least plan our next trip out here since I'm not totally convinced yet that I should move. And you four better be available for good times when Monroe and I get back!" she ordered, pointing to each of the guys.

They all smiled at her while Luke promised, "You got it, babe."

"I'm in. It was pure entertainment tonight," Stone noted. "Though, can we not be on a dance floor next time?"

Emme, Nikki, and I laughed.

Monroe gasped. "How dare you?" she shrieked.

He looked at her confused.

Surprisingly, it was Emme that spoke up. "Monroe is a dancer. You've just insulted her livelihood."

"In that case, maybe we'll come to California to see you dance," Stone teased as he cocked an eyebrow.

Monroe realized they got the wrong impression. "I'm not a stripper. I *teach* dance."

"We'll still come to California," Stone maintained, shrugging. "There are great mountains out there for riding. Besides, I haven't seen the beach in a while."

Fuck.

Emme looked to me and I saw the hurt in her face. I'm certain my pain registered, and it was like looking in a mirror when she saw me.

"Hey, are you okay?" Wes asked.

Shit.

"Yeah, I'm good. It's just been a long week and I've had a long day. We should really get going now, though," I suggested.

We said goodbye to the guys and as we made it to the entrance, we noticed that they were right behind us.

"What are you doing?" Emme asked. The panic in her

voice was evident.

Zane looked directly at her and explained, "There are lots of bad people in the world, sweetheart. Lou's lot is well lit, but we're not going to let you and your girls looking the way you do, which is hot as fuck, walk out to your car in the parking lot this late at night without making sure you get there safely."

Emme's eyes got glassy and I knew she was fighting not to break down. Nikki and Monroe understood the significance of what Zane just said.

To distract everyone from Emme, Nikki yelled, "Reason number six!"

Monroe and I giggled.

"What? What does that mean?" Luke asked.

Monroe answered, "Nikki is making a list. All the reasons she and I should move here. She's up to six now."

"How many reasons do you need?"

"I haven't decided yet," Nikki answered.

At that, everyone laughed, and the men walked us to the Jeep. I glanced to Emme as she mouthed a thank you to Nikki.

It was eleven o'clock Sunday morning. Emme and I had just bid farewell to Nikki and Monroe, who promised to let us know once they arrived back in Ventura. I had to admit how great it felt to have the four of us back together again, and I was really hoping they decided to make the move to Wyoming. The fact that they were even considering it was enough for me for the time being.

Wes had texted me shortly after I arrived back home last night to make sure we arrived safely and to let me know that he would be by to pick me up around one o'clock for my post-birthday lunch and private celebration with him. I could barely contain my excitement and couldn't wait to spend time with him.

Since I had some time before he was set to arrive, I decided to work on my art. Emme had gone back to bed for a nap after the girls left, so I figured I'd give myself an hour with my art before getting ready. I pulled out my supplies and got to it. An hour later, I did not stop and continued to work. It was twelve-thirty when I pulled myself away from it so I could get ready. Since there wasn't much time left, I kept my art where it was. I could take care of putting it away later.

I'd given myself just enough time to put on some clothes—a pair of black skinny jeans and a pale pink, off-one-shoulder knit sweater—fix my makeup and do my hair. Just as I turned off the curling iron, I heard the knock at the door.

"Hello, gorgeous," Wes greeted me when I opened the door.

"Hi, Wes."

"Ready?" he asked.

I nodded.

Once I grabbed my purse and locked up, Wes and I walked to his truck. He took me out to a local Italian restaurant for lunch. After we'd given our order to the waiter, we fell right into conversation.

"So, did you have a good birthday yesterday?" Wes asked.

"Yes, surprisingly, I did. I had no idea Nikki and Monroe were coming out to visit. They showed up at our door at six-thirty in the morning and we spent the day shopping and getting pampered at a spa before dinner and dancing at Lou's. It was hard to let them leave this morning. I miss them so much already."

"Did Nikki's list grow?"

I laughed. "I think she added number seven to the list. That being the fact that birthday celebrations would be much easier if we all lived close to each other."

"Not that I'm complaining, but why did you move in

the first place?" Wes asked and then took another bite of his chicken cheesesteak sandwich.

My stomach grew cold and I looked away from him.

Wes must have noticed my distress. "Hey, I'm just trying to get to know you. If it's not something you want to talk about right now, it's okay."

"I hate to disappoint you, but I don't think I'll ever be able to talk about it," I paused a moment. "I'll just say this, I have no plans to ever move back."

"Well, there is the bright side then."

After swallowing a mouthful of my vegetable stromboli, I asked, "Oh yeah, and what's that?"

"I don't have to worry about you leaving me," he clarified on a wink. Then, he continued, "So, what birthday was this?"

"The big two five," I answered.

"Same age as Elle."

And there it was.

My opening to discuss the situation from last night. There was no time like the present if I was going to do this. I was feeling full already and, with the subject I was about to bring up, I couldn't eat any more food. Setting my fork and knife down, I looked up at him.

"Listen, Wes, about last night and the situation with Elle—" I started before he cut me off.

"Charley, don't. It's fine. In fact, as much as it killed me to see you with tears in your eyes, especially on your birthday, I'm not upset or angry at you with how you reacted. In fact, it felt good."

"It felt good?" I repeated.

"Let me tell you something about me," he began. "I'm not that kind of guy. If I am with a woman, I'm with only her. As far as I'm concerned, the second night I walked you to your car and you said I could kiss you, you became my woman. A few days later when you said yes to me giving you snowboarding lessons with you wearing my gear, you really became my woman. Then, gorgeous, you officially became mine when you were in my bed a couple nights after that. Knowing you saw Elle and didn't know she was my sister but thought she was with me in a different capacity, and got upset shows that you want to be my woman. I'm not happy you got hurt, but it feels good to know that you like being my woman."

"I think I'm done eating and would like the rest of my birthday celebration to commence," I announced.

Wes' eyes heated. He took out his wallet, threw a couple bills down, curled his fingers around my hand, and ushered me out the door.

We had barely entered his home and were just inside the kitchen when Wes came up behind me. He brushed my hair off my exposed left shoulder and pressed his lips to my skin there. I tilted my head to the opposite side to give him better access. One of his hands was resting on my hip while the other cupped my breast, gently squeezing it. He pulled my body back against his and I could feel his arousal at my behind. I arched into him.

"Baby," he groaned, his voice rough.

Wes pulled my shirt over my head before he positioned his hands at the front of my jeans. Within seconds, my jeans and shoes ceased to exist. With my back still to his front, his hand slid inside my panties. His fingers immediately found the right spot, and I moaned as I arched my back even farther. My head fell back on his shoulder, my face turned toward his. His mouth captured mine while the fingers of his other hand swiped over the fabric covering my hardening nipple. Wes slid a finger inside me as I rolled my hips, inching myself closer to release.

"Oh, Wes," I moaned.

He continued and, seconds later, my body came apart, my knees buckling. Thankfully, Wes tightened his hold on me and took my weight. Moments after, he picked me up and carried me through the house to his bathroom. He set me on the edge of the sink and turned on the faucet for the massive soaking tub. Wes pulled his shirt over his head as he turned back to me and closed the distance between us.

"As magnificent as that was, Mr. Blackman, I'm thinking maybe we should have stayed at the restaurant so I could have finished my lunch," I began. My hands made their way to the waistband of his jeans. I went on, "I'm suddenly feeling very hungry."

I opened the fly of his jeans and pushed them, along with his boxer briefs, down his thighs. I got myself off the ledge of the sink and started to trail down his body, but was hauled right back up.

"Christ, gorgeous. I want nothing more than your mouth on me right now, but you aren't going to get on your knees on the cold bathroom floor."

Wes turned off the faucet and opened the drain. He turned, lifted me up by my bottom, and I wrapped my legs around his waist.

"Ever since that night in the parking lot when I massaged your legs while they were wrapped around me, I've been thinking about this," he started. "You pressed up against me, wearing next to nothing, with your legs wrapped around my waist. The real thing is so much better than the fantasy."

Wes lowered me to the bed before he settled himself on it, his back against the headboard. I began kissing and licking down his body, running my hands over every mouthwatering inch of him.

I finally got to my prize and gripped his length in my hand.

He groaned.

Hearing that sound, I licked my lips and looked up at Wes as I put the tip of him in my mouth. I flicked my tongue across the head, lightly sucked, and pulled away only briefly before I took more of him into my mouth. I held on to the root of his cock while I worked his length with my mouth. One of his hands fisted my hair, and I could hear the grunts and groans coming from him. His vocal appreciation made me work him that much harder.

Wes soon had his hands under my arms, pulling me up his body until I was face to face with him.

With one hand still under my arm and the other behind my head, his voice was low and gravelly when he praised, "This fucking mouth. I knew it was going to be good, but it's even better than I imagined."

And then he kissed me hard. It was wet and demanding. Wes snaked an arm around my waist and brought me up so I was straddling his lap. He tore his mouth from mine only so he could tear open the condom packet with his teeth and sheath himself.

I was then lifted in the air and brought down on him as he slammed into my body. I rode him while he gripped my hips and kissed my mouth. For the second time in a very short time, I felt it building again. I rode him harder, my movements quicker. Wes thrust up as my hips crashed down and we eventually found it together, exploding into pure bliss.

I sat there in his lap, my head resting on his shoulder, as he stroked his hands up and down my back. That felt really good. Several minutes of silence had passed when Wes finally spoke.

"I've got to get rid of this condom, gorgeous. Lift up."

"So sleepy," I murmured.

"You can take a nap. I just need to dispose of this first."

Begrudgingly, I hoisted myself up and off of him. I whimpered at the loss and collapsed on the bed beside him. He tried to suppress a laugh as he got up and moved to the bathroom.

I felt the bed dip moments later as Wes got in the bed and curled my body into his. My head was resting on his chest, my hand on his abs, and my leg thrown over his thigh. I loved feeling the length of his body against mine.

"What a great birthday celebration this has been," I marveled. "Thank you, Wes. And I'm sorry we didn't make it to the bathtub."

"It's not over yet, Charley. We have a lot of the day left still; we'll get it done."

"Next time, I want to feel you," I blurted.

"What?" he asked.

"I want to feel you," I repeated. "Just you, Wes. Nothing between us. I'm on birth control so we're covered with that."

"Are you sure?"

Nodding against his chest, I maintained, "Very sure. I'm clean, too. I've never been with anyone else without protection. I want that with you, though."

"Feels good to hear that, baby. Just so you know, I'm also clean."

I smiled inwardly and melted deeper into him. He traced his fingers along my hip as I closed my eyes and drifted off to sleep, feeling the happiest I had in a really long time.

Eleven

Charley

"WAKE UP, GORGEOUS."

My eyes fluttered open and I was staring up into Wes' beautiful face. I was on my back in Wes' bed, while he sat on the edge of it, his torso twisted backward so he was leaning over me.

"How long have I been sleeping?" I asked.

"About an hour," he disclosed, smiling down at me. Wrapping his fingers around my wrist and turning it, he placed a box in the palm of my hand. "Happy birthday, Charley."

"You got me a birthday present?" I asked.

"That's what you do when someone you care about has a birthday, isn't it?"

Admission that he cared about me. My belly warmed and the butterflies there had taken flight. I knew he liked me, and I had experienced the 'you're my woman' talk, but something about the way he said this made my heart squeeze and I was flooded with emotions.

I sat up in the bed, pulling the sheet up to cover myself and I looked down at the box. My throat got tight. I opened the box and the stinging I felt in the back of my eyes couldn't be blinked away. My eyes filled with tears as I looked from the necklace to Wes.

My throat constricted, I barely managed to rasp out, "Wes." Then, a single tear spilled down my cheek.

He looked at me, concern in his face. His thumb swiped the tear off my cheek and he held my face in his hand.

"Charley, talk to me. What's happening inside your head right now?"

I glanced down at the necklace again. It was a silver chain that attached on either side of a snowcapped mountain range. Not showy or overstated. Simple and perfect.

"It's perfect," I said, my voice still husky.

"I was hoping you'd like it, but I have a feeling there's more going on here," Wes pressed on.

I nodded. "Wes, I can't—" I got out before he cut me off.

"Listen, I know we've only just met not even two weeks ago. That doesn't change the fact that I feel something strong for you right now. I get that it might seem like it's too soon, but babe, no matter where this goes, you've got some shit that's eating at you. I saw it in your face the first night I walked you to your car. I thought maybe I was seeing something that wasn't there, but I've seen it several times since then—most recently, today at lunch and just now. You've got to get it out, baby. If you don't want to talk to me, fine, but you've got to talk to someone."

I remained silent, slightly shocked that he knew from the first day he met me that something had been on my mind.

"Now, I have no plans of intentionally upsetting you today, but I want you to know that the way I'm behind you when you're riding down a trail making sure you don't get hurt, I'll be there the same way for you with whatever this is. I'm not going anywhere, so whenever you are ready, I've got your back."

I leaned forward and wrapped my arms around him burying my face in his neck. Wes' strong arms wrapped around me and I couldn't deny the comfort and safety I felt there pressed tight to his body.

"Will you put this on me?" I asked, holding the necklace out to him when I pulled out of his arms a few minutes later.

"Absolutely."

Wes carefully took the necklace out of my hand and clasped it around my neck. He kissed me at my neck right before he kissed my forehead.

"Come on. You need a relaxing soak," he urged.

Following a bath, which was very relaxing, I found that Wes had set out one of his t-shirts for me. I pulled the shirt over my head and went to look for him. I made my way out to the kitchen and found him standing there at the island wrapping something in foil. He was wearing a pair of jeans and a white t-shirt that fit snug across his chest and arms.

Yum.

Wes glanced up when I approached. He stopped what he was doing to look me up and down. His eyes heated as he grinned at me.

"Do you eat salmon?" Wes asked.

The basics?

He said he could do the basics. I was beginning to think his definition of the basics was far different from mine.

"Yes," I answered.

He smiled and placed a tray holding two foil-wrapped packages in the oven.

"Can I help?" I asked.

"Next time. I've got it today, gorgeous. Would you like some wine?"

"Sure."

Wes poured a glass of white Pinot Noir for me before he went back to dinner preparations. I figured if he wasn't going to let me help make dinner, then I needed to bring the conversation.

"So, yesterday, you and Zane said that he is one of the top riders in the world and he's a better rider than you. Does the same go for Stone and Luke?"

"That's what they do. Though, Luke is a big mountain, big air rider."

"What exactly is that?"

"Big air is basically when a rider launches off a man-made jump and does tricks in the air. Of course, landing those jumps is critical."

"You mentioned they test boards for you. Are different boards needed for pipe riding or big air?" I asked.

He nodded. "Yeah. Boards will be different based on the type of riding you do, whether pipe, big air, freestyle, slopestyle, racing, alpine…" He trailed off, belatedly realizing that I probably had no clue what half of what he just said meant. Bringing himself back on track, he continued, "I'm currently working on the development of a new line of boards that we are calling the Elements Series. There will be four different models—Fire, Air, Water, and Earth. Each model in the series will have a variety of different designs in its group. The first step, though, is to get the boards made and tested, then we'll work on the design. The Fire model will be the first one released. It's made specifically for pipe riding. The second model will be the Air model, which is going to be designed for big air riding. We have not yet begun production or development on the Water and Earth models. I have ideas of where I want to go with those, but I'm still considering my options on that while we get the Fire and Air models squared away."

"That sounds amazing. I didn't realize how much went into producing the boards. I mean, all I ever see is a finished product. I never really took into consideration all the testing and data you probably need to collect before you can begin selling them. And then, they all need names."

"It's a bit of a process," he responded with a wink.

Wes moved back to the oven to pull the tray out. He plated our dinner of baked teriyaki salmon, broccoli, and rice. I was seriously impressed. We moved to the dining room to eat.

"Thank you for making this weekend so special, Wes."

"Could have done better had I known it was your birthday," he answered.

I decided to ignore that. Birthdays hadn't exactly been the easiest for me for many years, but they were always made special.

But when the one thing that made them special when they'd already been hard was no longer there, expectations for birthdays went out the window.

Sensing I wasn't going to address his comment Wes changed topics. "I'm thinking, if you don't have any plans yet, I'd like to spend Christmas with you."

I looked up from my plate to find Wes looking at me waiting for an answer. "Seriously?" I asked.

"I wasn't joking. Do you already have plans?"

"Um, well, not so much. I mean, Emme and I were probably just going to have dinner at home. We haven't planned anything special."

"Fuck, Charley. It's Christmas."

"Uh, I know."

"You and Emme don't have any family or friends coming to visit you from California?" he asked.

I looked down at my plate and felt my eyes start to sting.

"Shit," Wes mumbled under his breath. "Charley, I'm sorry. Forget I—" he started before I cut him off.

"I'd love to spend Christmas with you," I blurted before I could think too long and change my mind.

Wes leaned over to me and kissed me quickly. "Okay, gorgeous. Then we'll spend Christmas together. And just so you are aware, that involves a trip to my parents' house for Christmas breakfast."

Shit.

Shit.

Shit.

I should have kept my mouth shut.

"Your parents' house?"

He just smiled and nodded.

Damn.

Wes and I finished dinner. He took our plates to the kitchen and put them in the sink. I followed, thinking I could help clean up. Wes had other plans. He turned from the sink and looked down to see me standing right behind him. He put his finger under my chin and lifted. With my head tipped back, Wes' mouth came to mine, where he kissed me, long and slow. I noted that he seemed to do this a lot. Sure, there were moments that when it was necessary, Wes could do rough and fast, but I often found that he seemed to want to take his time, savoring me.

Wes deepened the kiss and dropped his hands to the sides of his t-shirt I was wearing and gently tugged the fabric up until his fingers were touching the skin of my legs. After his hands roamed up the sides of my legs until they were at my hips, he moved both to my ass, where he squeezed, pulled me closer, and groaned into my mouth.

He pulled away and looked at me curiously.

"No panties this whole time, Charley?"

I feigned innocence and just shrugged.

Wes laughed. It was the first time I'd seen and heard him laugh one of those laughs that came from deep in his belly. It was a beautiful sight to see.

He quit laughing, his eyes liquid, and ordered, "Turn around, baby."

"What?" I asked.

His voice was low, nearly a whisper, when he demanded, "Gorgeous, turn around."

I could tell he was serious, so I turned.

"I like seeing you in my shirt, but I'm going to like seeing you out of it better," he shared as he lifted the shirt over my head and tossed it onto the island.

Oh.

Okay.

Kitchen sex.

This I could do.

I saw the shirt Wes had been wearing land next to the one he took off me. Then, I heard the zipper of his jeans before I heard them fall to the floor. My body quivered in anticipation.

"Going to need your hands on the counter, Charley. And brace because I'm going to fuck you from behind," he paused and then brought his mouth to my ear. "Hard," he whispered.

Tingles ran up and down my body. I put my hands on the counter of the island. His hands ran over the cheeks of my ass and squeezed before one hand gripped my hip the other went between my legs.

"Always wet for me. Can't fucking wait to feel you with nothing between us" he proclaimed, his voice getting hoarse.

I loved hearing his voice like that.

He ran his fingers through the wetness, teasing me. He had me so close so quickly that when he pulled his hand away, I wanted to cry.

"No, Wes. Please."

I was begging, and I didn't care.

Before I could get another word out Wes slammed into me.

"Yes," I cried.

He hadn't lied when he said he was going to fuck me hard. As Wes pushed forward into me, I used my leverage on the counter and pushed my ass back into him. And he felt incredible.

"Charley," he growled.

He had a bruising grip on my hips and proceeded to pound into me. I was so close.

"Wait, Charley. You come with me this time."

There was no way. I wasn't going to be able to hold back.

"Fucking wait, Charley."

"Wes, please," I rasped out, barely holding on.

He continued slamming forward and I continued pushing back.

"Come for me, gorgeous."

I exploded around him as Wes groaned through his orgasm. My legs got weak, but Wes supported my weight from behind as we came down from the high, catching our breaths.

"Happy Birthday to me," I sighed.

Wes gave me another laugh. I smiled and felt my belly warm.

Wes and I were in his truck on the way back to my place. Following our kitchen sex session, I told him I wanted to get home since I had an early shift at the diner the next morning. We pulled up outside my place and Wes walked me to the door. When I stepped inside, I saw that Emme left a note on the table by the door.

Hey sweets,

Got a call for a shoot today. A client went into labor and wanted me there to capture the birth. I didn't want to text and interrupt your birthday festivities but wanted to leave a note in case you came back and didn't find me here. Be back soon (hopefully).

xoxo,
Emme

"Everything okay?" Wes asked.

"Yeah. Just a note from Emme letting me know she got a call for an unplanned photo shoot," I shared, glancing at the clock on my phone. "Do you want to come in for a bit?" I asked.

He smiled at me and his eyes warmed. "I'd love to, but I think you're right. Tomorrow is going to be an early day for me, too. I'll meet you at Parks Ridge for lessons, though."

"Okay. Thank you again for a wonderful day, Wes. It really means a lot to me."

"You're welcome, Charley."

Wes leaned in and gave me a sweet kiss on the lips before he turned and walked out. I locked the door behind him and went to my bedroom.

As I walked into my room, I saw that I still had my art out from earlier in the day. Since it was still a little early and I was feeling inspired, I figured I'd take a quick shower and then do a little drawing. I stripped off my clothes and made my way into the bathroom.

I finished in the shower, wrapped a towel around myself, and then took a few minutes to dry my hair. Stepping out into my bathroom, I came to a halt and gasped.

Wes was sitting on my bed with my drawings in his hands. He looked up at me and he had a look that I'd never seen from him before.

"Did you draw these?" he asked.

"What are you doing here?" I countered.

"You didn't answer my question."

I didn't want to answer his question.

He held my stare. This went on for several minutes. Finally, I caved.

"Yes. I drew them. Now, what are you doing back here? How did you even get back in?" I questioned, panic filling my voice.

"Relax, Charley. I was walking back to my truck and I saw your girl. Tiny little thing that she is and she was trying to carry what seemed like two hundred pounds of camera equipment. I carried her stuff in here for her."

My eyes got big and I asked, "Emme let you help her?"

He jerked his head back in surprise at the question, but still answered, "Yes."

"And then she let you in here?"

"Why wouldn't she let me in here?" he wondered, now becoming slightly frustrated.

I stayed silent.

"Charley, you've got to give me something here," Wes pleaded. "I've been trying to figure you out since we met. You are a waitress at a diner and you're a barista at a coffee shop in a ski lodge. You work all the time, and while I'm sure you make enough to live decent, you're driving around in a relatively new, fully-loaded Jeep. It's a Rubicon, babe. Fully loaded, that's going to run you well over forty grand."

He held some of my work out to me. "You've never mentioned anything to me about this. Do you do this professionally?"

I stumbled back at his question.

"No," I answered, my voice just a hair over a whisper.

"Why the fuck not?" he swore, his voice angrier than I'd ever heard.

Fuck. Fuck. Fuck. I was going to cry. I was standing in a towel in my bedroom with Wes sitting on my bed holding my artwork in his hands and I was going to cry.

It happened.

The tears spilled over my cheeks. Wes was up and had his arms wrapped around me in seconds. He held me tight as my body was wracked by sobs. I had held it together for so long, and I just couldn't keep it in anymore. Everything poured out of me.

"Christ, Charley. You've got to talk to me, baby."

I burrowed my face deeper into his chest. Wes didn't falter; his arms continued to hold me close. After I'd spent entirely too long sobbing uncontrollably, Wes' fingertips began tracing lightly up and down my shoulders and arms. He kept me pressed tight to him and I eventually started to calm down.

I had to give him something. I hadn't given anybody anything in nearly ten months, but I decided I was going to give Wes something. I took a deep breath.

"It's my brother's," I confessed.

"Not following you."

"The Jeep," I clarified. "It's his. Actually…correction. It *was* my brother's Jeep." I paused for several moments preparing to utter the words. Finally, I blurted, "It was his until he died nine and a half months ago."

"Jesus Christ," Wes mumbled under his breath. "I'm sorry, baby."

Wes picked me up and carried me to my bed. He set me down gently and I stayed right where he put me.

Catatonic.

My mind was racing, but my body wasn't moving.

Wes walked away, and I glanced up to him, fearing he was leaving. My breathing increased. He turned back around, sat on the bed, and put his face right in front of mine.

"I'm not going anywhere. Just getting you some clothes, gorgeous."

Blinking back the tears that had welled up again, I nodded.

When Wes came back from my dresser, he pulled a pair of panties up my legs and over my hips before he slid a shirt over my head. After, he shrugged off his jacket, took off his boots, and removed his shirt. I was hauled up into his arms, the covers of my bed were thrown back, and Wes put us both in my bed. He was on his side, my front pressed to his. My face was buried in his throat.

Wes held me.

He didn't ask questions; he didn't say anything.

He just held me.

We stayed like that for a long time. It felt good. I felt safe and comfortable.

And, because I felt good, I decided to give him something else.

"His name was Taj," I offered quietly.

Wes' hand at my hip started tracing my skin. I think he knew how much I liked that and how well it worked in comforting me.

He didn't respond. He just traced while I continued talking.

"My brother and I were close, Wes. I draw now when I'm feeling overwhelmed about things or when I'm reminiscing about happy times I had with him. I can't remember a time before Taj died when I didn't want to be a graphic designer, but I always doubted myself. My brother pushed me, told me I was the best he'd ever seen and that I was incredibly talented. He wouldn't let me give up. When I lived in California, I did end up with a few paid graphic design gigs, and I started gaining momentum in my career. I swear anyone who ever heard Taj talk about me would have thought I walked on water. He was so proud of me."

I paused, remembering the time I told him about my first paid job. One of Nikki's ex-boyfriends owned a tattoo shop. He needed a graphic designer for his website. He had someone who could write all the code and do all the technical stuff, but he wanted someone who'd kick ass on the design of the site. Nikki offered my services, even though I didn't officially offer services at that time. She just knew I had a passion and could get the job done. When I showed her ex some samples of my work, he hired me on the spot. I didn't make a ton of money, but I was beyond thrilled to have finally gotten paid for doing something I loved. When I told Taj about it, he lost it. He was so excited for me and insisted we go out that night to celebrate. He had said, 'This is just the beginning, Charms.' That was his nickname for me, insisting I was his lucky charm. Of course, until I wasn't.

"Wes, he was my biggest fan. When he died, part of me died, too. I moved here because everywhere I went in California reminded me of him. It hurt too much. I cried every single day after he died until I moved here. I can't pursue that dream of designing without him. I didn't have the confidence then, but I knew he'd be there to pick me up and keep pushing me. Now, if I pursue it and I fail, I'm alone."

"Gorgeous," Wes said gently. "First, you are not alone. You've got your girls, two of which came here to Wyoming from California just to spend your birthday weekend with you. That's got to count for something, no? You have friends at your jobs. I don't know how close you are with them, but from what I can tell at the coffee shop, it's friendly enough. And, baby, you've got me. I'm not going anywhere."

My hands balled into little fists, unable to handle what his words meant.

Wes continued, "Second, from everything you just told me, I'd bet my entire company that Taj would probably be pretty fucking pissed at you right now. If what I saw in that pile of artwork over there is any indication of what you are capable of, Charley, you need to not be making coffee and waiting on fucking tables. You need to be using that talent. You've got to know that if you pursue it now, there isn't a chance in hell that you'll fail."

I took in a deep breath and let his words sink in. "Wes, if you look at those drawings over there hard enough you'll see his name hidden in every single one of them. I do that so he's always with me. I can't do this without him."

He let out a sigh of understanding. "For the last week,

I've been so confused trying to figure out why a girl would move all the way here from her hometown and spend all her time working. You didn't move because you had a job transfer. You moved here to make coffee and wait tables. I get it now and I understand why you moved, but you don't give yourself anything else but mindless work. Unless there's something I'm not aware of, that's how it's been until I convinced you to snowboard with me. I'm not going to force you to do anything, Charley. Take some time before you decide, but really think about what you're doing with your life. You deserve so much more and you're wasting your talent. Do it for Taj if that's what you need to tell yourself, but baby, you really need to do it for you."

I didn't respond. I just snuggled closer to Wes. His hand tightened on my hip and he pressed a kiss to the top of my head. Exhausted from my most recent turn of events, I let sleep overtake me.

When my alarm went off the next morning, I was slightly disoriented. A moment later, it came back to me. Last night, I let my guard down.

My phone was on the nightstand closest to Wes. I had to reach across him to get to it. As I did, Wes wrapped his arms around me and kept me on top of his body. After I silenced the alarm, he pressed a kiss to my lips.

"Good morning, gorgeous."

"Morning, Wes."

He stared at me a little while and had a new look on his face, one I hadn't seen before.

"You good?" he eventually asked.

I looked back at him for a moment and thought about it. I thought I'd be freaked or anxious, but I wasn't. I felt calm and relaxed. And, Wes didn't give me the look that I'd been given every day of my life for the last three months I was living in Ventura. He didn't look at me like he pitied me.

"I'm good, honey."

He smiled at me.

"And thank you for staying with me last night. I'm sorry I lost it," I lamented.

"No need to thank me, Charley. I wouldn't have wanted to be anywhere else. In fact, I'm thinking I like waking up next to you," he shared, with a wink of his eye. "I need you to understand something, though. You don't ever apologize for what happened last night. I can't even begin to imagine how you manage to stay so strong. If something ever happened to Elle, I don't know what I'd do. If you ever need to cry it out, baby, you do it without concern for anyone else. Do you understand?"

"I understand."

His arms tightened around me.

"I've got to get out of here so I can get back home and get ready for work. I'll see you this afternoon, though."

I pushed up off him and got out of the bed.

I stood there in my t-shirt and panties watching Wes get dressed. When he finished, he stalked toward me. His hands went under my arms and lifted me off the ground. I wrapped my legs around his waist while his hands made their way to my bottom.

"Think about what I said last night, Charley. You deserve more than what you're giving yourself."

I nodded and answered, "I will."

"Good. Now give me a kiss that'll last until I see you this afternoon."

I smiled at him and did just that. I kissed him with everything I had.

Twelve

Charley

THE NEXT WEEK FLEW BY.

Apart from Tuesday when I covered for Hannah at the coffee shop, I worked every morning at the diner, followed that up with snowboarding lessons with Wes, and worked my shift at the coffee shop. I did make my way over to Wes' one night for a little fun, but since I insisted on sleeping at home and he wasn't thrilled with me leaving his place and driving myself home, he spent two more nights at my condo.

Over the course of the week, I did take the time to really consider what Wes had said to me. He insisted I wouldn't be making a mistake if I pursued my dream of becoming a graphic designer. As I considered this decision, noting there was just over three weeks left in the year, I realized it would be a great way to start the new year.

New year, new me. That's how the saying goes, right? Except, in this case, it was the same old me.

I was a bit freaked. After I'd thought about everything, I realized that maybe I was selling myself short. Wes had given me some new perspective and he was right. Taj would have been pissed at me for giving up. I decided that I needed to make a change.

One concern I had was about my current employers. First Tracks had enough staff that they'd manage without me. Brew Stirs was a much smaller operation. I didn't want to leave them hanging; so, I knew I needed to let them know immediately about my decision to leave. I planned to talk to Emme, Monroe, and Nikki about it today and then talk to Wes about it tonight. Once I had some reassurance from the people who supported me, I'd go into work tomorrow and give my official notice. That would make my last official day at both jobs two days before Christmas.

I had just woken up and gotten ready for work. I walked out into the kitchen to grab coffee and breakfast, but mostly I was hoping to catch Emme.

"Oh, thank goodness you are still here," I said, finding her sitting at the island having breakfast.

"Hey sweets, what's up?" she asked. "I feel like I haven't seen you all week."

"I know, honey. It's been so crazy busy, but that's kind of what I wanted to talk to you about."

"Sure. What's going on?"

"Remember the night after my birthday when you had the last-minute shoot for the mom in labor?"

She nodded.

"Well, Wes had just dropped me off and left. I got in the shower, but when I got out, he was in my room."

"Oh. Yeah, I had just gotten back from the shoot and got all of my camera equipment out of the car. Wes saw me and offered to help me carry it all. Actually, he didn't really offer to help, he sort of just took it all out of my hands."

I let out a small laugh. "That sounds about right."

"I'm sorry, I didn't think about letting him in since he had obviously just left. I assumed it was okay. Wait? Did something happen?"

I nodded. "Yep. I haven't really told you this, but you

obviously know that ever since Taj died, I haven't been pursuing any graphic design work. I know you think I've completely given up on it and while part of that is true in the professional sense, I haven't stopped drawing. I do it several times a week."

Surprise moved over her. "Oh, Charley. Why didn't you tell me?"

"I'm sorry, Em. It's just been something I've kept for myself," I paused, taking a deep breath. I went on to tell her exactly what happened when I walked out of the shower and saw Wes with my drawings.

Emme was staring at me, completely about to lose it.

I kept going. "I broke down and told him that Taj died less than a year ago. And Wes took care of me. He was so gentle through it all. He listened to me and held me, never demanding or expecting me to share more than I was prepared to share. We discussed my art and I explained how much Taj supported me with it."

"Oh my. I'm so sorry, Charley," Emme lamented.

"It's okay, honey. Ever since it happened, I feel different. So much lighter, happier. What I really wanted to ask you about was something that Wes said. He thinks I should be pursuing my graphic design career. In fact, he said that he was certain Taj would be pissed at me for giving up on it. What do you think?"

"Honestly?" she asked.

I nodded, biting my lip.

"He's right, Charley. I've thought that since the day you stopped. Of course, I realized you were going to need time after Taj, but you never went back to it. That's such a huge part of who you are, sweets. I never brought it up because well, you know, but I think about it all the time. Wes has already brought so much happiness back in your life, Charley. I haven't seen you this happy in so long. Listen to him on this. He's right."

"Wow. I thought you'd be torn and I was going to need to call Nikki and Monroe about it to get their thoughts. I guess I don't really need to do that now."

"They'll say the same thing," she assured me.

"Alright, I've got to go. Thank you for listening. I'll catch you later, honey."

"Love you, Charley."

"You too, Emme."

Much like the past few weeks had been, my shift at the diner flew by. As much as I'd miss my co-workers, especially Greg, I was really beginning to feel that I was making the right choice. My days were passing me by, I had very little time for myself, and I wasn't exactly doing something I loved. I finished my shift, hopped in the Jeep, and noticed I had several text messages. They were from Nikki and Monroe. Evidently, Emme was doing me some favors and spreading the news to them.

About time, babe. You need to be designing! You follow through with that, I'll add it to my list. Reason number eight for moving—my bestie is getting her life back and I need to be part of that!

That was from Nikki. Gosh, that girl could always make me laugh. I tapped out a reply to her.

Thanks, Nikki. I'm thinking two more reasons, you and Monroe better start packing! Love and kisses.

I scrolled to my next text message.

Hey Charley, heard the news. Go for it. You're the best at it and Taj would be so proud. You've got my vote and my support. Whatever you need. :)

Monroe, my faithful supporter. We always joked she was the mom of the group since she was always taking care of us. I sent her a quick reply, too.

Thanks, Mama. :) I'll keep you posted on the details when I get it all figured out. Love you.

I tossed my phone in my purse, started the Jeep, and drove to Parks Ridge. I pulled in and saw Wes was already there. I pulled up next to him, glanced over, and waved at him to come into the Jeep. He had a puzzled look on his face, but quickly made his way over and hopped in. He gave me a really nice kiss, but he didn't prolong it. I'm certain he knew I had something to talk about considering this was not the norm.

"I was wondering if we could skip the snowboarding today?"

Wes got a sexy grin on his face and asked, "Sure, gorgeous. Did you have something else in mind?"

I rolled my eyes at him. "If you keep that up, I'm going to start thinking you only want me for my body."

"You can't say that you blame me, Charley. It's a great fucking body."

My eyes flared. "You're incorrigible!" I exclaimed.

He chuckled briefly and then got serious. "Okay, so I'm guessing what I have in mind and what you have in mind are not the same thing. What's going on?"

"I've been thinking about what we discussed on Sunday. I think that maybe you are right. I think I need to do Taj proud. More importantly, I need to do myself proud. I wanted your honest opinion one more time before I decide to follow through with pursuing a graphic design career. Do you really believe I can do this?"

"Absolutely," he replied instantly. "There's not a doubt in my mind that you're phenomenal and will be successful at it."

I smiled at him. "I talked to Emme this morning; she gave her approval. She said a lot, actually. Mostly, she said you were right. And I just got texts from Monroe and Nikki."

"What did they say?" he asked.

"Monroe supports me, one hundred percent. That's who she is."

"And Nikki?"

"Nikki's up to reason number eight," I joked, smiling at him.

He leaned over and kissed me hard, wet, and deep. I tore my mouth away from his and rested my forehead against his.

I could feel the lump forming in my throat and my eyes starting to sting. "Thank you, Wes."

"For what, baby?" he asked.

With my voice strained and my eyes wet, I pulled my head back from his and looked at him when I answered, "You're giving me my life back."

Wes stared at me. The tears spilled down my cheeks. Through the blurriness, I could see he was clenching his jaw, fighting some kind of emotion.

His voice rough, he asked, "Are you working alone tonight?"

"No. I think Mark's on tonight until close, too," I answered.

"Think Mark can hack it by himself tonight?" he asked.

"Sure. I do it all the time. I don't understand."

"Gorgeous, stay here. I'll be right back."

"Where are you going?" I asked as he stepped out of the Jeep.

He looked at me and ordered, "Lock the doors. I'll be right back."

Wes closed the door and waited until I locked them before he walked toward the lodge. I sat there dumbfounded by what just happened. When Wes returned, he ordered me to get out.

"What's going on?" I asked, stepping out.

He took my keys from my hand, reached in and grabbed my purse, handed it to me, closed the door, and locked the car. Then, he tugged me by the hand and guided me over to his truck. Opening the passenger side door, he picked me up and put me in. Then, he closed the door, rounded the truck, and hopped in the driver's seat.

"Um, Wes. I need to go to work. What are you doing?"

"I took care of work for you tonight. Mark's got you covered. I'm taking you to my place," he explained as he pulled the truck out of the lot and headed in the direction of his home.

"What? You can't do that."

"Charley, I just did. Mark's good. You're covered. Let it go."

My mouth opened to speak and then it closed again. I didn't know what to say. I had no idea what had gotten into him, so we sat in silence all the way to his place. After we arrived and he led me to his bedroom, Wes stripped off his shirt and boots. I stood there in silence.

"Shoes off, Charley."

I took my shoes off.

Wes walked over to me and removed my jacket, shirt, and jeans. I was standing there in my bra and panties mentally patting myself on the back for putting on a cute, matching set today. He removed his clothes and stood before me in just his boxer briefs.

I swallowed hard and licked my lips. He was so beautiful.

Wes pulled me close to him, bent his head, and kissed me. Through this, he backed up to the bed and held me close. He fell back and pulled me down on top of him. As he removed my bra and our tongues danced, our hands roamed our bodies. There was moaning and gasping while our legs were tangled together. Wes eventually rolled us so that my back was to the bed. He took off my panties and disposed of his last article of clothing as well.

Then, Wes was in me.

He was propped up on his elbows and forearms with his hands framing my face. His eyes didn't leave mine. And his strokes were slow. Deliciously slow. As I looked in his eyes, I realized something was different. A look I hadn't seen before was there. It was soft and warm and tender. I registered what was happening.

This was not just fucking; this was love-making.

"Wes," I breathed, my voice tight.

He continued to thrust slowly into my body, alternating between kissing me and looking in my eyes, and with each thrust, my body grew hotter for him. I could feel it building deep in my belly.

"Get there, Charley."

His thrusts had increased ever so slightly in speed.

"Gorgeous, get there," he demanded, his voice rough.

A few strokes after, I got there. And Wes was right there with me.

I was naked in Wes' bed. He was spooning me, his fingers tracing delicately over the skin at my hip. I really loved the way it made me feel. We had just made love or, at least, I believed that's what it was.

"Got a plan?" he asked.

"I'm sorry?" I countered, not following him.

"You said you were going to pursue your dream. Do you have a plan?"

I took in a deep breath and blew it out. "Well, not a complete plan. I only planned today and tomorrow. Today's plan was to talk to you and to the girls about taking this step. Assuming I had everyone's support, tomorrow's plan was to give notice at the diner and the coffee shop."

"How do you think that'll go tomorrow?" he wondered.

"Not sure. I've been friendly enough with everyone, but nobody knows much about me. I think it'll catch them off guard. I just hope to remain friends with everyone, especially Greg and Hannah."

"Greg?" he repeated, as his fingers stopped tracing and his body tensed.

"Greg works at the diner."

"I figured that much, Charley, but I've never heard about him before," he remarked, sounding slightly annoyed.

"Are you jealous?" I teased.

"Should I be?"

"Considering Greg is madly in love with his boyfriend, Tony, I'm going to say no. But even if he wasn't gay and in love, I'd still say no."

Wes stayed silent and went back to tracing. Then he admitted, "Happy to hear it."

The silence lingered for a while before I spoke up. "I'm scared, Wes."

"You'll be successful, Charley. You've got too much talent not to be."

"I wasn't referring to that. I was referring to you."

I felt his body tense. "What are you scared of?"

"I've spent nearly ten months alone. Emme's there, but she's always been there. I've made friends at work, but I've not let anyone in. You come along with all your hotness and suddenly my mind starts listening to my body."

I felt the tension leave his body and the bed vibrate with his laughter. "What's your body saying?"

"My body really likes you."

"I told you it was a great fucking body," he reminded me. "I'm failing to see the problem here, gorgeous."

"The problem is that this is moving very fast. Lightning speed, if I'm being honest. I've opened up and shared things with you that I haven't shared with anybody else other than those who already know, specifically Emme, Nikki, and Monroe. You and I have only known each other about two weeks and I'm not going to lie, I'm feeling like I'm already in deep with you. I'm trying to see the good that's happening and embrace it, but sometimes I still find myself waiting for the other shoe to drop. It scares me because when that happens, I am certain I will be worse off than I was before."

Wes stopped tracing and squeezed my hip. He turned my body toward his.

"You shared some serious shit with me, Charley. I don't take that lightly. I know now that physically you are there, but your mind needs a little time to catch up. I'm good with that; I'm in no rush. That said, you need to know that I don't have any intentions of having this be just some fling. I can't make any promises about where this is headed, but I know where I'd like to see it go. If it doesn't get there, no matter what the reason, I want you to know now that I know your heart is fragile. I'll handle you with care, baby."

A tear slid from my eye. This man was absolutely amazing. I knew it hadn't been long, but he was different. He was special.

"There's more, Wes."

"What?"

"There's more," I repeated. "I shared with you about Taj and my artwork, but there's more."

"Fuck," he hissed under his breath.

"I need time, though. I'm not ready to let that go yet."

He closed his eyes. I had a feeling he was slightly disappointed. He opened his eyes, squeezed my hip and assured, "You'll get there...I'll get you there."

I pressed my face into his throat and snuggled into him. I was feeling seriously lucky.

"Happy as fuck you said what you did in the car today, Charley," he declared.

"I'm getting that now."

"I want you to know it means something to me."

That felt good to hear.

"I know, Wes," I began. "What did you do to get Mark to cover for me?"

"Asked what I needed to do to have him cover you."

"And?" I asked.

"And nothing. He said you were good. He said that even though you've only started working recently, you've been a great employee, never took off, and covered for others when they needed it."

"Wow. And now I'm going to go in there tomorrow and give my notice that I'm leaving."

"It'll be okay."

I cuddled into Wes and he squeezed his arms tight around my body.

"Since I have you for the rest of the night, I think I'd like to have you in the shower. Then, I'm going to feed you and we can follow it up by watching a movie. Is there any chance I can convince you to stay the night?"

"I can't, Wes."

If he was disappointed, he didn't let it show. He immediately replied, "Okay. Change of plans then. I'm still going to take you in the shower, but afterward, we'll go so you can get your car while there's still a bit of daylight. I'll follow you to your house where you can either drop off your car and then come back with me or I stay with you. Which do you prefer?"

"I love waking up next to you, Wes. Stay at my place."

Wes angled up out of the bed, picked me up, and carried me to the bathroom.

We showered.

It was hot.

Way hot.

When we came back out into Wes' bedroom, he had tossed some clothes at me. They were all brand-new women's clothes. All were Blackman Boards apparel.

"What's this about?" I asked.

"You're at my place enough. You don't have clothes here other than what you wear on your back. I have access to lots of gear. Now, you have clothes here."

He said it so matter-of-fact, like it was no big deal. And I had a feeling that if I tried to protest he wouldn't have any of it, so I kept my mouth shut.

"Smart move," he praised as though he knew exactly what I was thinking. "And just because you have that doesn't mean I don't want you to bring any of your stuff from your place here. I'm hoping you'll eventually bring some of that over here on your own, especially the sexy stuff."

With that, we dressed and left to get my car. When we got to my place, I cooked dinner, and Wes spent the night so I could wake up next to him.

The next morning, I felt sick. My nerves were on edge and I felt horrible about having to give my notice. My co-workers didn't know it, but they helped me through one of the most difficult times in my life by distracting me from all the bad that had happened around me in California. Wes tried to calm me, in more ways than one, and while I was doing marginally better, I was still mostly a wreck.

"If it gets bad, call me and I'll be there," he insisted before we parted ways that morning.

"Okay, Wes."

I drove to the diner and Robert and Carol were first on my list. They were the husband and wife owners at First Tracks. They were the sweetest, most loving couple. I knew once I told them everything they'd be happy for me, but it didn't make it any easier. Most of my anxiety at the diner was because I had no clue how Greg was going to react. I really liked all my co-workers, but I had grown close with Greg. Considering he didn't know what had happened in my life and I deemed him to be a close friend, I think it said something about the state of my mind pre-Wes.

Carol was at the front door when I walked in.

"Good morning, Charley," she greeted.

"Hi Carol," I began, feeling the knots in my belly twist. "Is Bob here? I need to talk to both of you."

"Sure, dear. Come on back to the office."

I followed Carol back to the office where Bob was already sitting at his desk going through some paperwork.

"Darling, do you have a minute? Charley wanted to have a chat with us."

"Sure. Come on in and have a seat," he answered.

We all sat and I told them what was happening. I did not give details about why I had moved here and what had happened in California with Taj, amongst other things. They would worry, and I didn't want that for them. I explained that I needed to get back to my true passion and focus on building a career as a graphic designer. As I had suspected, they were gracious about all of it and were very happy for me. Of course, they did tell me that there'd always be a spot open for me if I ever wanted to come back. I thanked them and left the office to start my shift.

Greg was on the morning shift with me, but I was too nervous. I decided to wait until the end of my shift before I broke the news to him. Fortunately, it was so busy that the time passed quickly. My shift was over before I really had a chance to fret and Greg caught a reprieve.

It was now or never.

"Hey Greg, I need to talk to you," I cautioned.

"Oh dear. This doesn't sound good."

"I talked to Bob and Carol this morning and gave them the news. I wanted to tell you about it too."

"News? Girl, if you tell me you're pregnant with Wes Blackman's baby, I'm going to have a shit fit."

I jerked my head back at his exclamation.

"Gregory! Bite your tongue!" I whisper-shouted. "I'm not pregnant. I gave my notice today. I'm putting my focus on building my graphic design career."

"Girl, I didn't even know you knew how to draw."

"I didn't give Bob and Carol all of the details of my life in

California, but I explained to them that this was my passion and something I needed to do for myself. I want to give you more of the details, but it's not something I want to discuss here. For now, I'll just tell you that before I moved here from California, I had been pursuing this career path and was doing really well up until just under a year ago. I had some really bad stuff happen and I gave up my dream."

"Does Blackman have anything to do with this?" he asked.

Oh no. I really hoped Greg wasn't going to give me a hard time about this.

"He's been helping me through a lot of stuff, Greg. And while he was initially the one to question why I was not doing it full time, the choice I made is something I've thought long and hard about it."

"He's good for you."

That was unexpected. "You mean that?" I asked.

Nodding, he explained, "You're different now. Happier. Lighter. Don't know what happened to you in California, girl, but always knew something was weighing on your mind. Wes comes into the picture and you're smiling, talking, laughing, and now leaving to take care of you. Yeah, he's good for you."

I stared at him.

"I'm happy for you, Charley. But if you leave here and don't call, I'll be pissed!"

I smiled. "I'll do one better. I'm going to plan an outing for all of us. You, Hannah, and me. We'll all go out and I'll bring you up to speed on everything."

"I'm holding you to that."

Greg and Hannah had known each other for years. They both grew up in Rising Sun and attended the same high school. I had gotten my job at First Tracks and when I mentioned to Greg that I was looking for another job, he told me that his friend, Hannah, mentioned they were hiring at Brew Stirs. He gave me her contact information and they hired me on the spot.

"Alright, Greg. I've got to get going. See you Monday. Tell Tony I said hello."

"See you later, Charley."

I pulled into the lot at Parks Ridge and made my way to my spot. As soon as I parked, I saw Wes pulling into the lot. He parked, came over to the Jeep, and hopped in.

He kissed me quickly on the lips and asked, "How'd it go?"

"Surprisingly well. I knew Bob and Carol would take it in stride. I was worried about Greg. He was happy for me, though."

"Happy to hear it," he started. "You feel up to riding?"

I smiled at him, "Absolutely."

Wes and I rode for a bit before I went to work and he went back to his office to supervise the final stages of a renovation project he had going on at the new warehouse location.

"Hi Mark. Hi Hannah," I greeted, as I arrived at the coffee stand.

"Hey Charley, you good?" Mark asked.

He was referring to yesterday. I nodded.

"I need to talk to you, Mark."

"You're leaving, aren't you?" he guessed.

I looked between Mark and Hannah. They were disappointed.

"I'm sorry. I need to give my official notice to you because I've decided to pursue my graphic design career. Before I moved here, I was pursuing my dream, and after some bad stuff happened, I let go of it. I need to go back to it."

"That's awesome, Charley," Hannah said. "Congratulations."

Okay, so Hannah was good.

"Thanks, Hannah. I still have to figure it all out and don't have a position lined up, but I know it's what I need to do."

"If there's anything I can do to help, let me know," she added.

I nodded to her and turned my attention to Mark.

Finally, he spoke, "Happy for you, Charley. You are a great employee and we'll be sad to see you go. If you need a reference, you can put me down."

I let out a sigh of relief. "Thank you, Mark."

"No sweat, honey. Now get your ass to work."

I smiled at him and got my ass to work.

Hours later, I was closing up and Wes was walking in.

"All good?" he confirmed as he walked up to me.

I loved that he cared about how it went.

"All good," I answered.

"Good. You feel like waking up to me tomorrow, gorgeous?"

Tomorrow was Saturday. That meant sleeping in and then waking up to Wes.

"Absolutely," I answered.

Wes walked me out and followed me to my place. We showered together, made BLT sandwiches for dinner, and I went to bed satisfied and smiling, for more than one reason.

Thirteen

Charley

MY BODY JOLTED AWAKE AT THE BLOOD-CURDLING SCREAM. Before I could even get out of bed, Wes was already up and moving out of my bedroom.

Shit.

I ran out of the bedroom and tried to pass him.

"Wes, I've got it," I insisted, running to Emme's bedroom.

"Like hell you do," he roared.

He kept moving toward Emme's bedroom at the opposite end of the hall. His legs were longer than mine so he made it there ahead of me. When he opened the door, he stopped and froze. I caught up to him and snuck in under his arm that was propped up against the door.

I ran over to Emme who was panicking, crying, and shaking in the middle of her bed. She was sitting up, her knees curled up to her chest with her arms wrapped around them. I got to the bed, wrapped my arms around her, and held on tight. She immediately tensed up.

"Shh. It's okay, honey. It's Charley and I'm right here with you."

She was frantic, but I just kept my hold on her. I glanced to the door as I held her and saw Wes standing there with another look I'd never seen before on his face. He was concerned, but it was more than that.

"I've got you, Emme," I whispered softly as I began rubbing my hand up and down her back. "It was just a nightmare."

After a few minutes, she began to calm down.

"Wes, can you give us a few minutes?" I asked.

He hesitated, but eventually nodded and closed the door as he backed out of the room.

We sat in silence a bit longer.

"I'm sorry, Charley," Emme apologized on a whisper.

"What are you apologizing for?" I asked.

"You had Wes here overnight and I'm a mess now."

"Don't you worry about Wes. I think he's a little freaked, but I'll take care of it. Are you okay? It's been a while since you've had one."

"They stopped shortly after we moved here. They started up again after your birthday. I've been having them ever since, but this was the worst."

"Oh, honey. I'm so sorry. It was too soon. Why didn't you say anything to me?"

"You're getting your life back, Charley. You are finally smiling and happy. I figured this would pass, but it's just getting worse."

"I'm here for you, Em. We've been through a lot. Just because I'm doing better now than I have in months doesn't mean you go at it alone. When you need me, you need to tell me. And get it out of your head that whatever you are going through is going to put a damper on any happiness I'm feeling. If I find out again that you are keeping stuff like this from me, I'm going to be seriously pissed off. Don't hide it from me."

She nodded. "What are you going to tell Wes?"

"I'm not betraying your confidence. Don't worry. I'll give him enough so he doesn't worry, but he won't get the details."

"Thank you."

I smiled at her. "Are you good? Do you need anything?"

"I'm good."

"Are you sure?"

She nodded and offered a smile.

With that, I got up and walked out of her room. I stopped in the kitchen to put on some coffee and noticed that it was already brewing. When I walked back into my bedroom, I found Wes sitting up in my bed, his back up against the headboard. He did not look happy.

"Hey," I greeted, trying to act casual.

His brows lifted. "Hey? Really, Charley? Care to enlighten me on what I just witnessed?"

I shrugged and tried to play it cool. "Emme had a nightmare."

"That was pretty fucking obvious. What I want to know is why she had one that you seemed not even remotely fazed about?" he pressed, clearly losing his battle with trying to remain calm.

I stayed silent, not sure yet how I was going to broach the subject.

After a beat, I shared, "She has them sometimes."

He clenched his jaw and narrowed his eyes. "Charley, that girl is fucking scared out of her mind. It's not just a nightmare she has sometimes. That night at Lou's you pulled her off the dance floor when she looked about ready to freak. Then, as you were leaving, she had the same look when my boys and I walked you and your girls out to the car. Not for nothing, gorgeous, but I've had a nightmare once or twice and I've never screamed like she did. At least now it makes sense why you never want to spend the night at my place. If she has a nightmare like that and nobody is here for her…Christ. There's something bigger going on than you are telling me about."

"Yes, Wes, there is. I am not going to lay it all out for you, but the stuff I told you with Taj is part of what she's dealing with. She's been through a lot, maybe more than what I've dealt with and she is trying her best to move on. I don't want to make it harder for her. The nightmares stopped for a couple months and they just started again."

"Fucking hell," he clipped, clearly pissed at this point.

I genuinely appreciated his concern for Emme, but I needed to respect where she was at mentally. I also needed to get Wes out of his mood.

I walked toward the bed and climbed up his body. "Wes, honey, will you please let this go for me?" I begged. "At least for now. I really wanted to sleep in today, wake up in your arms where I feel safe, and then spend the morning fornicating."

His eyes immediately softened, and he laughed. It was a good laugh that caused his head to tilt back.

"Interesting choice of words, gorgeous. Are you trying to distract me from the issue at hand using your body and this mouth?"

Since I knew I'd gotten him, I played the innocent card again. "I have no idea what you are talking about."

He laughed again. "You're too much, Charley."

He put his hands under my arms and dragged me the rest of the way up his body so that I was straddling his hips and my face was right in front of his. He kissed me, and I got reacquainted with his body.

After I got lucky with Wes that morning, we made our way to the kitchen for breakfast. Emme joined us and thankfully Wes was amazing. He made sure it wasn't awkward and I could tell she was comfortable.

"Hey, I'm glad I have both of you here," Wes started, pausing to take a sip of his coffee. "Since this will be your first Christmas in Rising Sun, you don't know the tradition. Lou hosts a massive party at his place on Christmas Eve. It's a good time with music, food, and karaoke of mostly Christmas songs. Would you two be up for it?"

"I'll go," Emme agreed, shrugging like it didn't matter one way or another to her.

I looked to her, surprised that she was willing to go and confirmed, "Are you sure, Em?"

She nodded, "I'm sure, sweets."

"Good. I'll come by and pick you both up for it. I know your other girls were just here, but if they come out for the holiday they're more than welcome to join us," Wes added.

"We'll call and fill them in. I'm not sure if they're planning to come out here, but it can't hurt to try," I reasoned.

"Besides, anything that will up the count on Nikki's list is worth calling them for," Emme pointed out.

She wasn't wrong.

We finished up breakfast, and Emme took off for a full day of holiday mini-sessions.

Wes and I spent the rest of the day doing my normal weekend routine but added some new fun activities that really involved Wes thrown in the mix.

I even shared more of my drawings with him. I showed him the ones I had done prior to Taj's death and then the ones following. He learned which were some of my favorites. I even told him about the one that meant the absolute most to me. The one closest to my heart was the first one I drew following Taj's death. It was an ocean wave cresting as the sun was setting behind it. There were footprints in the wet sand leading out to the ocean water. After showing him this one I decided, while sitting on the floor of my bedroom, to give him more of me.

"This is it," I divulged as I held up the drawing.

"Tell me about it, gorgeous," he urged, a pleading tone in his voice.

I took a deep breath and looked to Wes.

"Taj was a surfer. He was always in the water. At every opportunity he got, he would make me go out in the water with him. I guess that might be why I picked up the snowboarding so quickly. I had practice riding on a board. That first time I rode down the trail without falling and you were behind me, Wes, it was just like the first time I rode a wave with Taj by my side. I'll never forget it; I had been practicing for so long and I would continuously eat it. It was so frustrating, but Taj pushed me. One day we went out into the water and I just got it. When we got back on the sand after riding that wave, I burst into a happy dance and my big brother was so very proud of me."

My voice had grown thick with emotions.

Wes' eyes were warm, and he put his arm around me. "Baby…" he intoned gently as his voice trailed off.

"It's okay, Wes. I'm okay. I'm finding it's getting easier. Talking to you about him has been good for me. Thank you for listening."

"Anything you need, Charley."

I moved my body closer to his and snuggled my face into his neck. His arm tightened around me and he held me while I told him more of my surfing adventures with Taj.

Through this, I was beginning to realize just how lucky I was to have Wes come into my life.

Two weeks later, I finally finished my last day at work. This was not before Greg and I made plans to get together after the holidays with Hannah. I was honestly excited about maintaining these friendships for years to come, and they were both thrilled when I actually agreed to and settled on a date with them. They'd been asking for months, but I hadn't been ready.

On the new job front, I was actively looking for a position to get myself started and gain experience. Unfortunately, it was not going well. Still, I tried to stay positive and keep in mind that I'd only really been looking for two weeks and it was the holiday season. I was not regretting the decision and I knew financially I would not need to worry. Even still, it was slightly disappointing.

Emme and I had also reached out to Nikki and Monroe last week to let them know about Lou's Christmas party. Unfortunately, they were unable to make it out for the celebration, but since Nikki loved that Emme and I were going to be going out, she agreed to add it to her list. Monroe asked us if there were any special events happening for New Year's Eve. Of course, we had no idea, but we told them we'd ask about it. They were both hoping to make it out for a visit to celebrate and ring in the new year.

Emme and I had plans to go shopping tonight to find something to wear to the Christmas party. Wes was working late…again. He'd been working late a lot in the past two weeks. He said he had a few projects he was trying to finish up before the holidays in addition to dealing with the increased sales the company had received as the Christmas holiday approached. Sadly, the extra workload made it so that he was not able to ride with me for the last week.

I picked up my phone and decided to call him before heading out with Emme.

"Gorgeous," he sighed, his relief evident.

"Hey, honey. How's it going?" I asked.

"Better now. It's been a rough two weeks with everything going on here."

"I know. I'm sorry. Are the projects coming along okay?"

"Nearly complete. They tied up all the loose ends on the construction project in the warehouse earlier today, so after the holidays I'll start the process of transitioning everything from the old building to this one. One of the other projects I have going on, which is the more important one, should be finished tonight. What about you? How was your last day today?

"It was good. I've made plans to get together with Greg and Hannah in the new year, so I'm looking forward to that."

"Any luck on the job front?" he questioned.

I took in a deep breath. "Not so much."

"Don't worry. It'll happen when it's the right time. Are you heading out shopping with Emme soon?"

"Yeah. Missed you and wanted to hear your voice first, though."

I heard his breath catch. "Charley…I miss you, too. I'm sorry we haven't had much time together lately, but I am thinking about you all the time."

"Same here," I reassured him. "I better get going, though. I'm looking forward to seeing you tomorrow, Wes."

"Me too, baby. You and Emme should be ready by six tomorrow. I'll pick you both up then."

"Sounds good. Bye, Wes."

"Later, Charley. Be careful."

I disconnected the call, threw my phone in my purse, and walked out to the kitchen to meet Emme. She was ready, so we took off to the mall. We shopped for several hours until the stores were closing, but we both managed to find incredible outfits for the special occasion. Emme was a bit more hesitant, but I succeeded in talking her into the dress that only she, with her beautiful body, could pull off.

We got back to the condo and lugged all our bags in.

"I'm wiped, Charley," Emme declared.

I knew she was.

Over the last two weeks, I'd woken up with her almost every single night. Her nightmares were getting worse and I was seriously worried about her. I was hoping it was just the holidays approaching that she was experiencing so much anxiety. If this continued into the new year, I wasn't sure I was equipped to deal with it. That is not to say that I wouldn't do whatever I had to for her, but I think she needed more than what I could offer her.

"Me too. It's been an exhausting couple of weeks. I'm looking forward to not having anywhere to go tomorrow morning."

"How about it? I don't have any shoots scheduled until next year. I am so ready for a break after the holiday rush."

"I'm hoping to find a job to start the new year, but I think it'll be good for both of us to have a little bit of downtime. Tomorrow should be a nice way to kick off the break, though. By the way, when I talked with Wes earlier, he said that he'll be picking us up at six tomorrow."

"Sounds good. I'm going to head to bed now."

"Yeah, me too. I'll see you in the morning. Good night, Em."

"Night, Charley."

As I carried my bags down the hall into my bedroom, I heard my phone chime notifying me of a text. I dropped my bags on the bed and grabbed my phone out of my purse. Lighting up the display, I saw Wes had texted me.

You make it home yet, gorgeous?

He was always looking out for me. That made my insides warm.

Me: Emme and I just got in. Did you get your project finished?

Wes: Yeah. Got it done about thirty minutes ago. About to head out of here.

I missed him. As exhausted as I was, I missed him more.

Me: Glad to hear it. Any chance I can talk you into driving your truck here instead of your place tonight? ;-)

Wes: You miss me still?

Me: A little.

That was a lie. I missed him a whole lot more than just a little.

Wes: Be there in fifteen.

Me: Yay!!

Seventeen minutes later, Wes arrived. I opened the door and let out a huge sigh of relief. He stepped inside, locked the door, wrapped his arms around me, and kissed the top of my head. The two of us stood there holding each other for a bit before I tipped my head up and kissed him. We kissed for a bit before he pulled his mouth away and squeezed me tighter. I snuggled my face back against his chest, pressing my body into his.

"Are you hungry?" I asked.

"I ate a couple hours ago. I'm good. You?"

"Had dinner with Em."

"Exhausted, gorgeous. Want to get in bed with you and sleep."

I took in a deep breath, his scent filling my nostrils. Yeah, I could definitely go for that, too.

"Works for me," I answered.

Once we were in my room, I put on a camisole and a pair of panties while Wes stripped down to his boxer briefs. We got into bed and Wes curled his body around mine, his front to my back.

"Thanks for coming to me tonight," I said after we had been there for a few minutes.

"Anything you need, Charley," he replied, sleepily.

That was the second time he said that to me. I had to admit how good it felt. And being there wrapped in his arms felt especially good. I snuggled in closer to him, not feeling like I was close enough. It was in that moment that I grasped just how deep I was in this with Wes. It had become so much more for me the last few weeks, and I knew I was beginning to have real feelings for him. Feelings I knew that, if this ever went south, could completely obliterate me. My body tensed at the thought.

"What's wrong?" he asked.

Shit.

"What? Nothing," I responded.

"Charley, you're rock solid right now."

"Sorry. It's nothing."

He growled. "I'm worn out, baby. Think you can share it with me and not do the song and dance right now?"

"I apologize. I was just thinking about how good this feels and how much I appreciate your concern for me."

"Doesn't explain why you're wound."

"If this thing between us ends, it won't be good for me."

Wes squeezed his arms tight around me. "Not like it'd be a walk in the park for me. You aren't the only one with feelings in this. You mean something to me and I'm not going anywhere."

I snuggled in closer, though I'm not sure how that was even possible. Wes groaned. "Charley, sit your ass still and sleep."

"Okay, Wes."

Minutes later, wrapped in his arms coming to terms with how I was feeling about our relationship, I fell asleep.

When I woke the next morning, it was with familiar fingers tracing the skin at my hip. Another hand was cupping my breast while a thumb moved slowly back and forth across my nipple. Wes was still spooning me and doing very nice things to my body. I moaned and arched my back pressing my ass into Wes' hard length. He groaned and brought his lips to kiss the skin at my shoulder. Wes' hand at my hip moved south and slid into the waistband of my panties. His fingers began to tease the sensitive spot between my legs.

"Wes," I rasped. I was seriously turned on and would easily be coming apart within seconds. I was right on the edge when I lost his hand. "No, Wes. Please."

"Want to watch you ride me, gorgeous," he explained as he pulled my camisole over my head and my panties down my legs.

He fell to his back as he hauled me on top of his body.

I held his cock in my hand and guided him to my entrance. Then, I slammed my body down onto his. Wes' hands came to my hips and gripped them hard as I quickly moved over his length.

"You feel so good, Wes," I moaned as I leaned my body forward, putting my weight into my hands that fell at either side of his head.

Wes took this moment to glide his hands from my hips up the sides of my body to my breasts. I continued to roll my hips and was further encouraged that he enjoyed what I was doing with them when he groaned before taking a nipple into his mouth. This was my undoing. I was right back on the edge and Wes didn't let up. He began thrusting his hips up to meet mine while not relenting in his attention to my breasts. His groans came faster, and I threw my head back knowing he was right there with me.

"Eyes on me, Charley," he ordered.

My head snapped back down, and I looked him in the eyes as my body shattered. His hands were back at my hips, holding them in place while he drove up fiercely into my body.

"So beautiful," he growled as he came halfway through my orgasm.

I collapsed on top of his body while we both attempted to get our breathing back to normal. I stayed there on top of Wes while he lightly traced his fingers up and down my back, seeming to linger a little longer at the space on my lower back just at the top of my ass.

"I could stay like this all day," I told him. And I could have, no doubt in my mind. I was sated, and I felt safe there in his arms.

"I would like nothing more, but it'll have to be another time, Charley. I've got some things I've got to get done before tonight," he advised.

I whimpered. "I'll hold you to that, Mr. Blackman."

He squeezed me before he rolled us over so I was on my back, his hands brushing my hair from my face. "What do you have planned for this afternoon?" he asked.

"I am going to do some baking with Emme today. Depending on how much time I have left, I might draw for a little. Then, I'll need to get ready for tonight."

"You bake?"

"Em's the baker in the group; however, I've been told by many that people would pay money for my chocolate chip cookies."

"Is that right?" he challenged.

I nodded. "You just have to make them with love. Works every time."

"I'm going to have to try those then, baby," he insisted.

I smiled at him.

"I need to get going, Charley. I'll be back at six to pick you and Emme up," Wes promised as he got up and got dressed.

"Okay, honey."

Once he was dressed, I walked him to the door and kissed him. I worked on some art until Emme woke up. I was lucky enough to have time to talk to her about her nightmares before we spent the rest of the morning and all afternoon baking. Most importantly, I put a little extra love into my chocolate chip cookies.

Fourteen

Charley

IT WAS FIVE MINUTES UNTIL SIX, THE HOUSE SMELLED DELICIOUS, and Emme and I were nearly ready.

Emme was wearing a three-quarter sleeve black sequined mini dress that fit like a glove. The neckline was high, but when she turned around her entire back was exposed down to just above her ass. To bring a little Christmas spirit to her outfit, she donned a pair of red bottom Christian Louboutins. To not take away from the dress, she curled her hair and pulled it into a loose, low ponytail at the side of her neck. Her hair was off her back, cascading down over the front of her right shoulder.

In keeping up the sequin theme for the evening, I was wearing a deep purple sequined skirt, a black sleeveless top with a cowl neckline, and a pair of black patent-leather pumps. I added a chunky black and purple bracelet on my wrist and a pair of sparkly diamond studs in my ears. I put some loose waves in my hair and kept it down. I had also put on a very sexy pair of undergarments that I was hoping to show Wes later.

There was a knock at the door. Emme and I were in my bathroom putting the finishing touches on our makeup.

"That's Wes. I'll be right back," I declared as I tightened

the cap on my lip gloss and walked out.

On the way out of my bedroom, as I typically did whenever I was going out with Wes, I did a quick head-to-toe inspection in my full-length mirror. I assessed my look, gave myself a small nod of approval, and walked to the front door. When I opened the door, I pulled my bottom lip in and bit down at what I saw.

Wes looked divine. He was wearing a pair of jeans with dressy boots and a black wool peacoat. I could see the collar of his black, white, and gray plaid fitted shirt popping out of the top of the coat. In addition to my senses being assaulted by the sight of him, standing directly behind him was Zane, who looked rather breathtaking himself.

"Hi, um, hey. I didn't realize you were both coming," I noted, fumbling over my words.

This could be bad.

Wes gave me his wicked grin realizing I was having a hard time pulling myself together. "Yeah, I have a car service that's driving since it'll be packed. I also don't want to be drinking and driving tonight," he answered. "Are you going to let us in, gorgeous, or are we waiting out here for you?"

"Right, sorry. Come in," I urged as I moved out of the doorway and let them in.

As Wes walked in, he bent down and pressed a kiss to my lips, then whispered in my ear, "You look beautiful, Charley."

I swallowed hard and closed the door behind them saying, "I'm just going to go grab Emme. Help yourselves to anything in the fridge. Em and I also baked today, so there are tons of Christmas cookies on the island. Be right back."

My stomach was in knots as I scurried back down the hall to my bedroom to get Emme. I walked into the bathroom and saw she had just finished the last of her makeup.

"Ready," she stated, standing up from the stool in front of the vanity.

"Emme, sit down," I ordered.

"What's wrong?" she asked, and hesitantly sat back down.

"Wes is here," I said.

She stared at me like I was crazy. She knew Wes was picking us up. What she didn't know, which was also what I didn't know until about thirty seconds ago, was that he had Zane with him. So, I gave her the news and divulged, "Wes is here with Zane."

She sucked in a breath. "Oh."

"Honey, if it's too much and you can't do it, we can either go separately and meet them there or we can stay here. I'll come up with something. We can tell them you are feeling sick suddenly and—"

Emme cut me off. "Charley, it's fine. I will go. I need to try to start living a somewhat normal life," she explained, cutting me off.

I jerked my head back and stared at her. "You're sure?" I asked.

She stayed silent a beat and then answered, "Yes, I'm sure."

"Okay. If you change your mind and need to leave, you promise you'll tell me?"

"Promise."

With her promise, I went over and hugged her. We left my room and walked out to meet the guys. I made it to the kitchen first and saw that Wes and Zane were elbows deep in baked goods. Wes was standing on one side of the island, Zane sitting at a stool on the other side. When we walked in, they turned to look at us and smiled.

Zane's eyes held Emme's for a bit and then she spoke up, "Hi Wes. Zane."

"Hey, Em," Wes said as both he and Zane looked at her and grinned.

"You girls planning a party?" Zane asked.

"No. Why?" I wondered.

"This is a lot of fucking cookies for the two of you, don't you think?" he challenged.

He had a point. We had seven different varieties of cookies including traditional sugar with Emme's secret ingredient, iced oatmeal, lemon crinkle, chocolate crinkle, gingerbread, iced Italian almond, and my famous chocolate chip. We'd made double batches of each variety so there were, as he put it, a lot of fucking cookies.

"It's Christmas. You can never have too many cookies," Emme piped up.

She also had a point. Christmas, in my opinion, was synonymous with cookies. You couldn't have Christmas without cookies. Lots of them.

Wes chimed in, "They're really good."

"Thanks," Emme and I both said.

"You ladies ready to go?" Wes asked.

We both nodded and turned to head out of the kitchen. As we did, I heard a sharp intake of breath and a mumble from Zane that sounded a lot like, "Fuck me."

Emme and I both turned around. I didn't look at her, but I'm certain she had the same expression on her face as I did. That look was likely one of confusion.

"Is something wrong?" Emme asked.

"It's pretty cold out. Are you planning to wear something over that?" Zane questioned her.

Realization hit me.

Zane saw the back, or lack thereof, of Emme's dress and reacted. I bit my lip and looked to Wes who was smirking, shaking his head, and looking down at his boots.

"No. I figured it might be too warm in Lou's and then I'd take the jacket off and have to worry about keeping track of it all night. And then, if I misplace it, I'll be out a jacket."

"Sweetheart, the high today was just barely thirty degrees. It's a hell of a lot colder than that outside right now. Get a jacket. If you lose it, I'll buy you a new one."

She narrowed her eyes and explained, "A jacket will ruin this dress, though."

"Not much you can do to ruin that dress. Looks pretty fucking perfect to me. Get a jacket, Emme."

She tilted her head to the side, thought for a minute, and acquiesced, "Okay, I'll get a jacket."

With that, Emme and I both grabbed jackets, locked up, and left for Lou's. The ride to Lou's went better than I had expected. I had been worried about it being awkward, but thankfully everything went smoothly. Wes and Zane told us stories about Lou's Christmas parties from previous years before the conversation went to snowboarding. Zane had been training very hard recently prepping for a couple of contests he had coming up after the holidays. Wes was supporting his riders in their training along with continuing development on his new board series. Emme talked a little about her photography, mostly answering questions that Zane and Wes asked and I spoke a little about my recent unsuccessful job searches.

We finally arrived at Lou's, and Wes had not been kidding. It was still early, and the place was packed. The driver pulled up to the building, where Wes and Zane both exited the car first to help Emme and me out.

The outside of Lou's had been magnificently and tastefully decorated for the holiday festivities. We walked into the first-floor dining area of Lou's where we were greeted by none other than Lou himself.

"Charley. My pretty birthday girl. How are you doing?" he asked, pulling me into a big bear hug.

"Wow, Lou. You remember me?" I marveled, notably shocked that he'd met me once and remembered who I was.

"Darlin', Lou doesn't forget a pretty girl," he responded.

I smiled at him and beamed. "I'm doing well. How are you?"

"Best time of year, darlin'. Doesn't get any better than this. Now what I'm really wantin' to know is how you know my boys, Wes and Zane, here?"

I felt my face flush at the same time Wes' arm wrapped around my shoulder and pulled me into his side.

"Charley is my girlfriend, Lou," he answered. My belly fluttered. That was the first time I'd heard him call me his girlfriend. It felt good.

Lou looked at Wes, back to me, and back to Wes. He smiled and ordered, "Take good care of her. She's a good one."

I wanted to redirect the conversation, so I piped up, "Thanks, Lou. And so, Zane being an extension of Wes, I now know Zane."

He gave me a look of understanding.

"You remember my friend, Emme?" I confirmed, waving my hand over to my friend.

"I told you, Charley, Lou never forgets a pretty girl," he repeated, turning toward Emme. He asked her, "Are you with my boy, Zane, here?"

Emme's face flushed hard and her eyes got big. She answered, "No, Lou. We are just friends."

"Well, darlin', that's a damn shame. You two would make a good-looking couple; however, if you two aren't together, you might want to step away from him."

"Excuse me?" Emme asked as we all looked at Lou with confusion on our faces.

Lou lifted his hand and pointed above Emme and Zane's head. We all looked up.

Mistletoe.

I looked to Zane, who had a wicked, sexy grin on his face as he looked at Emme. Emme looked like she wanted to run. I'm certain Zane noticed her anxiety as he bent down, kissed her on the cheek, and grinned. "Merry Christmas, sweetheart."

"Give it some time. You're not together now, you're going to be soon," Lou reckoned, with a huge smile plastered on his face.

Emme's eyes nearly popped out of her head, and I turned to find Wes smirking.

"Lou, always a pleasure. We'll see you later," Wes interjected as he escorted me further into the dining room. Zane and Emme followed. We found a table that was open; so, Emme and I took a seat while Wes and Zane went to grab some drinks from the bar.

"Are you okay?" I asked the moment they were out of earshot.

"Fucking mistletoe," she replied. "My cheek is still on fire. He's hot; there's no denying that. And he seems to be very cautious…protective almost. At the same time, he is laid back and seems like he'd be a lot of fun. But you know where I'm at. I can't pursue anything like that."

"I know, honey. You need some time. I also know part of what you're saying about him being protective. Wes gives me that same feeling. Like he will do whatever he needs to just to make sure I am safe and happy. It scares the ever-loving shit out of me," I shared.

"How did you do it? How did you find a way to let go and be happy again, Charley?" she wondered.

"Honestly? He was persistent. He made me feel safe. And oddly enough, as soon as I told him about Taj, I felt better. The more I've talked to him about it, the better I've felt. Talking about it has been very, very good for me. Maybe you should talk to someone other than me, Nikki, or Monroe about your stuff. Someone like Zane, maybe? You never know until you try. Perhaps he can help you find your happy."

"I'm so not doing that. And I'm not holding my breath on finding happiness. I'll be happy if I don't have to worry about losing everything again," she offered. My heart broke for her.

"However, after the peck on the cheek what I think I need now is someone who would be willing to hold me and kiss me. I just need to feel for a bit; you know what I mean? Would it be wrong to ask for that?"

"Honey, you are beautiful. I don't think it'll be a hardship for someone to give that to you. That said, if you are thinking about Zane, I'm sure he'll be into it. I also think, though, you're going to have to be upfront with him."

"Ugh. Why does he have to be so fucking hot?" she wailed as she dropped her head to the table.

"I hear you, Em. Apparently, that's how they grow them out here in the mountains."

"What do they grow here in the mountains?" Wes asked as he and Zane approached the table with our drinks.

I looked up at him and bit my lip. "Trees," I answered quickly and took the drink out of his hand. "Thanks for getting this."

"Trees? Really Charley?" he countered.

I decided not to answer. I just gave a shoulder shrug and took a sip of the candy cane cocktail he brought me. So yummy.

We all sat and enjoyed the music playing over the speakers, talking and eating. It was evident that Lou knew how to celebrate. There was an endless supply of food, drinks, and entertainment. A little while later, the four of us made our way up to the second floor. When we got there, I noticed Stone and Luke were both there hanging with each other and a gaggle of girls. I waved to the guys and Emme smiled at them while Wes and Zane offered chin lifts of acknowledgment. Other than that, we didn't intrude on their fun.

Emme and I made our way to the dance floor for a bit before the karaoke started and the boys found tables close by. A few songs later Lou was up on the stage calling up the first brave soul for karaoke. We sat and enjoyed the entertainment for a bit. After a couple hours of Christmas music, dancing, food, and drinks, we decided to head out for the night.

The car brought us back to our place and the guys, as expected, walked us to the door.

Emme spoke up and asked, "Would you guys like to come in for a while? We still have cookies."

I whirled my head around to look at her and saw she was gazing, yes gazing, up at Zane.

"I'd fucking love more cookies," Zane answered.

Wes grinned, pulled me close, and looked to me when he admitted, "I'm good on the cookies for now, but I'm more than happy to stay a while."

We made our way in, and I asked the guys to give us a minute while I dragged Emme down the hall to my bedroom.

"Honey, you sure about this?" I questioned her.

"No, but if I don't take small steps, I'll never know. I told you before, Zane makes me feel safe. And both you and Wes are here, so if something happens, I know you're right down the hall. I figure I'll give Zane enough information and he can decide what to do with it. I'm not looking for a one-night stand or a relationship. I expect to be by myself for the very foreseeable future, essentially forever, but I don't want to be lonely on Christmas Eve."

My eyes welled up and my heart broke again for my best friend. "Okay, Em. I'm here for you if you need me."

"I know, sweets. Thank you."

I hugged her, and we made our way back to the guys.

"Hey Wes, I wanted to show you some of the new stuff I've been working on. Come with?" I hinted, extending my hand.

He smirked, catching my drift. "Sure," he answered, taking my hand and leading us back down the hall to my bedroom.

After we made it to my bedroom and I shut the door, I

turned to Wes and blurted, "I'm worried."

"About what?" he asked.

"I need details on Zane. I know he's your friend, but is he a good guy? Like a *really* good guy? My best friend is hurting a lot right now, and I think she just needs companionship that isn't me or the girls."

Wes' eyes warmed and he pulled me into his arms. "She'll be fine with Zane."

"I'm serious, Wes. I'm really worried about her. She's been having nightmares nearly every night and when I say she's hurting, I mean she's very fucking fragile."

"Did you forget I witnessed the result of one of those nightmares? Charley, baby, if for one second I even had a shred of doubt about your girl in Zane's care, I wouldn't be standing here right now. I promise you, she's good."

I squeezed him. "Okay, Wes."

"Now. Can I show you what this outfit did to me all fucking night, gorgeous?"

"If you like my outfit, I should warn you that I also bought some pretty spectacular undergarments," I teased, reaching up to press kisses to his neck and jaw.

He pulled me tighter to his body, where I could feel his arousal, and groaned.

And with that, Wes showed me just how much he appreciated what was under my outfit. Multiple times.

Fifteen

Charley

"Merry Christmas, gorgeous."

I rolled toward Wes, my eyes closed. I snuggled into his chest and felt his body move as he laughed.

"We've got to get up, Charley."

"What time is it?" I wondered, my eyes still closed trying to soak up every ounce of sleep I could get.

"Seven," he answered.

I lifted my head to look at him in disbelief. "I'm pretty sure you said it's Christmas. Unless one has a child living in their house or they themselves are a child, there is no good reason to get up this early on Christmas morning. Last I checked, there were no children living in this house, and you, my friend, are definitely not a child. You are all grown man; so, sleep it is."

I closed my eyes again and snuggled back in. He continued to laugh at me.

"I'm not sure what you're finding so funny, Wes."

"Damn it. Now there is a problem," he stated.

"Exactly. I'm glad you are seeing this my way. No worries, honey, just go back to sleep."

"Charley, I'm definitely not going back to sleep. The

problem is that you are being cute with that mouth right now. And that means I'm going to need to have my way with you this morning. The bigger problem is that, in doing so, we're going to be late for Christmas breakfast at my parents' house this morning."

My eyes shot open. I completely forgot about breakfast with the parents. I bolted up out of the bed and shifted my body to get out and get ready when Wes ceased my motions by wrapping his arm around my waist and tugging me backward. Then, I was on my back and he was on top of me.

"Wes, we *cannot* have sex this morning. I'm meeting your parents for the first time and you can't make me late for that. And I absolutely cannot go there having just had sex with their son," I informed him.

He grinned his sexy grin at me.

Shit.

We were going to be late for breakfast.

An hour and forty-five minutes later, Wes pulled into the driveway of his parents' house. We were fifteen minutes late. This was, of course, after Wes and I had sex that morning, which was worth being late for. It was also after I had gotten myself ready in lightning-fast time, and lastly, after I attempted to make sure that Emme was good.

That was a whole other issue I wanted to get into, but unfortunately, did not have the time to since I'd chosen sex over being on time for Christmas breakfast with Wes' parents. After I finished getting ready, I walked down the hall and found that Emme was not yet awake. I didn't want to leave without knowing she was good, but I also didn't want to wake her or interrupt anything. Thankfully, I didn't have to debate on what to do for too long because Zane walked out of her room about thirty seconds later. He had a strange look on his face that I couldn't quite read, so I asked him if she was awake. He nodded, but feeling unsure about the situation, I decided to go in her room. I gently knocked on the door, walked in, and saw her lying in her bed. I told her that I was heading out with Wes to his parents' house, but wanted to check on her first. She assured me she was good and that she'd call if anything came up. I explained that we'd be back later with plenty of time to spare so we could make and have dinner together and exchange gifts.

At that, Wes and I took off.

I sat, unmoving, in the passenger's seat looking at their house. It was a beautiful log home on a decently sized piece of property; though, it was not nearly as large as the land Wes' home sat on. This home also had incredible mountain views.

I hadn't said much on the drive over as I was too panicked about meeting his family. I had already met Elle, but our meeting was brief.

What if they didn't like me?

"Charley, baby, relax."

"What if they don't like me?"

"They will like you. Trust me," he insisted.

"You can't know that. They might not like me. And then, where will I be?" I worried still staring at the house, nervously biting my lip.

"Gorgeous, look at me."

I looked at him.

"If for some God-forsaken reason they didn't like you, which won't be the case, you'll still be right where you are sitting next to me because *I* like you. Now, stop panicking and let's enjoy Christmas. Okay?"

I swallowed and nodded. "Okay, Wes."

Wes came around the front of the Jeep and met me on my side to help me out. He took the tray of cookies that I insisted on bringing from my hands and carried it for me. I figured if there was even the remote possibility that they wouldn't like me I could possibly bribe them with sugary treats. Wes held my hand as we walked up the path to the front door. The moment we stepped in front of the door, it opened and an older, but a remarkably beautiful, petite, blonde-haired woman smiled at us.

"Merry Christmas, Ma," Wes greeted her before he turned to me. "Charley, this is my mother, Linda; Ma, this is my girlfriend, Charley."

"It's a pleasure to meet you Mrs. Blackman. Merry Christmas," I said.

She looked at me a moment, still smiling, and offered, "Merry Christmas, Charley. Please, call me Linda." She then moved to hug Wes. "Merry Christmas, honey. She's even more beautiful than you said."

My belly warmed at the words Linda exchanged with her son. He'd spoken to her about me. I took this as good news. He handed her the homemade cookies. Linda ushered us inside and, no sooner had she closed the door, an older man, who looked strikingly similar to Wes, joined us. He had a full head of salt-and-pepper colored hair, the same chiseled jawline, and a large frame; though, he wasn't overweight.

"Hey Pops. Merry Christmas," Wes acknowledged him, giving his father a one-armed man hug. He then put his arm around my shoulder and pulled me tight to his body. "This is Charley. Charley, this is my dad, James."

"Merry Christmas, Mr. Blackman."

Wes' father pulled me in for a hug and said, "Merry Christmas, darlin'. You call me James, though."

He released his hold on me and I stepped back and nodded at him.

"Come on in. Elle is in the kitchen," Linda urged us.

"Merry Christmas, Wes," Elle greeted him as we walked into the kitchen. She looked to me next and said, "Hi Charley, Merry Christmas."

"Merry Christmas," I returned.

Wes hugged his sister and wished her a Merry Christmas as well.

At this point, Linda had made her way over to the kitchen, so I spoke, "Thank you for having me here today. Is there anything I can do to help?"

"As long as you brought your appetite, we should be good to get started. We just finished making breakfast, so go ahead and grab a seat. Elle, James, and I will bring out the food."

I walked with Wes over to the breakfast nook where he pulled out a chair for me. He sat down next to me while Elle sat across from us, and Wes' parents sat at either end of the table. I don't think I had ever seen a breakfast spread like the one before me. I was thankful that Emme and I decided on having dinner instead of lunch since I was certain I would fall into a food coma after consuming this.

Everyone loaded up their plates and the conversation was easy. Wes' family asked about my graphic design career and I asked about Elle's music career. Of course, the conversation went to Wes, and I pushed to find out about his childhood.

"Wes always kept us on our toes," his mother declared. "There was never a dull moment with this boy around."

I looked to Wes and saw him grinning at me.

"I don't think anything will ever top the time he basically ruined Nan's walls with the pudding," Elle chimed in.

"Don't forget the BB gun incident with Grandpa," Linda added.

"Pudding? BB gun?" I asked, leaning forward curiously to hear all about this.

James explained, "Wes was spending the afternoon at my mother's house one day when he was about six years old. She was occupied with making his lunch but had given him chocolate pudding a bit before that because that's what grandparents do, apparently. While she was making his lunch, Wes decided to fill a balloon with chocolate pudding. Once he felt the level of pudding was sufficient, he blew up the balloon, and let it loose. The balloon darted all over the kitchen spraying her pristine white walls with chocolate pudding."

I stared, jaw dropped. "No, he did not," I gasped as I turned to Wes. "You did not!"

"Guilty," he confirmed. "I feel bad looking back on it now. Nan was running around the kitchen trying to catch the flying pudding missile and her kitchen looked like a war zone when it finally ran out of air. It was the only time I ever experienced my grandmother's ability to get angry at me," he confessed.

"That's the truth," James started. "She loved all of her grandchildren, no doubt about that, but Wes was special to her. His cousins live in Michigan and my mother, along with us, always lived here. That said, she grew attached to Wes. Of course, Elle came along and brought sunshine where there was the disaster of Wes' ways, but my mother didn't care. She loved him like no other."

"Oh my goodness," I said in murmured disbelief at what he'd done. "So, what happened with the BB gun?" I asked.

Elle answered, "My grandparents were divorced, and Wes had gone over to spend the day with our grandfather. He decided that using the BB gun in the house was a good idea. Unfortunately, he shot out Grandpa's kitchen window. He was very destructive as a child."

I looked to Wes and just stared, wide-eyed, at him. He grinned back at me, clearly proud of his childhood antics.

"One day, when Wes has children of his own, that's going to come back to haunt him," Linda put in.

At that moment, my mind whirled with thoughts of Wes with children. Visions of him chasing a little boy around his house trying to keep him out of trouble were heartwarming. My belly warmed, and my heart squeezed at the images of Wes as a father. I only hoped I'd be lucky enough to not only witness but also be a part of, that one day.

We spent a couple of hours after breakfast with Wes' family, and he had been right. I got along with all of them. I was so nervous about meeting them, but they welcomed me with open arms and it was never awkward.

Finally, Wes excused us, letting his parents know that we had plans to have dinner with Emme. Linda and James gave me hugs and told me they wanted me to come back for another visit soon. I took this to mean they liked me. I hugged Elle and told her to let me know when she was performing at Lou's again so I could come and support her. She told me she would. Afterward, Wes and I left.

We were in the car pulling out of the Blackman's driveway when Wes spoke.

"I'm going to take you to my place before we head back to yours, gorgeous," he began. "We won't be long. I just need to do something quickly."

"Okay, honey."

We drove to his house and talked the entire way about that morning's breakfast with his family. I expressed how much I enjoyed it and how much I really liked his parents and his sister. He told me that he knew I'd like them and that they would, without a doubt, have liked me.

Wes turned the truck into his driveway. Once we were inside, Wes asked me to have a seat in the family room while he went to get something. At this point, he was acting a little strange and the butterflies were fluttering madly in my belly. A few minutes later, he came out carrying a Christmas present. It was wrapped, nicely I might add, but it was huge.

"What is this, Wes?" I asked.

"Remember that project I told you about that I'd been working on?" he responded.

I nodded and stared up at him.

He held the gift out to me and said, "Merry Christmas, gorgeous."

My throat grew tight.

He had spoken of this project several times. I thought back to the conversations and remembered thinking how important it seemed to him. The only thing that existed for the last couple weeks for him was this project. And now, knowing it was a Christmas present for me, I was struggling to keep it together.

"Wes," I whispered trying to fight back tears.

"Open it, Charley," he urged as he placed it in front of me.

I stood up from the couch and tore the wrapping paper from the box. The box was white, nothing outside giving away its contents. I opened one end of the box and peeked in. Realizing what was inside, I looked back up to Wes and marveled, "You got me another snowboard?"

"This one's special. Take it out," he answered.

I pulled the board out of the box and spun it around. My knees buckled at what I saw.

Wes immediately wrapped his arm around my waist to hold me up. "Easy, baby. Are you okay?"

I stared at the board, my eyes filling with tears and my nose stinging as I tried to swallow past the lump that had formed in my throat. More than a month ago Wes gave me a board and a bunch of gear so that he could teach me how to ride. I appreciated what he had done so much, but this was too much.

This was *my* board.

The board has my drawing on it, the ocean wave cresting as the sun set behind it, Taj's footprints walking from the wet sand heading out to the ocean. On the top of the board, there was another one of my drawings dedicated to Taj, a simple sand dune with his surfboard spiked into the sand.

"I don't know what to say. How did you do this?" I asked Wes, my voice barely a whisper.

"I wanted to give you something special. I know how much those drawings mean to you, how much Taj means to you, and wanted you to be able to have him with you while you ride. I told Emme what I wanted to do. She got the drawings for me."

I didn't know what to say. My eyes were filled with tears and I stood there taking it in.

Do you like it, Charley?" he wondered.

"I love it, Wes. Thank you so much. This means everything to me," I murmured as I set the board down and curled into his arms.

"You're welcome. There's more, though," he went on.

"What? No. Wes, this is enough. More than enough," I insisted. "Besides, I feel really bad now because I don't have your gift here with me to give you. And my gift for you is nowhere near as magnificent as this."

"Charley, this gift has two parts. You just saw, and I explained the first part as to why I did this. The second part is still the board. I know you've been looking for jobs to get your career launched and you haven't had much success. I want you working for Blackman Boards. I've got the new lines coming out and they need designs. The second part of your gift is you seeing this board realizing that beyond what it means here," he emphasized, holding his hand to my heart. "It also needs to mean something in your head. Your work is phenomenal, baby. The best gift you could give me here on Christmas is to tell me you'll work with me at Blackman Boards as the senior graphic designer."

"Are you serious?" I gasped.

"Would I joke about this? Of course, I'm serious."

I was in deep shit. I loved Wes. Down to my bones, I knew I loved him. If anything ever happened to us, I knew I'd never survive it.

"I always loved Christmas," I started. "As a little girl growing up, Christmas was always a special time. Taj and I were so lucky. We had great parents who made sure that our Christmases were filled with joy. When I was fifteen, Taj had just turned eighteen. Our parents were killed in a car accident on their way home from a New Year's Eve party. Their car was hit by a drunk driver and they were killed instantly."

"Charley...Christ, baby."

"Ever since they died, though, Taj took care of me. We only had each other. He worked hard to make sure I had anything I needed. It was rough for the first few years, but despite that, Taj insisted on giving me the best birthdays and Christmases. I remember always thinking I'd never be able to repay him for everything he did for me. When he died, I didn't expect to ever do anything but just exist on holidays. But you came into my life and I have never had to experience a birthday where I just exist. And now Christmas is here, and you've proved again to me that it was worth giving in to every fear that I've had about becoming close to someone again. This Christmas has been incredible, Wes."

I stopped, taking in a breath. Wes continued to hold onto me and let me pause for a moment. Then, I continued, "Unfortunately, I know better than most, how precious time is and how short life can be. I don't want to live with things unsaid because I know time may take that opportunity away. So, I need to tell you that even though I know it's only been a very short time, I don't want to let another moment pass without saying this. I need you to know that I love you, Wes."

I felt his body tense, but he said nothing.

I went on, "I'm sorry if that's the wrong thing to say. I'm sorry if you aren't ready to hear it, but after this, I know I need to say it. In fact, I'll say it again...I love you, Wes."

I barely got the words out of my mouth before Wes lifted me up in his arms and pressed his mouth to mine. I wrapped my legs around his waist as he put his hands on my ass and continued kissing me. Wes carried me to his bedroom, never breaking contact with my mouth. He lowered me to my back in the bed while his body settled over mine. Finally tearing his mouth from mine, Wes framed my face with his hands and stared into my eyes. His emerald eyes were smoldering. After a few moments of silence, silence that said so much, Wes' mouth came crashing back down on mine. Not long after, our clothes were tossed all over his bedroom floor.

Wes put his hand between my legs. "My gorgeous girl. Always ready for me."

He teased me with his hands for a few minutes before positioning himself at my entrance. His hands went back to framing my face as he pushed inside me.

"Oh, Wes," I moaned.

His thrusts were deliciously unhurried, gentle, and controlled. I loved when he did this. He would build me up slowly and draw out my pleasure. Wes brought his mouth down to taste my lips, my jaw, my throat, and my shoulders. One of his hands made its way to my breast and his finger and thumb played with my nipple, rubbing and squeezing it. I kept my legs wrapped around his body as my fingers roamed through his hair. Wes strengthened his strokes ever so slightly and my breathing increased as I felt my orgasm rapidly approaching.

"Don't stop, honey," I begged. "Please don't stop."

Wes didn't stop. He continued to increase his pace indicating he was right there on the edge with me. I tipped my head back.

"Mouth, Charley," he demanded.

I immediately snapped my head back and gave him my mouth. Seconds later, I came apart with Wes. Our kisses drowned out the sounds of our moans. When Wes tore his mouth from mine, he looked down in my eyes.

"Now we absolutely must get back to my place so I can give you your gift," I shared, feeling sated and happy in post-orgasm bliss.

He laughed and pointed out, "Not for nothing, but what you just gave me was gift enough. I knew you were something special the moment I saw you, gorgeous." His words pulled me out of my post-orgasm stupor. "The more time I've spent with you, the more I knew I was right. The day you told me I was giving you back your life, I knew then how much you meant to me."

I knew when he took me back to his place that day that there was something more going on when he had me in bed. He had been making love to me then.

"So, I'm thinking what I just said wasn't the wrong thing to say, was it?" I asked.

"Not a chance, gorgeous. Pleased as fuck you did," he answered. "In fact, want to hear you say it again, baby."

My lips tipped up. "I love you, Wes."

"I love you too, Charley."

We sat in silence for a bit letting the moment sink in. Wes eventually broke it. "You haven't given me your answer—are you going to come work with me?"

I pressed my lips together and tapped my fingers on them as I pretended to think about it. "Well, it'll be highly inconvenient, but alright, I guess I can do this for you."

His face lit up and his eyes warmed.

I needed him to know just how much this meant to me. "Wes, in all seriousness, I would love to work with you at Blackman Boards. This means everything to me. Thank you."

He touched his mouth to mine and gave me a squeeze.

We stayed in his bed for a while, our limbs tangled. After a bit, we got up, I cleaned up, and we got dressed. I grabbed my new board and Wes drove us back to my place.

When we arrived, I was surprised to see that Zane was still with Emme. She and I made dinner while the boys hung in front of the television. I managed to get a few words in with her and made sure she was doing well after having spent the night before and then Christmas Day with Zane. She assured me all was good. I wanted more details from her but knew that she would share when she was ready. The two of us exchanged gifts while we were waiting for the food to finish in the oven.

After an amazing dinner and even better desserts, we all hung around in the family room enjoying the holiday. Emme seemed more relaxed than I'd seen her in a really long time, so I was grateful for the time the guys spent with us. A little while later, Zane said he needed to get going. We said goodnight, and Wes and I gave Emme and Zane some privacy while they said their goodbye. Once we were in my bedroom, I gave Wes his gift.

I handed him the wrapped box and said, "Merry Christmas, Wes."

He smiled at me and tore off the wrapping paper. Wes lifted the lid off the present and set it aside. He pushed the tissue paper out of the way and, after looking at the gift, looked up at me with an intense heat in his eyes.

As I stood there shifting back and forth on my feet, I bit my lip nervously.

He looked back down at the gift and gently ran a couple fingers across it.

"It's silly, Wes," I threw out, unable to handle the silence any longer. "Had I known you were going all out for Christmas I would have definitely gotten you something more—"

"Quiet, Charley," he demanded, interrupting me.

I immediately stopped talking.

My belly was full of nerves.

"Not magnificent?" he asked, incredulously. "Earlier today at my place you said that your gift to me was not nearly as magnificent as mine to you. Are you kidding me?"

I stared at him, unsure of how to respond.

"Do you like it?" I wondered.

"Is that a serious question?" he countered.

I nodded and explained, "I didn't know what to get you. You can get yourself anything you want, so I struggled to find something that I thought you'd like. This idea came to me and I talked to Emme about it. She was more than willing to help me make it happen. I've never done anything like this before."

Wes looked back down at the gift that sat in his lap. He pulled the picture frame out of the box and a look of pure adoration flashed across his face. Given the newness of our relationship, I didn't know how he'd respond to me giving him a framed photo of me from a boudoir photo session I did.

"Are there more of these?" he asked.

I nodded but said nothing else.

"I want them," he advised. "All of them."

"So, I guess that means you do like it?"

"Gorgeous…it's the best fucking present I've ever received. Now, get over here and let me love you."

With that, I joined Wes in bed and let him love me. It was a better Christmas than I could have ever imagined.

Sixteen

Charley

Blackman Boards closed on Christmas Eve and would not reopen until after the New Year. I would officially start working when the company reopened. Even though I was so excited to finally be able to do what I loved full time and could not wait to start, I had to admit that I was still very nervous about pursuing my dream. I asked Wes to take me to the warehouse so I could see where I would be working and perhaps help get myself a bit more prepared. It was three days after Christmas. I finally wore him down and convinced him to take me. We pulled into the lot outside of the building and parked. Wes met me at my door and took my hand in his.

"I am so excited to see where you work," I exclaimed.

"It's where you work now too, Charley" he replied as he gave my hand a squeeze.

We walked up to the front door, where Wes unlocked it and ushered me in ahead of him. Once inside, I took in the monumental space. Just through the front doors, I walked into a bright area. The sun shone in from all the windows surrounding that expanse, and there were hundreds of snowboards hung on the crisp, white walls. There was a reception area about ten feet inside the front door. Off to the right in front of the reception area was a lounge area with a couple of light gray couches that had black, white, and charcoal colored throw pillows on them. A fireplace enclosed by mostly gray stone that had hints of whites, blacks, and browns throughout was off to the side of the lounge area.

Also to the right, but behind the reception area, were lines of individual white desks. Each desk was furnished with a computer and the typical desktop necessities. A filing cabinet was off to the side of each desk, and a few of the desks seemed to have some personal touches, such as a picture frame or an ink blotter whose calendar was filled with notes. It was evident that not all the desks were being worked from yet, but at least half of them were.

"This place is beautiful, Wes," I stated, continuing to take in my surroundings.

"Thanks. I'm happy with the outcome of the office area. When I first bought the building, this space felt like a dungeon and I didn't want my employees working in that kind of environment. Everyone continued to work at the old site until the renovations were finished here. Now that the office renovations are complete I'm slowly transitioning the employees from the old space to this one," he explained.

"I love the boards hanging on the walls," I admitted.

And I did. I took them in and realized that one day I might walk in and see boards with my designs on them hanging on these walls. The thought filled me with joy.

As if reading my mind, Wes insisted, "I'm going to have you up there soon, gorgeous."

I glanced at him with a smile on my face and he winked at me.

"What goes on down here?" I asked.

"The lounge area at the front is for local clients waiting for a board repair when needed. Sometimes, we do tours as well. Reception is self-explanatory. The desks here are for my employees who handle all customer service and sales."

"So where do you work? I assume you have your own private office, right?"

He nodded and took my hand again. I followed him past the two rows of desks to the elevator that was located at the center of the back wall. He pressed the button to call the elevator.

"One of the conference rooms is there," he added, pointing to the room off to the left of the elevators. "Haven't had any meetings there yet since the staff is still split between the two spaces. Around the corner from the elevators here across from the conference room are the bathrooms. A little farther down the hall is one of the employee break rooms."

The elevator dinged and the doors opened. We hopped on and rode up to the second floor. When we stepped out, I found that despite the lights being off it was also a well-lit space. Windows lined both sides of the building, but only those windows on the right of the elevator gave a view of the outdoors. I walked behind Wes to the windows located on the left side of the elevator to find that those windows looked out into warehouse space.

"The boards and some of the accessories will be made down in the warehouse there," he explained. "Your new board was made down there."

My heart melted a little thinking of Wes out in the warehouse building the board for me.

"There's so much equipment and machinery there. And you have racks upon racks of boards. How is it all kept straight?"

"It's a bit out of sorts right now since the renovations were just completed. The guys who work out there will get it sorted the first week back after the holidays. I bought the place because we outgrew the old space, but this needed the renovation work before we moved full production here. We produce a lot of boards and, without the space being set up for us to produce efficiently, we would fall behind on production rather quickly."

"And what happens up here?" I wondered.

"The offices up here are for the staff not involved in sales, customer service, or production of the actual boards and accessories. Essentially, my office as well as the offices for the marketing reps, team riders, specifically, Zane, Stone, and Luke, as well as team coordinators, human resources, materials and design engineers for the equipment, and now the senior graphic designer, and ultimately, the team she puts together are all on this floor."

"I see. So, are you sure you weren't just trying to fill a position and an office space by hiring me?" I teased.

"Considering I'd like to have your office be in the same room with my office, no. However, I will leave that decision up to you. You can have your own office or after I show you mine, you'll see I have plenty of room to set you up in there. That said, even if you weren't my woman and I saw your work, I would have wanted to hire you. You need to start believing that you are that good, Charley."

"I think we should have separate offices," I stated. I knew if I was in the same space with him it would be unlikely that I'd be able to focus and actually accomplish anything.

"Okay. Let's go look at them," he said without hesitation.

We walked to the end of the hall and passed by several open office doors on the way. Wes stopped at a closed door directly in front of us and opened it.

"This is my office," he declared.

I frowned. "Well, see, now I'm rethinking the separate offices."

He chuckled.

His office was big.

No.

It was huge.

And it screamed sophistication. All of the furniture was sleek and modern, matching the vibe from the first floor. But what I loved most were the snowboarding touches. His coffee table had several snowboarding magazines adorning it and, like the walls downstairs, Wes tastefully added boards to his walls on either side of the room. In addition, there were pictures of snowboarders riding the pipe mid-air doing tricks.

I loved his office.

And he hadn't been kidding when he said that he could have comfortably fit me in the office with him and I would have still felt like I was in my own office. "You've got a great space, Wes. I must admit that it's certainly tempting to shack up with you in here. Can I see where I'll be working?"

"Sure. Follow me," he spoke as he strode to one of the two doors on the right-side wall of his office. Pointing to the other door, he noted, "That's the bathroom."

Okay, so he had his own personal bathroom in his office. I guess that was normal for the owner of a company like this.

Wes opened the other door and we walked into a mostly bare office space that was about half the size of his, but even still was a large office. Other than the desk in the middle of the room, the leather office chair behind it, and the love seat and two armchairs in the opposite corner from where we entered, the space was empty.

"This is a huge space, Wes. Are all of the offices on this floor at least this size?" I asked, suddenly a bit concerned.

I didn't want to come into the company as the girlfriend of the owner and get special treatment, which would likely lead to animosity from the other employees.

"I know what you are thinking, Charley. Get it out of your head," he ordered. "There are twenty private offices on this floor, and while not all are this size, a good majority of them are. You don't need to be concerned about getting preferential treatment. I want you close to me and this is as good as it'll get for me if you don't want to share a space with me. That said, nobody here will even think twice about you being in this space. You are highly qualified for the position and I treat all of my employees fairly."

I licked my lips. I loved that he not only knew what my concerns were without me needing to come out and express them directly, but he always took the time to address those concerns honestly. And what I loved even more was not only that he wanted me close to him, but also, and perhaps more importantly, his confidence in my ability to be a great graphic designer. I believed he trusted I would be an asset to his company.

His eyes dropped to my mouth and I walked closer to him. I rested my hands on his chest, tipped my head up, and proclaimed, "Okay, Mr. Blackman, this space will do."

"Happy to hear that, Miss Meadows," he returned giving me his wicked grin. "Now, I have spent several days sitting at my desk thinking of taking you on that very desk. Since we're here in your new office, I think I'd like to take you on your new desk. We'll get to my desk another time. Give me that pretty mouth."

I slid my hands up his chest and wrapped my arms around his neck before I gave him my mouth. He picked me up and carried me over to my new desk. Once there, he squeezed my ass and gently placed me on top of it. He quickly removed my shirt and bra while my hands made their way to the hard muscle of his abdomen. Wes helped me by pulling his shirt over his head and tossing it to the side next to mine. At the same time, I kicked off my sneakers. Wes' hands made their way back to the waistband of my yoga pants.

"Lift up, baby," he ordered.

I put my hands on either side of my body on the desk and lifted. Wes pulled my pants and thong down my legs and tossed them into the pile of clothes. Still resting back on my palms and my breaths coming quick, I watched with hooded eyes as Wes took my body in.

"So fucking gorgeous, Charley. Fuck, you're beautiful."

He put his hand under one of my ankles and kissed his way up the inside of my thigh. I quivered under the gentle brushes of his lips on my body. His mouth reached the spot between my legs and he swiped his tongue through my wetness. I moaned. He licked, sucked, kissed, and tortured the sensitive spot with his mouth. I could feel the tightening starting in my belly and, at that moment, Wes pulled his mouth away and stood.

I whimpered.

He was naked now having lost the rest of his clothes during the time he was working me with his mouth.

"I want you to come with me," he requested, his voice hoarse.

"Okay, honey," I gave in, my voice a breathy rasp. "Hurry."

Wes leaned over my body and took one nipple in his mouth. He nipped the hardened peak then soothed it with a swipe of his tongue before sucking it into his mouth. Turning his attention to my other nipple, he repeated the same. Finally, with his cock between my legs, his eyes came to mine and he pushed himself inside me.

"Wes," I groaned, dropping my head back feeling and loving the fullness of him.

He took his lips to my throat and pumped in and out of my body. His lips covered my throat, collarbone, and jaw with kisses before he took my mouth.

"Love this mouth, Charley," he growled.

"Harder, Wes. Please," I begged.

Wes gave it to me harder, gripping my hips tightly with his hands. He eventually slid his hands up my sides, under my arms, and wrapped his hands over the top of my shoulders pulling my body down harder on him. His pace quickened. I was on the verge of an orgasm when Wes took my mouth again and thrust several more times before planting himself to the root of his cock, the two of us coming together.

We were still breathing heavy minutes later when Wes spoke, "I think I'm going to love having you right next door to me."

I couldn't say I felt any differently. I laughed and agreed, "Me too."

"Love you, Charley."

"I love you too, Wes."

He pulled out of me and I made my way to the bathroom in his office to get cleaned up. When I walked out, I found Wes already dressed. He gave me a packet of papers from his office that I needed to review and complete so I could become a legitimate employee. After, we locked up and left. As we made our way to Wes' truck, my cell rang. I fished it out of my purse and saw it was Nikki calling.

"Hey Nikki!" I answered.

"Are the mountains ready for another dose of the California girls?" she asked.

I laughed. "Yay!! You and Monroe are definitely coming out?"

"We'll be there early Friday morning just in time for whatever the New Year's Eve celebrations will be on Saturday. We will stay through New Year's Day and leave on Monday morning to come home."

"Guess Emme and I are going to have to work our butts off coming up with one more really good reason to add to your list so that the next time you come out to Wyoming you don't have a return flight to Cali."

She laughed. "Yeah, you better get on that right away. Listen, my next client just showed up for her cut and color, so I've got to go. Just wanted to give you the heads up and let you know we were coming. Monroe is sending the flight details over to Em tonight."

"Okay, Nik. Love you," I said as Wes opened my door and I climbed into the truck.

"Love you too, babe."

I disconnected the call and Wes made his way around to the driver's side. He got in and started the truck.

"Are your girls making it out for New Year's Eve?" he asked.

"Yep," I confirmed with a huge grin on my face.

"You miss them, don't you?"

I nodded. "Every single day. They are my best girls and I really want them to move here. We joke about it with Nikki's list, but I'm not expecting that they'll actually make the move. They've lived in California their entire lives. This would be a huge change for them."

"Don't rule it out. You never know what could happen. In the meantime, do everything you can to show them what they are missing out on."

"Got any ideas?" I wondered, hoping he could offer some suggestions.

"When do they arrive?" he asked.

"Friday, early morning," I answered.

"I've got a few ideas then. I'll make a couple calls to the guys. We can spend Friday on the mountain as a group and get dinner out afterward. Then, we'll start the celebrations with a New Year's Eve bash at Lou's. New Year's Day we'll have everyone over to my place."

"That sounds like a great time," I bubbled.

"That's what it's about."

At that, Wes put the truck in drive and pulled out of the lot. We decided to grab some food for dinner on the way back to my place. I texted Emme to see if she wanted anything, but she said she wasn't home and would be in late. I found this odd but didn't press for details she may not have wanted to share. After dinner, Wes and I spent the rest of the night cuddling on the couch watching a movie before heading to bed.

Seventeen

Charley

"It hurts. Every spot on my body aches. I hurt so bad even my fucking fingernails hurt!"

That was Nikki. She and Monroe arrived yesterday morning and Wes, true to his word, came through and got the rest of the guys to clear their schedules just to show my friends a good time.

I had to admit, I was surprised by my girls. When I told them that we were going to spend the day on the mountain snowboarding, they were more than happy to go.

We arrived at Parks Ridge early yesterday morning and had the mountain mostly to ourselves for a good part of the morning. Monroe had done really well. I am certain her many years of dance helped with her ability to pick up riding quickly. She was certainly no professional, but she didn't wipe out much. Stone was clearly impressed by her. Zane stuck with Emme that morning giving her a snowboarding lesson. She did well, but she was mostly cautious as was her typical nature. She quickly recognized her limits and stuck to them. Any time she nearly went down Zane was there to catch her before she fell. If she went down, he went down with her. Seeing that made my heart squeeze.

And then there was Nikki. Poor girl. She tried so hard, but it was just not happening for her. She wiped out so many times; it was unreal. I had to give it to her, though, she was determined. By the end of the day, she managed to get down a smaller hill without falling. Luke stayed behind her the entire way and when she reached the bottom of the hill, we all cheered for her.

After the guys spent the entire morning and the better part of the afternoon riding with us, only briefly taking a break for some lunch in the lodge, I told them that we could probably use a break, but would love to watch them ride pipe. They seemed to have never-ending stamina and were all about it. The girls were more than ready for a rest and, secretly, I knew they were excited to see the guys ride. Em wanted to get some pictures, so Zane walked her back to the car to get the camera before they met us over at the pipe.

The guys took the next two hours to ride while we watched, chatted, laughed, and Emme took pictures. I knew I missed the four of us being able to be together all the time, but I had not realized just how much I not only missed being with them but also just how much I needed it.

Once the guys finished on the pipe, we all went out for dinner. Dinner went well, and the conversation was easy. I hadn't wanted Wes' buddies to feel put out by my friends and either they covered it really well or they were thoroughly enjoying themselves. I wasn't going to complain either way. Following dinner, Wes and his friends took us back to Emme's and my place. They hung out for a bit and eventually left giving my girls and me some time with each other.

We stayed up late, so everyone slept in this morning. The girls and I had brunch followed by some shopping and an early dinner before this evening's festivities. We were now in the process of getting ready for the New Year's Eve bash at Lou's.

Well, most of us were getting ready. Nikki was barely moving.

"Get your ass up now or you're going to make us all late," Monroe asserted.

"How do they do that every day? My body is going to need a vacation from this vacation. I'm serious. Something that results in feeling like this the next day and doesn't involve a series of orgasms preceding it is so not worth it in my book," Nikki declared.

"Don't worry, Nik. I'm sure if you let Luke know how fragile your body is right now, he'll take good care of you," I assured her.

"Yeah, I agree," Emme chimed in. "He seemed pretty cozy with you yesterday. I'm sure he'd be more than willing to help you heal."

"He's going to have to carry me around all night tonight at this rate. I can barely roll over in this bed," Nikki informed us.

"Luke's got enough muscles," Monroe added. "I bet he'd oblige you if that's how you want to play this. Either way, whether you walk or are carried, you're going to be ready on time so get your ass up."

"I'm going to need some Ibuprofen."

"I'll get it," Emme called as she walked out of the room.

After taking some Ibuprofen, Nikki got moving and we all finished getting ready. Just before the guys showed to pick us up, Emme grabbed her usual group photo of us. Minutes later, there was a knock at the door.

"I've got it," I stated.

I opened the door and the smile on my face grew. My handsome man stood there with his equally handsome friends and they all looked breathtakingly beautiful.

"Wes," I whispered softly, reaching my hand out to his and pulling him toward me. As his body collided with mine and he snaked an arm around my waist I looked behind him to Zane, Stone, and Luke and greeted, "Hey guys, come on in."

As his friends made their way in, Wes leaned into me and touched his lips to mine. "Hey, gorgeous. You look absolutely stunning."

"You're not so bad yourself, Mr. Blackman," I breathed before I put my lips to his.

"Hey lovebirds! I know it has been maybe fifteen long, grueling hours since you last saw each other, but the rest of us are still here," Nikki yelled to us when we were mid-kiss.

Wes laughed and then I spoke loud enough for everyone to hear. "I'm sorry, Wes. Nikki is a little moody right now. Her snowboarding lesson yesterday left her feeling sore in places she didn't know existed. She could barely get out of bed to get ready."

I glanced toward Nikki and saw she was glaring at me. My gaze shifted to Luke who was eyeing Nikki with concern.

Mission accomplished.

Monroe piped up and asked, "Alright, enough. Is everyone ready to go?"

"Since I have my camera out, do you guys mind if I get a picture of all of us together?" Emme asked.

Everyone was on board, so Emme set the timer on the camera on the tripod and we all huddled together for a photo. Then, we made our way out to Lou's in the limo the guys arrived in.

As per usual, Lou's was jam-packed with both locals and out-of-towners hoping to ring in the New Year with each other in the most fun way. I'd only been to Lou's a handful of times at this point, but it was never once disappointing.

"Elle's performing tonight," Wes announced as we walked in through the door and into the saloon.

"I know. She texted me earlier this week and told me," I offered.

Wes' body tightened, and he glanced down at me. "I didn't realize you and Elle had exchanged numbers."

I grinned at him. "Yep. At Christmas breakfast when you made a run to the bathroom. I like your sister. She's so sweet."

His face warmed as he looked down at me. He spoke softly, "I love that you get along with her."

"Me too, honey."

Wes and I followed our friends to a table near the front of the room so we'd have a good seat to watch Elle when she performed. Our first round of drinks arrived not long after we were seated. Minutes later, Elle showed up.

"Hey everyone!" she practically shouted as she made her way around giving hugs to Wes, his friends, and me.

"Hi El, you remember my friends Emme, Nikki, and Monroe?" I asked.

"Yes. It's great to see you all again."

"You too," Monroe and Emme said as Nikki nodded at Elle.

Elle turned back to me. "I heard you start the new job on Monday. Congratulations! But you better get to working right away, though. The X Games are only a few weeks out and I want to see your stuff on their boards when I watch the Games on TV."

My eyes got big and I turned to look at Wes. He chuckled and shook his head as if Elle hadn't just dropped big news on me.

"The X Games?" I asked him. My mind was racing, and my stomach was in knots.

"Oh boy," Elle said before Wes could respond. "You haven't told her about them yet, Wes? What are you waiting for? I've got to go get ready to get on stage. Have a great time tonight. I'll catch you all later."

"Later," Zane and Luke replied.

"Kill it, Elle," Stone added.

The girls thanked her and wished her luck.

Wes gave her a hug before she took off. When he sat back down, I was still staring at him.

"What's wrong, Charley?" he asked while laughing at me.

"The X Games, Wes? When are they?"

"Yeah, they're in Aspen at the end of January."

"It won't happen that quick, will it?"

"What?" he responded.

"My designs? They won't be on boards by then, right?"

"If you get some good stuff together...absolutely."

I bit my lip nervously.

His eyes dropped to my mouth. Then, he looked back at my eyes and he spoke. "Gorgeous, nothing happens unless you are comfortable with it. You approve all designs before they are used, but baby, you *can* do this. You've got to start believing in yourself."

"He's right, sweets. You can do this. We all know it. Now you need to believe it," Emme piped in from across the table.

My eyes got wet.

"And, just sayin'," Nikki chimed in. "If you get your work on boards at the X Games, that easily gets me to number ten on my list. Can't have one of my best girls that far away from me becoming famous and having nobody around to make her look glamorous."

Everyone laughed. I could always count on Nikki to lighten the mood. I looked to her and smiled. She returned a wink.

At that moment, Lou was up on stage welcoming everyone and introducing Elle. She took the stage and started her set. We spent the next hour listening and singing along with Elle and I very soon forgot about my anxiety with this huge life change.

"Be right back, honey. I'm going to head to the ladies' room," I explained, leaning into Wes as Elle finished up her set.

He nodded at me.

I walked to the restroom, did my business, and was standing at the sink washing my hands when a woman walked up next to me and spoke.

"I saw you come in with Wes," she stated deadpan.

I looked at the woman. She was about my height with far more curves. Her hourglass figure was accentuated by the sparkly gray, form-fitting, halter top sweater dress she wore. She had short brown hair that sat just above her shoulders and deep brown, almond-shaped eyes. She was beautiful. And, she was talking about Wes.

"I'm sorry?" I asked, puzzled.

She smiled. I didn't like it. I could tell she had a bad attitude and she had only said a few words to me.

"Wes," she repeated his name. "You came here with him. I'm surprised to see him take a break from the snowboarding and work to actually go out," she scoffed condescendingly.

Who was this woman and why was she being such a bitch?

"Forgive me, but do I know you?" I asked, still genuinely curious about this woman and a little concerned at this point.

"No, you don't," she said, pausing a moment. She continued, "But Wes does—"

"You've got to be fucking kidding me," I heard called from inside the room. I took that moment to look away from the woman and noticed the bathroom door closing as Elle stood just inside the door. She walked right up to Miss Attitude and came within inches of her face. "I think it'd be in your best interest to keep my brother's name out of your mouth."

Wow. Elle was typically such a sweet woman. Seeing her now, I made a mental note to never piss her off. Angry Elle was something else.

Miss Attitude laughed. I had to hand it to her. Seeing Elle like that sort of scared me and I wasn't the focus of her anger. This woman had balls to laugh in her face.

"This couldn't be more perfect. A reunion with the princess

herself," she remarked with a smirk on her face.

"You've got about five seconds to get your ass out of here. Stay away from Charley and don't even think about approaching Wes."

The bitch looked to me, still smirking. "Charley? It's been a pleasure," she offered as she approached the door. "Wish I could say the same about you, Elle. Until next time, ladies."

She walked out of the bathroom.

"Who the fuck was that?" I asked.

"Scum. Absolute scum. Her name is Dana. She's Wes' ex and she is, by far, the biggest bitch known to all of mankind."

"I guess it's safe to say you didn't approve of her?"

"Hell. No. I love my brother and support him in everything he does, but that bitch was the biggest mistake of his life. She broke his fucking heart."

I gasped. The thought of Wes being heartbroken hurt me. I suddenly had a very real understanding of Elle's rage-fueled standoff moments ago. Just thinking of someone hurting Wes made my stomach grow cold.

"Oh my goodness. I am such a horrible, selfish person," I concluded, my eyes tearing up and my nose stinging.

"What? What the hell are you talking about?"

"I've been so caught up in myself and everything bad that has happened in my life that I never even stopped to consider Wes. He's been so compassionate, thoughtful, and understanding and I've been taking everything he has to offer, giving him nothing in return," I told Elle, tears spilling down my cheeks.

Elle pulled me into a hug. "Charley, stop. This isn't my conversation to have with you, but know that Dana has been out of Wes' life for at least two years now. He has moved on to bigger and better things, the best of which is you. You may not think it, but trust me, you give him plenty in return."

I stood there in Elle's arms as my tears fell. After a few moments, she pulled back and did her best to clean up my face.

"Come on," she said. "Let's get you back out there so you can start this new year with your man by your side."

I nodded in acknowledgment. "Thanks, El."

She winked at me and we walked out of the bathroom.

As we approached the table, finding everyone else still having a great time, Wes looked over at us and must have noticed something because he immediately pushed his chair back, stood, and strode over to us.

"What happened?" he asked.

Before I could answer, Elle started rattling off the story.

"Your bitch of an ex is here. She saw Charley in the bathroom, cornered her, and was her usual pleasant self," she recounted with a roll of her eyes. Then she continued, "Now she's got Charley questioning and doubting herself."

Wes' eyes came to mine. He said nothing, but I could see him thinking. His face was filled with concern.

It figured.

He was the one who had his heart broken and he was concerned for me.

I walked to him, put my arms around his neck, and hugged him tightly. He wrapped his arms around me as I whispered in his ear, "I'm so sorry, Wes. You are amazing, and I've been a shitty girlfriend." His arms got tight at my declaration, but I ignored it and kept going. "I've been selfish. You deserve more. You deserve better than I've given. I promise to do better."

Wes pulled back to look at my face but did not loosen his grip on me. "Quiet, Charley. I'm not going to spend tonight discussing that woman. I don't know what the fuck she said to you, but you don't need to do anything different for me. I can see she said enough to mess with your head and I intend to fix that. For now, for tonight, let's forget about her. If you feel like you need to give me something, give me this. I want you to enjoy tonight with me and our friends. That's it. When we leave tonight, though, I want you at my place."

Our friends.

I loved that.

I took a deep breath and gave him a small smile. He wanted to have a good night tonight and I figured that if this woman made things miserable for him years ago, I was going to make sure she didn't ever do it again, especially not through me.

"Okay, Wes."

"That's my girl," he approved as he lowered his head to press a kiss to my nose. "You okay?"

I nodded.

"Good. Now give me that mouth, gorgeous."

I tipped my head back to give him access and kissed him. We eventually rejoined our friends and I went off with my girls, Elle included, to do some dancing while the guys watched. It wasn't long before I had forgotten about Dana and was able to really enjoy the rest of the night.

The guys joined us on the dance floor minutes before midnight. Wes had his arm draped over my shoulders, pressing the side of my body into his front. The countdown to midnight began at twenty and got louder at ten. Wes' mouth captured mine after everyone shouted, 'Happy New Year' and for that moment nothing else existed. It was just us.

I broke the kiss, put my lips to his ear, and shared, "This past year was the toughest of my life. I never thought I'd ever recover and be happy again. You have given me something good to remember about last year. It started horribly but ended wonderfully. I am so thrilled to be going into this new year with something to smile about."

Wes' arms tightened around my body. "I'm going to give you more of that, Charley. I want to see you continuing to smile."

"Happy New Year, Wes."

"Happy New Year, baby."

Eighteen

Wes

Charley and I were in the limo on the way back to my place. This was after we left Lou's and stopped at her place. Everyone had gone in and we all hung with Charley's friends for a few minutes while she packed a bag to take to my house.

I know she had been a little hesitant to spend the night with me at my place since Nikki and Monroe were here only one more night. Thankfully, they not only reassured her that it was fine but also encouraged her to go with me. Despite me not knowing the cause of Emme's nightmares, it was clear that Nikki and Monroe knew that Charley had never spent the night away from Emme. I'm certain that was part of the reason they pushed so hard for her to come and spend the night with me. This would be her first time spending the night at my place and I was very much looking forward to falling asleep and waking up in my bed with her wrapped in my arms. I was having everyone over tomorrow so I knew she'd be able to spend the day with her girls then.

After she packed a bag and everyone said their goodbyes, we dropped my boys off at Stone's place since they had all met up there. We told them we'd see them all tomorrow and were now alone in the limo going to my house.

Stone's place was about twenty-five minutes from my home, so the moment we were alone, Charley pounced. She straddled my lap and ran her fingers through my hair before dropping her mouth to mine.

Damn if I didn't love her mouth. My hands gripped her thighs and worked their way to her ass as I kissed her back.

"You are so damn sexy," she breathed as she pulled her mouth from mine.

"I think you're a little tipsy, gorgeous."

She smiled at me and rolled her hips. "Just tipsy enough to make this fun."

"Fuck, you've got me so hard," I admitted, squeezing her ass in my hands and holding her still on top of me as I thrust my hips upward.

I moved one hand up over her thigh and trailed my fingers under her skirt, right up to her pussy. I traced along the edge of her panties. She squirmed looking for more friction. I pulled her panties out of the way and gave her what she needed.

I learned several weeks ago that I'd never be able to deny this woman anything. Slipping two fingers in and out of her, I heard the beautiful sounds of her moans and watched as she climbed higher and higher toward her climax.

"Wes," she rasped out as her head fell back.

The sound of her voice when she was this close to orgasm was captivating. I could hear her call my name just like that every day for the rest of my life and never tire of it.

"That's it, Charley. Take what you need, baby," I encouraged her.

That's when she froze. Her head snapped forward, her eyes burning into mine, and she stopped riding my fingers. "What's wrong? Did I hurt you?" I asked, terror taking over.

She stared at me a moment before tears spilled down her cheeks.

I pulled my fingers out of her body and gripped her hips. "Charley, fuck...what's wrong?"

"I am so sorry, Wes," she whispered.

"For what? What just happened?" I asked.

"You give. You always give."

I shook my head, not understanding what she meant. "I'm not following you, baby."

She took a deep breath and then spoke, "From the first day I met you, you have looked out for me and you've taken care of me. You were there to walk me to my car every night at Parks Ridge. If I'm out running errands, you always call or text to check in on me just to make sure I'm okay or that I've made it home safely. You have been there to listen to me when I find that I need to talk about Taj. Before I even told you about Taj or my parents you gave me what I needed by making me feel safe and comforted all while being patient with me. You never pressured me to talk about it. And then you offered me my dream job."

I sat there staring at her not sure what to say, but also certain she wasn't finished.

"Up until a little over a month ago, I lived my life working constantly just to keep busy and get through each day. Now, I wake up feeling like I am the luckiest woman in the world. I want to soak up every ounce of joy you've brought into my life and draw out that happiness."

"Gorgeous, this all sounds like good stuff. I am still not sure I understand why you are in tears."

"Wes, you give. You give me you. You give me your compassion. You give me your kindness. You give me a comfortable, safe place to unwind. Most importantly, you give me your love. I was late in learning this, but you keep giving all you have to give. And me? I just keep taking."

Seriously? I had this woman on the brink of an orgasm and told her to take what she needed, and it brought her to this? Clearly, Dana did a number on her.

"You give, too. This isn't one-sided," I told her.

Her voice was so sad and downtrodden when she replied, "How? Wes, I don't give you anything."

Now I was pissed. She thought that little of herself?

"Don't ever fucking say that, Charley. You give me *everything*. When you ask me to spend the night with you because you like waking up with me, I get what I need knowing you want me next to you. When I learned that you refuse to leave your best friend home alone because she might have a nightmare, I got what I needed knowing you won't walk out on the people you love. When you call me two hours after you've just been with me simply because you miss me and want to hear my voice, I get what I need. When you call out my name with your raspy voice right before you come, I get what I need. When you told me you loved me for the first time because you didn't want another day to pass without letting me know how you felt, I got what I needed. But, most importantly, when you nearly jumped out of your boots in excitement when you knew you'd be watching me ride pipe for the first time, I got what I fucking needed."

I realized there was so much more I could tell her, but she pulled in a sharp breath at my last statement and the tears were still spilling down her cheeks. I took her face in my hands and swiped at her tears with the pads of my thumbs.

"That list I just gave you, gorgeous? Tip of the iceberg. I'm thinking maybe you get my point now, though. If not, I'll hold those other things for when I think you need more reassurance that you give me everything I need every single day."

The limo stopped. We had just parked in front of my house. After we got out and I sent the driver off, I took Charley by the hand and walked her into the house. Once inside, I picked her up and carried her into the bedroom and straight to the bathroom. I set her down on the countertop and turned on the shower.

We hadn't said a word to each other yet. As the water warmed up, I walked back to my woman and lifted her up to place her on her feet. I stared into her eyes as I placed my hands on her shoulders. Turning her around I captured her eyes again in the mirror. My hands went to the zipper on the back of her skirt. After unzipping it and letting it slide down her legs to her feet, I lifted her top over her head and tossed it aside. She stood there looking beautiful in her matching slate-blue lacy bra and panties with the intense sapphire heat swirling in her eyes. I stripped out of my clothes, my eyes still captured by hers, and removed the last two pieces covering her beautiful body.

Pressing my front to her back I dipped my head so my mouth was at her ear.

"Everything I need, gorgeous," I whispered. "Everything."

Her breath hitched.

I put my lips to the skin just below her ear and trailed kisses down her neck to the top of her shoulder. Turning her body so her front was pressed to mine, I continued to kiss, moving back in the direction I came from until I was at her jawline and finally at her mouth.

I took her mouth. She gave without hesitation.

Running her hands up my arms until they clasped behind my neck with her mouth still connected to mine, Charley wrapped her legs around my waist as I lifted her up. We kissed, and I walked us into the shower. The warm water hit our bodies and things grew more intense. Charley's back was now up against the wall of the shower and, without delay, I entered her body.

Just the same as in the limo, her head fell back against the wall and she groaned.

As I pumped in and out of her, she moved her hips to meet mine with each thrust. I loved the way she came alive when she was hungry for me.

"Wes, honey. You feel so good," she rasped out. Within minutes, I felt her tightening around me. "Oh, Wes," she called out.

I slowed my pace for a bit and helped her ride out that wave of pleasure. Watching her come apart was my undoing. I started moving quickly again, and a few thrusts later, I was on that same ride.

I held Charley up, keeping my body pressed to hers as we both came down from the euphoric high we had just experienced. I pulled back and looked at her beautiful face.

"You are fucking everything to me, Charley."

"I'm so thankful for you, Wes. Please tell me you know that."

I nodded. We finished up in the shower, I put a towel around her, grabbed one for myself, and we stood staring at each other. After a couple moments, I urged, "Come on, gorgeous. Let's go to bed."

The second we were in bed, I immediately had Charley on her back while I covered half of her body with mine.

"I'm sorry for what happened tonight that made you doubt your worth, especially to me," I lamented.

"You shouldn't be apologizing to me," she started, her voice broken. "Throughout this entire relationship, I've been—"

"No, Charley," I cut her off. "You aren't going to go back there. I've made some bad decisions in life. Dana was one of them. I didn't realize it then, started to realize it just after it ended, and definitely know it now. I also made some good decisions in my life. You are one of them. No doubt in my mind about that, baby."

She bit her lip. My eyes went to her mouth briefly and she asked, "What happened?"

I tilted my head, contemplating for a moment, and was

about to answer when she backtracked, "I'm sorry. I shouldn't have asked that. You don't have to tell me. It's just that tonight Elle told me that Dana broke your heart. When she said that, I saw red. It made me so angry to know that someone hurt you."

I smiled hugely at her. "Feels good, baby."

"What?" she asked.

"You feeling angry on my behalf...that feels good. Love you for it," I shared, pausing for a moment. "It also feels good to know that you get along with Elle. Dana never did. I should have realized then it would never work, but I was young and focused on what I wanted that I never stopped to really consider what I had, or didn't for that matter, with Dana. We got together when I was relatively new in the business. I was only riding at that point. The guys and I were doing well but hadn't gotten to the level we are all at now. We did well enough to win some contests, though. Blackman Boards wasn't a thought in anyone's mind at the time. I finished school and made the decision to pursue the business. Dana and I had been together for four years when I proposed to her."

I felt Charley's body tense underneath mine, but I needed to finish so she could understand what she meant to me.

I continued, "I didn't have much to offer her at that time, but I worked day and night to achieve my dream. I knew if I stuck with it and kept pushing I'd get to a place where I'd be able to give her anything. She was never into snowboarding. She was never excited about the prospect of seeing me ride. And she absolutely hated the time I spent building my business. I knew I wasn't around much, but I was doing what I was doing to be able to give her, to give us, the life I thought we both deserved. Six months after I proposed to her, I came home from a very long day of work to find all her shit was packed and gone. A note and the engagement ring were on the bed. She left me because she believed I was chasing an unattainable dream and she wanted me to grow up and get a real job. It's been more than two years since she left. Like I said, didn't realize it then, but now I know it was the greatest fucking thing she ever did for me."

Charley blinked her eyes in surprise. "She left because you were working hard to build a career doing something you loved?"

"Not sure she saw it that way, but yeah."

"She's probably kicking herself now. Serves her right. Wow, what a bitch."

I laughed. I loved seeing her fired up.

"I want you to understand something, Charley. You've been through a lot of shit in your life. The last year has been tough from what I can tell. That said, it's understandable that you've needed some emotional support. I'm happy that I could give you that. In all that, though, I don't want you to doubt what you are giving me in return. It meant everything to me the day you were excited to see me ride for the first time. She never gave me that. You did. And, it felt fantastic."

We sat in silence for a few moments before she teased, "And here I thought you only liked me for my body."

"Can't say that's a hardship either, gorgeous. This body and this mouth...I could probably be content with both for a very long time. But there's a whole lot more to you worth loving. I need to know you get that."

I felt the wetness hit my hand that was resting against her cheek. "Yeah, my girl gets it," I concluded, wiping the tears from her face.

"Love you, Charley."

"I love you too, Wes."

The minute the words were out of her mouth, I kissed her. Then, I showed her just how much I loved her.

I had a feeling it was going to be one of the best years of my life.

Nineteen

Charley

"WHY AM I SO NERVOUS?" I asked Emme, Nikki, and Monroe as I ran around the kitchen getting coffee and breakfast.

It was Monday morning and my first official day of work at Blackman Boards.

This was, of course, after the incredible weekend we had just had. Having spent my first night ever at his place, Wes took full advantage and I woke up yesterday morning feeling deliciously sore.

We then spent the rest of the day Sunday at Wes' house with our friends. I was so thankful that Wes seemed to like my friends enough to allow them in his home. It was important to me that they all got along and I was grateful that Wes was not only close by yesterday, but also gave me enough space so that I could spend some much-needed time with my girls before they went back to California.

I came home with them yesterday evening because I wanted to make sure that I not only spent the last couple hours they were here with them but also that I went to work separately from Wes today. He wasn't thrilled with it, but I insisted. In typical Wes fashion, he gave me what I needed. I'm not sure what or who I felt I needed to prove anything to, but I just knew that I felt very strongly about arriving on my own on my first day.

"No clue," Monroe started. "You are going to rock this job, Char."

"Yep. I am with Monroe on this. Nobody is worried about your ability to do well at this job because we all know how talented you are," Emme added.

"My only concern would be how you plan to stay focused on work all day when you know Wes is in the room right next door," Nikki chimed in. "If my man and I had a door separating us all day long, he looked like that, and he was as talented at giving the goods as you say he is, I'd be nervous that I wouldn't be able to get any work done at all."

"Lucky for you that you don't have a man then, right?" Monroe teased.

"I'm being selective right now," she shot back.

"Ladies, please," I interrupted. "I need help."

Emme piped up, "You don't need help, Charley. You've got this. I've never met anyone more perfect for this job than you. Of course, while I do think that Wes had other motives in putting your office right next to his, he is definitely not the kind of man who would hire someone who wasn't highly qualified for this position. You're going to be fine. Stop thinking about it being more than what it is. You'll be doing what you love and, in doing that, you get to help Wes do what he loves."

I stopped and thought about this for a moment. She was right. I was helping Wes do what he loved by doing what I loved most in this world. I smiled big at my girls.

"You know, I think you are all right," I announced to them. "I am awesome and I'm going to rock this job. Wes' office being right next door to mine will just be icing on the cake. Maybe I'll reward myself every time I come up with kick-ass designs by paying him a visit. I hardly believe he'll have a problem with that."

"That's our girl," Nikki approved.

"Does this outfit look okay?" I wondered.

I had spent a ridiculous amount of time mulling over what to wear and finally settled on a just-above-my-knee navy blue skirt with a crisp, white three-quarter-length sleeve scoop-neck sweater.

"Sexiest bitch in the room," Nikki declared.

We all laughed, and Monroe added, "You look fantastic, babe."

Emme nodded her approval.

"Okay. I need to go or I'm going to be late. Thanks for the pep talk, girls," I said as I hugged each of them. I then turned to Nikki and Monroe. "Wish you both would be here when I get home from work. I miss you already."

"We miss you, Charley," Monroe insisted as she looked from me to Emme. "Both of you. There's nothing I want more than our foursome back together again, but it's not easy for Nikki and me to just pack and leave."

I half smiled at her, feeling the lump form in my throat. I really missed having them around all the time, but I couldn't expect them to drop their lives because of what had happened in mine and Emme's. The two of us could only be thankful that our best friends took the trips out to visit us understanding why we couldn't go back to California to visit them.

"I know," I assured her. "I am really happy with how things have changed for me in a positive way in the last couple months, but sometimes I find myself longing for things to go back to the way they were before everything went to shit. When you and Nikki come out here, I get that back and it feels good. I just hate having to let it go."

She pulled me in for a hug as the tears fell down my cheeks. I looked and saw that Emme's eyes were filled with tears as Nikki was swiping her hand across her own cheek.

After a few minutes of silence, Nikki stepped in front of me, hugged me, and stated, "We love you, Charley. Have a great first day and call us later to let us know how it went."

I nodded, grabbed my things, gave them one last look, and made my way to the Jeep.

I tried to pull myself into a better mood on the way to work, but it was tough. Those two girls were such an important part of my life, and I hated having to see them go knowing it would be several months before I'd see them again.

I made it to work fifteen minutes before I was scheduled to start and was still feeling very heartbroken. I figured I'd get into my office and try to pull it together before I had to work. I entered the building and literally had to take a few steps back when I was greeted by the receptionist.

"Girl, you must be Charley," the beautiful, dark-skinned black woman behind the counter greeted me.

I nodded and stayed put as she made her way out from behind the counter to come face-to-face with me.

"My name's Florence, but everyone calls me Flo. Glad to see you really do exist. I almost didn't believe it when the boss told me about you," she shared.

Wes spoke about me to his receptionist. Good to know.

"Hi Flo. It's nice to meet you," I greeted, extending my hand. She pulled me into a quick hug instead.

After she let me go, I took her in. Flo was about the same height as me. She wore a pair of skinny black jeans that showed off her ample booty and wide hips. A short sleeved open front gray cardigan was covering her white camisole that covered her modest chest. She completed her look with a pair of black ballet flats, a delicate pink necklace, and matching bracelet. I was admiring the pair of large silver hoop earrings when I couldn't help but notice just how exquisite her skin was. Her round face had flawless skin that wasn't overdone with makeup, except for her eyes. Her almond-shaped, cocoa-colored eyes were dramatically done up, but somehow, at this hour of the morning, she rocked it. Immediately, I decided I liked her.

"Now, tell Flo what's wrong. Why do you look like someone who just found out that Santa's not real?" she asked with genuine concern.

"Is it that obvious?" I wondered looking around to see if anyone else was going to notice my sorry self. Thankfully, it appeared Flo was the only one currently in the office.

"You've got at least another half hour before the rest start rolling in here. It's just me and the big guys upstairs here. And yes, girl, it is that obvious. So, what's the problem?"

"My best friends from back home came to visit for the weekend. They are going back this morning. I had to say my goodbyes before coming in today," I answered.

"Where's home, darlin'?" she asked.

I pulled in a breath at her question. I hadn't thought twice about saying it when I did, but I realized once she asked that California was no longer home.

"They live in California," I responded, looking away.

Before Flo could respond or ask any more questions, I heard footsteps and saw Wes was striding toward us. He had a look of concern on his face as he approached.

"Good morning, gorgeous," he greeted as he pressed a kiss to my lips. "You okay?"

I nodded.

"Woman, if you ever need to talk, I'm your girl," Flo piped up, ignoring Wes briefly. After I gave her a friendly smile, she turned her attention to Wes. "Got yourself a good one here. I like her."

"I am well aware of that Flo. I like her, too, but I'm going to put her to work now."

"Have at it. Nice meeting you, Charley."

"Thanks, Flo. You too."

Wes took me by the hand and we walked to the elevator. As we stepped on and the doors closed, he turned to me.

"Why are you upset?" he asked.

"It's nothing. I'm just being silly," I explained, trying to brush it off.

"If something is upsetting you, it's not nothing to me. Tell me what's wrong."

I looked in his soft eyes to see that he wasn't being demanding. He was pleading with me to share what was on my mind.

I took in a deep breath.

"Nikki and Monroe leave this morning. It's going to be a couple months before I see them again. They're the only family I have left, so it's hard. I'll be fine, though. Sorry if I worried you."

"No need to apologize to me," Wes insisted as he squeezed my hand and the elevator doors opened. "Are you okay to do this today? I'm happy to take you back to your place so you can spend the rest of the morning with them."

I loved this man.

"Thank you, Wes. I really appreciate that, but I think I need to get my mind on some designs. I could really use the distraction."

"Whatever you need, Charley."

We walked off the elevator and down the hall toward our offices.

As we walked into my office, Wes spoke, "Wouldn't want to push you into something so intense so quickly, but the guys really want new designs for the Games. Would like to have you starting on those immediately."

I looked at him but said nothing.

"No pressure. I'll tell the guys you aren't ready for it if you want."

"No," I exclaimed. "Don't do that. They've been great to

my friends. I can do this for them...and for you."

He smiled at me. "I'm going to let you get to it then, but first I need to taste you. Give me that pretty mouth, baby."

I kissed Wes and got to work.

I was right.

Work was just what I needed to occupy my mind and help me focus my attention on something other than my friends leaving. I wrote down some ideas I had for boards for each of the guys. I also managed to start on the design ideas I had for Zane.

It felt like five minutes had passed when Wes walked back into my office.

"Hey, honey. What's up?" I asked.

"Planning to eat lunch today?"

I glanced at the clock. I had been so caught up in my work that I hadn't even realized how much time had passed. This was typical for me. I could so easily lose track of time when I was designing.

"Wow. That went quickly."

Wes' head tipped back, and he laughed. When he looked back at me, he noted, "Glad you are enjoying yourself in here. I'm going to assume you are liking your new job?"

"I love it, Wes."

He smiled. "Want to take a break and be my lunch date?"

I pretended to think for a minute and joked, "I guess I'll go with you. I mean, if you can't find anyone else to join you. I would absolutely hate for you to go alone."

He sauntered toward me, bent down so his face was inches from mine, pressed his thumb to my lower lip, and proclaimed, "Love this mouth. Even when you are being smart with it."

Wes captured my lips with his. He slipped his velvety tongue past my lips and into my mouth. I stroked his tongue with mine and moaned as I wrapped my arms around his neck. Wes groaned as he wrapped an arm around my waist and hoisted me out of my chair. He tugged my body toward his, and the evidence of just how much he really loved my mouth was pressing into my belly.

I pulled my mouth from his and responded, "Noted."

With the silence surrounding us, my stomach growled loudly. I felt my cheeks flush and I bit my lip.

Wes chuckled. "Come on, gorgeous. Let's go feed you."

That afternoon, we ended up at the most popular deli in Rising Sun, according to Wes. As we waited for our chicken salad sandwiches, I pulled out my phone and saw I had received texts from my friends all sending words of encouragement for my first day. I tapped out quick replies to let them all know that everything was going well and that my nerves from earlier that morning had been for nothing. Of course, they responded promptly telling me how they knew that would have been the case.

I tossed my phone back in my purse and looked up to find Wes holding our food. He motioned over to an empty table. As we ate our sandwiches and I found out that Wes was not kidding about the chicken salad being the best in the world, I filled him in on the progress I made on Zane's board design.

"Sounds awesome. I can't wait to see them all."

"I hope the guys like them."

"I'm confident they will. Don't worry," he reassured me. I smiled at him and took another bite of my sandwich. Wes continued, "I wanted to talk to you about the Games. What are the chances I can convince you to come out to them with us?"

I swallowed my food and stared at him. "Excuse me?"

"Blackman Boards will be one of the sponsors for the event. I need to be there, and I would like to have you there with me. The event is four days long, but we'll all need to head out a couple days early. We'd be gone about a week."

Damn.

I put my sandwich down and sat back in my chair, biting my lip. I really wanted to go. I also really did not want to leave Emme alone for an entire week.

Shit.

Wes studied me a minute and then added, "I was also thinking that I'd like to see if Emme's available to go with us. The guys will be debuting the boards from the Fire line up in the Elements Series. The Games will be the perfect place to get shots for our marketing materials. I've seen Emme's work. I asked her yesterday when everyone was over if she could send me some of the pictures she took from this past weekend when we all went riding. She emailed the photos over this morning and I was impressed. She took some amazing shots and I think she'd be able to get some great stuff for us to use for our marketing. I haven't said anything to her about it yet—I wanted to run it by you first."

My eyes got wet and the lump had, once again, formed in my throat. I seriously loved this man so much. He knew I wouldn't leave her and he didn't want me to have to make that decision.

"I love you, Wes. I really, really love you," I declared.

His eyes warmed as he smiled at me and asked, "We're going to Aspen, aren't we?"

"We are definitely going to Aspen."

Twenty

Charley

I WAS IN MY JEEP ON THE WAY TO MEET GREG AND HANNAH FOR brunch. It was Saturday morning and I had just left Wes' house. This was, of course, after I'd had morning sex with him following a marathon of nighttime sex.

Last night was the second night I had spent the night at his place. I was comfortable doing this because earlier in the week, a couple days after Wes asked me to go to Aspen for the X Games, we went to my place and Wes talked to Emme about it. Thankfully, her schedule was open for the dates we'd be in Colorado. The next day she told me that she was going to be spending the night out on Friday night at Zane's so that they could get up early and head to the mountain. He needed training time and she wanted to get some practice shots in before the event. I still did not know the full story on what was going on between the two of them, but she was happy and content so I was giving her some time to get it sorted before pressing her on it. I knew she'd share it when she was ready.

I had finished my first full week at Blackman Boards and I absolutely loved everything about my new job. My co-workers were great, especially Flo. She and I had really hit it off and I always spent a couple minutes chatting with her in the mornings. She was hysterical, and I realized after only two days why Wes put her in that position. Flo was always in a joyful mood, whether it was first thing in the morning or after a long day of work. Her people skills were exceptional, and she could multitask like no other. Wes hit the jackpot with her.

The workdays passed so quickly for me. From the time I got into my office until Wes would come in to get me for lunch, I was consumed with work. We'd come back from lunch and I'd dive right back in until it was time to go home. There were even a couple of days where I asked Wes if we could get lunch to go so I could hurry back to what I had been working on.

Zane, Stone, who I found out is actually named Xander Stone, and Luke had stopped into the offices briefly during the week. I had an opportunity to chat with them about what I had in mind for their designs, but I didn't get much time as they were all in a hurry to get back to training. They were mostly open to whatever I thought would look good and preferred that I put a few things together for them to choose from.

Needless to say, work did not feel much like work and before I knew it the week was over. Seeing as it was only my second night at Wes' place last night, we had a busy night. Tired was an understatement, but Wes made it so worthwhile. I told him before I left this morning that I'd be back after brunch with every intention of catching up on some sleep. He gave me his sexy half grin and kissed me goodbye before I walked out the door.

I was now pulling into the parking lot of the cafe Greg, Hannah, and I were meeting at and I was feeling famished. I guessed all the sex last night really helped with working up an appetite. The minute I stepped inside, I spotted Greg and Hannah.

Standing up to give me a hug, Hannah greeted, "Hey Charley. How have you been?"

"So good, Hannah. How are you?" I asked.

"Same old."

"Girl, you look well and freshly fucked," Greg announced as he gave me a hug.

"Seriously, Gregory? Could you say it a little louder? I'm not sure the other patrons heard," I chastised him.

He just smiled and winked at me.

We all sat down, and the interrogation began. They threw question after question at me, rapid-fire. The waitress finally came over to take our order and I was so grateful for the reprieve.

After placing our orders, I decided to lay it all out for my friends. I realized that's just what they had become. My friends. Even though I hadn't shared much of anything about my life with them when I worked at the diner and the coffee shop, I realized over the last couple weeks working with them and just now with how much interest they were showing in my life that they were true, genuine friends.

So, I gave it to them.

All of it.

I told them all about my parents, Taj, and the reason Emme and I moved here from California. I filled them in on what life was like for me after my parents died, and after Taj had died, but before Wes was a part of it. Then, I gave them the good stuff. I told them all about life since meeting Wes. Of course, they knew what he did to help me pursue my dream career, but they didn't know all the juicy details of our relationship. I gave them enough of that to satisfy their curiosity.

"So now you've got it all," I ended as I took a bite of my French toast.

"Damn. I knew he was something special, but now I'm just jealous," Greg grumbled.

"Did you forget that you've got a man already?" Hannah reminded him.

"No," he sighed as he rolled his eyes and shoveled a forkful of pancakes into his mouth.

Hannah got serious. "In all seriousness, I can't believe everything you've been through. How is it possible you're still standing?"

"It's Wes. He is the reason I'm sitting here with you right now sharing all of this. I'm not sure how he did it, but he helped me learn to live life again," I answered.

"I always knew there was something," Greg started. "You were such a great listener anytime I needed to vent to you about my parents and the whole situation with Tony, but you had this look about you sometimes. Like you could burst into tears at any moment. You always managed to recover quickly, and I'd think that I made it up in my head. I'm so happy for you, girl, so happy that Wes helped you heal."

I thought back to the times Greg would go off on a tangent about his parents and I knew precisely what he meant when he said I was about ready to fall apart several times. I hated that his parents couldn't be accepting of his relationship with Tony. Life was too short. I would give anything to have my family back in my life.

I tried to blink away the tears threatening to fall as I looked at him and agreed, "Me too."

"Okay. So, tell us all about the new job," Hannah changed topics.

I was so thankful for her quick thinking. I was glad they finally knew the story, but I didn't want to dwell on the sadness. So, I told them all about the new job before they updated me on all the happenings in their lives, the diner, and the coffee shop as we finished eating.

"It was so good to see you both," I insisted as I hugged Hannah and Greg just outside the cafe.

"You too," Hannah shot back.

"I'm calling your ass soon and we are going out. I'll bring

Tony, Hannah can bring her flavor of the week, and you bring Wes," Greg offered.

"Sounds like a plan to me," I responded. "See you soon."

"Bye, Charley," they called in unison as I waved to them and walked to my car.

Fifteen minutes later, I pulled my Jeep into the driveway at Wes' place and walked into the house through the open garage door.

I found Wes in the living room lounging on the couch, his legs propped up on the coffee table, and a book in his hand. He looked up as I walked into the room.

"Hi, gorgeous," he greeted softly as he closed the book and set it down.

"Hey, honey," I answered, making my way over to him.

"How was brunch?"

"After the marathon last night, I needed sustenance. Brunch provided that so I'm good now."

"And your friends?" he asked, holding his hand out to wrap around my waist and pull me into his lap.

I smiled at him. I loved that he cared enough about me to ask about them. "They're good. I filled them in on everything. They now know about my parents and Taj. They also know about you. Preliminarily, I get the feeling that you passed the test, but Greg is planning a get together with himself, Tony, Hannah, whoever her date may be, and us. He wants us all to go out together. I think he wants to check you out for himself."

"Sure. Just let me know when," he immediately responded.

"Really? You'll go?" I marveled. I was surprised by his quick answer and nonchalance.

"Why wouldn't I? Aren't they your friends?" he countered.

"Yes, but I didn't think you'd actually want to go."

"Do you want to go?"

"Well, of course. I mean, I've just recently started feeling like a normal human being again and if I'm going to be living in this town for the foreseeable future, I think it's best I maintain friendships with people who I not only like, but who also seem to care about me."

"Then that's even more of a reason why I will go. When are you going to realize I'll always do my best to give you whatever you need, Charley?"

"Today. I realized it at brunch, actually. I think it's just taking me some time to get used to the idea."

He gave me his sexy grin and promised, "I'll see to it that you get constant reminders then."

"Much obliged, Mr. Blackman."

I leaned in to kiss him and shifted my body to straddle his thighs. His hands went to my ass as mine fisted in his hair. I rolled my hips over his already hardened length. He groaned. I continued for a bit until Wes' hands moved to the hem of my sweater and removed it. He took my bra off and pressed his face into my chest, sprinkling kisses over every inch of my breasts. I wanted to feel his skin next to mine so I removed his shirt. Running my hands along the hard, lean muscle of his arms and chest only left me wanting more.

"You are so beautiful, Wes. And I mean that in every way that matters. Not only do you have an incredible body, but you are also so good to me," I shared.

"Seeing how this body is all yours, baby, I'm glad you like it."

"I really want you inside me now."

"Not going to say no to that, Charley. Lift up a minute," he instructed.

I lifted up and he pulled my bottoms off followed by his own. My hands were on his shoulders and he slid his fingers through my wetness.

"Always ready for me," he rasped out.

"I can't wait any longer," I confessed, moving one of my hands to him and positioning the silky-smooth tip of his cock between my legs.

On the initial downward glide, I felt an overwhelming sense of relief. Despite my earlier demand to get him inside me, I didn't move for a moment as I soaked that up and took it in. I could have stayed like that and been completely content.

Wes pulled me out of my own head and urged, "Ride me, gorgeous."

I did as he asked and rode him. Slow at first, followed by harder and faster. Wes put one hand between us and found my clit with his thumb. I found that feeling growing and knew I wasn't far from reaching my orgasm.

"I'm going to come, Wes," I rasped, my eyes fixed on his.

He didn't relent on my clit and easily pushed me over the edge. Only then did he ease up on my body as he watched me come down from the high.

"Didn't think it was possible for me to get any harder, baby. Then, I hear that raspy voice say my name right before you come and I feel it shoot straight to my dick. It's the most beautiful sound out of that pretty mouth."

I barely had any time to recover before his magnificent hands gripped my hips and held me firmly. I braced myself with my hands on his shoulders while he thrust non-stop into me. He was relentless and managed to work me up enough that I felt a second orgasm building. His fingers put a bruising grip on my hips that hurt just a bit and I knew he was right there with me. I kept one hand firmly gripping his shoulder while I used the other to reach behind me to cup his balls and squeeze them.

"Charley," he growled. "Fuck."

"Wes."

I came apart again as he, too, found his orgasm beneath me.

I collapsed on top of Wes and struggled to catch my breath. He held me there while he kissed my neck and shoulder. A few minutes had passed when he finally stood, still inside me with my legs now wrapped around his waist, and walked toward the bedroom. He didn't put me down until he entered the bathroom.

"Go ahead and get cleaned up so we can take a nap," he suggested.

"Okay."

I got cleaned up. One of Wes' t-shirts was folded on the edge of the sink, so I slipped it over my head. Walking out of the bathroom, I found Wes waiting in the bed for me. He was on his side, the covers at his waist, and he'd folded the covers back for me to climb under. As beautiful as he looked, I could tell something was wrong.

I climbed in next to him and fell to my back. When I tried to pull the covers over myself, Wes stopped me.

Nervously, I asked, "What's wrong, Wes?"

He didn't say anything. He just searched my face, concern littering his. His eyes moved from my face down my body where his hand was sliding under the shirt I was wearing. Wes still said nothing, but pushed the shirt up and exposed my belly. He winced as he looked down at me. I began to feel self-conscious, so I moved my hands to cover myself when he stopped me.

"Wes?" I called.

Finally, he spoke. "Marked you. Fuck, gorgeous, I'm so sorry."

"What? What are you talking about?"

He bent his head down and placed gentle kisses across my abdomen. He put his hand on one of my hips and with a strained voice he said, "Here, on both sides. I was too rough out there and put marks on your beautiful body."

I sat up on my elbows and looked down at my hips. There were two marks, one on each hip where his thumbs had pressed in. I remembered his grip getting tight right before he came.

"Look at me, Wes."

He closed his eyes for a moment before he looked at me.

"I'm fine. I don't even feel it. You didn't try to hurt me, and I know you never would," I tried to reassure him.

"I am so sorry. I would never hurt you like that, Charley. Ever."

"Wes, I know. It's okay. Honestly, if you weren't so upset about it right now, I'd say I think it's kind of sexy."

"What the fuck, baby?"

"You'd never hurt me, Wes. It makes me feel good to know I made you lose control for that brief moment. Trust me, honey. It's all good and it's kind of hot."

He stared at me like I was a crazy person. "I don't want to damage your ego now, but there's no excuse for me losing control and putting marks like this on your body. I'm glad you're feeling good about this and that I didn't really hurt you, but trust me, that is never happening again."

I fell back onto the pillow, curled my body into his, and wrapped an arm around his waist. He stayed tense, so I snuggled farther into him and ran my fingers up across his body. After a few minutes, he loosened up, put his head on the pillow, wrapped an arm around my back, and hauled me into his side. He gently traced his fingers across my back and hips as I rested my head and hand on his chest.

"I love you, Charley."

"Love you too, Wes."

"Get some sleep, gorgeous."

"Okay, honey."

It took a few minutes as my mind raced replaying the conversation we just had. I knew Wes would always protect me and that I'd always be safe in his arms. When those thoughts finally settled in my mind, I drifted off to sleep.

Twenty-One

Charley

After spending a lazy weekend with Wes that went by too quickly, the next few days of work went by even faster. It was now time to kick some ass. This was mostly because I decided that I wanted to have my designs on the boards at the X Games. It finally sunk in that this was what I wanted my whole life. I had the opportunity of a lifetime and could not let it go to waste. I told Wes about my decision and, as expected, he supported it wholeheartedly.

The first few days after making my decision I spent my time designing, making adjustments, and then reviewing those designs. Once I came up with some that I thought would not only represent the Fire line well but also would pay a bit of a tribute to the riders themselves, I took the designs to Wes. I had only ever had a few interactions with each of the guys and I didn't know if my interpretations of them were completely accurate. Given that Wes grew up with them, I figured he'd be the best source before I showed the guys the designs. I didn't want to insult any of them.

Before showing Wes what I came up with I made him promise me that he'd give me his honest opinion. The last thing I wanted was him to just approve of the designs because he was worried about my feelings. Not pushing me to be the best I could be would not benefit anyone. It wouldn't help me become a force to be reckoned with in my career and it wouldn't help Wes to sell boards that didn't have awesome graphics. Thankfully, he agreed to give me brutal honesty.

With that, I showed Wes the results of my hard work. He absolutely loved what I came up with for Zane and felt it suited him perfectly. For Stone, though, he gave me a few ideas to help tweak the design to fit him a bit more. There was a little more to the story with Stone that Wes didn't share, claiming it wasn't his story to tell, but he gave me enough for me to know the direction I needed to go with the design. He went through the rest of the graphics not specifically slated for Zane or Stone and found a couple that could be used for Luke's boards. Since Luke rode big air and the Elements Series boards for big air, the Air line, wouldn't be ready for testing until after the Games, Wes decided to put some of my designs on boards already in production that were meant specifically for the type of riding Luke did. Wes then picked out his favorite designs that he wanted to use for the Fire line boards that would be mass produced. In addition to those, assuming Zane and Stone were happy with their board designs, Blackman Boards would offer those as limited edition boards.

After I received input from Wes, I got to work on the revision for Stone's board design. It didn't take long at all now that I had a bit more information to work with. I completed the revision, went back to Wes and got his seal of approval, and put a call out to Zane, Stone, and Luke. Since it was crunch time and we did not have much time left before the final designs needed to be sent down and put on the boards, the guys agreed to stop in later that day to take a look at what I had come up with. I hoped they'd give their approval at the same time.

It was about a half hour before I was set to go home that

day when they arrived. They looked wiped when they came in.

"Looks like you guys had a hell of a day," I pointed out.

"We've been training hard since Monday after the new year. Today Stone and I were testing out a bunch of new tricks using a shortened pipe and the airbag. It's a little easier on the body when you test on the airbag, but since we're attempting new tricks it can be a bit more physically demanding," Zane explained.

"It can also make you question how far you should push things. If you keep practicing a new trick and it's just not working, you begin to wonder if you should move on to something else. It's a good thing and a bad thing all at once," Stone added.

Luke chimed in, "I worked on the airbag too, but not on the pipe. Big air is completely different. Regardless, we're all beat at this point in the day. It's time to recuperate and get back at it tomorrow."

"Well, I'm hoping that you get it figured out and are ready to rock in a couple weeks. More than that, I'm hoping you all are going to be able to do it in style. I've worked up some designs for your boards and wanted to get your opinion before we pushed them out to production."

"Sweet. Let's see them."

I showed them what I had come up with and they were blown away. Those were the actual words they all used. It was safe to say I had their stamp of approval, the three of them very satisfied with what I had put together.

I told them I'd get everything finalized so the boards would be done and ready to go before we left for Aspen and wished them luck on the rest of their training.

Stone and Luke excused themselves so that they could stop over to see Wes. Zane hung back for a minute. I had a feeling I knew where this was going.

"Hey Charley, I wanted to talk to you a minute about something," he cautioned.

"Sure, Zane. What's up?" I asked.

"It's about Emme. I'm not going to sit here and play games. I like her. A lot. But there's something going on with her that I can't figure out. She's only given me very little to go on and I am stuck. I want to pursue something more serious with her, but she is so cautious and hesitant. The girl won't budge."

I took a deep breath, not knowing what to say.

Zane spoke up again, "I'm not looking for you to betray any confidence of hers, but please give me something, Charley. What am I up against here? Is this going to go nowhere?"

"It's pretty bad, Zane. She's fragile. I can't tell you her story, but I will tell you this. I don't know if Wes has told you anything about me, but I came here to Wyoming because I *needed* to leave California. Ten years ago, both of my parents died in a car accident. I was devastated, but I got through it because of Emme, Nikki, Monroe, and most importantly, my big brother, Taj. Not quite a year ago, Taj died. Part of what I dealt with surrounding Taj's death is connected to Emme, but she's been through far worse."

Zane pulled in a sharp breath.

I kept going.

"I don't know you that well, Zane, but from what I do know you seem like a really great guy. If you are anything like Wes, I know that I'm not wrong in assuming you'd take care of Emme in all the ways that matter. I feel very lucky right now. Wes found me, and in that, I found a way to be happy again. I want that for my best friend. I need to believe that deep down she also wants it. Please don't give up on Emme. I promise you, no matter how long it takes, she's worth the fight."

He nodded.

"Thanks, Charley. I'm going to head over and say goodbye

to Wes before I leave, but awesome job on the designs. I can't wait to see the finished product."

"No problem, Zane. And thanks for the compliment."

Zane walked through the door connecting my office to Wes' as I followed behind him. Luke and Stone were both still there and, when Zane and I walked in, they looked to us.

"All good?" Wes asked.

I nodded.

"Some seriously kick-ass stuff she put together, man," Zane announced.

"No joke. We've been doing this for how many years now and have yet to see anything that good on any board ever," Luke chimed in.

My jaw dropped. Wes looked to me, smiled, and winked.

"Wow," I mumbled under my breath. I couldn't believe they thought it was that good. I was humbled by and so appreciative of their kind words.

"Alright, Wes. I need to get out of here. It's been a long fucking day and I need to eat," Stone declared.

"Okay, guys. Happy to hear it's going well out there for the most part. I'm going to try to make it out to one of your training sessions at the end of this week to check in and see what you've got planned. We'll get the designs over so they are ready to go as soon as the boards are finished in production. I was a bit worried since we were getting so close. Thankfully, since Charley did such a great job on them from the start we have now got enough time that it won't be too hard to finish them before we have to head to Aspen," Wes explained.

"Awesome. Heading out now," Luke said. He offered Wes a chin lift and directed his attention to me. "Later, Charley."

"Bye, Luke," I answered.

"Catch ya later, guys," Stone stated as he followed behind Luke.

Zane turned so he was facing me, reached an arm out

to put his hand on my shoulder, squeezed, and spoke quietly. "Thanks again, Charley. Just so you know, I'm holding you to your word. You said she's worth it; I'm going to keep fighting."

My heart melted, and I was overwhelmed with joy. I was so excited I squeezed his wrist at my shoulder, gave him a hug and reassured, "It may take some time, but I promise you won't regret it."

He pulled back, squeezed both of my shoulders this time, and nodded. He turned to Wes, gave him a chin lift, and walked toward the office door as he called, "Later, Wes."

"Later."

I had the biggest smile in the world on my face as Zane walked out. Zane wasn't going to give up on Emme and all of the guys loved the designs I came up with. I turned to Wes and noticed he wasn't smiling.

In fact, he looked a little angry.

I frowned.

"What's wrong?" I asked.

"What was that all about?" he scowled.

"I'm sorry?"

"With you and Zane. The whispering, the touching and squeezing of shoulders, and the hugging. What…was…that…about?"

My eyes nearly popped out of my head. Wes was jealous. "You can't be serious, Wes."

"Completely," he answered, his voice devoid of any emotion.

I stood there and stared at him in disbelief. After taking a deep breath, I stated, "I just received overwhelming support from you and your friends about the designs I put together being worthy of boards that are going to be seen by millions of people. That is *huge* news for me and I'm sorry, but I'm happy about that. Your friend just spent a few minutes in my office asking me about my best friend, with whom he's interested in pursuing a relationship. I told him she has been through a lot and that he'd need to be patient with her, but that she would be worth it. Just now, what you saw was him telling me that he was going to put in the effort and pursue things with her. I'm sorry if what happened made you uncomfortable, but that was not my intention. I simply reacted to the news that my friend might finally get what I know she so desperately needs...that she'd finally get what I got when you walked into my life."

I started to feel my throat constrict on my last few words and knew I was going to break down if I didn't get out of there. With the tears welling up in my eyes, I looked one last time at his face and turned to walk back to my office.

"Charley, wait."

I stopped but didn't turn around.

"Look at me, gorgeous."

I turned around to look at him as a single tear fell from each eye. Through the wetness in my eyes, I could see his jaw clenching.

"I'm sorry," he lamented. "I was wrong. I wasn't prepared for what I'd feel in seeing another man's hands on you and I overreacted."

"Zane is your friend. He's not just some random man."

"I know that, Charley. And I know he'd never cross that line."

"So, you know he'd never cross that line, but you doubt me and my loyalty to you?" I questioned, shock registering and filtering through my voice.

He stared at me and said nothing.

And then I knew.

"You don't trust me," I stated, my voice just barely above a whisper.

"It's not that," he insisted as he started to stride toward me. I kept my eyes on him as I took a step back with each step he took toward me.

I put a hand out in front of me cautioning him to stop. "Then what is it?" I countered. "Because it sure as hell feels that way."

He stopped and stood there with a mixture of emotions running through his features. Anger. Sadness. Guilt, maybe.

"Charley, I'm sorry. This was a great day for you. I don't want to ruin it by arguing. Please don't walk away from me."

His voice was strained on his last statement. I realized then what was going through his head.

"Oh my God. You think I'm like Dana," I accused, my voice now significantly louder than before.

"No. Not at all. You are nothing like her," he answered with conviction.

"I know that. I hear you saying it, but I'm not certain you believe it. You think I'm going to leave you just like she did."

He stood there in shock.

Yep.

He couldn't deny what I was saying.

We stared at each other for several minutes before I broke the silence and spoke.

"I'm going to go home now, Wes."

"Charley..." he croaked out.

I cut him off. "No, Wes. Please don't say anything else. Think about what you just did to me. Aside from Emme, Monroe, and Nikki, I have no family left. They are all dead," my voice cracked. I took in a breath and continued through the tears now streaming down my face, "I told you what you've done for me. Over the past couple weeks, you've become my family. Why? Why do you think I would ever do something to destroy that?"

He closed his eyes and dropped his head in defeat. When he opened his eyes again to look at me, I could see the pain registered all over his face. It broke my heart to see him like that.

But it broke my heart more to know that he didn't trust in my love for him.

I turned, walked to my office, grabbed my things, and scurried off to the elevator.

Wes didn't follow me.

Twenty-Two

Charley

THE PROBLEM WITH NOT HAVING A PLAN IN ANY EMOTIONAL situation is that you realize far too late that having an actual plan would have been a brilliant idea. This was my current predicament and the precise reason I was now standing in the bathroom around the corner from the elevator on the first floor of the Blackman Boards building.

I stepped off the elevator onto the first floor about five minutes ago and planned to walk out to my car when I realized I was going to need to walk past Flo. There was no way I was going to be able to walk out without her noticing that something was up. Since I'm not so great at handling this kind of pressure, I snuck off to the bathroom to give myself some time to come up with a game plan.

So far, I'd only come up with staying in the bathroom until everyone left. Unfortunately, if I didn't leave, my car would remain outside and then I'd likely have Wes looking for me.

Or maybe he wouldn't.

I wasn't sure which would be worse.

Finally, I realized I had no other means of escape and would need to face the music. Heck, if I didn't do it now, Flo would catch me on the way back in tomorrow. I looked over myself in the mirror, and though I didn't look horrible, I absolutely didn't look my best. She'd know something was up. I turned, walked out the bathroom door, and made my way to the front door.

"Charley girl, what's wrong? Did the guys not approve of the designs you came up with?" Flo asked as I approached.

I told her that morning that I was nearing completion on the designs and would likely be showing them to Wes and the guys today.

"Quite the opposite, Flo."

"That's great news. So, what's with the puffy eyes?"

"Wes and I had our first argument. But, I'm not sure I should be talking about this with you considering he's not only my boss but yours as well," I answered honestly.

"If you need someone to talk to, Charley, you talk to me. It won't prevent me from doing my job and doing it right."

I nodded.

"Okay, I'll keep that in mind. I will be honest, though. I don't think I'm ready to talk about this now. I haven't had enough time to really process it myself yet."

"You've got my number, girl. You call me. I want to know everything is alright."

"Thanks, Flo. I'll see you tomorrow."

She returned a friendly smile.

As I walked out the front door, my phone rang in my purse. Pulling it out of my purse, I looked at the display and didn't recognize the number. I decided to answer anyway.

"Hello," I said as I walked to my Jeep.

"Charley, it's Tony," I heard come through the line.

I was a bit thrown to hear Tony's voice over the phone. "Tony? What's up?"

His voice, laced with worry and anxiety, came through the line at lightning speed. "Greg was in a car accident. We were on our way home and I was following in my car behind him.

Charley, it was so bad. Someone drove through a red light and ran right into the driver's side door. They've rushed him off to Rising Sun Medical Center. Someone needs to call his parents, but I'm not sure I can do it," he panicked.

"I'm on my way now, Tony. I'll call Hannah to let her know and I'll meet you there in fifteen minutes," I assured him.

I called Hannah, told her what I knew, and she said she was calling Mark to cover her at the lodge. I threw my phone back in my purse, started my Jeep, and sped out of the parking lot toward the hospital.

Arriving in record time, I walked from the parking deck to the emergency room entrance and sent Emme a quick text to let her know where I was and why I was there. I added that I'd likely be home very late since I didn't quite know yet how bad it was. She replied almost instantly and told me that she was heading home from a shoot, but to keep her updated on Greg's status. She also said that she was going to stop in at home since it was on the way to the hospital so that she could change her clothes and drop off her equipment, but that she'd meet me at the hospital as soon as she could get there.

The sliding glass doors to the emergency room opened as I approached. I walked in and immediately saw Tony. He looked devastated. I went to him, wrapped my arms around him, and just held him.

After a few minutes of standing in silence, he spoke. "I can't live without him, Charley," he croaked.

"You won't have to. He's going to be all right. He'll be fine," I stated, not sure I believed my own words. I just knew that I needed to be strong for Tony and tell him what he needed to hear in that moment. "Come on, let's go sit and wait until they come get us."

We sat. Twenty minutes later, Hannah came barreling through the door.

"What happened?" she asked, tears streaming down her face.

"T-boned. Someone ran a red light and drove right into him. I was following behind him and watched the whole thing happen. It was like slow motion. I couldn't do anything to stop it or help him," Tony answered her. "He's in surgery right now. He's in such bad shape. Oh God, I hope he pulls through."

I couldn't help myself. In that moment, I started to lose it. Why was this happening? Greg was such a great guy and he was now fighting for his life.

"His parents," Tony began to fret. "Charley. Hannah. They need to know he is here. I know things are strained among them, but they need to know their son is struggling to survive right now. You know they don't agree with our relationship. They won't want to talk to me."

A deep voice then chimed in, "I'll call them for you."

I looked up to see Wes standing there, his face filled with concern. At the sight of him, I completely lost it. Wes immediately had his arms around me and I cried. Body-wracking sobs tore through me and I held on to Wes like my life depended on it. Several minutes later, I started to calm down and Wes finally spoke to me.

"Gorgeous, let me call Greg's parents and tell them what's going on. I'll be two minutes."

I nodded.

Wes got Greg's parents' phone number from Tony and walked out to call them. I sat there letting it sink in that he was here. I had walked out of his office after our first argument not much more than an hour ago and here he was by my side comforting me.

Minutes later, Wes walked back in and told us that he spoke with Greg's father. He and his wife were on their way to the hospital.

Wes sat down next to me and held my hand. I squeezed his

and looked up at him.

"How did you know?" I asked.

"I went to your place to make things right. Em was there and she told me you were here. I came right over."

"Thank you, Wes."

"I should have been with you," he sighed. "I'm sorry I wasn't."

"I left you, so it was a bit out of your control."

He winced at my words and I realized what I had just said.

"Wes…that's not what I meant," I clarified.

"Not now, Charley. Let's focus on Greg. We'll talk about us later."

I nodded.

Tony was sitting in a chair across from us. He stood and started to walk. "I'll be back. I'm losing my mind right now and just need to walk a minute."

"You need company?" Hannah asked.

He shook his head.

She nodded. "I'm here if you need me."

Tony took off around the corner and down the hall.

At that moment, Emme walked in followed seconds later by Greg's parents. I had never met them, but Hannah recognized them from back when she and Greg were in high school together. I could see a little bit of Greg in each of his parents. My stomach knotted thinking of him.

"Hi Mr. and Mrs. Williams," Hannah greeted. "I'm not sure if you remember me. Hannah Torres. I went to school with Greg."

"Yes, Hannah. I remember you," Greg's mom replied. "Have you heard anything?"

Hannah shook her head.

"These are some of Greg's other friends," Hannah said waving her hand to all of us. "Charley, who used to work with Greg at the diner, her boyfriend, Wes, and her best friend, Emme."

His parents simply nodded their heads in our direction.

"I'm sorry we are meeting under such horrible circumstances, Mr. and Mrs. Williams," I lamented as I stood, reaching my hand out to shake each of theirs.

Just then, a door opened behind the Williams and a surgeon walked out.

Wes stood next to me and held my hand.

"Family of Gregory Williams?" he asked.

Greg's parents looked to him and answered, "That's us."

"Mr. and Mrs. Williams, I'm Dr. Weaver. Would you prefer we go have a seat somewhere more private?"

"Please just tell me the news," Mr. Williams implored.

The surgeon nodded and took a deep breath.

I braced myself.

"Your son experienced horrible trauma to his body. The impact from the crash resulted in lots of broken bones and several internal bleeding injuries. We've managed to take care of the internal injuries, but there is a lot of swelling, particularly in his brain that we are extremely concerned about. As a result, we've put him in a medically induced coma to give his body time to rest and hopefully help him heal. The next twenty-four to forty-eight hours will be critical. We'll need to monitor him closely and see how his body responds over the next couple of days. We should know more then."

"Oh God."

I looked up to see Tony had returned and caught Dr. Weaver's update on Greg's status. He croaked out those words as he broke down into tears. Hannah immediately walked over to him and offered what little comfort she could.

Looking to Greg's parents, I could tell they were in shock. His mother finally spoke and asked, "Can we see him?"

"Yes," he answered. "Only two at a time and for brief visits, though, please. And I want you to prepare yourselves for what you are going to see. He's hooked up to a lot of monitors and machines. His body has taken a beating. Odds are that he's not going to look a lot like you remember. You can follow me this way."

Mr. and Mrs. Williams followed Dr. Weaver through the door to see their son.

"Gorgeous?" I heard Wes say from beside me.

I turned to look at him. He looked like he was in pain.

"What's wrong?" I asked.

"Give it to me, Charley. I know you are about to break down. You lost your parents in a car accident, you recently lost your brother, and now you are scared you're going to lose Greg, too."

"I'm okay, Wes. Really. I'm fine."

"Charley, you are not fine. I know this because your hand is squeezing mine so tight I can't feel my fingers anymore."

I immediately loosened my grip on Wes' hand.

"I'm sorry," I murmured.

"Don't need you to be sorry, baby. I need you to get it out. Forget what happened earlier today and give it to me. Whatever it takes, whatever you need. I will get you through this. Give me the burden so I can carry it for you."

With those words, I couldn't control it any longer.

My bottom lip began to tremble and I let him have it. "Oh, Wes. What if he doesn't make it?" I worried, my voice cracking and my body falling into his. My throat was tight, my nose stinging, and my eyes were filled with tears. "I can't lose anyone else, Wes. I can't go through this again."

"I know," he consoled me as he held me, running his hands up and down my arms. "From everything you've told me about him, Greg seems like a tough guy. He will be okay, Charley."

"What if he's not?" I pleaded.

"Right now, he's fighting for his life, Charley. I know he's important to you. You need to fight right beside him."

Aside from earlier today in his office, Wes was always rational and logical. I knew what he was telling me was true. I couldn't give up on Greg while he was struggling to survive.

"Please. You have to let me see him," I heard uttered from behind me.

I turned around to see Tony was speaking to Greg's parents.

"We've already told the staff members that you are not permitted to be in his room," Mrs. Williams asserted.

"Mr. and Mrs. Williams, with all due respect, this isn't what Greg would want," Hannah chimed in.

"I'm sorry, Hannah. This isn't up for debate. I will not support this charade," Mrs. Williams responded. Her husband stood beside her and looked absolutely devastated.

I was mortified by what I was hearing. Pure anguish washed over Tony's face.

I couldn't control myself. I walked over to the group and spoke.

"Excuse me, but you do realize that the only reason you are here right now and were able to be the first ones in to see your son is because of Tony? He was the one who pushed to have someone call you because he knows that that was the right thing to do, despite your feelings on his relationship with your son."

"Charley? I believe that's your name, isn't it?" Mrs. Williams asked me as I nodded. "You haven't even known my son a year. What makes you think you have the right to speak to me like that?"

"You're right. I only met Greg last year, but from the moment I met him, I knew what an incredible person he was. Somehow, despite the hatred you are spewing, you managed to raise an incredibly loving and genuine man. You may not like what I am about to say, but someone needs to tell you to wake up before it's too late. The reason I didn't meet Greg sooner is because I didn't live here. I moved here after my brother died. He was the only blood family I had left after my parents were killed in a car accident ten years ago. Unfortunately, for me and my brother, our parents were pronounced dead at the scene.

Lucky for you, Greg was not. When he pulls through this and realizes what you've done and how you are treating the man he loves it's likely you will have irrevocably damaged what was left of your already strained relationship with him."

I finished speaking to her, went to Tony and hugged him. I whispered in his ear, "I'm sorry for the outburst, Tony. As much as I want to stay here, I need some air. It's suffocating for me. There's too much pain for me in a hospital. I hope you get in to see him. I'm praying for Greg. I will be back, but I need some time."

"I understand, Charley. Thank you. Whether I get in to see him or not I'm not leaving without him," he answered.

I hugged Hannah, told her I needed to go, and asked her to call me if anything changed. I looked to Emme. Her eyes were filled with unshed tears. She knew where my head was.

"You okay, sweets?" she asked, fighting to stay strong.

I shook my head. I wouldn't be until I knew Greg was on the mend.

"Do you need me to go with you?" she offered.

"I need some time," I answered.

"Okay, I'll stay here with Hannah and Tony. One of us will call if we hear any news. Call me if you need me."

"Thanks, Em. Love you."

"Love you, too, Charley."

I turned back around to see Greg's parents watching me. His father looked broken and his mother was wound tight. "I know you don't want my advice, but I'm going to give it anyway. You love your son? Stop hating what you don't understand and accept what you do. And that's love. Love your son and accept his choice in a partner before you lose him forever."

I turned to Wes. "Can you take me home?"

He nodded, took my hand, and walked me out of the hospital.

Twenty-Three

Charley

I walked through the front door of the condo. Wes was right behind me. I was in no state to drive myself home after leaving the hospital, so I left my car there and had him bring me back. Even though we had had our argument not more than a few hours ago, I was in no position to be a hero for the sake of winning an argument.

I felt like a zombie as I walked down the hall toward my bedroom. I could still feel Wes right behind me. We hadn't spoken since before we left the hospital. My thoughts were overwhelming me, and I think Wes knew that I needed that time to try to process everything that had happened.

Once I stepped foot inside my bedroom door, I stopped, and it all hit me at once. My head fell forward as my eyes closed and I felt the harsh reality of my life. It seemed that no matter how hard I tried to stay positive, life kept dealing me blow after devastating blow. I wasn't sure how much more I could take. My body began to shake, the sobbing overtook me, and I was immediately hauled up into Wes' arms.

"When you cry, it's like my heart is being ripped out of my chest, Charley," Wes shared as he carried me to the bed.

He settled me on the bed before getting a t-shirt out of my

dresser. When he returned, he removed my jacket, shirt, and bra and replaced them with the t-shirt. I fell to the side and my head hit the pillow. Wes pulled my heels off, unzipped my skirt, and pulled it down my legs. Then he removed his jacket and boots and climbed into the bed with me.

With his arms wrapped around me, I snuggled into him and continued to cry. I don't know how much time passed, but it wasn't until Wes began to gently trace the skin at my hips with his fingertips that I finally started to calm down.

After sitting in silence for a long time with my face pressed to Wes' chest, I spoke. "Isn't it crazy how sometimes all it takes is for something horrible to happen for things to be put into perspective?" I asked.

Wes squeezed my hip in response.

"I'm sorry about what happened at work today," I apologized.

"Charley, you have nothing to be sorry for. I was an asshole. I know you think I don't trust you, but that's not the case. I do. Seeing another man's hands on you was not something I was prepared for. In this case, it was Zane and I do know that it's not only him that would never cross that line, but you as well. I was wrong, and I should have handled it better than I did."

"That may be true, Wes. But, I shouldn't have walked out on you in the middle of it. I've always been one to react first to my emotions and think about them later. My brother always told me I needed to work on that. I can't fault you for having that same tendency."

"I can't promise that I'll never react negatively to another man's hands on you again, but I do promise that I'll do my best to be mindful of how my reaction to that will affect you. I love you so much, Charley, and I'm not willing to have you walk out on me because of my ignorance of your feelings."

"I appreciate your apology, Wes. Thank you. Please know

that you mean a lot to me. If I walk away from an argument, it's not the same as me walking away from you. I promise that if that time should come, I would at least have the decency to have a conversation with you about it. I will not just abandon you without a word," I tried to reassure him.

He pulled me tighter to his body.

"Thank you again for being there for me tonight at the hospital," I began. "I'm not sure I would have handled it half as well as I did, which is saying something since I didn't handle it well at all, if you hadn't been there."

"I hate that you even had to be there. I'm sorry about your friend, Charley. Whatever you need me to do to help make this easier for you, I will."

"I just hope Greg's parents realize what they are doing. Tony loves him and makes him happy. If for no other reason, how could they not just put aside their pride for the sake of their son's happiness? He's not harming anyone." My voice cracked at the despair I felt.

"I don't know, baby. My parents have always supported Elle and me. I can't imagine how Greg must feel to not have that. If you want me to, I can get Tony into that hospital room," he responded.

I pulled back from him so that I could look up in his face. He glanced down at me.

"Really?" I asked.

He nodded. "My mom was a nurse up until she and my dad started a family. After Elle and I were grown, she went back to working part-time. Not because she needed to, but because she enjoyed the work and caring for people. She officially retired a few years ago, but occasionally goes in to volunteer. The staff knows her well and could easily be persuaded to listen to her. You want it done, Charley, I'll make it happen."

My eyes filled with tears *again*. "I love you so much, Wes. I don't want anyone to get into trouble, though."

"Don't worry about that. I'll take care of it," he insisted.

I smiled up at him and then snuggled back into his body. Minutes later, we heard the front door opening and Emme calling my name. She knocked on my bedroom door a few seconds later. Wes went to the door and opened it.

"Oh, I'm sorry," she said. "I didn't—"

"It's okay, Em. We were just talking. Any news on Greg?" I asked as I sat up in the bed.

She shook her head. "Nothing new yet. Tony got in to see him, though, and said he looks awful."

"How did he get in?" I asked.

She smiled. "After you left, Mr. Williams sort of lost it... on his wife. He told her that he was sick of the tension and turmoil in their family. He said that you were right and that she basically needed to get her head out of her ass. Essentially, he said that if their son pulled through this, they needed to make every effort to mend the relationship before there's nothing left. I guess you got through to one of them."

"Wow. Really? And she allowed Tony in?"

"Not exactly. Once Mr. Williams put her in her place, she walked out of the hospital and Mr. Williams made arrangements with the staff. He told them that Tony was more than welcome to go in to see Greg. Tony was so relieved. He's planning to spend the night at the hospital, but wanted me to tell you how grateful he was for what you said," she answered.

"Well, maybe something good will come of this after all," I mumbled.

"Zane texted me while I was at the hospital. When I told him where I was and what happened, he asked if there was anything he could do. I had my spare key for your car, so Luke dropped Zane off at the hospital. He followed behind me and drove your car back for you."

"Zane's here?" Wes asked.

"Yeah, he's out in the kitchen. He said he needed more

food after today's training."

Wes looked at me. "I'll give you two some time to talk. I'm going to go talk to Zane for a few."

I nodded.

Wes walked out of the room and shut the door. Emme came and got in bed with me.

"How are you holding up, sweets?" she asked.

"Exhausted. I think I'm all cried out at this point," I answered.

She put her hand on mine and squeezed.

"Coming here was your chance to start over. Greg is tough, Charley. He's going to pull through and you are going to get a different ending this time."

"I hope you are right, Em. For now, I'm happy to hear that Tony can be with him."

"Yeah, me too. Tony really couldn't thank you enough for saying what you did to Greg's parents," she stressed.

"I couldn't control myself, honestly. I could see Greg's dad was distraught and would likely be more easily swayed. I didn't think it would happen that quickly. His wife, though? She's got a bad attitude. Standing there listening to her I got so angry. She doesn't realize that her son is alive and that's what her focus should be on. What I wouldn't give to have my family back," I sighed.

"I know, sweets. I miss your parents so much, but more than anything I wish Taj were still here, too."

The tears spilled over her cheeks and I reached out to hug her. "Emme..."

"I'm so sorry, Charley. I'm so sorry he's not here anymore," she just barely managed to get out.

I held her and cried with her. We stayed like that for a while. Eventually, we calmed ourselves down.

"Are you okay?" I asked.

"I will be," she answered.

"Alright, let's head out there with the guys then."

She nodded.

I grabbed a pair of shorts, pulled them on, and Emme and I made our way out to the kitchen.

As we walked into the kitchen, Wes put his arm around me and pulled me into his side. Zane was sitting at one of the bar stools.

"Thanks for meeting Emme and driving my car back here, Zane. I really appreciate it," I said to him.

"Don't mention it. I'm sorry to hear about your friend," he offered his sentiments.

I nodded and curled into Wes' body. He squeezed me a little tighter.

"Sorry, but I've got to head out. I've got a long day ahead of me tomorrow," Zane declared.

"I'll just grab my keys and I'll be right back," Emme noted as she turned to walk out of the kitchen.

"Don't worry about it, sweetheart. I'm going to take Wes' truck home, so you don't need to go back out tonight," Zane advised.

Emme looked to Wes and back to Zane.

"Are you sure?" she asked. "You did me a favor. It's really not a problem for me to take you home."

He gave her a sexy half grin and chuckled.

"I'm sure. You can walk me to the door, though," he urged as he winked at her. Then, he turned his attention to Wes and me. "See you later."

"Good night."

"Later," Wes replied.

Zane and Emme walked out of the kitchen and Wes turned me into his body.

"I guess you are staying with me tonight."

"That's the plan, gorgeous. I'm not going to leave you alone after everything you went through today."

"That's good because I really didn't want to be alone tonight."

"Are you okay?" he asked.

"I will be as soon as I know Greg is in the clear."

Wes leaned down and kissed my forehead.

"I assume everything is fine between you and Zane," I guessed. Even though Zane didn't know about my argument with Wes, I hoped what happened earlier today didn't affect Wes' interactions with Zane.

"We're good. He knows where everything stands."

My eyes got big.

"You told him we argued?" I asked, shock filtering through my voice.

"I wouldn't say I told him we argued. I all but congratulated him on making the decision to pursue your girl. I told him I was mostly happy about this because I was ready to knock him out in my office today when he had his hands on you."

"Seriously?"

"He's a guy, Charley. If he feels even a fraction for Emme what I feel for you, he gets it. Based on his reaction to that dress she wore on New Year's Eve, I'm pretty sure he would feel the same if someone had their hands on her."

My breath hitched at his words.

"What's that about?" he asked, not missing my reaction.

Shit.

"Nothing. I'm exhausted. I know we have to go to work tomorrow, but I'd really like to stop by the hospital in the morning to check on Greg."

"If you want to take the day off, Charley, it's not a problem. I wasn't expecting that you'd be up to working," he clarified.

"No. I definitely need to work. It'll help me destress. But I really appreciate you giving me the option."

"Whatever you need. We'll go to the hospital first thing in the morning then. After, we'll help you destress by going to work. For now, why don't you go have a seat on the couch?"

"Wes, I'm ready for bed. I'm not really up for TV."

He looked at me and his eyes warmed. "I know, baby. I just want you to relax for a few minutes while I make you some food. You haven't had any dinner. Neither have I, for that matter. I'm just going to make some eggs and bacon if you are good with that."

I hadn't even realized that I never ate dinner. I loved that he was always looking out for me.

"I'm good with that," I replied as I smiled at him. "Thank you, honey."

I kissed him quickly on the lips and walked in the other room to sit on the couch. Emme had just come back from walking Zane to the door when she saw me on the couch.

"Everything okay?" she worried.

"Yeah. Wes is making food," I answered.

Her eyes softened, and she gave me a small smile.

Wes stepped out of the kitchen at that moment and looked to Emme. "Did you eat dinner?" he asked her.

She shook her head.

He jerked his head in my direction. "Have a seat with her. I'll make extra."

"Oh, no. It's okay. You don't have to do that," she stammered.

His jaw clenched. "Emme, sit on the couch with Charley. It's eggs and bacon, not Thanksgiving dinner. It's not a problem to throw some extra on. Consider it a thank you for bringing Charley's Jeep back tonight."

"Okay," she said meekly.

Wes shook his head, turned around, and walked back to the kitchen mumbling, "Fucking stubborn fucking women."

Emme looked to me, her eyes got big, and she laughed. I laughed right along with her, and I loved Wes for making that happen.

Twenty-Four

Charley

HEALING. Oftentimes, it takes longer than we'd like. And sometimes we might not ever heal completely. After Taj's death, it took me the better part of ten months before I even began to feel normal. I was certain, though, that I'd never fully recover from the pain of losing him.

It was now five days after Greg's car accident and he was still in the medically-induced coma. Greg had made it through the most critical period and he was improving. The swelling had gone down significantly, and the doctors had started reducing the medications he was receiving so they could wake him up.

I was just finishing up my day at work and was planning to stop by the hospital before going home tonight. Wes and I were the only ones left in the building. It had been a crazy week for me between work, needing to tie up loose ends before we went out to Aspen, and the constant worry over Greg. I had stopped by the hospital every day since the accident. Fortunately, I never ran into Greg's parents. Tony was there every single time I went, and Hannah had been there once as well.

The first day I stopped in following the accident Tony incessantly thanked me for having had the courage to put Greg's parents in their place. I explained my position to him and he understood where I was coming from. It was important to me that he knows that I never meant to humiliate Mr. and Mrs. Williams, but I couldn't stand and watch them make even more of a mess of such a horrific situation. Tony didn't seem to care either way what my reasoning was. He was just happy to be able to be at Greg's bedside.

Yesterday evening when I stopped at the hospital after my day at work Tony updated me on Greg's status. His vitals had been steadily improving and the swelling was going down. The doctors started making the adjustments to medications and, while they couldn't make any guarantees, they said that he could wake up as early as this afternoon.

As much as I had wanted to stay at the hospital today and not go to work, things were so busy with the X Games approaching that I really wanted to make sure I did my part to help make it a success. Thankfully, Tony promised to keep me updated and had texted me earlier that morning to let me know that Greg had woken up briefly, but soon fell back asleep. Several hours later, he texted again to update and let me know that he managed to have a conversation with Greg. I could not wait to finish at work and get over to see him.

"Hey, gorgeous. Any news?" Wes asked, looking up from his desk as I popped into his office.

"Tony said Greg woke up a second time this afternoon and they had a conversation. I haven't heard anything since then, though," I answered as I walked over to him.

"That's good to hear. Are you heading over there now?"

I nodded. "Yeah, I've been itching to go all day today."

"You could have spent the day there today, you know?"

"I do know, Wes. I wanted to do my part here, though. There's a lot happening right now, especially since we are leaving in a few days to go to Aspen. I want to be a part of the success of that, regardless of how small my part in it is."

"Baby, just putting together those designs for Zane, Stone, and Luke was huge. The effort you've put in over the past few days has been tremendous. I wouldn't consider your part in this to be small, and I'm grateful for all the work you've done," Wes praised me.

I smiled at him before making my way behind his desk. He pushed his chair out and held his hand out to me. With my fingers in his, he tugged me into his lap, where I settled and put my arms around him. I had missed him. Even though we worked in adjoining offices, I felt like I hadn't seen much of him over the past couple of days.

"Thank you, honey. That feels good to hear. I'm so excited that Greg seems to be improving every day. As much as I really want to go on this trip to support you and the guys, I was starting to rethink it with Greg's accident. Knowing that he's doing better and woke up this afternoon is comforting. I can't wait to see him today."

"Are you good to go on your own or do you want me to come with you?" he asked.

"I think I'll be good to go on my own today. Thanks for offering, though."

He nodded and pulled my hand up to his lips to kiss my knuckles. "Okay. I need to check on a few of the boards we're debuting at the Games with your designs on them. I want to make sure they are perfect. We will have some there for people to check out in person, but the website is also going to have all the new designs for the Fire model starting on day one of the Games. When we get back from Aspen, I want to have the Air model designs in the works. Luke will probably take a couple days off after we get back from Aspen to recover, but I know he's ready to start testing the models."

"I already have some ideas for the Air model so I will be

ready to go on those when we get back," I noted.

We sat in silence a minute. Sadness overtook me.

"What's the matter?" Wes wondered, his voice filled with tenderness.

My eyes welled up with tears and I looked away.

"Charley, talk to me. What's wrong?"

"It's nothing, Wes. I'm just being a big baby."

He growled. "It's not nothing. Tell me."

I looked back at him. The concern on his face was too much. "I'm sorry. It has been an exhausting and extremely busy couple of days. Between everything with work and Greg's accident, I have so many different emotions running through me. And when it really comes down to it, I'm mostly just missing spending time with you. I want to spend a day on the mountain riding with you. I miss that the most."

His eyes softened for a moment before he closed them and dropped his head, shaking it. "You're it, Charley."

My eyebrows drew together as I asked, "What?"

He looked back up at me. "Everything I need. You're it."

I stared at him and felt the warmth spread through my body. "Wes…" I rasped.

"There's no better sound in this world than my name coming from your mouth with that voice. Kiss me, gorgeous."

I missed him. Despite my mix of emotions, I knew that this was what I needed to feel the most. I leaned forward and kissed him.

My hands went to his hair and gripped tightly as I pressed my body into his. I rocked my hips back and forth over his erection. This caused him to groan and squeeze my hips.

He tore his mouth from mine, held onto me as he stood, and set my ass on his desk.

"I'm thinking now would be the perfect time to fulfill that fantasy and take you on my desk," he suggested playfully, sliding my skirt up my thighs.

"Please, Wes. I need hard and fast," I pleaded, putting my hands to the waistband of his pants.

"Whatever you need, baby," he assured me, pulling my panties down my legs. "Always."

Seconds later, he was giving me the goods. Hard and fast. It was exactly what I needed. It wasn't long before I was close to shattering. Wes kept giving it to me, knowing I was on the verge of orgasm. Mere moments had passed before I was coming apart around him. He didn't stop or slow down and continued to give it hard and fast. Then, Wes pulled himself from my body. I nearly cried at the loss. He brought his mouth down, kissed me hard, and moved his mouth to my ear.

"My greedy woman," he teased with a slight edge of amusement in his voice. "Don't worry, gorgeous. I'm not done with you. I want you bent over my desk so I can take you from behind."

His sexy smirk spread across his face.

He lifted me off the desk, onto my feet, and spun me around so that my back was to his front. One of his hands gripped one of my hips as I felt the tip of him at my entrance again. I braced my hands on the desk just before I felt Wes slam into me. He powered in and out as I pushed back into each thrust. Wes' free hand wrapped around the front of my body and found my clit. I was a mess of sensations and, somehow, despite having just had an earth-shattering orgasm I was on the brink of a second one.

"Fuck, Charley. I can feel you already starting to squeeze my cock again," he growled. "You feel so good."

"Oh, Wes. I'm going to come," I rasped out.

"Take it, gorgeous."

So, I took it. And, Wes took it right along with me.

Wes held my body up to support my now liquefied legs. He pulled himself from between my legs and turned me around to hold me for a moment before I took off to the bathroom to clean up.

After taking care of business, I walked back out into Wes' office. He was standing next to his desk as I approached him. Folding me in his arms, he looked down and apologized, "I'm sorry we haven't had much time for ourselves the past few days. I promise I'll get you back out on the mountain after we get home from Aspen."

Home.

Yes, this was home now.

I pressed my cheek into his chest and admitted, "I'm very much looking forward to that."

We stayed like that for a while, both of us needing the comfort of each other's embrace.

"I should head over to the hospital now," I suggested, breaking the silence.

"Okay. I'm going to be here for a little while yet, but I'll walk you out to your car first."

I knew how much work he had left to do and was going to protest, but it wouldn't work and would only delay him further, so I kept my mouth shut.

"Wise choice," he informed me as if reading my thoughts.

We walked to my car and Wes told me to call with any major updates. He also made me promise to call when I got home that night. I gave him a kiss and took off.

I arrived at the hospital and rode the elevator up to the fourth floor. When I stepped into Greg's room at the end of the hall, I nearly jumped for joy at what I saw. Greg was holding Tony's hand and smiling at him while Tony rattled on about something. Tony noticed me walk into the room and stopped speaking.

"There's our girl," he announced to Greg.

Greg turned his head to look at me and, while he still looked pretty beat up, seeing him there smiling and alive was one of the most beautiful sights I had ever laid my eyes on. My vision went blurry with tears, so I quickly looked away to try and stave off a total breakdown. It was useless.

"Oh dear. She's going to lose it," Greg warned.

His voice was music to my ears and my heart couldn't handle it. I broke down.

I felt strong hands grab my biceps while the voice encouraged, "Come here, girl."

Tony walked me to the chair sitting at Greg's bedside. I sat down, tears streaming down my face, and looked at Greg.

"I'm sorry. I am such a mess," I lamented.

"Girl, after what you've done for me and Greg, you take all the time you need," Tony insisted.

I shook my head. Telling Greg's parents how lucky they were that their son was still alive hardly felt like a chore. "It wasn't a big deal," I brushed it off.

"It was," Greg insisted. "My dad was here earlier today. He told me that once I'm well enough to get out of here and go home, he wants to take Tony and me out to dinner."

I sucked in a sharp breath.

"I never thought that I'd ever have that, Charley," Greg confessed.

"Oh, that's incredible news, Greg."

He nodded.

"Thank you," he started. "My dad told me that he's incredibly sorry for how strained things have been lately and he wants to make amends. He is obviously not happy that I landed in the hospital, but was extremely thankful to see that I've got good people around me. People who are so good they'll stand up for what is right. He was referring to you, Charley. He said it took the words of a little spitfire in the emergency room waiting room for him to realize that he was making a huge mistake. He told me that he prayed every day from that day that I'd wake up so he could right his wrong."

"I'm so happy for you…for the both of you," I expressed

looking between the two of them, unsure of what else to say. And because I was so overcome with emotion, the tears spilled over my cheeks again.

"What's wrong?" Greg asked.

It took me a minute or two before I could pull myself together enough to answer. I explained, "I'm so thankful that you are okay, Greg. I've had such bad things happen in my life and they didn't turn out so well for me before. Nobody I cared about made it through such tragic circumstances. I was devastated the day of your accident. I knew I wouldn't be able to handle having another person I care about not survive. When I saw your parents that night, I reacted to everything I was feeling over the loss of my parents and my brother. Your parents still had you and they were throwing away their relationship with you for no good reason. I don't have my family anymore and I'd give anything to have them back."

"I am so sorry, Charley. I hate that you have lost so much. Thank you, though, for giving me part of my family back. I could never thank you enough," Greg comforted me.

"Your mom hasn't changed her mind about things?" I asked.

He took in a deep breath and shook his head.

"I'm not sure if she will or if she's just going to need time. Maybe things will go well with my father and he'll get her to come around. I won't upset myself over it anymore. Life is too precious to spend it worrying about things you can't change."

"You've got that right," I agreed, reaching out to squeeze his hand.

I spent the next hour and a half with Greg and Tony. Greg fell asleep once during this time as he was still feeling the effects of the medication. He apologized to me, but I told him it was no big deal. I spent that time catching up with and getting to know Tony a bit better. Eventually, I told them I had to get going and that I'd stop in again over the next couple of days until I had to leave for Aspen. We made tentative plans to have a celebratory get together as soon as Greg was out of the hospital and feeling up to it. There was not a chance I'd be missing that.

I hugged Greg and told him I'd see him the next day. Tony walked me out and I made my way home. When I got there, I called Wes just as I had promised I would and let him know that I had gotten home.

Yes.

I was home and it finally felt good again.

Twenty-Five

Charley

"HOW COULD THIS POSSIBLY BE HAPPENING TO US RIGHT NOW, Charley? I feel like I'm waiting for the other shoe to drop."

"I know Em. It's crazy," I answered.

The limo we were riding in had just pulled up to the tarmac where the private jet Wes chartered to take us to Aspen was parked.

Yep.

Emme and I, both of whom have had just about the shittiest luck in the world, just had a very comfortable limo, outfitted with champagne, pick us up at our place this afternoon and we were about to board a private jet to Aspen, Colorado. It left us both wondering how it even happened.

To top it off, and quite possibly even better than all that, I looked out the window and saw four of the most gorgeous men in the world standing there chatting with each other. I put the window down, snapped a picture with my phone, and put the window back up. I sent that picture in a group text to Nikki, Monroe, and Emme.

If this isn't the ONLY reason you need to move here, I don't know what is!

Nikki responded almost immediately.

You two are the luckiest bitches in the world! That's a whole lot of panty-melting hotness in one photo.

Emme and I looked at each other and laughed.

Monroe's response came a few seconds later.

Who gives a shit about the list anymore? I could totally move out there right now and give up the goods for the blonde.

My eyes got big. For her to make a statement like that meant she really felt something for Stone.

I was about to reply when the driver opened our door. We tossed our phones in our purses and climbed out. As we did, the guys turned to look at us and dropped their heads, laughing. I stood there confused at this reaction and looked to Emme. She shrugged. Wes said something to them and they all started stalking over to us, which I found even more odd.

They finally got close enough and Wes spoke. "Who else is in the limo?"

My eyebrows drew together. "Nobody, why?"

"We're going to be gone a week, Charley."

"I know that, Wes," I answered with a bit of attitude since I had no idea what his problem was.

"How much fucking clothing do you need for one week?"

"Oh shit," Stone warned, his tone indicating he sensed a bit of danger in the air.

I looked to see that the limo driver had put our suitcases and bags out behind the limo.

"Seriously, Wes? Do you really need an explanation? There are five suitcases and four bags. Two of those suitcases are Emme's. Two of them are mine. One of my suitcases was used just to fit all the layers I'll need for being out in the cold considering I grew up in warm and sunny California. Then, I have the other one for normal clothes for when I'm not outside. That same suitcase also has clothes for dressing up in case we end up going out at any point in time. Forgive me, but I've never been to the X Games before, so I was unsure of what to pack. Lucky for you, Emme and I didn't want to overdo it so we shared the last suitcase to put all of our shoes in."

"Appreciate the courtesy," he teased, shaking his head while smirking.

"Moving on, of the four bags you see there? Once again, two of them are Emme's and the other two are mine. One of my bags is carrying my makeup, toiletries, and everything else needed to make me look half decent. I know it may be hard to believe, but I don't actually wake up looking like this. The other bag? Well, that one is filled with panties, bras, nighties, and other lace-trimmed—"

"Quiet," Wes cut me off. "The guys don't need to hear about that one."

"Fuck," Zane bit out.

"Hey, that's where her explanation got interesting. I'd like to know more about that last bag," Luke joked.

Wes' jaw clenched.

I then heard Zane ask Emme, "You and Charley pack similarly?"

She blushed and looked down.

Zane tipped his head back and looked at the sky as he sighed, "Fuck me."

"Lucky bastards," Stone pointed out.

Wes chimed in, "Charley, which bag is the goody bag?"

I had a gray bag and a black and pink striped one.

"The black and pink one," I answered.

He walked over to the bag, grabbed it, and then grabbed a suitcase. Then he asked, "Stone, Luke, can you grab the other suitcases?"

"I'll get the rest of the bags," Zane offered, looking at Emme with a sexy grin on his face.

The guys all started walking back to the plane. Emme and

I just looked at each other, smiled, and fell into step right behind the guys.

I had never flown on a private jet before, but it was something I could get used to. Sophisticated design details, unparalleled comfort, huge flat-screen televisions, and plenty of leg room were just a fraction of the perks afforded on this particular jet. I parked my booty in one of the roomy, cream-colored, soft leather window seats while Emme sat in the one directly across and facing mine. A few minutes later, the guys joined us. Wes sat next to me, Zane slid in next to Emme, and Stone and Luke sat in the seats facing each other on the other side of the massive aisle.

At that moment, both Emme's phone and my phone chimed notifying us both of an incoming text. I knew that it was from our group text conversation. About thirty seconds after that, they chimed again. We both grabbed our phones and looked at them.

Nikki had responded to Monroe's earlier statement about giving up the goods to Stone.

If moving means Monroe is FINALLY going to get laid, I'm packing my bags and purchasing a one-way ticket!!

Monroe then replied.

You act like I'm the only virgin left on the planet. Em? Char? Say it ain't so.

I couldn't help but laugh out loud. I looked up to find Emme biting back her laughter while Wes, Zane, Stone, and Luke looked at us like we were crazy. I tapped out a quick reply.

You're definitely not the last virgin on Earth, mama. We're on the plane now, though. I can put a good word in with Stone if you'd like. I'm sure he'd be more than happy to help a potentially dying breed. ☺

Nikki replied.
YES!!!!!!!!

Monroe immediately answered.

Don't you dare!

Emme chimed in.

We won't, but if this keeps up we're going to have to tell them something. Charley and I are not very good at hiding our reactions to this convo and we're already getting strange looks.

Ok, I'm out. Have a great trip. Keep us updated. Lots of luck. Love you!! xoxo

That response came from Monroe.

Nikki kept at it.

NO!! We need to make this happen for our girl. Look at that picture, Monroe. He's smokin' hot! And I've seen the way he looks at those legs of yours. He'd be all over this. Come on.

I replied.

As much as I agree with you, I can't do it, Nik. Guess you'll have to come out to see us again to take care of business yourself. ☺

Whatever. Boring! Hope you have a great time in Aspen. Picture updates, ladies!

This is one of those things I loved most about Nikki. She'd fight you on something until the bitter end, but she'd ultimately respect your wishes.

I tossed my phone back in my purse as I looked up to see Emme doing the same. I looked away from her to see all the guys looking at us.

"Sorry," I started. "Girl talk with Nikki and Monroe."

Luke and Stone nodded, smiled, and looked away. My eyes went to Wes.

"I love seeing you happy and laughing like that. I want to do what I can to help you convince your girls to move here," Wes offered quietly.

"I really love you for that," I shared, kissing him quickly.

"I mean it, gorgeous. Whatever I've got to do, I want to see you like that every single day."

I whispered back, "Your friends are hot." His jaw clenched. "Not nearly as hot as you, honey. But, to my friends, your friends are smoking hot. Stone is our ticket. If he could be interested in Monroe, that's how we make this happen."

"No shit?" he asked.

"No shit. But, I told you before that Emme was fragile and I needed to be sure about Zane. I need to be sure about Stone with Monroe because Monroe is something super special. Stone can't play her. This would need to be a long-term thing. If that's not his style, don't push it and we come up with another plan."

"I'll work on it," he said.

I rested my head on his shoulder and added, "Thank you, Wes."

He kissed the top of my head before he reminded me, "Anything you need, Charley."

Roughly two hours later, we had landed in Aspen. Wes rented two vehicles for us to ride around in. Of course, it ended up being Zane, Emme, Wes, and me in one car while Stone and Luke rode in the other. We had just arrived at the house Wes booked for the week we would be staying at here in Aspen and, I had to admit, it was absolutely breathtaking.

After Wes pulled up the driveway and parked, we all climbed out.

"Gorgeous, the guys and I will get the bags. It's cold out here. You and Emme head inside," he instructed as he handed me the key for the house.

"Wes, I can pull one of the suitcases and carry a bag," I replied.

Wes clenched his jaw. Through gritted teeth, he ordered, "Charley. Get in the house."

I saluted him and responded, "Yes, sir."

He dropped the keys in my hand, so I grabbed Emme and took off to the front door. As we stepped inside, we took in the beautiful space.

The foyer had a wide staircase off to the right leading up to the second floor. To the left was an open door that led into a den. The main living area was an open-floor plan housing the contemporarily-styled kitchen, cozy living room, and the not-so-formal dining area. While the furniture and decorative accents were beautiful, the best part of the entire space was the countless floor-to-ceiling windows. Every room was so bright, and the entire house felt spacious with all the natural light.

"If this is what the downstairs looks like, I can't imagine the bedrooms," Emme marveled.

"I'm going to guess we won't be disappointed," I replied.

We heard the guys come in the front door and turned to see them walking through with all the bags. They set the bags down just inside the door and walked to Emme and me.

"Everything good?" Wes asked us.

"Wes, this is real estate heaven. It's beautiful here," I shared.

"The views are incredible. I could be happy staying here for the rest of my life and never leaving," Emme added.

"Not going to disagree with that, but you'd need to be fully stocked with food. And there's shit for food here," Luke chimed in from behind the refrigerator door.

"Em and I will go get food," I piped up.

"We can order something in or go out for food today. You don't need to do that, Charley," Wes replied.

Before I could respond Emme spoke.

"I really appreciate you hiring me to shoot photos for this event, Wes. I appreciate even more that you are allowing me to stay in this spectacular home with all of you. We showed up at the airport today to get on a private jet you chartered, and I wasn't even allowed to carry my bags because of the testosterone that's been surrounding me all day. At this point, I would be offended if you didn't let me contribute by at least conceding on this and letting Charley and me take the car so we can make a run to the grocery store. We could whip up some chicken fajita quesadillas for dinner tonight," she suggested looking to me for approval on her menu selection.

Wes looked from Emme to me. Then he looked to the guys.

"If you don't give them the car keys, I'm taking them in the car I've got the keys to and driving them myself," Stone warned. "I'm fucking starved and they just promised a home-cooked meal."

I looked back to Wes with a wide grin spreading across my face and held out my hand. He reached in his pocket and pulled out the car key.

"Be careful," he ordered as he handed the key to me.

"Love you, honey," I responded. Then, I gave him a quick kiss.

"Love you, too. Here. Take my card to pay for the food," Wes said pulling his wallet out.

"No. We are buying the food. You've covered everything else. We're getting this," I declared.

"You want to take the car and go buy food?" Wes asked.

I looked at him and nodded.

"I'm giving in, but you've got to work with me. There are four guys here that'll eat more food in one sitting than the two of you will eat in an entire day combined. I'm paying for the food. End of story," Wes insisted.

I realized I wouldn't win this fight. And the guys were clearly hungry, so I conceded and took Wes' credit card to buy groceries.

"Wise choice, gorgeous. The guys and I will get the bags upstairs. All the bedrooms have their own ensuite bath. Any specific preference on a room?" he questioned.

"I'm good as long as I'm with you," I answered.

He grinned. Then, he looked to Em and asked, "Want to pick one out before you go?"

She shook her head. "Are there enough bedrooms here for everyone?" she wondered. "I'd be fine with the couch down here."

Zane spoke up, "There are six bedrooms here. Even if there weren't you wouldn't be sleeping on the couch, sweetheart."

Emme blushed and looked away. I knew she was now going to have to fight to not have a breakdown.

I decided to step in. "Okay, so any room will work for us. Now, we are going to head out so we can get back and make some food. Any last-minute food requests?" I asked.

"I'll eat anything right about now," Luke said.

Stone, Zane, and Wes nodded their agreement.

With that, Emme and I went to the grocery store. After spending about an hour there, we felt we had stocked up on enough food. As we pulled into the driveway, the front door opened. Wes and Luke came out to help carry in the groceries. We unloaded all the bags and got to work on making dinner.

Fifteen minutes after we'd completely assembled the quesadillas and slid them into the oven, we were all sitting down to eat.

There was a bit of moaning all around the table after bites of food were taken.

I looked to Wes and he winked at me.

"Good?" I asked.

"Phenomenal," he answered after swallowing a bite of his food.

"I think it's safe to say that you made a good choice in agreeing to have Emme and I go to the store for food so we could cook this week."

He chuckled and took another bite of his quesadilla. The

conversation then turned to some of the details for the upcoming week. I learned a lot about the X Games in general, what Blackman Boards sponsorship of the event would involve, what the expectations were of Emme as far as media coverage, and then a bit more about the actual snowboarding.

Zane and Stone would be riding the superpipe, which is essentially a halfpipe with walls that are twenty-two feet high on both sides of the flat bottom. It sounded incredibly terrifying. While Luke could keep up with the guys on the pipe, he preferred big air and would be competing in that event in the upcoming week.

There was a lot on everyone's plate for the next few days. Zane, Stone, and Luke wanted to get some practice runs in over the next few days and would then have to make appearances at the Blackman Boards sponsored event at the Games.

Blackman Boards was hosting two 'Keep Riding' events. One would be an ongoing thing set in a tent every day of the Games open to both the public fans, media, and the athletes. Multiple television screens would be set up with coverage of the event being streamed throughout the day. Blackman Boards gear would be on display. Non-alcoholic refreshments and finger foods would be available along with music being played by a live DJ. The other 'Keep Riding' event would be held at a local pub the last night of the Games, which we all hoped would be a bit celebratory for the Blackman Boards riders.

After dinner and conversation, everyone decided to call it quits for the night given the busy schedule ahead. I was more than ready to have some alone time with Wes. Everyone made their way upstairs. Zane showed Emme to her bedroom and Wes and I took off down the hall to ours. I inspected the room and bathroom and noted my favorite part was the glass-paneled shower that boasted incredible views in the secluded mountain area.

I turned to Wes.

"Honey, I'm not sure staying here is a good idea."

His brows pulled together, and he asked, "Why not?"

"Well, I'm thinking I could get seriously used to living in a place like this and I'm not sure I'll want to leave."

He smiled and assured, "I'll bring you back whenever you want."

"Wes, I wasn't suggesting that you needed to do that," I reasoned.

"I know you weren't, but it doesn't change the fact that I will do exactly that. I'd give you anything, Charley."

"Is that so, Mr. Blackman?" I asked, feeling a bit frisky.

"Absolutely," he insisted, his voice rough.

"Then I think I'd like to ask you to give me something now."

"Anything, gorgeous."

"Since Em and I made dinner I think it's only fair that you feed me dessert. I'd like you in my mouth now. Then, just after the sun rises in the morning, I'd like you to take me in that shower."

"One condition," he replied.

"And that would be?" I asked.

"You aren't the only one who gets to have dessert tonight."

I tilted my head, put my hands to the hem of his shirt and lifted it up. He helped guide it over his head. After tossing the shirt aside, I placed my hands on his chest and ran my fingers over the hardened muscle down his abdomen to the waistband of his jeans. I unbuttoned his pants, and as I began to unzip them, I teased, "I think that can be arranged."

And just like that, as is often the case, dessert ended up being way better than the main course.

Twenty-Six

Charley

Fingers gently traced over the skin at my hip. I kept my eyes closed and smiled inwardly at the peace I felt with those gradual movements. I was still feeling sleepy since our nighttime activities kept us up late last night. I wasn't one to complain, though, especially when said activities resulted in having three orgasms. After soaking up all of the goodness in Wes' teasing fingertips, I opened my eyes and tilted my head back to look at my beautiful man. It was still pre-dawn so while there was enough light to see him even though the sun was still not shining.

"Hey," I said to him.

"I could watch you sleep all day, gorgeous. But waking you up by just barely touching your skin and hearing your sleepy voice is way better."

I smiled and snuggled closer to him pressing my face into his chest.

"I love when you trace," I shared.

"What?" he asked.

"Your fingers on my skin like that. I love when you trace them over me. It calms and relaxes me. Everything else in my life could be a disaster and if you do that it makes it all better."

"I'll be sure to keep that in mind."

We stayed there for the next few minutes in silence. Wes continued to trace his fingers across my skin and I continued to breathe in his scent and settle into the peace he was giving me.

"I'm ready, Charley."

"For what, honey?" I asked.

"Decided I'd like to alter the game plan for this morning. I want to take you in the shower while the sun rises. If you still want me to give it to you after the sun has risen, I'll do it then, too."

I felt a tingle right between my legs and kissed the skin of his chest. He squeezed my hip in response. I kissed again, and he kept his hand firmly planted on my hip. I brought one of my hands up to cup his cheek, lifted my head, and shifted my body so that I could press a kiss to his lips. The hand that had been resting on my hip was now on my ass and pulling my body into his. Keeping his mouth connected to mine Wes knifed up in the bed and snaked his arm around my waist. Then, he carried me into the bathroom with my legs wrapped around him.

Wes tore his mouth from mine briefly so he could turn on the shower. Still holding me, he turned his head to look back in my eyes and stared. Surrounded by windows, I could see the color swirling in his heated gaze and knew just how much he wanted me.

Moments later, he carried us into the shower and my back was immediately pressed up against the glass wall. Wes bent his head to my breast and took one nipple in his mouth. He licked and sucked before moving to the other side. I kept one hand wrapped around the back of his neck and moved the other between us. My fingers reached for his cock and gently squeezed before I positioned him. Wes pushed himself inside and filled me. His mouth moved to the skin at my throat and collarbone as my head fell back against the glass. My hands moved all over him, through his hair, down to his shoulders, and to his muscled arms. Wes kept his hands planted on my ass to hold me up as he thrust himself in and out of me.

I began feeling that sensation deep in my belly and knew it wouldn't be long before I was sent over the edge. Wes continued his assault on my body and kept giving me the goods.

"Wes," I rasped out.

"There she is," he approved. "Love that, baby. Love the voice coming out of that mouth."

He picked up the pace pushing me closer and closer to the edge. My breathing became quick and shallow as I stared into his emerald eyes.

"Take it, Charley. Take what you need."

I did as I was told and took what I needed while the sun, which had just begun to peek out, lit up the room.

After Wes brought me down from my orgasm, he kept himself planted inside me and sat on the wide ledge at the end of the shower, opposite the shower head. He was sitting upright, and I was on top of him. His hands moved from my ass to my breasts. He rolled my nipple between his thumb and forefinger on one side while he lifted the other to his mouth. After a few minutes of delicious teasing, Wes pulled his head back to look at me.

"Move, gorgeous."

I moved.

Wes sat there with his hands gently guiding my hips, but he mostly let me take charge. I controlled the depth and the pace of each thrust. I started slow, torturously slow. I wanted to prolong his pleasure and make him want it that much more. It didn't take long for me to realize I was not only teasing Wes, but also myself. It was too much, and I began to move quicker trying to get myself there again. My body moved rapidly, and I braced my hands behind my body on top of his thick, strong thighs. I glanced down at his impeccable body. The beads of water from the shower on his chest and abs were glistening in the sun. I persisted in riding him hard. Wes' eyes moved from mine and worked their way down my body. His gaze stopped on my bouncing breasts for a while before moving further down to where we were connected. He watched as I continued to quickly lift my body and slam back down onto his cock. Finally, he moved one of his hands to where we were joined, and his thumb found my clit. That was all I needed.

"Wes," I rasped. "I love you so much."

"Love you too, Charley. Come with me, baby," he demanded.

That was when I had my fifth orgasm in less than eight hours.

It was a good thing Wes was sitting because I fell forward and collapsed on his body, sated and exhausted. He held me there for a while before he finally spoke, "You're going to prune if you don't get out of this shower."

"So tired," I responded.

"I know. I'll help you finish up in here and then we'll go back to bed for a couple hours. We have time today."

Begrudgingly, I sat up and lifted myself off him. Wes kept his hands on me until I was steady on my feet. We quickly finished our business in the shower before Wes shut it down. I dried myself and my hair as quickly as I could, made my way back into the bedroom, pulled on a nightie from my goody bag, and climbed into the bed. Wes settled in the bed a few seconds after I did. He slipped an arm around my waist and pulled my body into his so that he was spooning me.

"Sleep, gorgeous."

I'm not sure how many hours later it was when I finally woke, but when I did, I was alone. Knowing that Wes probably wouldn't be thrilled with me heading out to the kitchen in my nightie, I made a quick trip into the bathroom before I threw on a Blackman Boards t-shirt and a pair of sweats.

As soon as I walked out of the bedroom and walked to the top of the stairs, I heard voices downstairs. I went down and saw that everyone was already awake. Emme was standing at the stove making breakfast while the guys sat on the stools at the island. I must have made enough noise coming down the stairs because everyone turned to look at me.

"Morning, sweets," Emme greeted.

"Mornin', Em," I answered.

I got another round of good mornings from the guys while Wes got up and walked to me. He wrapped his arm around me when he got close and bent his head to kiss me. His lips moved to my ear and quietly asked, "Feel better that you got some sleep?"

I nodded and curled my body into his. Then I shared, "Didn't like waking up without you there, though."

"I'm sorry, baby. Had some calls I needed to make this morning. I'm just making sure preparations for everything leading up to the event are in order."

"There's no need to apologize, Wes. I know you are going to be busy this week. I just like having you there."

"But I'm never too busy to give you what you need," he reassured me.

I looked up at him, smiled, and declared, "I love you."

"Love you, too."

Wes and I rejoined the group. I immediately dove in to help Emme. She was making Belgian waffles and eggs for breakfast. I got the plates and utensils out and moved to pour the coffee. Minutes later, Emme had finished up the food. The guys shoveled the food in and discussed the plans for the day.

Zane, Stone, and Luke were going to be heading out to ride for a bit and Emme would be tagging along. Wes wanted her to be able to check out where she'd be shooting and how everything would be set up ahead of time. I had been worried about how she would handle being off with the guys without me, but she seemed to be okay with it. I made a mental note to get her alone before they took off.

Wes and I needed to stop by the pub this morning to confirm all the details of the post-Games 'Keep Riding' event and then we'd be heading over to the mountain to make sure all was being set up properly and according to plan in the Blackman-Boards-sponsored event lounge. I was beyond excited to see this completed because the Elements Series was being debuted here with the Fire line. This meant that my designs would be officially out in the public eye. I was nervous and excited at the same time.

After we finished breakfast, I went to clear the table with Emme when Wes instructed, "Leave this. The guys and I will take care of clean up. Why don't you and Emme go on upstairs and get ready?"

"You four want to clean up breakfast dishes?" I asked, incredulously.

Stone chimed in, "Not sure any of us *wants* to clean up anything, babe. That said, two reasons we are willing to do this right now. First, considering you both cooked last night and this morning, we can offer a little bit of help in the way of clean up. Second, and probably most important, we've got to get to the mountain sooner rather than later to get a good day of practice in. For reasons that none of the men in this room can understand, especially with women who look the way you two do, women take way too fucking long to get ready. Since your girl is riding with us, we need her to go start getting ready now if we are going to have a chance at arriving there anytime soon."

"Valid point made," I reasoned.

"Breakfast, much like dinner last night, was awesome. Thanks for cooking this morning," Luke said to Emme.

She nodded and smiled at him. "You're welcome, Luke."

I looked to Zane. He had a look similar to the one Wes gave me the day we had our first argument. Jealousy. I guessed that was a good thing. I looked to Wes. He saw Zane's reaction, looked down to the floor, and chuckled.

"I think now is a good time for the girls to go get ready," Zane clipped through clenched teeth.

"Okay, that's our cue. Way too much testosterone in the room right now," I pointed out.

With that, Emme and I went upstairs to get ready. I went to her bedroom with her since Wes and I leaving immediately wasn't as crucial as Emme and the guys.

"So, is this all good with you?" I asked as I sat down on her bed.

She turned to look at me, eyebrows drawn.

"You going with Zane, Stone, and Luke today," I clarified. "Do you feel comfortable with that?"

Emme started setting out her layers of clothing for the day. The high was going to be hovering right around thirty degrees that day and, despite having been in Wyoming for almost a full year, we still didn't fare well in the cold.

"Surprisingly, yes. I can't explain it, but it's all Zane. While I don't know Luke and Stone that well they seem like genuinely good people. Regardless of them, I feel like Zane would move mountains for me. That's not to say that I'd ask him to do that, but it helps my comfort level. Aside from that, I'm doing this for you, Charley."

"Me? What do you mean?" I asked.

"Sweets," she began. "Do you realize how huge this event is? Your work is being debuted this weekend and I've been given the opportunity to capture that for marketing purposes for one of the biggest names in extreme winter sports. You better believe I'm going to do everything I can to support this *huge* accomplishment."

"Emme..." I murmured, my throat growing tight.

"You have come so far over the last year. I am so happy that you met Wes and he has given you what you needed to help you to realize your dream, believe in yourself and reach this level of success. Charley, I'm so proud of you," she praised as the tears pooled in her eyes.

I got up off the bed, went to my best friend, and hugged her tightly.

"Thank you, Em," I whispered.

A few moments of silence passed before I pulled away from Emme and said what I needed to say.

"I want this for you, too, Em. I want you to find happiness again," I shared.

"That doesn't exist for me anymore, Charley," she shot down.

"I know why you think that, honey, but you're wrong. I thought the same thing and now that I'm here I realize how big of a mistake that would have been. I won't push it, but you've got to consider trying to move on so you can find it."

She shrugged and closed her eyes.

"Okay, I'm going to let you finish getting yourself ready. I'll see you later today when Wes and I get to the mountain. Have fun this morning."

"I'll do my best," she promised.

I turned to walk out and head to my bedroom.

"Hey Charley?" she called out.

"Yeah?"

"Love you."

"Love you, too, Em."

Twenty-Seven

Charley

"I THINK I MIGHT THROW UP."

That was the truth. I was standing in the doorway between the bathroom and bedroom looking up at Wes. It was the first day of the X Games. I was excited that the day had finally arrived, but I was more nervous about the launch of the Fire line.

The past couple of days had been absolute insanity. Wes and I spent long days working with other Blackman Board employees to get everything ready for the 'Keep Riding' lounge. Zane, Stone, and Luke spent time riding a bit, but also resting a lot. Emme shuffled between snapping shots of the guys riding and helping us out where she could.

"Charley, relax. It's going to be great," Wes tried soothing me.

"What if it's not? What if it's such a flop that you don't sell any boards? I will have ruined the entire Elements Series!"

"That's not going to happen. It will be fine. You need to trust me. We've got to get going, though, or we're going to be late," he instructed, holding out his hand to me.

I took a deep breath and walked to him.

We made our way downstairs to find Zane, Stone, and

Luke gathering up their bags with everything they needed for the day. Emme came out of the kitchen with a bunch of brown paper bags in her hands and held them out to all of us.

"Breakfast on the road today," she announced.

"Awesome. Thanks, sweet cheeks," Stone said.

Luke looked to Zane and warned, "If you don't lock this shit down, I'm swooping in and staking my claim." Then, Luke turned to Emme with a smirk on his face and stated, "Thanks for breakfast, beautiful."

"You aren't claiming shit, but a big air win this week. She's off limits," Zane seethed.

Emme was beginning to look a bit uncomfortable.

Wes chimed in, "Alright, guys. Let's focus on what we've got to get done today. Thank you for breakfast, Em."

She nodded to him and then reached out to hand me a bag.

I shook my head saying, "I can't. I'm going to throw up."

"What?" she asked. "Why?"

"Nerves," I answered.

Everyone stared at me.

"What?" I asked.

"Nerves over what?" Emme pressed.

"The Fire line product launch. I could be responsible for destroying the entire Elements Series if people don't like it."

Luke turned and explained, "We've been riding a long time, Charley. Seen lots of cool shit on boards. Never have any of us seen anything like what you put together. And that is a really good thing. We already told you the work you did was awesome."

"You do know you are going to have three of the best riders in the world using boards with your work on them, right? People will love that. You've got nothing to worry about, babe," Stone put in.

I stayed silent.

Finally, Wes spoke up and added, "I told you, Charley. Not a chance it won't go over well. Trust all of us and believe you've got incredible talent."

I thought about it for a beat before saying, "Okay, I'll try to relax."

"Good. Take breakfast with you," Wes urged. "Everybody ready?"

Everyone nodded. The guys gathered up their bags and split Emme's camera equipment bags among themselves. With that, we all piled into the cars and made our way to the mountain.

Several hours later, the place was packed. Thousands of people had arrived. The Blackman Boards 'Keep Riding' lounge had a steady flow of visitors throughout the morning. We expected that would increase as the day went on. The best part of the day to this point, at least to me, was hearing about the reviews we were receiving on the Fire line. A pre-order had been launched on the Blackman Boards' website and Wes got word that the orders had already started flowing in. The news helped to take the edge off.

My nerves hadn't completely settled because I was now getting ready to watch Zane and Stone go into the qualifying rounds of the men's superpipe event. Along with experiencing excitement jitters for them, even though it was likely they didn't need me to be, I was also rooting for my girl. Emme was about to take photos for one of the biggest events in extreme sports. She was already a very successful photographer, but I knew this opportunity could easily catapult her career to the next level. I couldn't be more excited for her because she deserved this.

Wes and I stood there as we saw Zane at the top of the pipe with Stone. They'd just given each other that manly hug that guys do, slapping each other's back. Zane turned to look down the pipe, strapped his second foot into the board, took a deep breath, and went for it. I glanced over to where Emme was, her camera up at her eyes, completely focused on her target. Zane dropped in, went up one wall of the pipe, did his trick, landed, and continued up the wall on the opposite side of the pipe. Emme stayed focused on him the entire time. He completed his tricks and landed each of them. When he landed his last trick, the crowd erupted. Wes and I were right there with the rest of the crowd cheering for him.

I looked to Emme. She had pulled the camera from her face, but her focus was still on Zane. The grin on her face was bigger than I'd ever seen. It was then I thought about it and really hoped she would allow herself to let go of the past so she could find a way to be happy with him.

Not long after the cheering died down, Zane's score was posted up. He was currently in the lead, which made the crowd burst into applause again. Moments later, our attention was directed to the top of the pipe again. We watched four more riders make their runs. One rider wiped out when trying to land his final trick. The other three made clean, respectable runs, but they were nothing like Zane's. He seemed to soar out of the pipe so much higher than the others. Finally, it was Stone's turn, so I stripped off one of my gloves.

"Can you hold this for me a minute?" I asked Wes, handing him my glove.

"Sure. What are you doing?"

I pulled out my phone and held it up to him.

"I want to get Stone's run on video so I can send it to Monroe. She and Nikki asked for updates from the trip so I'm sending her what I think will be a very crucial update," I explained with a mischievous grin on my face.

He chuckled at me then looked up above the pipe.

I switched my camera on the phone to the video setting and hit the button to record as soon as I saw Stone turn himself on the board and start heading toward the pipe. He went up each side of the pipe flawlessly and did his tricks effortlessly. I didn't know enough yet about riding to know the names of any of the tricks he did or if they were done correctly from a technical standpoint, but it all looked amazing to me. I'd have given both him and Zane perfect scores. I sent the video off to Monroe.

Much like they did for Zane, the crowd roared for Stone. Evidently, Zane and Stone were the favorites in the men's superpipe competition. Stone's score was only two hundredths less than Zane's. We watched the rest of the riders in the lineup, and while some were very good, our guys stayed in the top two qualifying spots following all the qualifying rounds. I felt my phone vibrate in my pocket notifying me of an incoming text. I pulled out my phone and read Monroe's text.

Damn, he's beautiful…and I can barely see his face.

I tapped out a reply.

I thought you might like that. Wish you were here, mama.

She instantly responded.

Me, too. You know, I was totally serious earlier. I can dance anywhere. If I had a really good reason, I'd definitely make the move.

My heart squeezed. Monroe wanted love. I wanted my girl to have that.

You'll get your reason. I promise.

With the superpipe riding finished for the day, we had just under an hour to kill before the big air qualifiers began. Wes and I went back to the lounge to grab some food. Zane and Stone were already there. We walked up to them and Wes did the man hug thing with each of them.

"Sick runs," he said to Zane and Stone.

"Thanks, man," Stone started. "Pipe was awesome today. Hope it stays that way over the next couple days."

I chimed in. "Congratulations. I don't know much about

what you did, but it all looked amazing and way better, in my opinion, than the competition."

"Thanks, Charley," Zane replied.

"We're going to grab some food and head over to watch Luke," Wes told them.

Zane looked around and shared, "I'll grab something after Luke rides. I'm going to head over there now."

He turned and walked out of the lounge. Emme hadn't returned to the lounge, so I had a feeling he was going to look for her

Wes, Stone, and I quickly ate some food while Stone talked about his runs and his plan moving forward into finals.

After we shoveled in some food, we made our way over to show our support for Luke. Big air was set up parallel to the superpipe. We had arrived with about two minutes to spare.

"So, they are going to have a fifteen-minute jam session for qualifying," Wes stated.

"What does that mean?" I asked.

"Basically, there will be five riders and they'll round robin it for the next fifteen minutes getting in as many runs as they can until the time is up. Of all the runs they make in this qualifying round, they'll keep their two best scores."

"Got it," I began. "And how does Luke stack up against the competition?"

Wes smiled at me and answered, "The competition is tough. A lot of these guys put it all out there when they ride. That said, Luke's gotten the gold in this event the past two years and silver for the previous two years."

"Wow. So, he's got to defend his title then. Think he's nervous?"

Wes shrugged and shook his head. "We've been riding for so long. Sure, there's a little added pressure for him since he's at the top of his game and everyone expects him to kill it, but he's pretty good at staying focused and not letting himself get too much inside his own head. I have no doubts that he'll do fine."

"Well, I'm nervous for him," I admitted, turning from Wes to see the first rider dropping in. Wes stood behind me, wrapped his arms around me, and squeezed.

Luke was second to go. I held my breath as Luke dropped in. He picked up speed down the ramp, hit the jump, then spun and flipped through the air. Once again, there were names for the tricks he did, but I had no idea what they were. Luke landed, and the crowd shouted their approval at his run.

At the end of the jam session, Luke and the four other riders managed to each get in five runs. Luke had done a phenomenal job and was currently in the lead.

Day one of the X Games proved to be a success all the way around. The guys were all riding extremely well, my designs had been well received, Wes was more than happy with the launch of the Elements series, and Emme had landed her first extreme sports gig. I was feeling fantastic at how great the day had gone and was looking forward to the next few days.

I turned in Wes' arms and wrapped mine around his neck. "Wes?" I called to him.

"What's up, gorgeous?"

"I think I'd like to go back to our rental and celebrate the incredibly wonderful day we've had here."

"Is that right?" he asked, a sexy grin spreading over his face.

I nodded slowly keeping my eyes on his. Then, I lifted up on my toes and pressed a kiss to his lips.

"Lucky fuckin' bastard."

I turned my head to the side and saw Stone looking at us. I had forgotten he was there.

I bit my lip.

"Sorry," I apologized.

"No, she's not," Wes insisted. "She can't help that she

loves me so much."

Stone shook his head and laughed. "I'm going to head back to the lounge and get my stuff rounded up."

"We're coming right behind you," Wes responded, staying put.

Stone took off at that moment while Wes stood there with his arms wrapped around me. He looked at me a moment before he spoke.

"Feeling better than this morning?" Wes wondered.

"Much better," I answered.

Wes squeezed me tighter and shared, "I'm so proud of you, Charley."

I smiled back at him. "Thank you, Wes. Thank you for believing in me and for taking a chance on hiring me."

"No need to thank me. It wasn't exactly a tough decision to make. I knew from the moment I saw your work that you were meant to do this. I'm just happy that I was able to give you the opportunity so you could see just how good you are."

I hugged him back tighter and pressed my cheek into his chest.

After a few moments, he muttered, "Come on. I want to warm you up. You ready to go?"

I nodded.

Wes kept his arm wrapped around my shoulder as we walked side-by-side back to the Blackman Boards' lounge. When we arrived back at the lounge, we located Emme, Zane, Stone, and Luke. Wes walked over to Luke with me and we congratulated him. After Wes took care of a few business things the employees were handling in the lounge, we loaded ourselves into the cars and went back to the house.

While Zane, Stone, Luke, and Wes took off to shower, Emme and I made dinner. Earlier that morning she had done some prep work, chopping vegetables and beef for his beef minestrone soup. While she got to work on the soup, I took to carving out the bread bowls. Since we had a bit of time to kill while the soup simmered and thickened up, Emme went to shower and I went in search of Wes.

I walked into the den and found Wes sitting at the desk with his laptop open.

"Hey, honey," I said walking over to him.

"Hi, gorgeous."

"We have some time before the food is ready. I was going to head up to take a shower and try to get some feeling back in my limbs again."

"Okay. I have a few things I need to finish here, but I'll be up in a minute."

I took off to the bedroom and hopped into the shower. After I finished, I walked out of the bathroom to find Wes in the bed, shirtless, with the sheet pulled up just far enough to cover his lower half. A shiver ran through my body at the beautiful sight, knowing what was waiting for me beneath that sheet.

I bit my lip.

"I was going to put on something from the goody bag for you," I admitted.

"It's going to end up on the floor in about five seconds anyway. Surprise me with it later. Come here," he demanded.

I dropped my towel, walked over to Wes' side of the bed, and was grasped around the waist. He pulled me over his body, put me on my back, and settled himself over me.

Framing my face with his hands, he shared, "You should know, baby, that I looked at the pre-orders for the Fire line. I've done pre-orders before and while they've always been good, you knocked this out of the park. Our pre-orders were more than double what they've ever been in a single day. And, keep in mind, the day's not over yet."

I looked up at him in shock. "Really?"

A sexy grin spread over his face. "You think I'd make this

up?" he asked.

I bit my lip trying to suppress my smile. Wes' eyes dropped to my mouth then back to my eyes. "I'm so proud of you."

My eyes filled with tears and I barely croaked out, "Wes."

"Give me your mouth, gorgeous."

I lifted my head and gave Wes my mouth. He took. I continued to give. I wanted to give him everything I could. He had given me so much and I needed him to get that back from me. As I moaned, Wes pulled his mouth from mine.

"Love this mouth," he said running a thumb along my bottom lip. "These lips."

I decided to tease him a bit, so I parted my lips and just barely ran my tongue along the tip of his thumb. Wes groaned.

"Make love to me, Wes."

Wes didn't make me wait. He made love to me.

After, we joined the rest of the group for dinner. Following dinner, the guys decided to make it a quiet evening so that they could rest and be fully prepared for tomorrow.

I decided to surprise Wes with something from the goody bag.

He decided he liked surprises.

Twenty-Eight

Charley

"And once again, I'd like to extend congratulations to Blackman Boards' riders Zane Cunningham, Xander Stone, and Lucas Townsend on the clean sweep at the X Games this week!"

The crowd roared and the frontman of the live band at the pub started his set.

We were currently at the Blackman Boards 'Keep Riding' party. The X Games had come to an end and our boys brought it home. Zane had taken first in the men's halfpipe, Stone took second place, and Luke won the men's big air competition. Now, everyone was enjoying the celebration.

I, too, was having a great time. I was feeling such relief at how well the past few days had gone. Wes kept tabs on the Elements Series pre-orders for the Fire line and even he was amazed by how well they did. Of course, Zane and Stone taking wins in the competition only helped drive up the pre-order sales. I was relieved and, despite how much I was enjoying Aspen, there was a small part of me that was excited to get back to Rising Sun so I could start working on the designs for the Air line.

"I know I gave you shit about it before we left Wyoming,

but I've got to admit that I am definitely okay with all of the suitcases and bags you brought with you," Wes remarked. He was standing behind me, his front to my back, and had his head bent so his lips were at my ear.

I arched into him and leaned my head back to rest on his shoulder. I turned my lips to his ear and teased, "Is this your way of apologizing, Mr. Blackman?"

He growled. I felt the length of him harden at my ass.

"Not sure I should be apologizing. This dress is killing me, Charley."

I smiled inwardly. I knew what this dress would do to him when I decided on it. It was a sleeveless, royal blue dress that made my eyes pop. The dress fit like a glove, had a scoop neckline, and had a hem that sat mid-thigh, making my legs look a lot longer and leaner. The best part of it was the back, though. The entire back was open, and the material sat just at the curve of my ass. I certainly didn't have the booty that Emme had, but I had enough to make an impression.

"I thought you might like it," I began. "If you like the dress that came out of one of the suitcases, wait until you see what I have under it. That came from the goody bag."

"Fuck, gorgeous. I do have to stay here a little bit tonight considering Blackman Boards is hosting this party. Do you think you could take it easy on me for the rest of the night?"

I turned and pressed my front to his while wrapping my arms around his neck.

"And what fun would that be?" I questioned, smirking at him.

I felt someone gently press a hand into my back as Wes' eyes looked over my shoulder. I looked to find Emme standing there.

"Hey, Em. What's up?"

Her gaze shot between Wes and me, but she leaned into me, and quietly shared, "I just wanted to let you know that I'm going to call a cab and head back to the house."

I turned completely from Wes, though he kept his arm wrapped around my shoulders.

"What's wrong? Are you okay?" I asked.

Her eyes glanced toward the bar and restroom before she clarified, "Yeah, I'm fine. It's been a long couple of days and I'm just feeling pretty tired."

Something was wrong. I looked back to Wes.

"I'm going to take her back," I advised.

"No, Charley. I'm fine. I just wanted you to know that I was leaving so you didn't worry. I'll call a cab," she interjected.

"We can take you back, Emme," Wes chimed in.

"I appreciate that, but it's a big night for the company, Wes. I don't want to take you or Charley away from that. You've both worked hard, and I want my friend to have this experience. Besides, I would really like some time alone if that's okay."

"Not for nothing, Emme, but you aren't leaving here in a cab. Did you drink anything tonight?" he asked.

She shook her head.

"If you want alone time you take one of the cars back. I'll just grab Zane and get the keys for the other one from him."

Emme's eyes completely bugged out of her head and I knew something was really upsetting her. I had a feeling it had something to do with Zane.

"Wes?" I called.

He looked to me.

"Can we just give Emme the keys to the one we drove here, please?" I asked, my eyes pleading with him.

Wes stared at me a beat, searching my eyes, and conceded. He looked to Emme and instructed, "Come on. I'll walk you to the car."

She let out a breath. Pulling me into a hug, she whispered, "Thanks, Charley."

I squeezed her tight and told her to text when she got back so we knew she was okay. She agreed and stepped back.

Wes bent down to kiss me quickly and assured, "Be right back, baby."

Twenty minutes later, I got a text from Emme that she had made it back to the house, was going to take some ibuprofen, and head to bed. Thirty minutes after that, Zane had appeared. Every time I saw him, Stone, or Luke throughout the night, they had been tied up with either promotional stuff or the occasional fan that insisted on autographs or pictures. The guys were good about obliging their fans.

"Hey, have either of you seen Emme?" he asked, his eyebrows drawn together.

Uh oh.

"She left about an hour ago," I disclosed.

A look of concern washed over his face.

"What? Where did she go? Is she okay?" he worried.

My heart broke. I still had no idea where he and Emme stood, but Zane was really such a great guy. It was very clear to me he cared a lot for her.

I answered him. "She was feeling tired after everything the past few days, so she went back to the house."

He stayed silent, confusion still marring his features.

Wes spoke up, "She wanted to take a cab. Charley and I offered to take her back, but she insisted on going herself, so I let her take the Tahoe."

Zane reached into his pocket, pulled out the keys, and handed them to Wes.

"Here. I'm going to catch a cab back."

I looked to Wes. I didn't know if this was a good idea.

"We're ready to get out of here anyway. We can all just head back now. We'll let Stone and Luke know. Let them enjoy the rest of the night. I'm sure they'll have no problem getting back safely."

Zane nodded but stayed silent. As Wes took off to find Stone and Luke, I stood there with Zane and my heart continued to hurt. Surprisingly, I realized my heart hurt for Zane. At the same time, it shattered for Emme.

"Zane, I'm sorry."

"Nothing to apologize for, babe."

"I feel like I need to do something."

"She's wound tight and it's been a struggle to get in there. Not sure what else I can do. She's not giving me anything and, swear to God, I'd do whatever I could for that girl."

My eyes welled up with tears.

"Zane. If you only knew...she needs someone like you more than you know."

His eyes cut to mine, but he said nothing.

Wes came back and announced, "Luke and Stone are covered. They're going to hang and have some fun. They'll call if they need rides, but something tells me they'll be fine. Ready?"

Zane was already heading toward the door. Wes looked to him and back to me.

"Come on, gorgeous."

The first five minutes of the car ride was silent. I couldn't stand it and I knew that I needed to give Zane something to let him know that Emme needed him to stick with her, despite what she might currently be showing him.

Wes was driving, I was in the front passenger's seat, and Zane was in the back seat behind Wes.

"Okay, I need to say something," I broke the silence as I turned in my seat to face them. My nerves were back at it again and I was certain I was going to throw up. I was suddenly feeling very hot, so I took my jacket off.

Wes turned to look at me a minute and immediately pulled over.

"Are you alright, Charley?" Zane asked. "You don't look so good."

My eyes filled with tears.

"Charley?" Wes asked, reaching out to grab my hand.

I took a deep breath.

"I've *never* talked about this. Ever. I need to do this now, though. Not so much for me, but for Emme," I revealed, tears streaming down my face.

Wes squeezed my hand and Zane sat forward.

I looked to Zane and, through my tears, squeaked out, "Don't give up on her. She is so worth the fight. I promise you, Zane."

"I'm frustrated, but I'm not going anywhere."

"I'm sorry to do this today. It's supposed to be a happy occasion and—"

"Fuck the happy occasion, Charley. Get it out," Wes demanded, cutting me off.

I looked to him and then back to Zane. He nodded to me. I took this as indication that he didn't give a shit about the happy occasion either.

"Emme carries around a lot of guilt. And when I say a lot, I mean *a fuck ton*. You both already know that my brother, Taj, died. What you don't know is that he was murdered and that Emme blames herself for it."

As soon as I croaked out the last few words I turned, opened my door, stumbled out, and vomited. Seconds later, I felt Wes pulling my hair away from my face and holding it back for me. When I felt I had sufficiently emptied the contents of my stomach on the side of the road, I stood up. I'm not sure if it was from the cold or the shock of finally having told someone the truth, but I was shaking and shivering. I turned to Wes and pressed my face into his chest, gripping his shirt in my hands. Then, I felt him settle his jacket on my shoulders before wrapping his arms around me.

"Christ, baby. Let's get you back. Zane's had a couple drinks so I've got to drive. You going to be okay?"

I nodded.

He helped me back into the truck before rounding it and sliding back in behind the wheel. Once he pulled away, I felt something tap my left shoulder at that moment. I looked to see a water bottle being handed to me from Zane.

"It's mine from the pub. Grabbed it on the way out."

"Thank you, Zane."

The rest of the drive home was silent. We all made our way inside and Wes said, "Taking her up. Catch you in the morning."

I looked up to see Zane nodding at Wes. He then looked at me.

"Thanks, Charley. I'm really sorry about your brother, but thanks for giving me an idea of where her head is."

"She deserves to be happy," I stressed. "Be patient with her. What she needs from you…if you give that to her, I promise she'll give it back. Tenfold. She just needs some time to realize you are what she needs. There's more to her story, but that's hers to give."

He nodded at me.

"Let's go, gorgeous."

Wes wrapped an arm around my shoulder and walked with me to the steps. When we got to the bedroom, Wes walked over to my goody bag. He found a nightie and a pair of panties. He walked back over to me and removed the jacket he'd draped over me earlier. Sitting me down on the edge of the bed, Wes pulled off my heels and slipped the straps of the dress down my shoulders. When he got to my waist, he instructed, "Lift up."

I lifted, and Wes continued to slide the dress and G-string down my legs. He kept his eyes on mine and my heart squeezed at the warmth I saw in his eyes. He pulled my panties up my legs and then the nightie over my head. After, he stood and held out his hand. I stood and put my hand in his.

"You want something to eat?" he asked.

I shook my head.

"Okay, go ahead and brush your teeth."

I walked into the bathroom and did what I needed to do. Wes came in to brush his teeth while I washed my face. When I walked back in the room, I found Wes had stripped out of his clothing and was standing in a pair of boxer briefs.

"Let's get in bed, baby."

I climbed into the bed with Wes and curled into him. He was on his back, had an arm wrapped around me, and had his hand resting at my hip. It wasn't long before his fingers started tracing circles on the skin at my hip.

After some time had passed, I said, "Thank you, Wes."

"For what?" he asked.

"For being there when I need you. Not sure what I'd do without you."

"Don't plan on ever letting you have to figure it out, either."

"I'm sorry I didn't tell you sooner about Taj."

"Always told you from the start that I wouldn't pressure you to tell me anything. That's still the case. You'll tell me whatever you need to tell me when you are ready. I'll always be there when the time comes."

I squeezed him and snuggled closer to him.

"I love you, Wes."

"Love you, too, gorgeous."

Minutes later, we both fell asleep.

Twenty-Nine

Charley

WE RETURNED FROM ASPEN ABOUT A WEEK AGO. I SAT STARING out the window of my office at Blackman Boards, thinking. I was still trying to process the past two and a half weeks, including all the success of the new Fire line launch, the situation surrounding Emme and Zane, Greg's recovery, my newfound sense of peace surrounding Taj's death, and my relationship with Wes.

First and foremost, the X Games had proven to be wildly triumphant for the company. Between the results of the contest with our boys winning and the sales on the new product release, Blackman Boards was certainly riding a huge wave of success. Over the course of the last week, I put my effort into the designs for the Air line even though there was not nearly as much pressure to get them completed as there had been with the Fire line.

Upon returning from Aspen, Luke took two days off from riding and was ready to get back at it. Since he was the best big air rider on our team and one of the best in the world, he was heading up testing of the new boards. It would still be several weeks before the designs would be needed. Regardless, I was determined to do my part to make the Wind line at least as successful as the Fire line.

While things were going really well with the company, I was heartbroken that the same couldn't be said for things between Emme and Zane. Following the last night in Aspen where I had spilled my guts, literally on the side of the road and figuratively about Taj's death, the situation with Emme and Zane had grown tense.

This was partly because I saw that Emme had done a lot to avoid Zane during breakfast that next morning. She accomplished this by mostly keeping occupied with cooking and talking with everyone but Zane. It was also partly because when breakfast was over, everyone went about the business of packing up their things for the return flight home. About fifteen minutes after Emme had gone to her bedroom to do this, Zane came out of her room, slammed the door, and stalked off looking extremely ticked off.

This is where things went from bad to even worse. I was certain nobody had shared any news about Taj's murder with Stone and Luke, but it would have been impossible for them to not feel the shift in dynamics between Emme and Zane. Everyone either heard or witnessed the door slamming incident, so it was no secret that things weren't good. At this, Luke didn't help in alleviating any of the tension. Rather, he pushed the issue further by being overly attentive to Emme.

When she had finished packing up her things and was pulling the suitcases out of the bedroom, Luke saw her and carried everything down the stairs for her. Once we were on the jet, it still hadn't eased. Emme sat in a seat and Luke dropped into the seat right next to her. When Zane stepped on the jet a minute or two later and saw this, his hands curled into fists as he clenched his jaw. Ultimately, he turned his head and moved to another seat facing away from Emme.

I was then sitting there thinking about my role in all of this. I thought I had done the right thing by telling Zane about

Taj and where Emme's head was, but at that point, I wasn't so sure.

Wes came and sat next to me. He reached over, put my hand in his, and squeezed. I was thankful for his silent support. He always seemed to know just what I needed without me needing to ask for it. I pulled my knees up to my chest, shifted in my seat, and rested my head on Wes' shoulder.

He kissed the top of my head and whispered, "It's going to be okay, Charley. Promise you."

That said, they hadn't really gotten any worse. The flight back to Rising Sun was relatively uneventful and mostly quiet. When we landed, Wes took Emme and me home in his truck that he left at the airport. Zane, Stone, and Luke all took their own cars home.

Needless to say, it had now been a week since we returned and things weren't exactly okay yet.

Everything sort of fell back into sync for Emme and Zane, individually. Emme hadn't talked about the situation with Zane and he hadn't stopped in my office at all to discuss it. I decided it would be best to let things settle before pushing either of them on the subject. I knew Emme was really upset, more than she had been in a long time, but I understood her reasons for keeping her distance, despite how much I disagreed with them.

To distract myself from the situation with my best friend, the day after we returned from Aspen I went to visit with Greg. He was finally home from the hospital. I had been in touch with him while I was in Colorado and knew he was doing much better but still wanted to check in with him in person. It was such a relief to see him home with a lot of the cuts healing and bruises fading.

What made the visit even more wonderful was seeing and hearing the excitement he was feeling over his newly revived relationship with his father. Greg's mother had still not come around; however, his father had been to see him several times and Tony cooked dinner for the three of them one night.

Before leaving Greg and Tony's place, Greg had insisted that we set a date to go out together. I was worried it was too soon after the accident, but he all but demanded that we get it figured out. Apparently, the accident made him realize just how precious life is and wasting time sitting around was no longer an option. We planned to get together two weeks from then at Big Lou's since Elle would be performing.

This is what I never thought I'd have again. Outside of Emme, Nikki, and Monroe, I hadn't expected I'd have new friends that I cared about like they were my family. I never expected or hoped that I would ever recover from the loss of my brother. While I could never forgive what happened to him and I'd absolutely never forget the happiness I felt around him, I was beginning to feel more at peace with his death.

I knew, beyond a shadow of a doubt, that Wes was solely responsible for piecing me back together and helping me really learn to live life again. And live life is exactly what we had been doing since we got back. Before heading out to Colorado, I told Wes that I was missing the laid-back feel we had experienced in the beginning of our relationship. He promised to give that back to me when we returned. He'd held true to his promise. We hadn't yet gone riding, but we had taken plenty of time to slow down and spend time together, just the two of us.

Just as I was sitting there in my office thinking through all of this, I heard the door between our offices open. I turned to see Wes walking toward me.

"Let's go, baby," he said.

"It's lunchtime already?" I asked, glancing to the clock.

"Yes, but shut everything down for the weekend. I'm taking you to lunch and we are going to go riding afterward. I want to get back out there and, more importantly, I want to give you what I promised I would."

My face lit up and I grinned at him.

"Really?" I asked.

"Fuck."

"What?"

Shaking his head, he answered, "Nothing. I just realized I'm ruined. Looking at you with that look on your face, I realize there isn't anything I wouldn't do to make you feel that happy every day."

I stood up and walked to him, my body colliding with his. "You already do. I was just sitting here thinking about you. It took almost a full year to feel this way again, but you are the only reason that it's happened. I don't know that I'll ever be able to thank you for it."

"It takes the fucking cake that you are this excited for not just spending the time with me, Charley, but that you want the time with me doing something that I love. That, gorgeous, is all the thanks I want," he expressed.

I smiled up at him.

"Now, give me that mouth and then go shut everything down for the weekend," he demanded.

Considering he'd made good on his promise to give me what I needed I figured it was only fair that I give him what he needed. So, I gave him my mouth before I shut everything down.

"Oh, fuck!"

Wes roared with laughter as I shouted obscenities at him. It had been entirely too long since I was last on a board, made evident by the fact that I was now sitting on my ass coming down the mountain.

"Are you okay?" he asked, stopping in front of me and

holding out a hand to help me up.

I reached out to grab his hand and complained, "What the hell? I thought this would be more like riding a bike. You know, like once you learn the skill, you don't forget how to do it."

"It is. But, you only just learned how to do this and you did not get out here enough to continue practicing. You've only fallen a handful of times and we've been out here for a couple hours already."

"It's incredibly frustrating and so exhausting. Who knew that falling took so much out of you? What time is it anyway?"

"Dinner time. You ready to eat?" he asked.

"Wow. It really has been a couple of hours. I guess I don't feel so bad now. I didn't fall *that* much over the last five hours. I suppose I could eat now."

We finished riding down the mountain to head into the lodge. Thankfully, I didn't fall again. As we walked through the lodge, I stopped by Brew Stirs to say hello to Hannah. We confirmed plans for next weekend at Big Lou's before I took off with Wes back to his place for dinner.

Wes and I had settled on grilled cheese and tomato soup from a local café for dinner. After spending the better part of the day on the mountain, I found that there was nothing better than a bowl of soup to warm up with. That, and cuddling up with my man in front of the fireplace.

We sat on the floor at the coffee table in Wes' great room eating dinner. After dunking my sandwich into my soup, I took a bite and looked around the room.

I finished chewing, swallowed, turned to Wes and asked, "Why haven't you finished?"

"Come again."

"Your house. You've got enough furniture and essentials to live and get by, but you don't have decorations or personal touches. Why haven't you finished it?"

Wes took a bite of his sandwich, chewed for a moment, and answered, "Couple of reasons. First, I've been too busy with everything in the company. Putting in late nights, all I want to do is come home, eat, and sleep. Second, when I started carving out more time for my personal life a few months ago, the only thing I was interested in doing with my free time was you…and maybe a little bit of riding. And last, I'm a guy and know shit about decorating a house. In my opinion, if there's furniture, it's decorated."

I rolled my eyes.

"Well, that's just ridiculous. You could have at least put up a couple of pictures," I suggested.

"I did. In my bedroom, on the nightstand," he reasoned with his sexy grin spreading across his face.

"That, my friend, does not count. I gave you that for Christmas. And I had to guess on what kind of frame to put it in since I had no idea what your style was."

"It's a picture frame. Does it really matter? Besides, I really only care about the picture that's in it."

I stared at him, dumbfounded.

"You cannot be serious," I exclaimed.

He gave me a look that said he absolutely was serious. I just shook my head at him.

"I like your style. You picked out a good frame," he teased me.

I didn't answer him. I smiled inwardly and went back to my soup.

"Decorate for us, gorgeous."

I dropped my spoon.

"Excuse me?" I asked.

"Decorate for us."

I swallowed hard and asked, "What do you mean *us*?"

"Are you my woman?" he asked.

I nodded.

"So, decorate."

After staring at him in silence for a moment, I explained, "It's your house. I can help you decide on things that will look good together, but our relationship is still relatively new. I don't want to put my style here and then if things don't work out—"

"Don't even fucking finish that statement, Charley."

I shut my mouth and looked at him. He was not playing around. I bit my lip. His eyes dropped to my mouth for a beat before coming back up to my eyes.

"This, what we have between us, isn't a game for me. I'm at a point in my life where I know what I want and when I find that I'm smart enough to not let it go. And baby, I don't give a single fuck about a wreath on my front door or candles all over the place. But *you*? I want *you* all over this house."

He stopped speaking for a moment, letting that sink in. It barely got through the surface before he started speaking again.

"I want you to move in, baby. I'm more than happy to have just you here, but I realize that women are into all that pretty shit. I'm good with whatever you decide to do if that means your head is on the pillow next to mine every night."

"You want me to move in with you?" I marveled, my voice barely a whisper.

He laughed. A deep throaty laugh. I loved that sound and while it would normally make me smile, I continued to sit there staring at him. Wes' face got serious again.

"Seriously, Charley?"

"Isn't it a bit quick?"

"You just said you were my woman. And I just told you that I'm not going to let go of what I want. Time isn't going to change that in a bad way. So yeah, gorgeous, I want you to move in."

I didn't know what to say so I stayed silent.

"It doesn't have to be today. I know you need to figure shit out with Emme. But soon, okay?"

I pushed my soup bowl back from the edge of the table. Then, I turned toward Wes. He leaned his back against the couch while I climbed over into his lap and rested my head against his chest. He wrapped his arms around me as I spoke. "Okay, honey. Soon."

Thirty

Charley

"A SEXY DRESS, A PAIR OF HEELS, AND A NIGHT OUT WITH friends always does the trick."

I was currently trying to convince Emme to come out for the night with all of us. She'd been back to work with editing photos from the X Games on top of her other clients. That was the only part of her life that had gone back to normal, or the new normal, since we returned from Aspen. Other than that, she was much quieter, and I knew she was still feeling very sad about the whole situation with Zane. I attempted to get some details on that whole issue, but she had not been willing to discuss. I respected her choice, at least for now.

It had been a week since Wes asked me to move in and I was too caught up in trying to figure out how I was going to bring up the whole Operation Move In With Wes to her. My life was at a point now where I was enjoying living and I wanted everything that went along with that, including moving in with my boyfriend. As much as I wanted that, I would never abandon Emme.

In an effort to try to lift her spirits and possibly loosen her up a bit so that she'd start talking about the Zane situation, I figured a night out with a little alcohol might work.

"I'm not really up for it," she mumbled.

"I know. And that's exactly why you need to go. You've been really bummed since we've come home from Aspen and it's been hard seeing you this way again. I get it, Em—I really do, but I can't keep watching you live inside your head. I am not going to push you to pursue anything with Zane, even though I think he's really great for you, but I am going to push you to live a little."

"I understand what you are trying to do, Charley. I do appreciate your concern, but I'm just not feeling up to it."

"Then you leave me no choice. I'm going to have to cancel with Greg, Tony, Hannah, and Wes and tell Elle I can't come watch her tonight because I'm staying in with you. We will then call up Nikki and Monroe and tell them all about why we are staying in," I offered, knowing that she wasn't going to let me give up my night out.

She gave me a death stare, pushed up off my bed, and grunted, "Ugh, fine. I'll go out."

I rolled from my belly to my back and shouted to her as she walked out of the room, "That's my girl! And you better have a sexy dress on that ass, Em!"

A couple of hours later, I had just put the finishing touches on my makeup. Emme walked in and I was shocked to find that she had listened to me. She was dressed in a pale pink, spaghetti-strap dress. The top of the dress had a plunging neckline which did wonders for her cleavage. The dress pulled in at her waist and pulled tight in a crossover pattern mid-thigh. She curled her hair, which only made her massive amounts of hair even bigger. Smoky eyes, pink cheeks, and a hint of gloss on her lips finished off her look. The girl was sex on a stick.

"You are one smokin' hot lady, Em," I complimented her, walking out of my bathroom.

She rolled her eyes and shook her head at me.

"You're not so bad yourself, sweets."

I looked at my reflection in my full-length mirror. My carnation pink dress also came to mid-thigh but was a body-con style with a V-neckline. It was sleeveless but had straps that covered the entire top of my shoulders. The whole front of the dress was ruched to the center and met in the middle at the rope-like pink band that ran down the front middle part of the dress. The look gave me curves where I didn't necessarily have them.

I smiled back at Emme and confirmed, "Ready?"

I told Wes that we'd meet him there. He was initially not happy about it, but when I explained that I was bringing Emme along he understood and conceded.

"Physically? Yes, I'm ready to go."

"It'll be a great time, Em. Come on," I reassured her as we walked out of my bedroom.

We locked up and made our way to Lou's. After we parked, we walked up the steps to the saloon where Elle would be performing. I was surprised to see Lou just inside the entrance.

"Charley! Emme! How are my pretty girls doing?" he asked pulling us both into hugs.

"Hi, Lou. We're doing well. Thanks," Emme answered.

"Yeah, we came to hang with some friends and watch Elle tonight," I added.

"Elle always draws my biggest crowds. Love that girl as if she was one of my own. Go on in. I saw Wes inside already," he replied. Then, he turned his attention solely to Emme and said with a puzzled look on his face, "Sorry darlin', didn't see Zane yet."

She looked to me and back to Lou. I chimed in, "No worries, Lou. We'll just head in and see if any of our other friends are here yet. Good to see you again."

"Same to the both of you. Have a good night, girls," he called as we walked away.

As soon as we got out of earshot of Lou, Emme tugged on my arm and stopped walking. I turned to her and she questioned me. "Is he going to be here?"

"Honestly? I don't know, honey. I haven't seen much of Zane since we got back from Aspen. I used to see him frequently in the offices, but I've seen him twice in the past couple of weeks. He hasn't talked much either when I did see him."

Her eyes grew big.

"Really?" she asked.

I nodded.

She swallowed hard, her eyes welled up, and she began to fret, "Oh, God. Do you think he's really mad at me?"

I felt for my friend. What she was going through wasn't easy, but I knew she needed to hear the truth on this.

"I can't say for sure as I haven't seen him much since we got back home, but I know that he really likes you. He's spoken to me about it a couple of times. Initially, I only told him that you had been through a lot and that it might be tough to convince you that a relationship is right for you. That last night in Aspen when you took the Tahoe back to the house while we were all still out, I told Wes and Zane about Taj."

Emme's eyes snapped to mine. "What?" she asked.

"I only told them that he was murdered and that you feel responsible. They don't know anything else and I won't divulge that. It's yours to share if you want. That said, I really do think that if you shared with Zane, it would not be a bad thing. And, it might help to bring a little understanding of the situation for him."

She nodded but said nothing.

"I want you to think about this, but let's not worry about it tonight. Come on, Em. I want you to have a good time."

"Okay, Charley, let's go."

We walked into the room where Elle would be performing

and immediately spotted Wes. He was standing next to Elle. His back was to me, but Elle saw Emme and me enter and acknowledged us with a bright smile and a wave. Wes turned to look at us and his face warmed when his eyes locked with mine. Then, his eyes traveled the length of my body. His face went from warm to smoldering in seconds.

We walked over to them and he wrapped an arm around my shoulders, pulling my body into his.

"It's nothing new, but you should know you look amazing," he whispered in my ear.

"Thank you, honey. You are looking pretty delicious yourself."

And he did.

"Come on, Wes. Stop hogging her and let me say hello to Charley," Elle demanded, taking me out of my own little world with Wes.

He chuckled and loosened his hold on me. I turned to Elle and gave her a hug while Wes greeted Emme.

"I was just telling Wes that he needs to bring you by the house again. Mom and Dad haven't stopped talking about you since Christmas. If Wes doesn't bring you by again soon, Mom is going to send out a search party."

I looked to Wes and he confessed, "She probably will."

"Then we better go soon," I suggested to him.

"I'm going to head back and get ready to go up here shortly. I'll talk to you later tonight. Enjoy the show."

"You've got it. Rock it, El!"

"Good luck, Elle," Emme chirped.

Wes bent his head, kissed her on the cheek, and wished her luck. It warmed my heart every time I saw his closeness with his sister. Seeing that always made me remember the close relationship I'd had with Taj.

As Elle walked off, I turned back to Wes and asked, "Have you seen Greg, Tony, or Hannah yet?"

He began shaking his head, but stopped mid-shake and pointed out, "Looks like they just walked in."

They spotted us right away and walked over. Everyone exchanged greetings and we all grabbed seats front and center to watch Elle. Everyone ordered a round of drinks and I told Wes that I wouldn't be having more than one since I thought Emme needed a night to loosen up a bit more than I did. He acknowledged this with a nod.

I turned toward Hannah and stated, "I thought you were bringing a date."

"I was. Then I decided not to," she replied, shrugging.

"What she really means is that the guy she was seeing is no longer in the picture," Greg added. "But, it's for the better. He wasn't good for her. Nice guy, but way too rigid. Hannah needs someone who is much more flexible. This guy scheduled everything!"

"He liked routine," Hannah barked back.

"Yeah, that's all good until he wants to start scheduling sex," Greg shouted back at her.

Tony, Wes, Emme, and I all just laughed.

Wes decided to break up the banter between Greg and Hannah and asked, "So how's the recovery coming, Greg?"

"Really well, Wes. Thanks. Other than a few bruises marring my to-die-for body, you wouldn't know I was even in an accident that bad."

We all laughed again. Leave it to Greg to make light of such a serious situation.

Lou was up on the stage at that moment introducing Elle. Everyone cheered for her and she rolled right into her set. With the music, the drinks, and the conversation, we were having such a great time. I noticed that even Emme had started to really get involved in the conversation. Since she was typically very quiet in situations like this, I knew I had accomplished my mission.

Three or four songs into Elle's set I felt a hand at my back and turned to see Stone there. Behind him were Luke and Zane.

Uh oh.

Wes cut in, greeted the guys, and thanked them for coming to support Elle. I exchanged greetings with all of them, and they did the same around the rest of the table. When Zane got to Emme, he simply dipped his chin and offered, "Em."

She replied, "Hi, Zane."

That was it. I saw the sadness wash over her face and her eyes well up with tears while the frustration washed over Zane's. Neither acted on these feelings, though, and Emme managed to pull it together before she fell apart.

The guys had pulled up a couple of chairs and joined us. Despite the tension I noticed between Zane and Emme, everyone still had a great time.

Elle finished her set and joined the group. The music began pounding over the speakers, so I got up to go dancing with Emme, Elle, and Hannah. Greg joined us briefly, but eventually went back to hang with the guys. After dancing for a long while, the four of us took off to use the restroom.

We finished up in the bathroom and made our way back toward the table. The girls and I were wiped and were ready to call it a night. As we approached the table, Hannah and Emme were ahead of Elle and me. They turned around to face me and both worried, "Oh no."

"What?" I asked.

I looked beyond them to the table to see Dana sitting in *my* chair with her hands on *my* man. Wes' back was to me.

"You've got to be kidding me," I heard Elle said beside me.

She started to take off toward the table when I grabbed her by the arm.

"It's okay, El. I've got this."

I walked up calmly and all eyes at the table came to me.

All eyes, except Wes' and Dana's. She still hadn't noticed I was there.

I heard her speaking, "You've obviously changed and are making time for things other than work in your life. You know we would be much better together. I miss you, Wes."

He pushed her hands off his arm and leg and asserted, "I'm making time for other things because they are important to me. Charley is important to me. It's over between you and me and there isn't a chance in hell that we'll be getting back together."

"Oh, Wes, we're so good together. I mean, she's—"

"Standing right behind you," I cut her off.

She turned to look at me and she actually had the audacity to smirk at me. Wes was looking at me with concern on his face. I decided to immediately calm his fears.

"It's okay, honey. Despite everyone else here understanding what you said and knowing what that means, you aren't speaking in a language that she understands," I explained to him. Then, I directed my attention to her, "Last week, Wes and I sat in his great room in front of the fire and he asked me to decorate his place. Actually, correction—he asked me to, and I quote, decorate for us."

Her eyes rounded and her jaw dropped.

"Now she gets it," I heard Greg say.

I decided not to let it go at that.

"That's right. Wes asked me to decorate, which ultimately led to him asking me to move in with him. You had your chance with him. You decided to walk away from that. I'll be damned if I sit by and watch you attempt to ruin what I have with him. Now, before you make yourself look like even more of an ass, I suggest you leave."

She waited a moment, looked to Wes who had his eyes on me, and got up to walk away. As soon as she had gotten far enough away, I took my focus off her. My eyes were pulled toward Emme who had stepped into my line of vision. She looked completely sobered up and sad.

Shit. I just dropped major news on her via an altercation with Wes' ex.

"Em, I'm sorry."

A tear slid down her cheek. She broke my heart.

Where was Greg when I needed him to lighten the mood?

"Emme, please. I didn't want you to find out this way. I've been struggling with how to tell you, but—"

She cut me off by holding her hand out in front of her. When I stopped speaking, she spoke. "Wes asked you to decorate his house and move in?" she asked.

I nodded. "I need you to know that it's not happening immediately, and that—"

She cut me off again.

"This happened a week ago?"

I nodded again.

"And you didn't think it was a good idea to tell your best friend?"

"I'm sorry, Emme."

"Why?" Her voice was practically a whisper.

I stayed silent. I wasn't sure how she'd react to my reasoning. I also knew that I would not lie to her. So, after a good minute, I decided to tell her the truth.

"Because I really want it. I *really* want to move in with him. I've started living life again and it feels so good. And I didn't know how to tell you. I don't want to just up and abandon you. And, to be honest, it feels a lot like abandonment."

"Charley, I'm so disappointed that you didn't think I could handle this news. You're my best friend. You are supposed to share things like this with me. We're supposed to celebrate it. And you didn't think I could handle this? You didn't think I'd be happy for you?"

"It's not like that, Em. I am just worried about you."

"I get that, but Charley, come on. Don't you think it would finally be freeing for me to know that my life isn't continuing to ruin yours? I'm the reason Taj is no longer here. You think I wouldn't want this for you?"

Oh. My. God.

She thought she was a burden in my life.

"You haven't ruined my life, Emme. And Taj's murder is not your fault. I don't know how to make you see that."

"Are you kidding me? It was my psycho ex-boyfriend who decided to pull the trigger."

"Exactly. He's the one responsible. Not you."

"I called Taj. I never should have called Taj that day. If I hadn't called him, he'd still be here," she cried, shaking her head back and forth as the tears streamed down her face.

"And it's very likely you wouldn't be. You barely survived as it is, Em."

"What the fuck?" I heard Zane explode from behind me somewhere.

I forgot for a moment where we were and that we had an audience. I turned to look back at my friends and my boyfriend. Everyone had a look of concern on their face. My attention was turned back to Emme when she started speaking again.

"That's right, everyone. It was almost a year ago when Taj was murdered, and I nearly died right next to him. My ex-boyfriend beat the shit out of me for months, years actually. And that wasn't even the worst of it. I decided to call Taj one night because it had gotten so bad I knew I wouldn't make it out alive if I didn't get to the hospital. He managed to get me out of there to safety, but he was ultimately shot and killed. So, you see, the problem is that Taj succeeded in saving me, but lost his own life in the process."

With that statement, Emme turned and walked away.

Thirty-One

Charley

"MOTHERFUCKER!" Zane roared as he pushed his chair back from the table.

"Dude, chill out," Stone ordered, placing his hand on Zane's shoulder.

"Chill out? Did you just fucking hear the same thing I did? Emme was beaten by some asshole to the point she was hospitalized and nearly died. Not sure how the fuck I'm supposed to calm down right now."

Luke chimed in, "I'm just as fucking pissed about that shit as you are, but you need to calm down because the last thing that girl needs right now is someone with a short fuse around her. Chill the fuck out and go find her or I will."

Zane held Luke's eyes for a moment, took in a breath, and stalked off in the direction Emme had gone.

"Oh God," I began to fret as the tears started streaming down my face.

Wes took me in his arms and held me.

Moments later I heard Greg, Hannah, Elle, and Tony surrounding me.

"Charley, girl, I'm so sorry," Greg started. "I had no idea."

Hannah's hands wrapped around my shoulders while Wes

continued to hold me. "So sorry about Taj, babe."

I pulled out of Wes' hold and looked to my friends.

"Thanks, guys. I'm sorry I ruined the night."

"Ruined?" Elle challenged. "Charley, love, that whole showdown with Dana earlier was pure entertainment. Sorry about the situation with Emme, but you two will work it out."

"Thanks, El."

Wes' voice filtered in. "Did you drive your car here or did Emme drive hers?"

"I drove," I answered.

Luke walked up and instructed, "Give me your keys, babe, I'll get your car home. You ride with Wes."

"Oh, Luke, you don't have to do that. I'll be fine."

Holding his hand out to me Luke ordered, "Babe. Keys."

I reached over to my purse at the table and dug out my keys. I handed them to Luke and he grinned before he praised, "You verbally kicked Dana's ass tonight. That was awesome."

"Seriously fucking awesome, Charley," Stone added. "I'll follow Luke and give him a ride from your place to his."

"Thank you, guys."

"No problem, babe. Wes, catch you later," Luke said.

"Later," Wes returned, offering a chin lift to his friends.

"Can I catch a ride home with you guys?" Elle asked Greg, Tony, and Hannah.

"Girl, you are a superstar. Of course you can ride with us," Greg answered.

"Elle, I can take you," Wes insisted.

"Wes, you need to be with Charley right now. I'm a big girl," Elle responded.

Tony chimed in, "It's okay, Wes. I'll get her home safely. You take care of our Charley girl."

Wes nodded to Tony.

Everyone said their goodbyes as we made our way to the parking lot. Wes hauled me up into his truck and we took off.

"Are you good with going to my place?" he asked.

Trying to swallow past the lump forming in my throat, I barely got out, "I'm worried about her."

Wes pulled out his phone, tapped on the screen a few times, and held it up to his ear.

"You with her?" he asked.

He paused for a moment.

"Was going to take Charley to my place, but she's worried about Emme."

He waited again while I assumed Zane was responding.

"Right. Keep me posted." Another pause. "Okay, man. Later."

"Zane is with her. He will take care of her, Charley. I swear that to you. He knows what he's dealing with and would never hurt her. He said she's really out of sorts now and pretty upset, but he's handling it. Zane knows she is fragile. He said for you to come with me to my place and to give him the time to help her now. He'll call if he needs us."

I nodded.

Wes and I sat in silence the rest of the way back to his place. When we got there, I walked through the house to his bedroom. I could feel him following behind me. Once I entered the bedroom, I stripped out of my dress, pulled on one of Wes' t-shirts, and climbed into his bed. He stripped out of his clothes and joined me. Wes wrapped an arm around my waist and pulled my body toward his, my back to his front. He had left the bedside lamp on.

"You've got to know, gorgeous, we'll do whatever we have to and see her through this. All of us—not just me, you, and Zane. I also want you to know that even though the night ended the way it did, I was pleased as fuck to hear you say what you did. First, what you said to Dana because that was hilarious. And second, when you told Emme that you really wanted to move in with me. Made my year, baby."

"I really do, Wes. I love you and want to start making a life together with you. I just don't want to hurt her in the process. I don't want to leave her alone."

"You want my thoughts?" he asked.

I nodded.

"She loves you, Charley. She wants you happy. We all know that what happened to her and to Taj is not at all her fault, but it's no surprise she blames herself. She is feeling responsible for you experiencing the pain you have over the last year and finally seeing something good happening in your life will help how she's feeling. She might even begin to realize that, despite what happened, there can still be good to come of it."

I wiggled and turned my body so that I was on my back. I looked to him and wondered, "Are you sure you aren't just saying this to get me to move in with you sooner?"

He grinned at me. "If it helps my cause, then I'm going to use it. That said, I wouldn't say it if I didn't honestly believe it were true."

I smiled up at him. "Thank you, honey."

"For what?"

"You always make it better. No matter what it is, you always make it better for me. Thank you."

His face warmed as he looked down at me.

"So, what room are you going to start with?" he questioned.

"What?"

"Decorating. What room are you going to start with?"

"Oh, see? You do care about it more than you like to admit."

"Not a chance. But, I'm amazed at how you can say decorate to a woman and she finally understands some deeper meaning."

I smiled at him. "Women think differently than men. I knew Dana would get the significance of that statement and realize she no longer had a shot with you. I don't regret saying it. To answer your question, though, I think the bedroom would be the first place to start."

"Really?" he asked. "I thought the bedroom was the one place that was half decent as far as decor goes."

"It's missing something, though, and I need to rectify that. It needs a little more me next to, on top of, underneath, and beside you," I teased as I gently pushed his shoulder so he was on his back. Then, I climbed on top of him to kiss him.

"Works for me," he replied. "I have a feeling I'm going to love what you do with the space."

He barely got out the last word when I captured his mouth with mine. I went on to show him just how good I was at decorating. And I found that Wes knew a thing or two as well.

The next morning, I woke to an empty spot next to me in the bed.

I frowned and sat up in the bed. Just then, the door to the bedroom opened. Wes came in carrying two cups of coffee and a frown.

"Damn. Sorry, baby. I thought I'd be back before you woke up," he remarked.

"You come bearing gifts. You are forgiven," I replied taking one of the mugs out of his hand.

I took a sip, closed my eyes, and swallowed.

"Good?" he asked.

I nodded.

"I talked to Zane a few minutes ago," he shared.

My eyes shot to his.

"How is she?" I worried.

"She's still asleep. Took a while for her to settle last night. Zane said she's only been sleeping about two hours," Wes told me.

I closed my eyes at the news.

"She's going to be okay, Charley. I promise you—whatever it takes. Zane is understandably pissed about the situation and the role he played in any distress in her life over the last few weeks, but he's hoping he can make up for that now. He really cares a lot for her."

"I know she is attracted to him. And I know that she has enjoyed being around him. Prior to the X Games, the time she had been spending with him was good for her. She was the happiest she had been in years. I hope he can get through to her and that she allows him to help her through this."

"If there's anything I know about Zane it's that he doesn't quit. He won't give up on her, especially now. Give it time. He'll get her there."

I smiled meekly at him and took another sip of my coffee.

"So, I figured since Emme is probably going to be asleep for a bit and my parents are hankering to see you again, I thought maybe we could stop over there this morning and visit with them if you're up to it."

I thought about it for a moment and agreed, "Yeah, I think I'd really like to do that."

"Okay. I'll call Ma and let her know. Go ahead, get showered and ready," he urged, placing a kiss on my forehead.

Forty-five minutes later I was ready. I was thankful that I made the decision a few weeks ago to bring over some clothes to Wes' place. Of course, he had already stocked the place with a ton of Blackman Boards apparel for me, but sometimes a girl needed a few familiar pieces from her wardrobe. Wes didn't seem to mind that I brought them over. In fact, he encouraged me to bring more.

"Ready?" he asked as I walked out into the kitchen.

I nodded.

He wrapped his arms around me and bent down to press a kiss to my lips. Because I was feeling extra loving and frisky this morning, I decided to give him a little more than just a peck back. I gave him my tongue and then ran my hand along the front of his pants.

He groaned into my mouth.

I pulled my mouth away briefly and questioned, "What time do we have to be at your parents' house?"

"Fifteen minutes," he answered.

"Damn," I muttered. "I had the urge to play a little. I was hoping to take you in my mouth before we left."

"Christ, Charley. You are going to make me get into the habit of being late to my parents and not giving one single fuck either."

"We can't make a habit of it, Wes."

"Okay, well, we can worry about being on time the next time we visit. Today, we are going to be late. I'm not waiting until later today to have fun with you."

Wes picked me up and I wrapped my legs around his waist. He walked us over to the couch in the great room and sat down with me in his lap.

I pulled his black, waffle knit shirt over his head and worked my way down his body. Running my hands and lips all over his chest and abdomen, I found that Wes' breathing quickened. He was seriously turned on, and I was feeling extraordinarily powerful. I brought my hands to the waistband of his grey cargo pants and undid the belt, button, and zipper. I freed his cock from his boxer briefs and wrapped my hand around the top of the shaft. I traced my tongue up the underside from root to tip before taking just the head into my mouth and gently sucking.

"This fucking mouth," Wes' husky voice filtered into my ears.

I took that statement as words of encouragement and took all of him that I could into my mouth. I worked him in a slow rhythm before I picked up the pace. I then alternated between sucking him into my mouth and licking up and down his shaft. Seeing the heat in his eyes, I grew turned on and started moaning. I reached my other hand up to massage his balls. Between the moaning and massaging, I'm not sure which did him in, but he was soon tapping me on the shoulder and saying, "Charley—fuck, baby, you've got to stop or I'm going to come."

I pulled my mouth off of him, looked him in the eye, and admitted, "I want it, honey. Give me your pleasure." Then, I took him back in my mouth until he came.

Once he finished, I pulled away and smiled up at him.

"Destroyed me, gorgeous. Love this mouth," he hummed as he lifted me up and set me on the couch beside him.

He gently pushed me back so that my shoulder blades were against the armrest. He lifted one foot and removed my boot before moving to the other.

"What are you doing?" I asked.

"I'm going to take care of my woman," he shared.

"Is that so?"

He unbuttoned my jeans and pulled them down my legs followed by my panties.

"Damn right it is."

"You know I didn't take you in my mouth just to get you to do this for me, right?"

"Doesn't matter what your reason was, gorgeous. I'm still doing it. Now are you going to stop talking so I can eat you?"

I bit my lip and nodded.

Wes chuckled, put his hands under my ass, lifted me, and ate. He ate like he hadn't had a meal in months. Wes always made comments about my mouth; but if I was being completely honest, I had to admit that he had one talented mouth. It wasn't long before Wes had me calling his name and trembling underneath him.

When I came down from the Wes-induced orgasm, I

reached a finger out to touch his bottom lip and whispered, "This fucking mouth."

He threw his head back and roared with laughter.

"Good one, gorgeous, but that's my line."

I shrugged and smiled at him.

A few minutes later we were in the truck on the way to visit Wes' parents. We were late, but his parents didn't seem to mind.

Three hours later Wes and I were leaving his parents' house and heading to check on Emme. We pulled up to the condo and I sat in the passenger's seat, staring.

"What's going on in that head?"

"She's my family, Wes. My heart breaks for her."

"It'll be okay, Charley."

"She was so angry with me last night."

"That's allowed, gorgeous. If she's your family, she can be angry at you. But once she's had time, she'll look at it all and realize that she loves you more than she's angry at you. Trust me."

I stayed silent. Wes was right. Emme and I were family and our love for each other wouldn't allow this to come between us.

"Okay, honey. I'm ready to go in," I declared.

Wes hopped out of the truck, came around to open my door, and held my hand as we walked to the door.

Amid everything that happened last night, I was surprised that I remembered to take my house key off of the ring with my car keys so that I'd have a way into the house. I put the key in the lock, opened, and we pushed inside.

Upon entering we found Zane in the kitchen, but no Emme. He looked like he hadn't slept all night.

"Where is she?" I asked immediately.

"Shower. She just woke up a little while ago," he answered.

"How is she doing?" Wes pressed for more information.

"It took a lot to calm her down, but she finally did and slept. I'm pretty sure it was just exhaustion that overtook her. She's been quiet this morning. To be honest, I didn't learn a whole lot last night, but with the stuff that she did share it was pretty fucking difficult to keep my shit together."

I closed my eyes and dropped my head. Wes wrapped an arm around my shoulder and pulled me into his body.

"Sorry about your brother, Charley. Sounds to me like he was a stand-up guy who, if given the choice, would do it again."

I looked back up and locked eyes with him. Speaking through the tightness that had formed in my throat and the tears that had spilled over my cheeks I confirmed, "In a heartbeat."

He nodded at me.

I looked between him and Wes and stated, "I'm going to go check on her."

Wes squeezed my shoulder, kissed the top of my head, and reminded me, "No matter what, remember she is your family and she loves you."

He let me go and I walked down the hall toward Emme's bedroom. I knocked lightly on the door, turned the handle, and let myself in. She was standing in front of the door to the balcony looking out at the mountains. As I walked in, she turned to look at me. I stopped just inside the door.

We stared at each other for several minutes saying nothing.

"Em," I rasped, my voice cracking. "I'm so sorry."

She held my eyes a beat before a single tear spilled over her cheek and she turned back to look out at the mountains. I didn't move. My breathing quickened. She wasn't going to forgive me. I had lost my parents and my brother. I could not lose one of the girls who had become my sister.

"Emme. Please. Yell at me, throw something, do whatever you need, but please talk to me."

She didn't turn to look at me, but she finally spoke.

"Regret is something else, Charley. Isn't it? You make a choice on something, follow through, and then hope you don't regret that choice. Every day. Every single day I regret my decision. I never should have called Taj that day. Maybe I could have still survived, and he'd still be here. But I can't change it. I can't go back and choose again," she stated, finally turning to look at me. "If I had the choice to do it all over again, I never would have called him."

"Taj loved you like a sister. He loved you like he loved me. I'm sorry that things went down the way they did last night. I'm sorry that part of your story was told to a group of people that you don't know all that well. But I'm not sorry for what I'm about to say. Em, he wouldn't want this. You need to stop blaming yourself. You need to start living your life without regret and find happiness. You need to listen to what I'm saying and do it because if you don't, then Taj died for no reason. I understand how hard it is. It took me a very long time to get here, but trust me, *you* can get there, too."

She was crying at this point, but managed to get out, "I'm so scared, Charley."

I went to her and wrapped my arms around her. "That's okay. You can be scared and cautious. But you are still here, Emme, and you need to live. He would want you to live. He would want you to be happy. He did what he had to do to make sure you survived. Please, honey, don't let him be gone for no reason."

She cried for a long time. We both did.

Eventually, after we both settled, I clarified, "I'm not looking for any guarantees, but can you promise me one thing? Promise me you'll try. Do it for Taj, Em."

She looked me in the eyes when she resolved, "I promise I'll try."

I smiled at her. She grinned back and asked, "So, Wes

asked you to move in with him?"

I nodded.

"You know, I wasn't upset about the fact that you wanted to move in with him. I'm so happy you found someone who will give you the world. I was hurt that you didn't tell me about it. Then, when I had the time to think about it, after having a complete and utter meltdown here last night, I realized that I haven't exactly been the most forthcoming either. I've kept a lot to myself lately and I'm sorry. It was really hypocritical of me to get angry with you when I haven't shared much about what's going on in my life."

"It's okay, Em. I know you'll share those things when you are ready," I assured while winking at her.

"Is Zane still here?" she asked, hope filtering through her voice.

I nodded and responded, "Yeah. He's out there with Wes. This isn't me pushing you, but Emme, you should really think about that one. He cares a lot for you and, honey, I think he's one of the good ones."

She nodded and then looked out the window. She stayed quiet for a moment and I gave her that time. I think she knew that what I said about Zane was the truth, but it would understandably take her some time to get there.

"Think we should go out there?" she asked.

"We've got two extremely hot guys out in our kitchen and we're standing here. I absolutely think we should go out there," I answered.

I turned to walk to the door and she called, "Charley?"

I looked back at her. "Yeah, Em?"

"Love you."

My soul warmed. Yeah, Emme was absolutely my family. I responded, "I know, Em. Love you, too."

We walked out of Emme's bedroom and down the hall toward the kitchen. I smelled something delicious. As we stepped into the kitchen, I saw Zane bringing a stack of plates over to the island as Wes set two boxes of pizza on the island. Both guys stopped what they were doing and looked to us. Concern was written all over their faces.

I decided to break the silence.

"You ordered pizza?"

Wes and Zane both let out the breath they were holding.

Wes smiled at me and confessed, "Yeah, you girls want to eat?"

I looked to Emme and smiled.

"Well, you two can't exactly eat all of this on your own," I pointed out, hopping up on one of the stools gesturing to the two boxes on the island.

They laughed.

"Peppers and onions or mushrooms?" Wes asked me.

"Peppers and onions," I answered.

Wes put pizza on a plate for me and then for himself. He came over to sit next to me, leaned into me, and whispered, "All good?"

I looked away from Wes to see Emme walking over to Zane. He handed her a mushroom slice on a plate, which was her favorite and I hadn't heard him ask her, and quietly confirmed, "Are you doing okay, sweetheart?"

I didn't wait to hear her answer. I turned my attention back to Wes and with a huge grin on my face I declared, "All good."

He pressed a kiss to my temple and took a bite of his pizza. The four of us spent the rest of the afternoon together, eating pizza, talking, and even playing some board games. I'm not sure if Wes and Zane were the type to play games, but they went along with it and seemed to be having fun so I didn't dwell on it. It was a really, really nice time. Nobody brought up the events from last night and even though there was plenty of opportunity for it to be awkward, the guys made sure it never went there. I was so thankful for them.

Before I realized how late it was, Wes stood up and announced, "Early day tomorrow at the office and a crazy week this week. I've got to get some sleep."

"Yeah, I'm ready to drop," Zane added as he stood.

I looked to Emme and her eyes were worried. I took that as my cue to give her some space.

"Why don't you just crash here tonight? We can ride in to work together tomorrow," I suggested to Wes, as I got up off the couch.

"You actually want to go in with me? Didn't you insist on being independent and showing up on your own?"

"I figure if I am going to move in with you, I need to start getting used to having company on my drive in to work."

His sexy grin spread across his face and he conceded, "Okay, gorgeous, I'm all yours tonight."

"You better be all mine every night."

I turned to Emme and saw she was still sitting on the couch, looking down at the floor. I walked over to her.

"You okay, Em?" I asked, quietly.

She shrugged.

"Wes can go to bed ahead of me. I'm good to stay up for a while with you," I offered.

"I'll be alright, sweets. Thanks," she said.

"Okay. If you need me, you come and get me. Got it?"

She nodded.

I hugged her tight and said good night. Then, I walked to Zane, pulled him into a hug, and whispered, "Thanks for taking care of my girl last night and today."

He whispered back, "She's not just your girl anymore."

I froze in his arms at his statement, but quickly recovered and pulled back. He winked at me. My heart melted.

"Good night," I said, turning to Wes and wrapping my arm around his waist.

As we walked down the hall toward my bedroom, I turned my head to look back at Zane and Emme. She was standing up next to the couch and looking him in the eyes. His hand came up to brush down the side of her cheek. I smiled inwardly. Zane was right. She wasn't just my girl anymore. I just had a feeling she didn't know it yet.

Once we got into my bedroom, I stopped and turned to Wes.

"I love you."

His face warmed. "I love you, too."

"Thank you," I began, pausing for a moment. "There are so many other things you could have done today, but you spent it here with me and my best friend, well, and your best friend, and you did that because she needed us here with her today."

"Charley, I was here for you. Sure, I knew that Emme needed to not be alone today, and if nobody else was here, I would have stayed with her. But I would be doing that for you. Today, I was here for you because you needed me. Nothing else that I could have done today is more important than giving you what you need."

I pressed my cheek into his chest, hugged him, and breathed in his scent.

"Let's go to bed, gorgeous."

"Okay, Wes."

Thirty-Two

Charley

COUNT YOUR BLESSINGS. ISN'T THAT HOW THE SAYING GOES? Undoubtedly, my life up until about three months ago had been dismal. That's a lie. I had an extraordinary life filled with lots of blessings until I was fifteen. Then my parents died, and I tried to stay focused on the good I still had in having my brother with me. But when he died, and it became extremely difficult to remain positive.

Three months ago, a man walked into my life and changed everything. He made me see the good again, and I was so thankful for him. I began counting my blessings.

After an exhausting weekend, I had been looking forward to a relatively stress-free week at work. Lucky for me, I got just that. And aside from the two weeks leading up to the X Games, I had never really been stressed at work. It never felt like work and I thoroughly enjoyed what I was doing. Blessing number one.

Correction. That was blessing number two. Blessing number one was the realization that after Saturday's turn of events there should have been a much bigger fallout between Emme and I and there wasn't. I was so worried then that the doom and gloom was headed my way, but she surprised me with her understanding of my predicament and we were able to move quickly on to much happier topics.

So, blessing number one was my kickass best friend slash sister slash roommate who had a heart of gold. Blessing number two was a stress-free week of work.

It was now Friday afternoon. Everything was still going smoothly in my life. Wes and I had just gone out to lunch where he told me he had something he needed to show me when we got back into the office. The excitement filtered through my body as we stepped off the elevator and walked down the hall to Wes' office. Once inside, he told me to have a seat on one of the couches. He grabbed an envelope off his desk and handed it to me.

"What is this?" I asked.

"The Fire line has been doing phenomenally well, Charley. Blackman Boards has always done well with board sales. We make a quality product, our riders are some of the best in the world, and our designs were decent. With the Fire line, we retained the same product quality, our guys are still riding at the top of their game, but we've added you and your designs. The Elements Series has exploded with just the first line. The Air line is nearly completed. We've already received numerous inquiries on when they'll be released. I expect the Air line will do just as well as the Fire line did. I'm so proud of what you did with the designs."

"Thank you, Wes. That's awesome news. I'm so happy to hear that the series is off to such an amazing start."

"I had some ideas about what to do with the Water and Earth lines before I even met you. Once I met you, saw your work, and learned about Taj, I decided what I wanted to do with the Water and Earth lines. My plans for the rest of the Elements Series are in that envelope."

I looked down at the manila envelope I held in my hand and back up to Wes.

"Nobody else knows my thoughts yet. I want your opinion and your blessing on it before I proceed with it. Open it and tell me what you think."

I had butterflies fluttering madly in my belly. The anticipation was too much to bear, so I quickly tore open the envelope and pulled out what was inside.

My stomach tightened at what I saw. Staring back at me on the first page was Wes' idea for the Water line. My nose began to sting, my eyes welled up, and the lump quickly formed in my throat.

I looked to Wes, tried to swallow past the lump in my throat, and croaked out, "Is this for real?"

He nodded.

I looked back down at the paper I held in my hands and took it all in. This was it. I knew beyond a shadow of a doubt that this is what the Water line should be. The paper was adorned with the front, back, and side profiles of a surfboard.

"Charley?"

I looked back at him. The tears spilled down my cheeks.

"I love it, Wes."

He let out a breath.

"One more thing, gorgeous. I want to dedicate this line in memory of Taj. I did some research after you told me about him. He was a phenomenal surfer. Everyone knew who he was and they loved him; he had quite a following. I think we should give his fans a little piece of him if you are good with it."

"Wes," I rasped, my voice barely a whisper as I set the papers down and stood to wrap my arms around him. He held me for a while before I could speak again. "Thank you, honey. This means everything to me. You could give me nothing else for the rest of my life, but this and you will have given me the world."

"Fuck, baby. Couldn't be certain, but I was pretty sure and

really hoping you'd be happy about it. But I honestly didn't think you'd feel this deeply about it. I love that it means so much to you."

"Wait. What's the Earth line idea?" I asked, suddenly realizing that I didn't get past the surfboards and the Water line.

I turned back to the papers on the table as Wes sat in the chair across from the couch.

"Honestly, it doesn't even matter at this point since I'm more than happy with your reaction to the Water line, but I think we're going to branch out into skateboards for the Earth line. Basically, the idea is to make Blackman Boards the leader in board production for some of the best extreme sports in the world."

I picked up the papers and flipped through until I reached the Earth line. I quickly scanned the page and then looked back at Wes. "You are a genius, Mr. Blackman. And I find that to be incredibly sexy. In fact, I'm extremely turned on right now thinking about this brilliant mind of yours."

"Well I would never want you to be turned on and me not do anything about it. Come give me that mouth."

I walked over and straddled Wes on the chair. Then, I gave him my mouth and he did something about me being turned on.

A couple of hours later, as we were leaving work, I was still riding the high of the news Wes had delivered to me in his office that afternoon. I could not wait to start the designs for the Water line. Without a doubt, these designs would all be inspired by Taj. I was so caught up in feeling giddy and excited that I almost forgot to acknowledge my third blessing.

"I know we did some celebrating in my office this afternoon, Charley, but I'm not quite ready for it to end. Stay with me at my place tonight?" Wes requested as he turned on the truck and pulled out of the lot.

"Yeah, I think I'd like to do that. Let me just call Em quick and let her know I won't be home. I want to make sure she'll be okay."

He nodded at me.

I pulled out my phone, brought up Emme's contact card, and put the phone to my ear. After two rings, she answered.

"Hey, sweets. What's going on?"

"Hey, Em. Wes and I are celebrating a great end of the week at Blackman Boards today. I just wanted to let you know that I was thinking of spending the night at Wes' place tonight."

"Happy to hear that. Awesome."

"Are you working tonight?" I asked, not sure if she had a shoot.

"No, nothing for a few days," she answered.

"Oh." I bit my lip and turned toward Wes. "Well, Wes and I could come there tonight if you are going to be alone."

"Charley. Stop. Go and celebrate with your man. I'll be fine. I have a bit of news, though. Zane is going to be coming over tonight to take me on our first official date."

"*Oh my God! Are you serious?!*" I screeched.

"What the fuck is wrong, Charley?" Wes worried.

I held my palm over the speaker of the phone and whispered, "Sorry, honey. Zane's taking Emme out tonight on their first official date."

He shook his head and mumbled, "Fucking women."

Emme continued, "Yeah. I just found out a little bit ago. He called me up and asked me out on an official date. I promised you that I would try to find a way to live life happy for Taj, so I'm making sure not to break my promise."

"Oh, Em. I'm so happy for you. Are you good with outfit, hair, and makeup? I can stop by quickly and we can video chat with Nikki and Monroe to make sure you've got it all covered."

"Charley, relax. I already called Nikki and Monroe. In fact, I was on the phone with Nikki when Zane called me. I told her

I'd call her back. When I did, I told her about it and she went crazy. She got Monroe in on the whole thing and they decided on the perfect outfit for me. I've already taken care of my hair. Go celebrate and enjoy your night with your man."

My eyes filled with tears. "Have a great time tonight, honey. Send me pictures before you go!"

"I will. Love you, Charley."

"Love you, too, Em."

I disconnected the call and tossed my phone back in my purse. I stared out the front window and tried to let it all sink in. Blessing number four.

"Wasn't that good news?"

"Yes. Why?"

"Well, why does it look like you are going to cry?"

"I'm a woman. Sometimes, we get emotional."

"Really?" he asked in disbelief.

"Emme is going to try, Wes. She's going to try to get what she deserves. I can feel it in my bones and it's slightly overwhelming. You should know, though, that if Zane hurts her, I will personally kick his ass."

"Trust me, baby, you don't need to worry about that."

"How can you be so sure?" I questioned.

Wes pulled the truck up the driveway to his house and shared, "Sunday afternoon you were in talking to Emme while Zane and I waited in the kitchen. He told me about what he went through with her Saturday night into Sunday morning. His reaction to what he learned told me everything I need to know. He's got it bad for that girl."

"Did he actually say that?" I continued to quiz him, as he turned off the truck and hopped out.

When he came around my side of the truck and opened the door, he explained, "He didn't need to. I heard him say enough other stuff that was eerily familiar to things I was feeling and would have said about you if the roles were reversed."

My eyes rounded and my mouth parted slightly.

"You understand now? He's got it bad for her. She's in really good hands, Charley."

I nodded my agreement.

"What are we going to do for dinner tonight?" I asked as we walked through the house.

"I bought some steaks earlier this week. Was going to cook for you tonight, but I want to take a quick shower first. Then, I'll get started. Are you okay to wait a little to eat?"

"Yeah, that's good. I'm going to check in with Nikki and Monroe. I haven't talked to them since earlier this week and we now have big news to discuss," I replied with a big smile adorning my face.

Wes walked into the bedroom and through to the bathroom. I heard the shower turn on as I sat down on the bed and I pulled out my phone to call my friends. I chatted with my girls for a bit and ten minutes later, Wes walked from the bathroom to his closet in a towel. He came out of the closet in a pair of jeans that sat low on his hips as he pulled a crisp white t-shirt over his head. Wes winked at me as I continued talking and then gestured that he was going out to the kitchen to cook. I nodded back to him. He kissed me on the top of my head and left the room. I finished up my call with Monroe and hopped in the shower.

After I was done in the shower, I put on some lotion and threw on a pair of panties, shorts, and a camisole. I ran the hair dryer through my hair for a few minutes before walking out into the kitchen. When I entered the kitchen, I did it quietly and looked at Wes standing over the island pouring two glasses of wine. He hadn't noticed me yet, so I drank in the sight of him for a bit. I definitely considered myself to be one lucky woman because, amongst all of his other qualities, Wes was breathtaking. Easily blessing number five.

I scanned his body from head to toe. When my eyes made

it back to his face, I realized I'd been caught. Wes was smiling at me and joked, "Like what you see, gorgeous?"

I shrugged and nonchalantly admitted, "I mean, it's alright."

"Liar. I'm surprised you didn't draw blood."

"What?" I asked.

"If you bit that lip any harder, you'd be sucking on some ice right now."

Shit. I looked away.

Wes walked toward me. He put his finger under my chin and tipped my head back so my eyes could no longer avoid his. Damn, and he smelled so good.

"Don't be embarrassed, baby. You can look all you want. It's all yours anyway."

"I know."

He took my hand and walked me the rest of the way into the kitchen. Wes grabbed the glasses of wine off the island and handed them to me.

"Take these over to the table. I'll grab the food."

I took the wine glasses into the dining room and waited while Wes followed behind me with the food. He made steak, roasted red potatoes, and brussels sprouts. I cut a piece of steak, which was cooked to perfection, put it in my mouth, closed my eyes, dropped my head back, and moaned.

When I opened my eyes, I saw Wes' eyes were intense.

"I'm sorry, honey. This is delicious."

"It's okay, Charley. But it's going to be difficult to get through dinner if you do that after every bite."

"I'll try to control myself," I joked.

"Appreciate it."

We took our time with dinner, enjoying conversation, and each other's company. I quickly realized I could get used to this every single day. We finished up dinner and cleaned up together.

After putting the last of the dishes into the dishwasher, Wes went to the fridge and noted, "Dessert is on the couch tonight."

When he turned around, I saw he had a bowl of strawberries cut up. He held them up and asked, "Do you prefer them with whipped cream or chocolate?"

I tilted my head and gave him a look that told him I was in shock.

"Is that even a real question, Wes? Chocolate, of course. If you ever give me the choice between chocolate and anything else in the world, I'll always choose chocolate."

He laughed at me. "Good to know."

"It'll serve you well to never forget that fun fact," I insisted.

Wes pulled out the chocolate hazelnut spread and put some in a bowl. He grabbed the strawberries and the chocolate spread while I grabbed the wine and we went to the couch. After I cuddled up next to him, Wes took a strawberry, dipped it into the chocolate, and brought the dessert to my mouth. The scent of chocolate hit my nose and my lips parted. He gently rested the fruit on my bottom lip. Opening my mouth a little wider, I took a bite of the strawberry. I moaned again. I chewed slowly, savoring it, and swallowed. Wes' gaze grew heated.

Taking a strawberry out of the bowl, I dipped it into the chocolate and fed it to Wes. He took it in one bite. Then, he brought the strawberry I hadn't finished back to my mouth. I decided it would be fun to tease him a little, so I opened my mouth just enough to take the remainder of the fruit and the tips of his fingers into my mouth. I licked his fingers as I pulled the berry into my mouth. He groaned, and his eyes never left my mouth.

When he focused his attention back to my eyes, I grabbed another strawberry to feed him. As soon as he had it between his teeth I decided, "I think we should do this more often."

He swallowed and pointed out, "You'll need to be here more often if we're going to make that happen."

I took the bowls and set them on the coffee table. Then, I climbed onto his lap and kissed him. He tasted so yummy.

"Well, maybe you'll have to convince me to be here more often," I teased. "Got any ideas on how you can accomplish that?"

With his hands framing my face and an intensity in his eyes I'd never seen before he pleaded, "Marry me."

My eyes rounded and I gasped. "What?"

Wes' thumbs brushed back and forth across my cheeks.

"You're it, Charley. I've said it many times before, but you are it for me. I love you. I want you here with me every day and every night from now until the day I die. You are all that I want. And for the rest of my life, I'll spend every day doing whatever is necessary to make sure you always feel loved. Please tell me you feel the same and will be my bride."

I stared back at Wes, shocked by his unexpected grand gesture. "Oh my God," I barely whispered.

His eyes searched my face for any indication of what I was thinking. I'm not sure if he found it because I, myself, had no idea what I was thinking at that moment. Well, except for one thing.

I began nodding and cried, "Yes, Wes, I will marry you."

His mouth was on mine in an instant as he wrapped his arms around me and stood, taking me with him. I crossed my ankles behind him while he supported my weight keeping one hand under my ass and the other on my bare thigh. Wes effortlessly walked us into the bedroom, kissing me the entire way.

He made his way to the bed, planted his knee into the mattress, and gently put me down on my back. He kissed the skin under my lips, on my chin, down my throat, and kept going down until his lips pressed against the skin on top of my beating heart. I'm certain he could feel it was about to beat out of my chest. My emotions were running wild and I felt the tears fall from my eyes.

"I love you, Wes."

He pulled back to look in my eyes. Then, he stood and walked away from the bed. He went into the closet and came back seconds later carrying a tiny box. I sat up in the bed.

"I want you wearing only this tonight," he explained as he sat back on the bed opening the box in front of me.

Staring back at me was a rather large round cut diamond, surrounded by a halo of diamonds, on a thin band that I assumed was platinum. It was beautiful.

Wes pulled the ring out of the box, took my left hand in his, and gently slid the ring on my finger. It fit perfectly. I looked down at it sitting on my hand for a moment before I looked back up into his eyes.

"Wes," I rasped out.

Before I could say anything else, his mouth was on me again. He started at my hand and worked his way up to my shoulder. Wes peppered kisses along my neck as he reached for the hem of my camisole. He tore his mouth from me only briefly so that he could pull the material over my head. Then, he planted a kiss right over my heart, down between my breasts, and down my abdomen. When he reached the waistband of my shorts, he dug his fingers into the sides of them and my panties and pulled both down my legs. He divested himself of his clothes and stood there.

My left hand had come to settle on my abdomen. Wes looked down at my hand and back up into my eyes.

"Most gorgeous thing I've ever seen and you're all mine," he said, his voice hoarse.

"Honey?" I called. "I think I've finally found something I'd choose over chocolate."

He laughed, brought his body to rest over mine with his

mouth inches from mine, and stated, "I fucking love you, Charley."

"That's good, Wes, especially considering you're going to be my husband."

He smiled at that but said nothing, so I continued, "I love you, too. And now I'm feeling the need to celebrate all the goodness that has just happened."

"Whatever you need, gorgeous. Always, everything you need."

With that, Wes gave me the goods and we celebrated blessing number six for most of the night.

Thirty-Three

Wes

A COUPLE WEEKS AGO, STONE SAID SOMETHING TWICE THAT WAS now ringing true in my head. I was a lucky bastard. I pretty much agreed with him then, but now it was undeniable.

It was early Saturday morning and I'd only gotten a few hours of sleep. I spent most of the night last night making love to my future wife. Charley was currently cuddled up against me, her front to mine, while her face was pressed to within inches of my chest. I could just barely feel her warm breath as it hit my skin.

I had myself propped up on one elbow, my head resting in my hand. My other arm was draped across her body while my fingertips traced along the skin at her hip. I loved doing that to her and she loved when I did it. I sat there looking down at her and knew I'd be content to spend the rest of my life waking up and doing this every single morning.

She started to stir. It usually took a few minutes of touching her, but she always woke in a great mood when she woke like this. Her eyes fluttered open and I watched as she mentally inventoried last night and realization hit her. I knew the instant she became aware of what had happened because she closed her eyes again, bit her lip, and cuddled closer to me.

"Good morning, gorgeous."

She tipped her head back to look up at me

"Good morning, Wes."

If I didn't love the sound of her raspy voice first thing in the morning, especially when she said my name. And now, I'd have a lifetime of hearing that.

"How are you feeling this morning?" I asked.

She pulled her lip between her teeth before she answered, "Like a well-loved fiancée."

"Happy to hear it."

She pulled her hand up to look at her ring. When she smiled, I couldn't help but feel a huge sense of pride at seeing my ring on her finger.

"I can't believe we're engaged, honey. Do you think everyone will think we are crazy because this is so fast?"

"I don't really care what anyone thinks about it other than you. There's not a single doubt in my mind that you were made for me, Charley."

She was about to say something but stopped herself.

"What is it?" I asked.

"Nothing, Wes. It was stupid. Never mind."

"It's not stupid. Obviously, it's something. Just tell me."

She hesitated a moment, then looked me in the eyes, and explained, "I was just going to ask if you felt that way before. You know, with Dana?"

I closed my eyes for a second before I looked at her. I hated that she had doubts about this and the fact that she wasn't the only person I'd ever been engaged to. I answered her honestly. "Not at all. Dana was comfortable. She was all I knew for so many years; it just seemed like the next logical step. This, baby—you and me, is everything I've needed. It's never dull or routine. It's not me feeling like I'm working to provide a living for someone who will never be satisfied. It's about being with someone who shares a true joy for my passion and who cares about other people. It's about being with someone who makes my life better simply by sharing hers with me."

"Wes," she purred, her voice just a hair over a whisper. I smiled back at her knowing what she wanted to say, but couldn't find the words for.

She pushed past it and asked, "Did you know all day yesterday that you were going to propose?"

"Don't you think I would have prepared a little bit more and made it perfect if I had known I was going to propose?"

She shrugged. "I don't know, Wes. It felt pretty perfect to me."

"See, gorgeous? That was it. I knew a few weeks ago that I wanted to marry you. I started searching for rings before we left for Aspen. Picked this one up a few days after we got back. I was just waiting for the right time to give it to you. Then yesterday, in my office, you said one thing that made me realize that it was the right time. I didn't know I'd actually ask you yesterday, but then the opportunity presented itself and I didn't want to hold back anymore."

She drew her brows together. "What did I say?" she asked.

"After you saw the Water line idea, you stood in front of me and said that I could give you nothing else but that for the rest of your life and that I would have given you the world. Felt that deep in my gut, baby. I knew right then that I'd spend forever trying to give you the universe."

"Oh, Wes. I think I'm going to cry," she warned.

"Don't cry. Kills me to see it."

She took a deep breath in to stave off the tears and argued, "They would have been happy tears, Wes. I'll try to keep them in check."

"Obliged."

"What are the plans for today?" she asked.

"Anything, Charley. Whatever you want."

She bit her lip. My eyes dropped to her mouth. I was certain that mouth would kill me one day.

She looked up at me through her hooded eyes and gushed, "I'd really like to tell my friends the good news."

I couldn't wait for the world to know that this woman was mine, so I was on board.

"Okay, so let's get up and get ready. I'll text Zane to make sure Emme is home and we can go to your place so you can tell her in person."

"Don't text Zane. If she's there and he's with her, I don't want her to know anything before we get there. Let's just take a chance on them being there."

I nodded and squeezed her hip. "Whatever you want. Do you think you can handle one more round before we go?"

"Because I'm feeling extra loved by you right now, I'm willing to give you two more rounds."

What did I say? Lucky fucking bastard.

It was just after nine that morning when we left our house. Charley insisted on picking up breakfast, in the form of donuts, before going to see Emme. We arrived at the condo right around nine-thirty that morning.

"They're here," Charley announced as we pulled in to park. "See? There's Zane's truck and Emme's car."

I glanced at her and saw she was beaming from ear to ear. The things I'd do to see that look on her face every day. She was bouncing in her seat with excitement.

I took the box of donuts from her hands as we walked up to the door because I was certain with her level of eagerness they would end up on the floor. We reached the front door, where she slid her key in and opened it.

As we entered the kitchen, we found Zane and Emme already there with cups of coffee. She was sitting on one of the bar stools at the island while he was standing on the opposite side of the island leaning on his elbows. I wasn't sure if we interrupted something important, but as soon as we walked in both of them had looks of surprise on their faces.

Charley walked right up to Zane, hugged him and greeted, "Good morning, Zane."

He returned the sentiment as Charley made her way around the island to Emme. She pulled Emme into a hug. "Morning, Em."

"Morning, sweets. Hey, Wes," Emme offered.

"Emme," I said, nodding in her direction.

Charley came back to me and stated, "So, Wes and I wanted to come by this morning and bring breakfast."

She took the box of donuts out of my hands and set them on the counter.

"Um, thanks?" Zane responded hesitantly, as he looked to me knowing something was off.

"Zane, relax. Of course, while I plan to get details of your date with my best friend, I wouldn't intentionally barge in on that. Though, I must say the fact that you are here is especially good news. Wes and I wanted—actually, it was just me who wanted—to bring the donuts. I felt they were needed. You see, I figure the only proper way to celebrate things this early in the morning with our friends is with donuts."

"Sweets," Emme started. "It was one date. Don't you think a celebration is a bit overboard?"

"Two answers to that. First, no it's not because you haven't had a first date in what—nine years? Second, that's not what these donuts are being used to celebrate. Though, if you want to add your first date to the list we can."

"I feel like we missed something. What's going on?" Zane asked, a confused look washing over his face.

"Well," Charley began and then paused as she looked to me. "Do you want to tell them?"

"It's all yours, gorgeous. You can do it."

She smiled up at me and then looked back at Zane and

Emme. "Last night, Wes asked me to marry him."

Charley held out her left hand to show off her ring and declared, "We're engaged!"

"Oh my God!" Emme shrieked as she jumped off the bar stool and ran over to pull Charley into a hug. "This is amazing! I'm so happy for you, Charley. Congratulations!"

While the girls stood there hugging each other, Zane walked over, slapped me on the back, and offered, "Congrats, man. You picked a good one."

"Thanks, Zane. Without a doubt, she's the best for me," I admitted.

Seconds later, Emme was wrapping her arms around me. "Congratulations, Wes. Thank you for choosing my best friend. She deserves all the happiness in the world and is so lucky to have you."

I hugged her back. "Thanks, Em. I consider myself to be the lucky one, though."

I glanced over to Charley and winked at her. Zane congratulated her.

"Okay," Emme spoke up. "Now the donuts make sense. Who wants one?"

She opened the box and we all grabbed one. We then spent the morning with the girls mostly rehashing the entire unplanned proposal. Several times throughout the entire story, I'd glance over at Zane and see him looking at Emme's reactions to it. Yep, he was just as fucked as I had been when I'd first gotten involved with Charley.

After she had recounted all the details, Charley asked the group, "Can we go out tonight to celebrate?"

"Yes!" Emme shouted.

"Fuck. You've been so quiet since I've met you," Zane stated, his attention on Emme. "Didn't think you had it in you to be this loud. That's good to know, sweetheart."

She blushed and looked away.

To help take the attention off her, I affirmed, "Elle is performing at Lou's tonight if you want to do it there. In fact, my parents are even going to this performance. I can call Stone and Luke, tell them to meet us there. Charley, you can call Greg, Tony, and Hannah. We'll tell everyone the news there."

"Yes, that sounds awesome, but first I have to call Nikki and Monroe."

"I'll grab my laptop and we can Skype with them," Emme advised.

She ran out of the kitchen to get the laptop and came back not even thirty seconds later with it. The girls sat on the stools on the opposite side of the island while Zane and I listened from out of view of the computer screen.

"Hey, babe. How was your date?" Nikki asked. "Fuck. Charley is there, and I don't see a hot guy, so this can't be good news. I really thought Zane was a good one. What happened?"

We heard a ringing sound again.

"Hey Em! Hi Charley," Monroe greeted. "Oh shit. The date didn't go well. I'm so sorry, babe."

Zane nudged me and quietly asked, "What the fuck?"

I couldn't help it. I just shrugged and laughed. Sometimes women were crazy. Couldn't say I didn't love that about Charley, though.

Emme glanced at him over the top of the computer screen and smiled. Charley spoke up.

"Zane is still here, ladies. In fact, he's just heard everything you both said. Wes is also here."

"What? So why are you both sitting there calling us instead of hanging out with Hottie Number One and Two?"

Emme explained, "Charley has some news she wanted to share."

With excitement in her voice, Monroe practically burst, "Oh my goodness."

Holding her left hand up in view of the camera Charley

shared, "I'm engaged!"

Screaming ensued.

See? Crazy fucking women.

The girls congratulated Charley who then pulled me over next to her so that I was now on the screen.

"Hello, ladies."

With tears in her eyes, Monroe spilled, "Congratulations, Wes. You've made our girl so happy."

"Thanks. She does the same for me," I reassured her.

I directed my attention to Nikki. "You better take care of our girl or you'll answer to the rest of us."

"I'd expect nothing less," I insisted with a smile on my face.

"Congratulations."

I nodded at her.

Zane walked over to stand next to Emme so that he was now on the screen. Monroe and Nikki directed their attention to him. "Just so you ladies are aware—Emme and I had an amazing fucking date and it went really well."

Emme looked away as Nikki shouted, "You gave her the goods, didn't you?"

Emme was quick to shut it down. "Okay, we're done now. Charley wanted to share her news with you before telling anyone else. We're going now."

"I want details later!" Nikki yelled.

"Call me later, babe," Monroe said to Emme. "Congratulations again, Charley and Wes. I'm so happy for you both."

Everyone said goodbye and Emme closed the laptop. The girls decided they needed to go shopping for a special celebratory dress. I hated shopping. Zane did too. At that moment, though, we were both completely fucked because we'd have agreed to anything either of them wanted. They promised to make it as painless as possible and swore we'd be no more than two hours. I had no idea why anyone needed two hours to pick out one dress, but I wasn't going to ruin the day for Charley.

The girls kept true to their promise and were done with a half hour to spare. We dropped them off at the condo to get ready and told them we'd be back later to pick them up. Zane offered to be the designated driver since Charley and I were celebrating.

A couple hours later I was on my way back to the condo. I decided to drive there so I'd have my truck there in the morning. I knocked on the front door and was nearly knocked on my ass when Charley opened the door. Despite having been there when she bought the dress, I hadn't actually seen it.

She was wearing a dress that hugged her body in all the right places. It was a short, pale-pink dress that showed off her long legs. As if that wasn't torture enough, the top half of the dress would have me fighting myself to not get hard all night. It had thin straps holding up pieces of fabric that covered her breasts. The dress was so low cut in the front I could immediately tell that she wasn't wearing a bra. The dress had a satin ribbon around the waist and sequin designs all over.

"Hey, honey. You look amazing. I just want to put a pair of earrings in and I'll be ready to go. Emme is ready and Zane just got here. Come on in."

She turned around to walk away. I saw the back of her dress and reached my hand out to grab her arm. Other than the two thin straps that held the dress on her shoulders her entire back was exposed.

"Gorgeous. You look so beautiful—I'm not sure I want to go out anymore."

She tilted her head and replied, "Thank you, Wes. I'm happy you like it, but we *are* going out tonight. I want everyone to know that you are mine forever."

I smiled at her and teased, "Already trying to lay down the law, are you?"

"You know it."

I laughed and ordered, "Give me your mouth first, then you can get your jewelry."

I kissed my woman good before she took off to finish getting ready. A couple minutes later, the four of us piled into Zane's Ford Raptor. We arrived at Lou's not long afterward and made our way up to the saloon.

Elle and my parents were already there as were Stone and Luke. I didn't see Greg, Tony, or Hannah yet. By the time we walked over to where everyone was, I turned back to the door to see Charley's friends walking in.

I leaned down and whispered in her ear, "Greg, Tony, and Hannah just arrived. We can tell everyone together."

She nodded and grinned at me.

After everyone exchanged hellos and caught up briefly, Charley gave me a look that said she was ready.

"Hey guys, I want to make an announcement," I boomed over the group.

Everyone turned their attention to me as Charley curled into my side.

"We're so glad all of you are here tonight because we have some news. Last night, I asked Charley to marry me."

Charley held out her left hand to show off her ring.

Elle, Greg, and Hannah screamed. My parents were beaming, especially my mother who had tears in her eyes. Stone and Luke looked shocked, but immediately shouted out well wishes to both of us. Tony took a cue from them and came up to congratulate both of us.

Elle settled long enough to come over, wrap Charley in a hug, and announce, "I'll finally have a sister! Congratulations!"

After Elle pulled away, she looked to me and tears filled her eyes. She stayed silent for a beat as a single tear fell down her cheek. "I'm so happy for you," she started as she walked to me and hugged me. I hugged her tightly as she whispered, "She's the one for you, Wes. I've known it since the first day I saw you with her. I see how happy she makes you and that makes me super happy. Congratulations, big brother. I love you."

"Thanks, Elle. Love you, too."

My parents congratulated the both of us next, followed by Greg and Hannah. Just as we got through all the shock for everyone, Lou was up on stage getting ready to announce Elle. She tapped him on the shoulder, whispered in his ear, and then he looked out at us.

Only Elle.

"Ladies and gentlemen, I'm going to announce our hometown favorite here in a minute, but I just received some fantastic news. My boy, Wes Blackman, is officially off the market. He proposed to one of my favorite pretty girls, Charley Meadows, last night and they are now engaged. Please join me in congratulating them."

Everyone cheered and shouted their well wishes.

"Wes, Charley—love you two together. I'm honored you chose to celebrate this wonderful occasion here at Big Lou's. Drinks for your entire party are on the house tonight. Wishing you both a lifetime of happiness."

I nodded up to Lou who then announced Elle. She immediately dove into her set. Everyone enjoyed her performance and she even threw in a couple extra covers specifically dedicated to Charley and me. Shortly after she finished up, my parents called it a night, but not before praising me on my decision to make it official with Charley. I was beyond thrilled that they loved her for me so much.

After my parents left, the girls got up to dance while I hung at the table with the guys, minus Tony and Greg. The two of them had taken off somewhere.

"Wedding bells, man? I still can't believe it," Stone declared.

"I wasn't going to waste any more time. That girl is it for me," I responded honestly.

"I'm still shocked. It was quick. Either way, I'm happy

for you. Think you made a good choice with that one," Luke noted.

I looked to Charley on the dance floor. Her body was moving to the music and she had just tossed her head back to laugh at something one of the girls said. Sitting there watching her, I realized that, without a doubt, she was the best decision I'd made in my life.

"Thanks, Luke. Appreciate it. What about you two? Planning on settling down any time soon?" I asked.

"Fuck no, dude. I'm completely content being single," Stone shared.

"Yeah, besides, we've got this one here to worry about next," Luke pointed out, as he nodded his head in Zane's direction.

Zane was watching Emme and didn't even acknowledge what Luke had said. I wasn't convinced he even heard us.

"Yo, Zane," Stone yelled.

Zane turned his head back to us.

"What's up?" he asked.

We all laughed before Stone asked, "You next?"

"For what?"

"Getting married."

"Not planning on going at lightning speed like this one here," Zane began as he pointed to me. "If I was going to settle down with anyone, I'd do it for that girl. She's going to take a little persuading, though."

"Looks like it's just you and me from this point forward," Stone concluded, looking to Luke. "These two are down for the count."

"Maybe you should try finding a single someone to be with instead of a new person every time you are out," I suggested.

"You two got lucky with Charley and Emme. There aren't any women like that out here. Besides, a new person every time keeps it fun," Luke maintained.

"May I remind you that they have two other friends?"

"Yeah, both of whom don't live here. I'm not planning on moving to California, and I'm definitely not into having a long-distance relationship," Luke replied.

"But if those girls moved here, you'd consider something?" Zane asked.

"Not me," Stone began. "I'd have no problem showing Monroe a good time, especially with those fucking legs of hers, but that's it for me."

I decided not to push it. I remembered my conversation with Charley a couple weeks ago about Monroe. She never gave me specific details, but she was very serious in what she said when she told me that if Stone wasn't into the idea of a long-term relationship, then we shouldn't push it. Even without details, I knew that Charley took her friendships very seriously and, if or when, she needed to share details she would.

A little while later, Luke and Stone were off. I assumed it was to find a woman for the night. I was thankful to be well past that stage in my life. The girls came back to the table and Charley, who was slightly tipsy, took a seat in my lap. She kissed me on the lips and then moved her mouth to my ear.

"I think I'm ready to go home, honey."

"Yeah?"

She gave me a sexy smile and nodded.

"Hey, Zane—you ready?" I asked.

Zane looked to Emme. She nodded.

"Okay, gorgeous. Let's say goodbye and we can head out."

Greg and Tony had reappeared. Everyone congratulated Charley and I once again and we all took off for the night.

The four of us got into Zane's truck and he drove us back to the condo. The girls were in especially good spirits, having had a bit of alcohol in them. Charley's head was in my lap and she was chatting about all the things she wanted to have at the wedding. I didn't know what half the shit was and, to be honest, I wasn't sure she'd remember anything she was saying anyway. I let her talk. It was a bit comical to watch. Charley would say something she absolutely wanted or something she refused to have at her wedding and Emme would immediately agree with whatever Charley said.

We made it back to the condo and Zane and I had to all but carry the girls to the front door. I pulled the key out of Charley's hand and opened the door. We said goodnight to Zane and Emme and, after grabbing two bottles of water from the kitchen, I took Charley down the hall to her bedroom.

I closed the door and set the water bottles down on the nightstand. When I turned back to look at Charley, I saw sadness had washed over her face.

"What's wrong, Charley?"

"Our engagement day is over," she pouted.

I tried to suppress a laugh. "It's okay. Tomorrow, you can start with all that planning you want to do for the wedding. Don't be sad about this."

She sighed. "Okay, honey. I'll be happy that it was, without a doubt, the best day of my entire life."

"Well, I plan to top today at some point in the future, so you better be prepared."

"I love you, Wes Blackman," she beamed as she wrapped her arms around my neck.

"And I love you, Charlotte Meadows."

Her eyes rounded as though she had just realized something. "I'm going to be Mrs. Wes Blackman soon."

I couldn't wait for that.

"That's right, gorgeous. I can't wait."

I crushed my lips to hers and took to making love to my future wife. The two of us hadn't gotten much sleep the night before so after giving her three orgasms in final celebration of our engagement, I wrapped an arm around my woman and knew I'd never sleep another night without her by my side.

Thirty-Four

Charley

I HEARD MUMBLING.

"I *can't* stay."

More mumbling.

I opened my eyes, reached over to the phone closest to me on the nightstand, and saw that it was just before ten o'clock. I rolled to my back and looked over at Wes. I could tell he had just woken up as well.

"Did that wake you up?" I asked.

"What the hell is going on?" he asked in response.

"I don't know, but..."

I was cut off by Emme yelling, *"Stop, please. Zane, you have to let me go!"*

Wes and I jumped out of bed. He pulled up a pair of jeans in no time at all and tossed me a pair of shorts. Thankfully I already had a pair of panties and a camisole on. We ran out of the bedroom and down the hall to find a distraught Emme and a not-so-happy Zane within inches of each other.

She looked terrified.

"Zane, what the fuck is going on?" Wes roared.

"Fuck if I know. I was asleep and woke up to her zipping that shit up," Zane answered as he swung out his arm.

I looked to the side to see one of Emme's suitcases there. When I looked at my best friend, she wouldn't make eye contact with me, or anyone for that matter.

Zane continued talking, "I've asked her what she is doing about ten times already. She won't explain anything to me. She just keeps saying that she needs to go and she can't stay. Says she doesn't want anyone else to get hurt. Do you have any fucking clue what that means?"

"Oh my God," I quavered, my stomach clenching.

All eyes went to me, but I looked only at Emme. I walked to her.

With my hands framing her face I asked, "Did he contact you, Em?"

The tears spilled down her cheeks from her puffy eyes and she nodded.

"He call?" I asked.

She shook her head.

"How?"

She didn't say anything. She didn't move.

"Emme. How?"

She waited a moment before reaching into the pocket of her hoodie. She pulled out a piece of paper. I took it from her and opened it.

You think you can run away from me, you whore? You're mine. You better get rid of your snowboarder before he gets a bullet, too. You'll always be mine.

"Oh, Em," I cried as the tears poured down my cheeks.

"Charley?" Wes asked with concern.

I handed him the note. He read it and looked at us.

"How did this get here, Em?" he asked.

"I found it this morning when I came out to put a pot of coffee on. I saw it on the floor in front of the door. I think he slipped it under the door."

"He?" Zane asked taking the note out of Wes' hand.

"My ex, Seth."

Zane read the note and clenched his jaw.

Wes asked, "You mean he had someone do it for him?"

We both shook our heads. Wes looked to me, clearly confused.

"After Seth killed Taj he was never caught. He went into hiding and they never found him. Emme and I moved here not only to get away from the painful memories but to make sure that he'd never find her."

Zane walked out of the room with his phone to his ear.

Emme was still in the corner, distraught.

I was frightened. Not for me, but for my best friend. I needed to know she'd be safe.

Wes walked over to me, wrapped his arm around my shoulders, and whispered in my ear, "We'll find that bastard, Charley. And, we'll make sure he never touches her again."

With those words, I breathed a sigh of relief. In an instant, he soothed my panic because I knew, beyond a shadow of a doubt, that Wes Blackman would always give me everything I needed.

Preview of *Everything I Have*

Prologue

Ventura, California
Emme

"THANKS FOR SUCH A GOOD NIGHT GIRLS. I NEEDED THIS bad!"

I was sitting in the front passenger's seat of Monroe's SUV on a Friday night, heading back to my house. Monroe was driving; Nikki and Charley were in the backseat. My girls had just taken me out for my twenty-fourth birthday celebration.

Today was not my birthday, though. My actual birthday was next week. Today was simply the only day that I would be able to safely escape to thoroughly enjoy a night out with my three best friends in the whole world.

Seth, my boyfriend for the last eight years, left three days ago to go out of town on a business trip. Yes, I've been with Seth since I was sixteen, which sadly, feels like a lifetime. I often found myself reminiscing about the early days of our relationship when we were so in love.

But oh, how things have changed.

Now I need to prolong a night out with my friends for days or weeks at a time because I can't get away. Because if I dare to leave the house for anything other than work when

Seth is home, I'll pay for it.

"We love you, Em. We'd never let your birthday pass without a celebration...even if we have to do it in secret," Monroe stated.

"Yeah, but it's awful that we need to wait until he's not around so we can spend time with you," Charley chimed in.

My friends knew that things had changed in my relationship with Seth. I didn't exactly share how bad it had become with them, but they knew enough to know that they didn't like him very much anymore. Their opinions of him would drastically change if they knew everything.

I sighed. "I know, but can we not talk about this now? I've got a mere five minutes left with you three. Can we please have this end on a happy note?"

Nikki spoke. "So, is it just me or did anyone else think that Miss Monroe was a bit harsh with Mr. Blue Eyes tonight?"

"Oh, come on. I'm a sucker for a pair of baby blues, but I just wasn't into him," Monroe retorted.

Charley added, "I've got to agree with Monroe on this one. She's something special and has every right to be picky."

"I'm just saying, you aren't going to find a good one if you don't give any of them a chance," Nikki pointed out.

And just like that, Nikki managed to turn the conversation away from my current relationship. I looked back at her as Monroe began to protest. I mouthed a 'thank you' to her, and she gave me a quick wink. I know she wasn't thrilled with my relationship with Seth either, but she also cared enough about me to respect my choice.

If only it were my choice anymore.

Two minutes later, we pulled up in front of my house.

"You sure you don't want to stay at my place tonight, Emme?" Monroe asked.

"I'm sure. Thanks again for the fun tonight. I'll call tomorrow. Love you girls," I called as I stepped out of the car.

"Love you, Em. Happy Birthday!" I heard Charley yell from the backseat.

Monroe and Nikki both wished me a happy birthday again as I closed the car door and turned to walk up to the house. After pulling my key out and shoving into the lock, I turned to wave at the girls. Once I walked into the house, I closed the door and flipped the deadbolt.

Shower and bed.

In that order.

I had two more nights alone before Seth returned and I intended to enjoy them fully. I walked up the steps and went down the hall to the bedroom. As soon as I stepped inside the room I stopped dead in my tracks.

Seth was standing about five feet away from me. I took a step back, shocked to see him there.

Shit.

"It seems as though my instincts were right," he seethed.

I said nothing. I knew that would put me in no better position.

"I knew you couldn't be trusted. I purposely told you I had a meeting on Monday morning and wouldn't be coming home until Monday night just so I could come back early and confirm what I knew to be true." He paused a moment looking me up and down, a look of disgust in his eyes, before continuing, "Look at you. Dressed like a whore. What were you doing, Emily? You think you're going to find someone else and leave me?"

"I'm sorry, Seth. The girls wanted to take me out for my birthday. I haven't seen them in such a long time and I really missed them. I'm sorry," I confessed as my entire body tensed in anticipation of what I knew was coming.

"Did you think you could go and I wouldn't find out?" he countered as he stepped closer to me.

"I swear, Seth. We just went out for dinner and drinks. I

was only with the girls," I answered, my stomach tightening.

"*You lying bitch! You think you can leave me?*" he roared as he leaned into me.

I shook my head.

And that was when Seth struck.

His fist came up and cracked my jaw. My body jerked back and my hands came up to shield my face from any further blows. That's when he punched me in the stomach causing me to drop my hands. He clocked me again in my face. This time, he hit me in my right eye. I tried to protect my face, but he struck again splitting my lip open. When my hands moved to my mouth, he came at me from the other side and punched me in the left eye. I bent over trying to protect my face; so, he grabbed me by my hair and threw me to the ground. Seth stood in front of me and repeatedly kicked me in the stomach before he moved behind my back and kicked my ribs. This was the worst I'd ever experienced his rage. I wanted to scream from the intense pain I was feeling, but I couldn't.

I could barely breathe.

"Stupid fucking whore! You are mine," he yelled as his kicks moved from my ribs to my lower back. The pain was unbearable and I was certain I would die.

Incredibly, after what felt like hours, he stopped. I could only see clearly out of one eye, my other already beginning to swell, but I saw him walk out the bedroom door. As he walked out, he muttered, "Waste of my fucking time."

I stayed put, fear having taken over me. I hoped he would leave, but knew better than to expect that that would happen. Instead, he made his way down the hallway into the bathroom. I heard the water in the shower turn on. I waited a few minutes and listened, making sure that he was actually in the shower before I moved.

It was in that moment I made a decision.

Despite the excruciating pain radiating through my body,

I knew I had to get up and get help. I crawled over to my purse which had fallen on the floor just inside the bedroom doorway. I pulled my phone out of the purse and called the only person I knew who was close enough and could help me.

The phone rang once before I heard, "Hey, Em. What's up?"

"Taj." I barely squeaked out.

"Emme? Are you ok?" he asked, his voice laced with concern.

"Please help. He's going to kill me."

"Who, baby girl? Where are you?" he asked, now on alert.

"Seth. He came home early. The girls just dropped me off," I paused to pull in a breath, then continued. "I need to get to a hospital, Taj. Please."

"Stay with me, Em. I'm already on my way."

"I can't," I winced, attempting to breathe. "He's in the shower. He'll be out soon."

"Two minutes, baby girl. I'll be there in two minutes."

"I have to go, Taj. The key is under the flower pot next to the stoop."

I disconnected the call and put the phone back in my purse. I didn't have the strength to move from the spot I was curled up in on the floor.

Even though it felt like an eternity, I'm certain it was less than two minutes later when I heard the front door open. Thankfully, Seth was still in the shower. I heard Taj's footsteps as he quickly climbed the stairs. He made it into the bedroom, looked at me, clenched his fists and jaw, and murmured, "Motherfucker."

"Taj," I whispered from the floor.

I heard the water turn off in the shower.

He bent down and picked me up off the floor. My body screamed in agony at the movements.

"I'm sorry, Emme. We've got to get you out of here."

"Thank you, Taj."

Just as Taj began walking toward the stairs, the bathroom door opened and Seth stepped out to find me in Taj's arms. I felt Taj's fingertips dig into my skin ever so slightly.

"What the fuck do you think you're doing?" Seth demanded, standing there in a towel.

Taj ignored Seth, quickly moved around him, using his body to shield mine, and carried me down the steps. After he descended the stairs, Taj walked out the front door and brought me to his Jeep. He opened the door and put me in the passenger's seat.

"Be back, Em."

"Taj, he's not worth it. Come on," I pleaded.

"Emme, I'll be right back. Use my phone and call the police. This motherfucker is not getting away with this."

I located his phone in the center console and called the police. I gave them my address and explained what had happened. They had units on the way.

And that was when I heard it.

The gunfire.

I froze in the seat willing Taj to walk out the front door. As the seconds ticked by and he didn't come out, I decided to go back in. I began to climb out of the car. I winced in pain with each step I took. I finally made it to the front stoop. Hunched over, I pushed the door open and walked back into the house. I looked up as I stepped inside and lost it at what I saw.

"Oh, God. No! Taj," I managed to yell somehow. Taj was lying on the floor in my living room with blood pouring out of his body. I made my way over to him and crouched down next to him. I framed his face in my hands. "Taj, please. Oh, God. I'm so sorry."

"Tell Charley I love her," he whispered. "Tell her I'll always be with her and that she'll never be alone."

"No, Taj. Don't you dare. You stay with me," I cried as I

took his hand in mine.

"Get safe, baby girl. Go get safe," he managed to whisper through his short, quick breaths.

I stayed right by his side, curled up next to him because I couldn't move anyway, and I felt the life leave his body. Tears streamed down my face as I heard the sirens approaching. I heard the back door to the house slam. I assumed that was Seth running, but I wasn't going to leave Taj. The front door finally opened. Two officers made their way over to me. Several others followed behind them. I heard lots of orders being barked by the officers, but I didn't pay much attention. I felt one of the officers wrap his hands around my shoulders.

I tensed.

"Not going to hurt you, darling. You've got to get up so we can help him. We have to do that even if he's responsible for what happened to you," the officer said.

"He saved me," I whispered.

"Come again?"

"I called him to come get me and take me to the hospital." I pointed to my body and face and said, "My boyfriend did this to me. Taj saved me. He died so he could save me. Oh God. What will I tell Charley?"

"Who's Charley, darling?" the officer asked.

"My best friend. She's never going to forgive me. This is her brother," I explained as I kept my face pressed to Taj's chest and my breathing became rapid. "I killed my best friend's brother."

"She's going into shock," I heard one officer yell out to whoever else was in the room.

I suddenly felt very tired.

Exhaustion came over me and everything went black.

acknowledgements

I'm not sure my first novel would have ever been possible without having some pretty incredible people in my world. First and foremost, to my amazing husband, Jeff, thank you for encouraging me to pursue this dream and making me realize that I am capable of so much more than I allowed myself to believe. My former, virtually pro-snowboarder, many thanks to you for the wealth of knowledge you've given me on snowboarding and riding half pipe. Without you, I'm not sure I could have told this story. You've supported me in ways that not many are cut out for; and for that, I'm eternally grateful. Your love means everything to me.

To my two beautiful boys, who've wholeheartedly accepted Mommy writing 'love stories' and graciously gave me the time to do it, thank you. When I seem to need it most, you offer snuggles, cuddles, love, and laughs. I love you both more than I could ever put into words.

To my family and friends who knew about this journey and supported me along the way, thank you from the bottom of my heart.

To S.H.—Thank you for the gorgeous covers! You always manage to give me exactly what I want when I offer no suggestions.

To E.M.—Thank you! A million times over, thank you! Your dedication to your clients is unparalleled. Even when you already have a full schedule, you never hesitate to squeeze me in. I appreciate you more than these words could ever express.

To S.B.—It's one thing to read a great book. It's something else entirely to read it when it looks beautiful. Thank you for all the little touches you add to make it special.

To my readers—Thank you for letting my characters into your hearts. I hope you'll continue on this journey with me.

Connect with
A.K. EVANS

To stay connected with A.K. Evans and receive all the first looks at upcoming releases, latest news, or to simply follow along on her journey, be sure to add or follow her on social media. You can also get the scoop by signing up for the monthly newsletter, which includes a giveaway every month.

Newsletter: http://eepurl.com/dme06z

Website: www.authorakevans.com

Facebook: www.facebook.com/authorAKEvans

Facebook Reader Group: www.facebook.com/groups/1285069088272037

Instagram: www.instagram.com/authorakevans

Twitter: twitter.com/AuthorAKEvans

Goodreads Author Page: www.goodreads.com/user/show/64525877-a-k-evans

Subscribe on YouTube: bit.ly2w01yb7

Other Books by
A.K. EVANS

The Everything Series
Everything I Need
Everything I Have
Everything I Want
Everything I Love

The Cunningham Security Series
Obsessed
Overcome
Desperate

Solitude (Coming February 2019)

About
A.K. EVANS

A.K. Evans is a married mother of two boys residing in a small town in northeastern Pennsylvania. After graduating from Lafayette College in 2004 with two degrees (one in English and one in Economics & Business), she pursued a career in the insurance and financial services industry. Not long after, Evans realized the career was not for her. She went on to manage her husband's performance automotive business and drive the shop race cars for the next thirteen years. While the business afforded her the freedom she wouldn't necessarily have had in a typical 9-5 job, after eleven years she was no longer receiving personal fulfillment from her chosen career path. Following many discussions, lots of thought, and tons of encouragement, Andrea decided to pursue her dream of becoming a writer.

Between her day job, writing, and homeschooling her two boys, Evans is left with very little free time. When she finds scraps of spare time, Evans enjoys reading, doing yoga, watching NY Rangers hockey, dancing, and vacationing with her family. Andrea, her husband, and her children are currently working on taking road trips to visit all 50 states (though, Alaska and Hawaii might require flights).